Table of

Dedication

To my Dad, Keith Thomson, who has been my hero and biggest supporter, always there when I needed him. You have shown me what true strength and love look like, and I am grateful for every moment we share.

To my Stepmum, Jill Clements, who has been a source of support, a shoulder to cry on, and a sounding board for advice. Together with my Dad, your joint wisdom and compassion have guided me through life's challenges, and I am so thankful to have you in my corner.

To my Husband, Niall McKay, my soul mate, who always puts my needs first and works tirelessly to create opportunities for me to pursue my dreams. Your unwavering belief in me has given me the courage to chase after my passions, and I am forever grateful for your love and support.

To my children, Bronwyn, Jacob and Alex McKay and their respective partners, Jay, Caitlin, and Becky, for their unwavering love and support. You have surrounded me with warmth, laughter, and strength, and I am so proud to call you my family.

To my grandchildren, Mia, Oakley, Chase, and Scarlett, who bring me immeasurable joy and light into my life. Your smiles and laughter remind me of the beauty and wonder in the world, and I am blessed to be your Nana.

Lastly, to my Book Dragon Team, for their incredible support in helping me to publish my book and keep my writing aspirations alive. Your dedication and passion for literature have fuelled my own creativity, and I am grateful to lead such a wonderful team. Thank you for believing in my Dragon and supporting my dreams.

© Kirsty F. McKay 2024 First Edition
Published by: The Book Dragon
6 West Row
Stockton on Tees
TS18 1BT
United Kingdom
ISBN: 978-1-7395159-5-9

British Library cataloguing in Publication Data. A CIP record for this book can be obtained from the British Library.

Titles by the Author

The Morvantia Chronicles
The Veils of Valoria
The Guardians of Valoria
The Sands of Elyssia (Releasing November 2025)

Standalone Titles
Gentle Ben (Releasing July 2024)
The Gift That Keeps On Giving (Releasing July 2025)

The Four Realms

Character Cast

Morvantia Universe
    Kyle Haven - Knight of the Order of Morvantia. Father of Finn. Married to Myrialle.

Myrialle Haven – Wife of Kyle and Mother of Aaron and Finn.

Mercadia – Elder of the Council (Governing Body and Mystic Protectors of Morvantia.)

Jarrow – Elder of the Council (Governing Body and Mystic Protectors of Morvantia) – Killed by the Master's Assassin's protecting the Selensia.

Master Quaid Morgan – Socialite & Former Friend and Rival of Finn.

Nyrvallia – Once known as Laybardi, a mortal from the Realm of Morven with the ability to Astral Travel. Infected & transformed into the Demon Warrior with powerful & deadly supernatural & weapons skill.

Aaron Haven – Eldest Son of Kyle & Myrialle. A Master of the Mystical Shroud and its new Eye.

The Chosen One – A Shade entity brought into this world by The Master also known as 'The Dark One.'

The Gydgen – Army of the Dead - Warlocks born from Death.

Elios – Elder of the Council (Governing Body and Mystic Protectors of Morvantia.)

Siegfried – A mouse and the Familiar of Elios.

The Fallen – Shadow Nightmares given physical form by the Warlock Kane. They are part wolf and part bison with thick leather hides, amber eyes, elongated snout, and teeth. They can run at incredible speeds, dissipate into shadows and regenerate via a cocoon shell created from their own mucus. They are weakened by light.

Finn Haven – Youngest Son of Kyle & Myrialle. Gifted Tracker & Shapeshifter.

Biscuit – Black Scottie Dog, companion to Bessantia.

Enwen – Tree of Life that is Messenger for the Universal Living Energy Morvantia.

The Weavers – Parasite creatures that are born of the Yellow Eyed Demon. They weave their viscous tentacles into the minds of other beings and take control, poisoning the host with fear, adrenaline and keeping their victim in a recurring nightmare state that eventually kills.

The Master – A demonic being of unknown origin with unfathomable powers.

Kane – Warlock & Commanding Officer of The Master's Army. Grandson of Rhydu. Son of Kyranna, Nephew of Ardella.

Yellow Eyed Demon – Of unknown origin, summoned by the Master.

Black Eyed Demon – Of unknown origin, haunts Rowan's visions.

Bessie – Also known as Bessantia, a Powerful Mage. Sent to Earth to wait until the time of the Prophecy and to aid the Guardian.

Barrock – The Fallen & First Officer.

King Gregor – Ruler of the Capital of Elyssia.

Drey Balor – The Master's Assassin and Former Love of Council Elder Mercadia.

Morbae – Guardian of the Mistress.

The Mistress – Sorceress of unknown origin.

Hymorious – An Ancient Father, prophet and powerful druid mage.

Gallo – The Fallen and assigned Guardian of Warlock Kane.

Mendip – The Fallen.

Symiar – The Fallen.

Grinn – The Fallen.

Mikoss – The Fallen.

Rivik – The Fallen and assigned Guardian of Warlock Kane.

Mortimus – Morvantian Citizen / Magical Hare belonging to Bessie.

Albion – Morvantian Dwarf / Magical Dragonfly belonging to Bessie.

Order of Morvantia – Thirteen Knights Sworn to uphold and protect the will of Morvantia.

Queen Lilly – Ruling Queen of all Fae.

Indigo – Mage Friend of Finn.

Roark – A Braeden Dragon.

Losiah – A Breaden Dragon.

Abaddon – A creature created from the bones and flesh of injured beasts and citizens of Morven following the Master's conquering of the realm. His creations could not be controlled due to the merging of so many tormented essences in one body, each with its own conflicting will and desire. These hideous creatures were banished and imprisoned.

Alyssa – A gifted mage and Warlock Kane's true love.

Ardella – Custodian of the Shroud, Daughter or Rhydu, Sister to Kyranna, Aunt of Kane.

Rhydu – Father of Ardella and Kyranna, Grandfather of Kane.

Kyranna – Kane's Mother, Daughter of Rhydu, Sister to Ardella.

Ursula – Second wife of Rhydu.

Great Valorian Temple Monks – A Brotherhood of Seven Druid Mages. Descendants of the bloodline of the Ancient Father Hymorious.

Mordreya – Twin of Morvela, Daughter of Ancient Father Gideon.

Morvela – Twin of Mordreya, Son of Ancient Father Gideon.

Freya – Wife of Ancient Father Gideon, Stepmother to his twins Morvela and Mordreya.

Boy in vision – Freya's Orphaned Nephew, Thommen.

Guardian of the Compass – A creature created by the Ancient Fathers to guard the compasses. A writhing, serpentine horror of oily black scales and razored fins with needle sharp teeth, that was neither fish nor eel but some awful amalgamation of the two.

Earth – World of Humans
Rowan Montgomery – Human born. A Clairvoyant born in Teesside, possessing strong psychic ability.

Christine Montgomery – Mundane human and mother of Jake and Rowan. Wife of David Montgomery (deceased.)

David Montgomery – Father of Jake and Rowan, husband to Christine. Now deceased.

Eddie Throston – Mundane human who befriended Finn.

Lizzie Thomas – Mundane human, Girlfriend of Eddie.

Sidney – Siddoms, pet poodle of the Throston family.

Jen Olsen – Mundane human and best friend of Rowan.

Sandra Olsen – Mundane human and mother of Jen Olsen, wife of Derek Olsen.

Derek Olsen – Mundane human and father of Jen Olsen, husband of Sandra Olsen.

Youth on train – Infected by the Fallen's bite.

Ticket Inspector – Mundane human.

Mother & Children on Outbound Journey – Mundane humans.

Mother & Children on Inbound Journey – Mundane humans.

Elderly Gentleman Passenger & Wife on Inbound Journey – Mundane humans.

Stan – Mundane human and bouncer of the Public House The Celtic Thistle.

Jake Montgomery – Mundane human and brother of Rowan. Bartender at the Public House The Celtic Thistle.

Simon – Mundane human and boyfriend of Jen.

Nicki – Mundane human and girlfriend of Ronan, Sister to Jimmy & love interest of Warlock Kane.

Frances Hardinge – Author.

Old Lady McGinty – Mundane Human and Neighbour of Bessie.

Duncan & Vera – Mundane humans.

Dr Herbert – General Practitioner of Duncan and Vera.

Jessica – Mundane human & Museum Assistant at the Witchcraft Museum.

Owner Bed & Breakfast – Mundane human.

Maori Elders – An ancient tribe of settlers dating back to 1300 CE known as 'People of the Land.'

Spirit Realm
     Charles – Rowan's Spirit Guide.

Aliyah – Spirit Guide of Christine Montgomery.

Lightkeepers – Spirit Protectors of the Human Realm.

Harry – Jake's Spirit Guide.

Daniel – Jen's Spirit Guide.

Eleanor – Spirit and Sage Master.

Nicolai – Lightkeeper & Ascended Master.

Raphael – Spirit and Lightkeeper of the Hall of Records.

The Lost Ones – Human spirits cast out to wander the first spirit plane that enshrouds the human world.

Glossary of World Building References

B rethren – Brothers.

Shadowlands – A deathly parallel realm that encompasses the four realms of Morvantia.

The Shroud – An energy source of unknown origin, no mage knows what lies at its core but it is believed that every magical artifact that has ever been created is done so from its power, and is therefore returned to the Shroud once it has fulfilled its purpose. The Shroud is an Energy Source that can be wielded to hide and shield the mind and body.

The Eye of the Shroud – A mystic of great power chosen by the Shroud to entrust its secret and keeper of all magical artefacts born from the Shroud.

Season's – Equivalent to three months passing in the human world.

The Silver Stag – The First Key.

The Sacred White Stallion of Valoria (Spirit) - The second Key.

Buckbear – A small hybrid creature which is mostly bear and part deer. Buckbears are believed to bond for life and will bring peace and love to their homestead.

Protector of the Keys – A Guardian appointed by Morvantia to protect the Keys. The Keys when united will open the bearer to her universe and subject her will to theirs, enabling them to travel into the Cosmos and seek ultimate power.

The Selensia – A force field and protective veil that prevents physical crossing from one realm border to another. Manifested and powered by the Council of Elders.

Solarius – Sun orbiting the realms of Morvantia.

Solarius Constellation – Sun stars that change position every three hundred seasons to a new constellation.

The Dreamscape – A place where the human spirit travels when sleeping and where dreams unfold.

The Thirteen Sacrifices – The omens of the apocalypse.

The Twelfth Sacrifice – The penultimate omen that sees the purest of Morvantia waters, the Samsara run red with blood.

The Samsara – Lake.

The Thirteenth Sacrifice – the final omen, the gateway cracks and releases the dead. The Ancient Fathers and their armies who died in the war long before, and whose essence was banished when they turned away from Morvantia's light and will. They are bound in death.

The Final Edict – Morvantia's final test and instruction that must be adhered to in order for a mage to prove they are worthy to take their place on the Council of Elders and become a Mystic Protector.

The Ancient War of the Fathers – Eight Mystics and Original Founding Fathers of Morvantia's Realms. Two Fathers to each realm balancing the light and dark. They were born from Morvantia herself before all other life was created.

Hymorious Table – Hymorious, an ancient father, prophet and powerful druid mage who carved the table and infused magic to manifest any artifact that the table has once touched no matter where the table lies.

Lemure – A spell that uses reflective surfaces to allow the spell caster at each end to connect, see, and touch each other, no matter their location.

Citrine – A manifestation crystal.

Fablekeepers – Morvantia's entrusted storytellers of the past, present and future.

The Void – A corridor between the Morvantia Realms and the Great Hall.

The Great Hall – Morvantia's Ancient Records Hall of the Fablekeepers.

Scorpion's Tail – Transformative Powers. Little is known of the Red Scorpions that hide beneath the desert sands of Elyssia and the full extent of the magic that they carry.

Lyboria Bite – Serpents used to keep their prey submissive. Only when a serpent has been captured, and surrendered its will, can the venom be used to magically harness the will of a victim chosen by its master. In all other instances the bites prove fatal to those unfortunate enough to encounter these serpents and the body is eventually consumed.

Gantalei – A Trial of Combat initiated to determine the Alpha / Leader of The Fallen

Arvantis – Sacred Cauldron of the Mistress.

The Mistress Brooch – Silver Brooch, infused with the bones of the Lyboria serpents, magically infused by the Mistress to alter the bites power.

The Margorian Compasses – 5 compasses crafted by Hymorious to allow their bearers to navigate the currents of time itself. Believed to be destroyed in the Ancient War of the Fathers.

The Margorian Shades – Beings born from the poisoning of Enwen's fruits. Living energy orbs that when taken without Enwen's consent and used for a dark purpose become Shades once that purpose has been fulfilled.

Four Realms of Morvantia – Moren, Valoria, Elyssia, Astyllis.

Calla Essence – Milked from the Stem of the Calla Flower. Only one Calla will pod instead of flowering.

Calla Pod – Every ten years the Calla Pod opens and releases a seed that marks a male Valorian giving them the power of convergence of mage and beast. The branding of the Calla identifies the son and takes place on their tenth birthday.

Rowan's Amulet – A oval pendant hung on a silver chain with a large emerald jewel at its centre. The Pendant is of unknown origin and is believed to unlock Rowan's powers and abilities, enabling her, as a human, to safely travel through the portal into Finn's world.

Enwen's Pearlescent Orb – Power source of the Knights of Morvantia blade and possess an energy crystal gifted by Morvantia to use as Enwen deems fit. This is only given to the pure of heart and worthy.

The Meridian – An energy field that belongs to Morvantia, gifted to Bessantia following her sacrifice and used to protect those in great need. The Meridian enables a connection between the cosmos and those who are deemed worthy by Morvantia to access certain powers and knowledge. The Meridian then teaches those who have been chosen to wield the gifts they have been given.

Voices in the Meridian – Little is known of who they are but they are believed to be supreme beings that reside in the cosmos beyond Morvantia's universe.

The Hall of Records – An energetic place that holds the Akashic records, memories, and life records of the human soul.

Akashic Records –

Chamber of Illumination – Great Hall where the Ascended Masters, Lightkeepers and Spirit Guides converge to discuss matters of importance and gain the blessing of the Divine.

Ancestors of Old – Ancient mortal Druids and Pagans with magical abilities and gifts.

Toki - a symbol of strength, the Toki carries with it deep meaning and symbolism associated with mana, reverence, strength, and bravery.

Oath of Dragoria – A Dragon is sworn to obey and protect its Rider. The Oath can be initiated when the actions and decision of the Rider would place them at significant risk of harm or death.

Nether Plane – A plane of existence where nothing living exists and essences freed from their physical body drift for all eternity.

Morvela's Orb - An orb that could see into the hearts of men, reveal their deepest desires and darkest secrets.

Mordreya's Staff – A staff imbued with the ability to control the minds of others, to bend them to her will.

The Eye of Malachite - An ancient stone imbued with the power to prevent dragons from shifting form.

Prologue

Before the Great War of the Moren
The Winter Tower, Astyllis, Morvantia

With his sword gripped tightly in his hand, Kyle stood alone and waited for the inevitable to come. It was the second time that he would face death, only this time it would be permanent. There would be no resurrection, and no opportunity to make amends for his past mistakes. His family, although safe from the creature that had infiltrated their world and destroyed his brothers, would continue to suffer in the wake of the lie that he and the Council of Elders had created. A necessity, Mercadia had told him, yet the burden of guilt did not ease any less.

Kyle's heart ached for the son who believed his father to hate him, never knowing how terribly sorry he had been for his reaction on that day. His eldest son, now forced to step up and take responsibility for the family, and for the woman who had captured his heart all those years ago.

My dear sweet Myrialle, how I regret leaving you and betraying our love.

As he blocked his sight against the memory of the pain inflicted, a deep rumble sounded in the distance, confirming his fate. With a heavy heart he turned his gaze to the darkness. Solaria's light had been vanquished from the sky, the realm plunged into sudden nightfall. It heralded the last of three signs.

His armour provided little warmth as the temperature plummeted further, and a breeze stirred the air around him. It gathered momentum, howling a warning to all who would listen of what was to come. Shifting closer to the arch window, Kyle watched and waited.

A crack of thunder in the distance, accompanied by zigzags of silver, momentarily lit the darkness and revealed the arrival of winter's storm. Concealed within the icy blizzard, the Nyrvallia's chariot travelled closer. As predicted in the ancient texts of Hymorious:

'When the thirteenth star falls from the sky, and Regan's blade is forged,

Morvantia's blessings will dry, and her will shall be no more.

Unholy blood will bind pure heart, and from death's ashes arise

Nyrvallia born of man and beast, the whisperer of lies.

Seven will slide from Enwen's grace, their betrayal will feed his flesh,

And with their blood he will rejoice, the harbinger of death.

As Spirits released poison Winter's cup, the light inside will end.

A doorway opens from the Fountain's seal, and the sire of evil ascends.'

Sadly, the texts made no mention of what was to become of the last surviving member of the Order of Morvantia, but

Kyle could guess, and it seemed that the Elder Council had drawn a similar conclusion.

Following Mercadia's confession, and the discovery of the long-forgotten scrolls, his closest friend and confidante, Elios, had read every scripture and journal Hymorious had ever written, determined to find the answer and put a stop to the prediction. But it was too late. The Elders concluded that Kyle was deliberately omitted from the texts, for one purpose alone, and so the decision was made. Kyle was forced to leave his wife and sons behind, without explanation, complying with the oath that he had sworn. Now there would be no time for him to put right his mistake, or to say goodbye.

Kyle's death would guarantee that his family be freed of the same fate that had bound him to the creature. Mercadia promised that no harm would befall them.

A sudden swish of cloth across the dusty floor disturbed his thoughts, and he spun in the direction of fingers that snapped in the darkness. The chamber flickered into light.

Kyle waited patiently for her to replace the torch to its sconce. "You should not have come, Mercadia."

"I could not stop myself," she replied, and hurried towards him.

Heaving a long sigh, he laid his sword gently against the stone wall. His arms opened to draw her in, and embrace her tightly. The last comfort he would ever know.

"Not enough," she whispered.

His heart acknowledged her words, but for different reasons. For had there been more time, he surely would have done things differently.

"We always knew this day would come," he said, careful to mask his thoughts.

Mercadia lifted her gaze to meet his. "Still, my brothers and I had hoped to have found another way."

He shook his head. "My fate is preordained; there is nothing you or I can do to change that."

She pulled away from him. "I wish it were not so."

Kyle reached for her hand, his thumb lightly stroked her skin. "There are many things that I wish were..." He struggled with his next words as her violet eyes pleaded with him. "Perhaps, in another time, you and I could have been more to each other."

"Please don't say anything else," she begged.

Kyle's thoughts once again turned to the family that he had deserted. "You must know that even if I should survive this night, it has to end for us here."

Her confusion was evident. "But after last night, I thought I meant something to you?"

"You do..." his voice trailed away as he sought for the right words. "It's just that I—"

Mercadia silenced him with her lips, her mouth gently teasing his, urging him to give back all that she offered. When Kyle did not respond, she stumbled backwards, her eyes misted.

"You must let me go," he said stiffly.

She winced and wiped furiously at the tears that had formed, her voice almost muffled by her sleeve. "I thought I could say goodbye to you, but I cannot. The thought of you gone is more than I can bear."

Kyle's resolve sharpened like a knife, and his back snapped ramrod straight at the sheer idiocy of her words. She must see sense!

"You are an Elder of the Council. You cannot escape your responsibilities any more than I can escape mine. Neither of us holds the power to stop what is happening," he rebuked.

There was a flicker of understanding in her eyes as she finally acknowledged him, her voice cold and miserable. "I'm sorry. I had not intended to make this harder for us both."

"Then why did you come?" he asked.

Her gaze lowered momentarily, "Jarrow wanted to know your last wish. The Council owes you that at least, for the sacrifice you make."

"The condemned man's last meal," he said bitterly. "Strange that Jarrow should send you, knowing what is to come," he challenged.

"I should have asked you last night, but I couldn't bring myself to do it. Not after what we shared."

"It is for you to decide what you tell Jarrow," he said. "I only have one wish, and it's yours alone to grant."

She raised her eyes to meet his. "What is it?"

He paused for a second before reluctantly voicing the request he knew would hurt her. "My family must never know about us, and what we were to each other."

Mercadia frowned. "You are asking to take away my right to mourn you."

"I ask that you spare my wife and children from further pain," he snapped. "They must never know of my betrayal."

"Is that why you do not return my affection?" she demanded. Hurt and anger hung in the air, yet there was little he could do to ease her suffering. The truth could not be denied.

"Before you arrived, my thoughts were of my wife and sons, and of what we did. It was wrong; the Council should have found another way."

She huffed like a petulant child. "You know as well as I do that unless the cord was severed, the Nyrvallia would have sought its revenge, and murdered your family. We had no choice."

"Be that as it may, my son believes that I died hating him." His stomach churned with self-loathing. It had been disappointment, and not hatred in Kyle's eyes that day.

Disappointment in the young Master Quaid, and his actions that had triggered the start of Finn's transformation. The incident ill-timed, as the warning of the Nyrvallia's approach into Valoria forced him to create the illusion of his death and see the Council's plan through to its bitter end. It was too damned late!

Kyle had been prevented from explaining the secret of the change to his son, unable to reassure him that he was not a freak of nature. There would be no support; his boy would face it alone, for Myrialle had also been kept in the dark. The secret exchanged only between father and son. Kyle's own father long deceased.

Mercadia sighed heavily. "It is unfortunate, I do agree, but at least he lives. You know it was Morvantia's will that you be brought to Astyllis, and be prepared for this night."

"Spoken like a true Elder," Kyle bit back, unable to curb his anger with the Council, but mostly with himself.

She winced from the sting of his reproach. "That's unfair... I-"

The crack of a branch breaking indicated the force of the storm was upon them. Their time had run out. Mercadia's desperate look confirmed that she knew it too.

"It was not Morvantia's will that I betray my wife with you." His words brooked no argument. "Please, I must know whether you will grant my request?"

Her gaze skimmed to the dark entrance of the stairwell. "I cannot refuse you," she answered sadly, "I-"

A sudden biting gust blew through the chamber and extinguished the torch. Kyle immediately seized his sword and pointed it in the direction of the arch. The pearlescent orb glowed furiously from its hilt. "The creature is here; you must leave now."

Footsteps echoed from below and began their ascent of the winding staircase, every step a torment of the horror to come. They had but seconds left.

Mercadia briefly caressed his cheek. "You will always be remembered. I promise you, I will keep your secret."

She hurried to the stone window, and climbed onto its ledge.

"I will never forget last night, and what we shared," Kyle called back, knowing it was what she had hoped to hear. It was the last kindness that he could grant.

"Thank you," she said softly.

Crimson eyes seared the darkness. "Such a touching scene," the Nyrvallia sneered, "and what an unexpected pleasure to find you here, Elder."

"One that I feel sure will leave you bitterly disillusioned," Mercadia fired back.

The creature snarled and clapped its hands together, muttering an incantation beneath its breath.

Kyle shielded his eyes and blinked rapidly as he attempted to adjust to the harsh iridescent blue light that poured into the chamber. All his senses were on high alert to the Nyrvallia's next movement. "Go now," he shouted.

There was a sharp intake of breath, yet despite her fear, Mercadia's voice never faltered. "You will not succeed, Nyrvallia. I've made sure of that."

Leaping from the window, she did not wait for its reply.

"No matter, I shall still have what I came for," the Nyrvallia hissed.

"The fountain is destroyed," Kyle gloated. "Even the likes of one such as you can sense it is too late. You will die with the knowledge of your failure. May the 'Dark One' reunite with you, and make you suffer for all eternity." Raising his sword, the last Knight of the Order of Morvantia propelled forward, and cried, "For Morvantia!"

The Nyrvallia unsheathed two swords from its back, and swiftly blocked his attack. A deafening clang of metal rang through the chamber, and sparks of power flew in all directions from each blade.

"Oh, I think not," Kyle's enemy sneered.

From above the Winter Tower, the eagle circled and cried out her despair as she waited for fate to determine the outcome.

Chapter One

Aaron

Present Day, Lake Samsara, The Moren

Aaron inhaled sharply, and slowly raised his gaze to the cool lavender eyes that studied him closely from beneath the dark grey cowl. The hand of the Chosen One tapped long spindly fingers impatiently as the Master's latest servant awaited his response. With his body held rigid under its grip, Aaron's mind darted in various directions, and he explored each possibility. To refuse the request was tantamount to suicide, yet the thought of taking his mother's life was abhorrent. Anger churned in his stomach as he thought of the lives that he had already taken. Why had it not been enough?

Now the very name he had prayed he would never hear a death sentence uttered for stabbed repeatedly at his heart.

With a firm shrug of his shoulder, Aaron pulled free from the Chosen One's hand and took a deliberate step backwards. His face hardened into a scowl, his fists clenched tightly at his sides as he fought to calm the rising storm.

The Chosen One simply arched its hideous brow and sneered. "Your body betrays you, Warlock."

Determined not to let the real reason for his emotion show, Aaran ignored the innuendo and raised his chin defiantly into the air. "I didn't join the Master's Faction to be his damned Executioner," he said, and pulled his frame tall. "As you pointed out yourself, I am a Warlock. Get the Master's other minions to conduct the order. You know that I can serve him in better ways."

The Chosen One tilted his head, "And yet he has nominated you for this task. Why is that, I wonder?"

Aaron held onto his nerve, his thoughts protected by the Shroud. "I have given him no reason to doubt my loyalty." His gaze locked onto those long spindly fingers as they tapped against the Chosen One's protruding chin.

"Perhaps, yet you seem to have difficulty with this small request."

"Taking another's life is hardly a small request," Aaron scoffed. "Surely you realise that my mother is no mere damsel."

A bony finger stabbed at his chest. "Then surely you realise that this would require someone with more power than the Master's simpleton minions," the Chosen One flung back at him with an equal measure of sarcasm.

Aaron sighed and released the tension from his body. Knowing that he had successfully distracted the Chosen One from the truth brought little comfort. It was a point well made. There were not many mages that came close to matching the abilities that his mother carried, although it had been a long time since she had fought in a war.

"My apologies," he said, and gave a slight bow of his head. "With the awakening of the Gydgen, I had hoped that the time had come for me to play a more prominent role in the Master's plans against the Council."

The Chosen One's stance relaxed. "I understand your desire. But it is I, and I alone who holds the power to control the Gydgen. They are born from death, and only one such as I can wield their thirst for blood and lust for vengeance. The Council made a fatal error of judgement imprisoning them in the Margorian Abyss."

Aaron could not help his curiosity. "But how can death be delivered to such creatures who are themselves born from death?"

"There is a way, but only I have that knowledge, and by death's decree I cannot share it, even with the Master."

Aaron considered for a moment. "And what if you should die? How is the Master to control them then?"

The Chosen One laughed. "Indeed," his only response.

Aaron swiftly changed the subject. "If I am to kill my mother, I would like to know why? What does the Master hope to gain by her death?"

"You know full well that the Master never explains his decisions. It is his will, and so you must obey."

"But surely you have your thoughts?" he pressed.

"I have my suspicions. The mind still fights this body not to betray its former keeper. But have no fear, young Warlock, I shall soon discover it all."

The Chosen One's words paused Aaron's thoughts. "What do you mean? He cannot still be locked within?"

"He is my prisoner for all eternity. No release can be granted for such a betrayal."

"Not even for an unconscious one?" Aaron challenged.

"It matters not."

He shook his head. "And you are confident you can keep him quiet? What if he fights you for control?"

His words were met with a scowl. "It is too late for him. There is only a small piece of his life force remaining, and even that is tainted by the scorpion's blood, the rest consumed by the transition. What is left will soon evaporate."

"But—"

"No more questions, Warlock. You delay unnecessarily with your foolish curiosity."

Biting back his swelling temper, Aaron acquiesced. "Very well; I shall see that the task is done, and I will inform the Master."

The Chosen One appraised him once more before nodding and then finally evaporating into the mist.

Aaron cursed under his breath and scrubbed the summoning rune from the sand. He walked to the opposite side of the lake, his senses searching around the perimeter to ensure he was alone and that the Chosen One had truly departed.

Confident there were no residual traces of its energy, Aaron reached into the opposite pocket, from which he had withdrawn the black onyx shard. Only this time, he removed a quartz point generator, the Elder's crystal.

Seated in the lotus position, taught by the Great Valorian Temple Monks during his brief retreat to the mountains of Elyssia, he chanted the sacred mantra until he felt the crystal thrum with light and energy. His connection to the sphere of Solaria opened.

"It is done. The thirteenth sacrifice made; the Gydgen are free."

"I am sorry it has come to this," Mercadia replied.

The sphere gently chimed with the touch of her hand as she activated its sight and enabled Aaron to see her. As the holographic image appeared within the generator, he noted with disappointment that Elios was not in attendance. For the first time since their meeting, he witnessed the sorrow and regret in her eyes, and was surprised by her genuine concern for the situation the Council had placed him in.

"I knew the risks. It was my decision." He heaved a deep sigh.

"How long do you have?" she asked, although he knew that she could see the answer for herself. The blackness that had seeped into and consumed his aura at an alarming rate could not be missed. Even to those who were not as awakened as he.

"For this last deed, the darkness has spread exponentially. It will be the final time I communicate with you, for once this night passes, I am lost from the light."

"Did you heed Elios's warning, and complete the spell before the sacrifice was made?" she asked, her teeth worrying at her lip.

"Yes. What was left untarnished now sits below the water. My brother is the only one who can save me, and retrieve it from its depths, but even then it will be difficult for him. For the Master will not release his grip on me so easily."

"He is stronger than either of us gave him credit for, but your brother..." She shook her head slowly, as though a memory had disturbed her. "It appears that we have all underestimated him, including the Master."

"How does Finn fare?" Aaron asked, a small stab of pride pricking at his heart.

Mercadia blew out a breath, her frustration evident. "With Bessantia gone, I cannot know or hope to foresee his path."

Aaron's temper sparked. "Gone? What do you mean, gone? Is she dead? How is that even possible?"

"I did not say she was dead," Mercadia assured. "She has simply gone, separated from him for a spell. An unavoidable risk, required to save your brother."

Aaron rose to his feet and furiously paced the shoreline. He sensed her eyes following him as his mind foraged through the pool of knowledge transferred from the previous keeper of the Eye. "Without her, we cannot hope to..." his words trailed away as he fought to control his emotions.

Mercadia's eyes narrowed, and she pushed at the barrier he had been quick to raise. His mind steeled against her intrusion.

"We cannot hope to what?" She cursed loudly, defeated by his power of the Shroud. "What is it you know? I demand that you share it with me."

"It does not matter. My brother cannot succeed against the Master without Bessantia's aid. You got him into this mess; I fully expect that you get him out of it. You owe me this."

Mercadia laughed. "You do not see it all, for it was not I that drew him into this web. He had already opened a connection with the girl. How, I do not know. But after the Silver Stag, it was not difficult to convince him to undertake this quest and retrieve her. As for Bessantia, I agree, and there is a way to bring her back. But I am advised that it is the girl who must undertake this. Jarrow believed that she is the only one with the gift to do so."

"Then she must be protected at all costs," Aaron insisted.

Mercadia smiled. "Have no fear of that. Your brother is in love with her. He will do whatever it takes to ensure her survival, and I believe she, his."

"And what about you?" he questioned. "It is not just the prophecy that motivates you, I just can't figure—"

She cut him off, "All you are required to know is that I made a promise to both your parents, and I will not break it. Let that be enough. You have my aid in this matter."

"Very well. But speaking of my mother, the Master has sentenced her to death. He has ordered it by my hand."

"I feared this," she said.

"Then why did you...?" He curbed his emotions. "Do you know why he wants my mother dead?"

"No, unless he..." Her voice broke with a sudden realisation. Of what, he could not be sure, but it was enough for the colour to drain from her cheeks.

"Unless what?" he demanded.

"It does not matter," she said, dismissing his question in turn.

Aaron's heart beat a wild rhythm in his chest. "Why does he fear her?" he pressed. "They have never crossed paths. Granted, her healing ability is widely known, but that would not in itself be enough for the Master to feel threatened by her."

Mercadia hesitated a moment, "To divulge would be to risk her life further. Others would seek her out."

"But the Master knows something?" Aaron persisted.

"I cannot be certain that he does. Only the Council Elders and one other, who cannot be named, knew the truth. A closely guarded secret with serious ramifications should it ever be disclosed," she warned.

He shook his head. "He suspects something that has identified her as a danger to him, I know it! It must be the other confidant that betrayed this secret. You must tell me."

Mercadia stamped her foot. "Never! They would not align to the Master and take such a risk and destroy us all."

"Who wouldn't?"

She refused to answer him.

Aaron ran a hand through his hair. "Damn it, you know that I cannot disobey him. By dawn, the darkness will have taken over; there will be nothing left to pull me back. My mother will die by my hand unless you act now."

"I am forbidden to interfere before the prophecy comes to pass," she snapped.

"If my mother dies, all will be lost." A hideous image ruptured his mind. "Saints preserve us," he gasped, "a Nyrvallia newborn!"

Mercadia released an agonised cry. "No, it cannot be!"

Aaron took no care as he forced his way into her mind and scoured through her thoughts and memories, searching once again for the image he had witnessed. It laid unprotected in the wake of her panic.

"You are afraid of the truth," he said, skimming further ahead as he sought more answers. The identity of the other confidant eluded him, but her desperation to protect their identity revealed a memory that diverted his attention: a memory associated with the first Nyrvallia, Laybardi.

"I...I...." she stuttered in her shock at his invasion, her emotions at a turbulent force sent her power skittering. Solaria's sphere beamed an amber light, a warning that she was losing control of herself. It would shatter if she did not get a grip.

"You've sensed it," he said, stalling for time.

Despite the warning, and the crack that appeared in the generator, Aaron forced his senses forward. He had to know the truth. Using the power he had gained from the Shroud, he created a backdoor entry to the one memory which had disturbed him in the rising tide of her emotions.

"Your magic doesn't lie," he muttered, with a final turn of the key.

"I had prayed it was just a nightmare." Mercadia's voice was barely audible.

Aaron frowned as he viewed the memory he had unlocked through to its devastating conclusion.

"The vision was not given to you by the Weavers' desire. A Nyrvallia is indeed rising," he said, still distracted by the disturbing scene he had witnessed.

"Does the Master know? Was it by his doing?" she asked.

Aaron clenched his fists to his side. "He does not know of this development, and I myself have only discovered it this night. That, and..." he paused. Back and forth he swung until he finally accepted the truth. Should he declare what he now knew? The light and dark battled within him: to forgive or punish her, make her suffer as his family had suffered?

Mercadia had used his silence to gather her wits and she thrust his energy away. "You've invaded my mind, how?" she demanded. Angry tears shone in her eyes.

Aaron could not help himself and smirked, torn between pity and bitterness. "Surely you did not expect me to undertake this foolhardy quest without an appropriate payment?"

"What do you mean? What is it you have done?"

He paused and considered. All that remained of the goodness within spoke first.

"She must know the truth," it said.

"Before she is punished," the dark added with a lascivious growl.

Aaron sighed and nodded. "The time I have spent in the Master's faction has allowed me to recover certain texts, and one thought to be lost following Moren's downfall."

"Deliberately so. I cannot believe you've desecrated his tomb." Mercadia's voice shook with outrage.

"I had no choice, you've exposed me and mine to great danger. And we now both know that it is you who cost me my father," he spat back.

He sensed Mercadia almost slip into unconsciousness, and with great difficulty, and much reluctance, he allowed her the time to gather herself once more.

Her hand reached out to hold onto the solid gold table the sphere rested on. "You should not have seen that memory."

"Too late. Your fear of the Nyrvallia is caught up with your feelings for my father. I would not have sought it, had you not revealed it to me."

"I didn't...I mean, I didn't mean to. I made a promise to him," she started.

Aaron refused to let her finish. "You broke my mother's heart, and you left a young boy believing his father hated him. Hardly a promise worth keeping."

"Do you think that I do not regret what happened? Kyle died to save our world."

"My father died with betrayal in his heart. He poisoned the fountain the moment he destroyed it, did you realise that? It all makes sense now. The Dark One...The Master, they are one and the same! And now once again you have placed my family in peril."

"No, he loved me, his heart was pure!"

"You're a fool if you believe that. Open your eyes. You and your accursed affections for my father. It was your fault his death was in vain."

"But the prophecy-"

He cut her off. "Our actions determine our fate, not the damned prophecy."

Mercadia's voice grew in strength. "You are wrong."

"Am I? Seems to me as though history is repeating itself. You put all your eggs in one basket, it is a dangerous and reckless plan. Because of you—"

"No! It is you who is a fool. The darkness has made you lose your senses. Your brother will prove that I'm right."

"And if Finn and my mother should die in the process? My father? My mother? My brother? All dead by your hand. Rest assured that I will come for you and the Council."

"You forget yourself, boy. I am an Elder," she snapped, barely containing her temper, her violet eyes murderous. The sphere beamed a final warning to them both.

Aaron could not help himself, the laughter bubbled up and tumbled out. A wave of energy slapped his cheek. He pressed a hand to the red welt that throbbed. "Feel better?"

"Hold your tongue," she fired.

His smile never reached his eyes. It was one that would have sickened his mother to witness. "Be careful, Mercadia. An Elder you may be, but I am the Eye of the Shroud."

"Impossible," she raged. "No mage alive could have survived such a transformation. Not even the Master. The time of the Eye is no more; the last disintegrated into dust long ago."

Aaron's eyes turned cold as he captured her gaze, his power rising, demanding that she acknowledge his words. "Look within the vortex, if you dare, and know that I speak the truth."

Her thoughts spilled clumsily into his mind. Could it be? What have I done?

He sensed her panic, the powerful and formidable Mercadia shaken to her core.

"Once the Master discovers what I am, he will not stop at enslaving the Council. Instead he will use me to annihilate you. There is nothing you can do."

Mercadia's mind continued to whirl out of control.

Is it too late to kill him? What will Elios say? Should I tell him? He must know of a way.

"Your thoughts betray you," Aaron said, his mind too strong for her to retaliate and cause a fatal effect. The sphere would indeed shatter at the first sign of bloodshed and it trembled close now.

"Stay out of my head," she snapped.

"Then shield better," he retorted.

Her lips pressed together, the turmoil evident as she fought to safeguard any further invasions and focused her mind on calm. He knew her ego to be scorched, and pride severely wounded. It would be a long time before she would forgive him for this night, if there was anything left of him to forgive.

Aaren blew out a breath and seized control of his temper, his thoughts now of his brother, Finn. The one who had turned his back on any hint of magic, and refused to study and heed their father's teaching. Now Aaron's survival was in his hands, and those of a stranger, a being from another world.

As much as he could hope, Aaron had to consider the real possibility that after tonight, he would truly live the rest of his days as a monster, the Master his puppeteer.

Mercadia's voice returned to its cool and composed self. "You must leave the Master's faction. You are far too dangerous a weapon. Return to Astyllis at once! Elios and I will find a way to repair the damage that has been done to you."

Aaron raised his sleeve and gestured at the mark. "You see it, don't you? What has been started cannot be undone, or be prevented. The information I have given you this night is my first and my last act of redemption. To be forewarned is to be forearmed."

Mercadia groaned, her hands clutched at her skirts, as she silently mouthed a steady stream of words not becoming of a Lady, nor an Elder.

A thought struck him, and he reached into his gown and pulled a vial of pearlescent liquid from his predecessor. Holding it up in the air, he whispered an incantation. The spell manifested from deep within the Shroud's vortex.

"What is that? I have never heard of such an enchantment."

"It is Tears of the Eye, and will help you to save my mother. I shall leave the vial protected within the reeds; only the Queen of Fae can retrieve it."

"How do I use it?" demanded Mercadia.

"Speak to Elios. Have him research the Hymorious texts. The answer lies within."

"Very well. You have my word as Elder of the Council, that I will do all within my power to save your mother."

Aaron nodded, although her word meant little to him now. "There is one other thing that I ask of you," he said, his stomach churned tight with regret.

"You know that I am in no position to refuse it," she sighed. Her heart ached as she remembered a similar conversation and promise to his father.

"With the wheels already in motion and the cogs turned in the Master's favour, there is no stopping what is to come. I have given you a slim chance, if my faith in Elios can be relied upon. Should I fail, tell my mother I am sorry. I would never willingly harm her or cause her pain. To my brother, let him know he must not blame himself."

Aaron released the connection before she could reply. He would converse with Mercadia no more. Time was of the essence.

With a heavy heart, he tossed the quartz generator deep into the Samsara. Silently he moved to place the vial within the reeds that lay on the cusp of the Selensia border. Dawn would soon be upon him, and with it his mother's fate sealed. Aaron prepared the portal to return to the Master's faction and stepped through. It was too late to look back.

Chapter Two
Mercadia

Aystyll's Keep, The Council of Elders, Astyllis

Mercadia delayed for a few moments more, allowing the time to collect herself and calm the storm of emotions. As much as she prided herself on her own ability and power, this time, she would have to acknowledge that it was impossible to avoid seeking her Elder Brother's counsel. Following all that she had discovered tonight, the stakes were even higher, and it was imperative that Elios be updated on the events.

I may be vain but I am no fool, Mercadia thought, as she considered the mistakes of her past. Her mind cast back to the vow that she had made the night Kyle had died, and her oath to the Saints that she would never let her pride get in the way again.

In the wake of Jarrow's death, a devastating loss to their triad of power, Elios remained the only Elder she could turn to with her fears. Despite their tumultuous relationship, Mercadia accepted that she must have faith and trust in his abilities and strength, and at the very least until the Council Initiate had atoned for her misdeeds, fulfilling the seventh and final edict.

Bessantia's sacrifice to the Nether plane, to save the girl and tracker, had satisfied the sixth edict, but at what cost? She had placed herself at great peril. Such a brave yet foolish act. Mercadia could only hope that her old adversary had been savvy enough to secure her identity and mask herself from the entities that resided. The entities that sought a key to their freedom. The Council could ill afford adding another string to the Master's bow. In the war he had waged, the rise of the Gydgen had been terrifying enough, although an expected threat. Their release from prison had also been cited in the prophecy. It would be down to the girl to bring about their destruction for the last time.

The final edict, as determined by Solarius's constellation, therefore, would only be satisfied when the girl was returned safely to their world, and had fulfilled the first half of the prophecy.

Mercadia's thoughts returned to the immediate horror of Aaron's revelations. His words crawled like insects beneath her stoic exterior and fed on her fear. The confirmation that the rise of a second Nyrvallia was indeed a reality, and not a nightmare somehow implanted by the Master's creatures. The truth could no longer be wished away, instead torturing her mind and sending her emotions spiralling into chaos.

Take a hold of yourself, she scolded inwardly, hugging her arms to her chest, her breathing erratic as she fought for control. The first Nyrvallia had risen before the Master's arrival. What would the combined evil of the two mean for this world, and its inhabitants, should they join forces in the war against the Council? Would either foe accept the other as the superior?

"Deep breath in, and out," she repeated, until the panic subsided.

Ever since the Council had enlisted Aaron into the Master's faction, her conversations with the young warlock had become increasingly grim, to the point of trepidation as to what evil he might reveal next. The Master's hunger for supremacy clearly knew no bounds, and his knowledge of their history was astounding. He was an unknown quantity, in respect to both his origin and his abilities. Where did he come from? How did he know? Who was feeding him this information? Could Aaron's words be true? Were the Master and the Dark One the same being? Impossible, it has to be! The Dark One would not have waited to emerge and claim its victory. What possible motivation would there be for such a delay? Damnation, Bessantia, I need to talk to Morvantia. Why could you not have foreseen this? It cannot be true, it simply cannot!

Mercadia considered that whatever game the Master was playing, he played it well. Somehow, he had acquired the knowledge of the creation of the Gydgen, long after they had been defeated and trapped in their murky prison, and many seasons before the Master had forced his way into their realm.

His knowledge of the Gydgen was dangerous to all that was light and good. These ancient warriors, a shadow army, freed and able to spill magical and non-magical blood once more, dripped poison into the minds of the innocents, and turned family and friends against each other, stripping away all that was pure and leaving nothing but an ugly shell to use as nourishment.

The guilt churned in Mercadia's stomach, exacerbated by the sickening rise of apprehension of what was to come. Her hand quickly rose to smother her mouth and prevent the release of its contents. She grimaced and swallowed down the bile. Her own weakness and fears lit a fuse of fury. She stormed to the heavy oak mirror that hung on the wall and scowled at her reflection.

'Foolish woman,' she chided, and slapped her own face. 'Remember who you are!" she commanded.

Her reflection raised a hand to touch its burning cheek, and in so doing sent more chaotic thoughts tumbling through her mind.

The Knights of Morvantia are no more. How will you defeat the Nyrvallia?

And what of the cost in enlisting and encouraging Aaron to follow the Master's orders?

Look what he has become, because of you! Was the information imparted worth the sacrifice?

Your selfishness and ego has sired something you cannot control. What would Kyle think of that? Would he ever forgive you?

Mercadia groaned and massaged her temporal lobes, easing the tension as her heart acknowledged the truth. Kyle, indeed, would never forgive her for using his eldest son. He had died to protect his family, and she, despite her promise, had been the one to carelessly thrust not just one, but both of his children into grave danger. If that was not enough, by shielding Myrialle and placing her under King Gregor's protection, she had awakened Myrialle's abilities further, and sentenced Kyle's first, and in truth, his only love, to death.

"I am not to blame," she said, wearily, hoping that somehow her words would carry across the distance, and reach Kyle's essence in the world beyond death. "I could not foresee what our actions would lead to. You must believe that."

It came only as a small measure of reassurance that she was not alone in both her poor judgement and lack of foresight. Bessantia's mind had also remained closed to the rising danger where Aaron was concerned.

Reflecting on past events and discussions, Mercadia questioned the strength of Bessantia's gifts, and Enwen's choice as Council Initiate.

Bessantia had failed to ward herself against the external forces that moved, and so had succeeded in blinding her sight to the rift that had torn through Morven's veil, allowing the Master his entry into their world. And now, she had failed to predict Aaron's transformation, and his obvious ability to interpret the ancient writings contained in the secret journal of Hymorious, the first descendant, and prophet of the Eye.

Although the combined knowledge of the Elders was vast, and had previously served them well, Mercadia knew that there were areas deep within the Shroud that no mage or Elder, regardless of their power, could penetrate. She too, had tried so many times, and failed miserably. The Eye, it seemed, was invincible to all spells and enchantments. Behind those magnificent doors it guarded, within the centre vortex of the Shroud, lay an unimaginable source of power, invocations, and antiquities. It would undoubtedly turn the tables on the Master and this war.

Mercadia screamed inwardly. She had handed the key to the greatest power on a plate to her enemy. She had been a fool to disregard Elios's initial warnings about the journal. Instead of listening to him, she had sided with Jarrow, the one who had always demonstrated the strongest prophetic knowledge without wrapping himself up in books and texts. Now she cursed her Elder brother for convincing her to dismiss the foolish ramblings of Hymorious and ignore the youngest Elder's warning. Age clearly was no indication of strength or power.

Elios had also been adamant that the Master was the one referred to in the Hymorious texts as the sire of evil, the 'Dark One.' Yet she and Jarrow had again disagreed, and in their naivety, believed the Fountain was destroyed, and Regan's blade sadly lost.

But Jarrow is dead!

Mercadia gritted her teeth. She must not make the same mistakes. With the rising of both the Gydgen and a new Nyrvallia, she must give credence to the belief that the Master was the true sire of evil.

Regrettably, she had done her youngest brother a great disservice. As the truth awakened, Elios had been accurate in his convictions and interpretations all along. This time she had to heed him, and enlist his aid.

Mercadia turned away from the mirror and all its revelations, her temper much deflated. Rolling her shoulders back and assuming a more confident posture, she marched with purpose to Elios's chambers. But as she reached to knock on the heavy oak door, her hand momentarily froze in mid-air, and colour flooded her cheeks. On the other side of the door she could hear a clock ticking, its hands of doom shattering her sudden resolve. She fought to get a grip on her emotions and to do what needed to be done: admit the truth she had been trying to deny, and push her pride and fears to one side, for they served no purpose.

It was bad enough that her fiancé had escaped his banishment, knowing that she was the one who would have to face him, and finally end his life. But to face the Nyrvallia too, without the hope of the Knights of Morvantia, and without a full Elder Council, left her reeling and floundering in the dark, a helpless bird that was about to be eaten. Not the bird of prey she had once been.

"If I walk away now, Elios will be picking my bones out of the Lion's teeth," she muttered. "For goodness' sake woman, get a grip; you are not powerless!"

Mercadia smoothed down her tresses, composed her thoughts, and rapped loudly on the door. Yes, the news she had to impart would not be welcome, but her determination not to repeat the mistakes of the past overrode her anxiety. She recalled her previous foolhardy decision to shield her brothers from the rising of the first Nyrvallia.

Mercadia, on that occasion, had attempted to deal with the creature alone. Even as the oldest mage to sit on the Elder Council, she had seriously overestimated her own power at the time, and her ego had almost cost their victory. And when her eyes had fully opened to the mistake that she had made, it had been far too late to retract the lies that had already been spun; the die was cast, and a family destroyed in its wake. Kyle's life, along with his warrior brothers, sacrificed. Now she questioned if they had even secured the victory they believed they had. What truth would finally be revealed?

As the seasons had passed, Mercadia had mourned Kyle, her heart heavy with the pain of his loss. That was until the day Drey had walked into her life, and for the very first time, she'd realised she had fallen in love.

Mercadia had known then that what she had thought she had felt for Kyle for all those seasons had not fed her pain, but raw, unequivocal guilt. The chance to make things right, lost forever. Drey's own duplicity, and his descent into darkness, had been the mirror that she'd needed to see the truth: her betrayal with Kyle, hurting a woman undeserving, and the forced separation of a father from his children, unforgiveable.

And now, not only did the Master have the Gydgen army and a Nyrvallia behind him, but he would also have control of the Eye, and thus every mage in the realm. Have I made a mess of things yet again? The great and powerful Mercadia, caught at last in the Spider's Web?

It had been her decision to enlist Aaron and send him as a spy into the Master's faction. For a second time, it seemed that she had underestimated the power of darkness, and how rapidly it had consumed the light, even one as brave and pure as Aaron. She knocked more firmly.

Elios's deep voice, muffled behind the solid oak, bid her entry to his private chambers. She steeled herself for the anger that was to come, and paused the speech that she had begun to formulate in her head. He was buried beneath a pile of scrolls, wisps of white hair peeking from above, as he muttered a loud curse.

"How do you fare, brother?"

Elios's head poked around the mountain of scrolls. He scowled, and said, "From the look on your face, much better than you."

"I have news." Mercadia inhaled and released a deep breath before plunging forward. "I'm afraid my news does not bring good tidings."

Elios's chair scraped back noisily against the floorboard. His robe caught on the side of the desk as he rose, and earned another profanity. He tugged the material free and muttered a steady stream of blasphemies as a loud tear echoed around the room.

Mercadia waited for him to finish his tantrum.

"You appear out of sorts today," she said, and tried not to smirk.

"Yes, and it would seem that you are not here to improve my mood, nor my day."

She knew she was stalling as her gaze swept across the numerous scrolls. "What are they?" she demanded.

Elios flicked his hand back towards the desk and groaned loudly when his fingers collided with paper. The mountain of documents were sent scattering across the floor. His eyes blazed with annoyance, and he stomped his foot.

"These are from King Gregor's vaults, and that blithering idiot who has the gall to call himself a librarian had left them buried behind seven barrels of mead and three crates of blue fire powder! If it were not for Siegfried's perpetual appetite for a good piece of parchment, they would never have been discovered. Imagine that!" he cried.

Siegfried, Elios's chosen familiar, scrambled his small furry white body onto what little remained on the desk and gave a loud squeak of pride, earning a scathing look.

Mercadia crinkled her nose in disgust. She could never understand why Elios had elected a mouse as his chosen familiar instead of something more majestic and deserving of an Elder Council member. Elios had insisted that he had his reasons and chosen to ignore her disparaging remarks.

"And what did Siegfried's little snack reveal?" asked Mercadia.

Elios raised a knobbly finger into the air, marking his point. "Well, the piece of scroll that my good fellow here did not manage to swallow speaks of an underground passage that leads directly from the castle to a Magorian Compass."

Mercadia's heart suddenly lit with hope. "But I thought all the compasses were destroyed in the Ancient wars of our Fathers?"

"It seems that one survived," he tutted. "And had our fool of a librarian looked harder when he was sent to retrieve all the scrolls, a proper inventory would have been completed. Think of the possibility if we had been alerted to this information sooner?"

Mercadia fully understood his annoyance. "But we have this now," she said, and clasped her hands together. "It could not have come at a better time. We can use the compass and balance our hand, which presently fares less than that of the Master."

Elios's face pulled back into a scowl. "And herewith lies the problem," he snapped. "You see, I have searched all the remaining scrolls, and not one sheds any light as to the location of the passage. My furry little associate has eaten the exact location, and the incantation to open the door."

"Well, get it out of him," Mercadia demanded. "Can't you make him regurgitate it or something?"

"Humph, I have no idea when Siegfried digested this important piece of information."

"Ask him," she said.

"To a mouse, one parchment looks pretty much like another," he said, rubbing his forehead. "I've a blasted headache from my transformation, and crawling through numerous nooks and crannies in search of his droppings. Not a snit of paper can I find to restore the original parchment."

"You've examined his mouse droppings?" Mercadia asked incredulously. "Elios, you really do need to get another familiar."

He shook his head. "Siegfried has served me perfectly well, and will continue to do so."

"Stubborn old goat," she muttered.

"Be that as it may, we know that one compass has survived intact. I will find a way to locate the passage and the opening incantation if it is the last thing I do." He folded his arms and cast a glare to Siegfried, who squeaked an apology.

"Now that's sorted, what unfortunate news do you wish to finish me off with?"

She sank into a velvet armchair, and closed her eyes as she counted to ten.

"A Nyrvallia has risen," she said.

Elios simply stared at her. "I'm sorry, but could you repeat that?"

"I said a Nyrvallia has risen," she repeated louder.

"Yes, I heard you the first time," he snapped.

"Then why...oh, forget it. You know what this means, don't you?"

"Of course I do. I'm not a simpleton."

He slumped in the chair opposite to hers. Siegfried followed, and curled himself on the arm. His long pink tail jerked out of the way as Elios drummed his fingers on the worn fabric.

"I suppose the only thing that stands in our favour this time around is that you told me before you went on and did something foolish."

"May I remind you that my power and knowledge have grown since that time?"

"Yes, and despite the growth in both of our powers, we are still an Elder down, which severely weakens us. We can barely hold the Selensia between us."

"We've defeated the Nyrvallia before."

He arched a brow. "And where do you propose to get another Morvantian Champion from?"

"I'm aware of our predicament," she said snippily.

Elios leaned closer to appraise her. She shifted uncomfortably beneath his scrutiny.

"Your power is severely drained. You need to rest."

"Oh, so does that mean you are ready to take over, rather than continue to hide behind your books and papers?" she asked, gesturing to the floor. "The Master is relentless in his desire to break the Selensia. Drey and his companions are obliterating our villages as we speak, and I am afraid the

Nyrvallia will soon join them. Not to mention the Gydgen army and..." She paused for breath.

"Then it is lucky for us that Myrialle's healing has worked wonders for me. I wish she could work a miracle with that damned parchment," he replied, scowling at Siegfried.

"Well, you do appear more like your usual cantankerous self," she sniffed. "But do take care. The Master's power is growing, and each hole he tears in the Selensia is bigger than the previous. Until we have our third Elder, we remain at significant risk."

"What a reassuring picture you paint, dear sister." He frowned. "It would be prudent for Bessantia to return to us now, so she can complete her oath and take her place."

"I am afraid that is impossible. My other unfortunate news is that Bessantia is in the Nether plane."

"What the blazes is she doing there? I thought Jarrow had taken steps to ensure that part of the prophecy did not happen."

Mercadia rose and paced the floor. "He lied to us. There was nothing in his chamber that could help her at all."

"What of his book?"

"It revealed nothing of use, and you should know that there were pages ripped out. I fear by Jarrow's own hand. In the fireplace I found some ashes, and what remained untouched by flame made no sense to me. I gave her the only spell I knew to spare her essence, should that part of the prophecy happen. She is out of our reach."

"Then we are in this strange girl's hands."

Mercadia stopped her pacing and knelt, placing a hand on Elios's knee.

His gaze softened.

"Do you miss him as much as I do?" she asked.

He nodded. "There are moments when I can still feel him, reaching out for help. A foolish notion," he said.

"I miss him so much. How did neither of us see that his mind was in such torment? I would never have sent him out to fight that night."

Elios patted her hand. "Our brother hid his secrets well. He did not want to worry us until he knew the time was right. You know as well as I do that he is...was...the only one who could be sent to fight. It was the right decision to make, and one that allowed King Gregor's men to live and fight another day."

"The Master's attack gave us no time," she complained. "No time to discover his secrets or to say goodbye." She moaned and crumpled to the floor, her chest heaving beneath the folds of her heavy embroidered gown. Mercadia drew her knees towards herself and suppressed the pain once more.

"Who informed you of the Nyrvallia?" Elios asked.

"Our valiant spy. And I've seen it too, in my dreams," she said, her mind still distracted by the grief.

"Did he say rising or risen?"

"Does it matter?" she asked.

"Rising is not yet risen," Elios replied. "I shall consult the Hymorious texts."

"You found nothing the last time to help. Why is this time any different?"

"Why, indeed, but I trust my instincts. Without a Morvantia warrior at our disposal, or Regan's blade, it is all that I have."

"There is one more thing I'm afraid I must mention."

"You really do know how to brighten my day," he grumbled.

"Aaron claims to be the Eye of the Shroud."

"Impossible," he scoffed. "I secured the text myself. No-one could find it in that ruin, let alone transcribe his journal."

"He did, and he has."

Elios remained silent for a few moments. She watched, and waited for the outcome of the information to dawn on him. It did not take long.

He leapt out of his chair, and furiously threw his hands into the air, causing Siegfried to leap from his perch and scurry away. Where to, Mercadia did not care.

"What have you done, woman?" Elios yelled.

She rose swiftly, and glared at him. "What I had to do," she said, jabbing a finger into his chest. "The information he shared has aided us so far. You cannot deny that, brother."

He spluttered, "Those titbits in no way compared to the weapon we have all but gift-wrapped and deposited in the Master's hands."

"Those titbits have saved lives, and if that damned journal was so dangerous, then you should have destroyed it before you showed it to Jarrow and agreed to bury it," she argued.

Elios's mouth snapped shut. Mercadia suppressed a smirk.

"Humph. Well, it is to be hoped that your valiant spy's contaminated essence doesn't tip the balance of the Shroud. Otherwise, none of us are safe."

"What do you mean, tip the balance?"

Elios rolled his eyes upwards. "The Shroud is neither Dark nor Light. Therefore, the Eye is neither Dark nor Light."

"Yes, I know that," she snapped.

"The Eye therefore may choose not to serve the Master and so remain neutral, allowing all mages to continue to draw on its power and gifts, or it could decide to drop us all into a steaming pile of horse manure... still, the last Eye was never swayed to truly turn its back on the light."

"I fear you may be grasping at straws," she replied. "I have seen his aura; it's black. The last sacrifice cost him dearly. By dawn, he will be as he was no more."

"Bah," Elios said, and stormed over to his desk. Picking up a quill and a piece of paper, he began to scribble furiously.

"What are you doing? This is not the time for sitting on your backside. We need action."

"I am contacting an old friend of mine. He can help with the Eye."

"Who?"

"Not your concern at this time," he flung back. "Now, instead of gawking—and I assume you have finished ruining my day—I would urge you to go and rest. We will need you at full strength."

"What about the Selensia?"

"I'll take care of it, after this," he muttered.

Mercadia moved silently to the door. Her hand hesitated on the handle. Should she mention that he had been right all along? That the Master and the Dark One were one and the same? What proof did she have?

"Elios?" she asked, not looking back at him.

"What is it?"

The words would not come to her lips. Perhaps it was best to leave this news for now. She'd laid enough burdens on his shoulders as it was.

"Despite our differences, I do trust you," she said, and hurried back to her room.

The little mouse poked his head around the small, yellow door carved into the wall of Elios's study and squeaked.

"Well, well, well, Siegfried," Elios exclaimed. "Perhaps there is hope for us, yet."

Chapter Three
Finn

Achavanich, Scottish Highlands, United Kingdom

The Fallen howled his fury into the night sky as each attempt to penetrate the Meridian failed. "What is this enchantment?" the creature growled, shaking off the effect of his recent blow. He attempted once more to force his way through the thorny barrier, and was met with the same punishment.

His fellow brethren cringed at the sudden spurt of silver light as their brother's enormous leathery hide crashed to the ground once more.

"Attack," he all but gasped the order to the others.

The smallest of the two shook his head, and limped to his brother's side.

"I am injured, Gallo. The wound will not heal. We must go back."

Gallo slowly rose to his feet, his reply cut off by a loud roar, and a second quake of the earth. Cold amber eyes glared in his direction.

"Mendip is right," their third complained. "To continue this assault is madness."

"I thought better of you, Grinn," Gallo snapped. "For one who claims to be no coward, you whine like a sow."

Grinn's large muscles moved spasmodically, and the flesh sucked noisily around his bones as he stretched out his hideous limbs and gave a roll of his shoulders. A crack reverberated, and he released a sharp hiss. "I have no desire to continue this foolish game of cat and mouse. Let the Commander try; his magic far surpasses our own."

"He'll burn our hides if we don't retrieve the Tracker and the girl," Gallo said wearily.

"Then let him see this enchantment for himself. Call for Rivik," Mendip pleaded.

"We must succeed," huffed Gallo.

Grinn spat out an inky globule and gestured towards the Meridian. "They have gone, Gallo, and we only waste time here with these futile attempts. Dawn approaches, and we all must regenerate. The Commander can deal with whatever this is."

The minutes dragged by before Gallo reluctantly nodded his accord. The Fallen turned together and miserably retreated back into the night.

In his current equine form, Finn edged closer to the boundary of the Meridian. His ears twitched for further sounds of the creatures that had pursued them. He gave a snort of relief and stomped his hoof in celebration at his victory.

Now, all that could be heard from the darkness was Rowan's harsh breathing and the slight snuffles and scratching of material as the little dog tried to fight its way out of the bag with little success.

Finn gave a soft whinny of reassurance and lowered to the ground, a signal for Rowan to dismount. She duly obliged and then moved away, allowing him the privacy to change back into his true form. A sigh escaped his lips as he stared down at his fully clothed body, relieved that it had been protected in the transformation.

"I thought you'd be naked?" she said, as he tapped her shoulder, and then lifted the bag free.

"You sound almost disappointed," he joked. He loosened the material, avoiding the sharp teeth of one seriously annoyed Scottie dog.

Biscuit wiggled free and then sprinted towards the hedging. He growled as he cocked his leg and released a spray of yellow liquid that steamed in the fresh night air.

Rowan did not respond to Finn's remark as she dissected a blade of grass. "What do we do now?"

"I hadn't thought that far ahead," Finn admitted.

"Helpful," she muttered. "How did you know the Meridian would stop them?"

"It called. Did you not hear it?" he asked gently. In the moonlight, he could see the tears that gathered in the corner of her eyes.

"If you remember, I was a little preoccupied back there," she sniffed.

"How could I forget? You knocked the Fallen right on its arse." He hoped his humour would catch and alleviate her shock and fear.

She did not return his grin, however, and instead stared at her hands as though they were alien to her. "I've no idea where it came from. It just happened."

"Do you think you can do it again, if you need to?"

"I've no idea," she replied. Her glum expression broke his heart.

He lifted her chin. "Hey, why the face?"

"I'm human, Finn. These things do not happen in my world. It's totally freaked me out."

"Wait a minute. Me turning into a horse didn't freak you out, but shooting energy bolts from your hand did?" he asked incredulously.

"Are you kidding me?" she spluttered. "You're a...from a...and I'm..." She paused and then finally started to laugh.

He simply stared at her, unsure of what to do next.

"Oh man...not in my wildest imagination could I...I mean, you were a dream, and poof, here you are. And we are being chased by an evil warlock, and an army of devil monsters. I rode you as a stallion..." she giggled, flushing. "Perhaps I should rephrase that? On second thoughts, nope...and after all that I've seen and heard... I'm having a meltdown, as I can shoot laser beams from my hands. Like I'm some sort of Wonder Woman..." she continued to guffaw. Her body flopped onto the grass, as she held onto her sides.

Finn casually laid himself back, staring up at the stars as he patiently waited for her hysterics to subside.

Rowan ceased her laughter, and suddenly sat up. "The Meridian, that's where my power came from," she said soberly. "I felt it changing me somehow, but..." She turned to face him. "What else has it done to me?"

"Prepared you," he said, and pulled her towards him.

She sighed as he placed a kiss on her forehead before he gently wrapped her in his arms and held her close.

Finn could not be sure how much time had passed before she broke the comforting silence they had lapsed into. "We can't stay here. They'll come back, won't they?"

"With Kane and reinforcements, I imagine. Wait a moment, let me try..."

He reached for his connection to the Council Elder.

Mercadia did not respond, her mind completely blocked against his invasion.

"Damn that woman. When I don't want her, she is there, like an annoying insect, and then when I do..." he growled.

"Charles is not replying either. I don't know if it is the Meridian still affecting his ability to connect with me."

Finn rose and reached for the rucksack. He whistled to Biscuit, who was trotting around the circumference of the Meridian. The dog stopped and held his gaze for a moment or two before he sat on his haunches. Finn nodded, pleased the instructions had been received. "There is someone who may be able to help us."

"Who?" Rowan asked as they walked to join Biscuit at the edge of the Meridian boundary. She stooped to scratch his ears.

Finn, confident that this was the same spot which Bessie had led him to previously, lifted Biscuit and shoved the little dog inside the bag. He cursed at the sudden nip of a finger before passing the bag to Rowan with a look of disgust.

"What are you doing?" she hissed, pulling the squirming bag onto her shoulder as Finn lowered himself to the ground and delved his fingers into the earth.

"Shush," he said, hoping she knew he meant the dog and not her.

Minutes passed and nothing happened. Finn frowned and ran a dirty hand through his hair. Rowan stared at him quizzically as he shrugged his shoulders.

"I thought that would work."

"Be still, Biscuit," she scolded. "Try it again."

Silence returned to the Meridian as Finn closed his eyes and reached deeper within himself. He willed for her to come and gasped, leaping to his feet as the ground trembled beneath them. His face broke into a wide grin. Rowan simply stared as the magnificent tree burst through the soil, its branches swirling and spiralling upwards. White and silver blooms sprang forth and bathed them both in a warm light. He reached for her hand and pulled her back before she had the chance to touch the bloom that had tipped forward and displayed a pearlescent orb.

"How beautiful," she murmured.

"Thank you, child," Enwen replied.

Finn smothered his laughter as she gaped at the tree.

"Did it... just..." she trailed off.

"She," he confirmed. "Her name is Enwen, and she's a friend of Bessie's."

"I'm so sorry for my rudeness. I was just surprised," Rowan said softly.

"There is no need for apologies. In this world, one is not used to seeing," Enwen reassured.

Finn cleared his throat. "Thank you for heeding my call. I did not know I could summon you, at least not without Bessie."

"And where is Bessantia?" Enwen asked.

Rowan shook her head. "We do not know. I assume—that is, I hope she is safe and still at the cottage. She ordered Finn and I to run when Kane and his creatures attacked."

Enwen fell silent. The minutes passed by but still she did not speak. Rowan glanced uncomfortably at Finn.

"Enwen?" he pushed gently.

"You must leave, this very moment. The Meridian's energy is being redirected. It must preserve and protect. It cannot help you here."

"How?" Finn asked. "Kane and his creatures are here, we cannot escape their reach, and I am unable to call on Mercadia. The blasted woman has blocked the connection for some reason, and right when I need her." His fists clenched at his sides.

"Do not be angry with her. She has good reason," Enwen said calmly. "The Elders have had their paths altered. Bessantia, too. I can send you where you need to go. Have you decided on a location?"

"Home?" he ventured.

Rowan freed the hand he still gripped. "No, the amulet. We have to find it first."

"Hurry, young one. Time grows short. The Meridian as you know now is dwindling. I must leave," Enwen urged.

Finn ran a hand through his hair, his mind hurriedly casting through all the possibilities. His thoughts shifted to the day he had first arrived. The hand of friendship extended as he'd been lifted from the floor. Eddie's features slowly came into focus. "That's one way to make an entrance, mate," he had laughed, offering Finn his coat and covering his nudity and embarrassment. The memories skipped on to the laughter they had shared on the walk back to Eddie's house. Finn's first taste of tea following a night spent sharing childhood stories.

"I have it," Finn said, and excitedly pumped his fist into the air, as the jovial face he remembered gave a cheeky wink.

Rowan's expression was not at all convinced.

"Trust me," he said. He squeezed her hand and then quickly released it to catch the pearlescent orb that Enwen had suddenly let fall from her branch.

"Step back," the magnificent tree warned, as Finn threw the orb up into the air.

It spun slowly at first and then gathered momentum, free from the constraints of gravity. A familiar melody played with each complete turn. The orb's size increased exponentially, until it had almost reached the height of Enwen herself.

Finally it stilled, giving a low gentle hum. The Portal had been opened, and waited for the couple to pass through.

Finn turned his attention back to Enwen, to thank her for coming to their aid, but she had already disappeared beneath the ground, her farewell response whispered to him on a tender breeze. He clutched Rowan's hand tightly before she could so much as utter a complaint and pulled her into the sphere.

A sudden jolt, and they both toppled through the very same doorway he remembered, and landed with a thud on the mahogany floor. The tavern fell into complete silence. Two silver-haired gentlemen frowned. A blonde-haired woman in the corner smothered a giggle.

Finn burst into laughter as a younger man with warm hazel eyes, dark floppy locks, and a spattering of freckles over his nose suddenly spurted his pint over the table. "Bloody hell mate, again?"

"You know how I like to make an entrance," Finn said, rising and lifting Rowan gently to her feet. "Are you alright?" he whispered.

She scowled and brushed at her legs. "A little warning next time."

The younger man's face beamed at them, and he banged his pint glass down on the table, his chair falling over in his eagerness to greet them. He gave Finn a huge hug. "It's good to see you."

"You too, Eddie," Finn said, receiving a friendly slap on the back.

The tavern resumed its normal chatter, and all attention shifted away from the two strangers.

Eddie chuckled. "At least you're fully clothed this time."

Rowan arched a brow as Finn's friend lowered his voice and whispered, "And you've brought a female Martian too."

"I'm from Teesside, not Mars," she said dryly.

Eddie guffawed, and Finn, unable to smother his own amusement, joined in.

"Have you both quite finished?" Rowan asked, with a hint of a smile.

Her posture had become more relaxed now that they were no longer the centre of attention.

Eddie could not stop grinning. "Can I get you both a drink?"

"After the day I've had, I could do with a large white wine," she said.

"The usual for me. Does the tavern allow dogs?" Finn queried.

Eddie gestured over to the corner, where the silver-haired gentlemen were seated. "As long as they are well behaved, the owner doesn't object. That's his old German Shepherd over there."

"Then perhaps a bowl and a jug of water for our small friend," Finn suggested.

As if on cue, Biscuit's head popped up from inside the rucksack.

"He's a cute fella. What's his name?" asked Eddie.

The little dog growled a response.

"Biscuit, and he objects to the word cute," Rowan said, pulling the bag from around her shoulder.

"I can't see why he should, with a name like that," Eddie quipped.

Rowan lifted Biscuit free, and whispered loudly in his ears to ignore the pair of them.

"I'm sure we can manage a drink and some grub for him," Eddie said good-naturedly. He wrapped an arm around Finn's shoulder and steered him towards the bar. "It's so good to see you again, mate. For a while there, I'd thought I'd dreamt you."

Rowan covered her mouth with her free hand to cough.

"You too," Finn said. He glanced back and noted the affection in her eyes as she followed slowly behind. "Sorry," he mouthed, knowing he had been forgiven.

The pretty young female behind the bar flashed a smile. "Well, hello, stranger. I see you're dressed for the occasion this time, although you do keep managing to trip over your own feet."

"Hey Lizzie, how are you?" Finn asked. He could sense a slight shift in Rowan's mood as she appraised the woman in front of them.

"Much better now this big lump has finally grown some balls and asked me out."

Eddie laughed. "Aww babe, how long are you going to hold that one against me?"

"Six months Eddie! How many hints does a girl have to drop?"

"Well, this is a world of equal rights and opportunities. You could have easily asked me out," Eddie said, and blew her a kiss.

Lizzie offered her hand to Rowan. "Men, bloody useless at introductions. I'm Lizzie."

"Rowan, nice to meet you. This little fella is called Biscuit."

Finn smiled as Rowan's mood visibly relaxed.

"He's gorgeous," Lizzie exclaimed, reaching across the bar to tousle Biscuit's fur.

"I see he doesn't object to that word," muttered Eddie.

"So, are you two together?" Lizzie asked.

Finn wrapped an arm around Rowan's waist. "She's the one I've been searching for," he said. Rowan blushed as he pressed a gentle kiss to her cheek.

Lizzie reached across the bar and gave Eddie a light smack. "Why can't you be that romantic?"

Eddie answered her with a brief brush of his lips. "You know I love you, baby."

She grinned, obviously happy to let him off the hook. "What can I get you, then? Eddie, the usual?"

"Yes. Finn will have a pint of Coke, and Rowan a large glass of white wine. Can you manage a bowl of water and some grub too for the gorgeous fur ball?"

"Sure, there's some spare dishes out in the back," Lizzie said.

She disappeared for a few moments. Rowan turned to Eddie. "What day and time is it?" she asked.

Eddie's eyebrows wiggled teasingly. "And I thought you said that you weren't a Martian?"

"Funny," she replied. Rowan's eyes flicked to the watch on his wrist. "I take it that does tell the time, and is not a mere decoration for you to impress the ladies?"

"Yes, all six grand's worth. It's ten thirty."

Rowan frowned, and she bit down on her bottom lip.

"I'll bring the drinks over," Eddie said as Lizzie returned. "Oh, and Finn? Try to make it to the table this time, mate." He gave that same cheeky wink and turned his attention back to the barmaid.

Finn led Rowan to a quiet booth in the corner. Biscuit nestled below the table against their feet.

"What was all that about?" he asked.

"The time we left the Meridian and the time it is here, they do not add up. Somehow we have gone backwards in time. My guess is around 4 or 5 hours. How is that possible?"

"Likelihood is, it was the only way that Enwen could be sure that we would meet up with Eddie. It would have been far too dangerous to have attempted to move us forward in time."

"No wonder I felt dizzy. Although strange that I have not lost my memories for those last 4-5 hours." She rubbed at her temples. "I really am riding that train to crazy town."

"Excuse me?"

"Never mind," she muttered. "Your friend, he seems like a nice guy. I do like him."

"Ah, so you have warmed to his charms. Should I be worried?" Finn joked.

She met his gaze. Finn's heart pounded in response.

"I know," he said quietly and reached for her hand, gently running his thumb across her fingers. "You feel okay now?"

"The dizziness has worn off, but my head is still jumbled and trying to make sense of everything that has happened," she replied.

Finn glanced over to the bar. Eddie had lifted their drinks and two silver dishes onto a black tray.

"So what's this about dressing for the occasion?" Rowan asked.

Finn's face heated. "When I first arrived through the portal, I landed in the very same spot right in front of Eddie, without a stitch on me."

She laughed. "Seriously? You were stark naked?"

"Totally humiliated. I would not have put it past Mercadia to have done it on purpose. Thankfully, Eddie came to my rescue."

"I'm a bloody hero," his friend replied, placing the two silver dishes underneath the table before sliding into the booth next to Rowan.

Finn lifted the glass of dark, effervescent liquid and took a long drink.

"Steady mate, the fizz will get to you," Eddie warned.

When he had returned the glass to the table, Rowan took a quick sniff of his drink. "Is there anything in that Coke?"

"No, I make sure this one does not touch alcohol. Who knows what it would do to him? You know, with him being...erm...from another country."

Rowan nodded and took a sip of her wine.

"So, do you have somewhere to sleep, or do you need a place to crash?" Eddie asked.

"I was hoping you'd ask," Finn said.

"No problem, stay as long as you want, although tomorrow night you will have the place to yourselves, as it is Lizzie's twenty-first. I would invite you along, but her grandma is a battle-axe and a stickler for numbers."

"That's fine we..." Finn's voice trailed away with the increasing pressure over his third eye. He gave a loud groan. "Perfect timing," he muttered.

"Something wrong?" Eddie asked.

Finn rolled his eyes and moved his hands to his throat, as though he were about to throttle himself.

"Oh, the erm...imaginary friend?" Eddie smirked. He quickly drained the contents of his pint. "I'll go grab another one before last orders."

"He knows about Mercadia?" Rowan hissed when they were alone.

"Sort of," Finn mumbled, allowing the connection to open to the Council Elder.

He sensed the light against his lids and acknowledged it was daytime in Valoria. Mercadia, despite her insistence on connecting with him, was remarkably quiet. Finn remained silent and listened in.

A man's voice trembled as he spoke. "All of them."

"Dead?" another voice responded. Finn was all too familiar with this one. The shock and anger evident in King Gregor's voice.

"Forgive me, Your Highness, but yes, all your men are dead."

Finn sensed the King's struggle to maintain control. "You mean to tell me that the entirety of my second guard have all been slaughtered? Except you?"

"I'm afraid so," the voice quivered.

"And how is it that you survived?" Mercadia demanded.

"I am to deliver the message."

"What message is that?" she asked.

"Death is coming to you all," the voice replied.

"What the..." A strange gargling sound echoed in Finn's ears.

"Someone help him," King Gregor shouted.

The sound of crashing metal was followed by a choking plea for help.

"By the Saints!!" King Gregor's voice was filled with fear.

A pungent aroma assaulted Finn's nostril, causing him to cough. He fought a violent urge to be sick.

"Stand away," ordered Mercadia.

The scream made Finn's blood run cold, bringing back unwanted memories of rotting corpses on enemy lines.

"Mercadia, what was that?" asked the King.

"I don't know." Her voice was much calmer than Finn sensed her emotions to be.

"Get rid of it now," King Gregor ordered.

Footsteps hurried across the floor. The sound of someone vomiting in the background churned Finn's stomach.

"My chambers immediately, Mercadia." The King's voice was dejected, and not at all as compelling as it usually was when he barked out his commands.

She sighed heavily. "I must speak with Finn first."

"Very well." King Gregor's footsteps faded into the distance.

Finally, they were alone.

Finn's senses pulled forward into motion. "Where are we going, Mercadia?"

"The gardens. I need the fresh air," she replied, her voice unsteady.

He understood the need. Although the pungent smell was gone, the memory of it still lingered. "Was it as bad as I heard?"

"Worse," she replied. Her breathing deepened as she pulled the air into her lungs. Finn was greeted by the scent of sprite lillies and elderthorn. He took a few moments to appreciate the delicate aromas too.

"Our situation here is dire. The Elder Council has weakened following Jarrow's death. It is taking everything we have, as we must maintain the Selensia. Without the third Elder, we remain vulnerable."

Finn ran a hand through his hair. "Then initiate the third Elder. How hard can it be?"

"An Elder's place cannot be given, it must be earned."

"Is there no-one worthy of taking Jarrow's place?"

"There was one, but it has become much more complicated now. In her attempt to save you and the girl she had to invoke a spell. I'm afraid she is gone."

Finn's heart galloped in his chest. "Bessie? Is she dead?"

"No, Bessantia lives, but for how long I am unsure. She is out of our reach in the Nether plane."

"What spell did she invoke?"

"The only one she could. Bessantia's history is quite complex. She cannot risk encountering the Master, not yet. Her sacrifice has afforded the Council some protection. But time is slipping through our fingers. It will all be for nothing if we do not find a way to set her free."

"And how do I do that?" he asked.

"Not you, the girl. She is the only one who can," Mercadia replied. "Has she located the amulet yet?"

"No. We search tomorrow," he confirmed.

She was silent for a moment and then asked, "Who distorted your time?"

"Enwen. It was our only means of escape. Kane and the Fallen trapped us in the Meridian."

"She did not mention your encounter." Mercadia sighed heavily.

"Enwen has returned to our world?"

"I had no choice but to summon her. We have gained another foe in this war. One whom I believed I would never have to face again."

He had never heard her sound so defeated. "What else do I not know?"

"I would gladly tell you it all, for a moment's peace, and to relieve the burden carried, but I cannot risk you becoming distracted from the task at hand. The only way you can aid us now is to find the amulet and return with the girl and Bessantia. You need to hurry."

"Easier said than done," Finn grumbled.

"I must go. King Gregor's patience grows thinner by the day. The loss of his second army has put him in an extremely bad mood."

"I would imagine the deaths of at least one hundred and fifty soldiers would put anyone in a bad mood," he said, unable to keep the sarcasm from his tone.

"I didn't mean it like that," she snapped. "Of course it is upsetting, and I do feel for their kin. But when Gregor is in a mood he tends to make rash decisions, and with all that is against us, we cannot afford another error of judgement."

"What do you mean, another error of judgement?"

"An attempted surprise attack on the Gydgen before they could grow in strength. I shall be speaking to Elios most severely. He should never have agreed to lift the veil and allow the King's army to pass through, particularly after our—" her words broke off. The connection instantly dissolved.

Finn seethed inwardly. The Elder Council was clearly in trouble, and still they refused to let him return home. A slight cough had him turn his attention from his frustrating conversation and towards his friend.

"You're back, then. Did you enjoy your little nap?"

He glanced at Rowan. Her expression was one of concern.

"Sorry about that," he said.

"If you don't mind, Eddie, I think it best that Finn and I get some sleep."

"No problem, I'll let Lizzie know."

Finn waited for Eddie to leave before turning to Rowan. "Thank you."

She downed the last of her wine. "We need to talk, alone."

"Tomorrow, I promise. Tonight let's just get some sleep."

He knew she wasn't happy, and he was grateful she had chosen not to press the issue. Instead she bent to retrieve Biscuit who was snoozing under the table. The little dog growled his disagreement at being placed once again in the rucksack. Finn rose and reached for her hand.

Eddie waved for them to join him at the entrance. He gestured towards a line of strange-looking cars parked on the opposite side of the road. "I guess you are too tired for the walk?"

"Truthfully, I'd appreciate the taxi to yours," Rowan answered.

Finn nodded his agreement and followed her across to the other side.

Rowan climbed straight into the back, Finn beside her and Eddie sitting in the front passenger seat. The taxi set off along the main road once Eddie had given the address. They headed South.

Rowan laid her head against Finn's shoulder. He stared out of the window, his senses on full alert now that they were moving again. He scoured the area for any sign of Kane or his minions despite the probability at that time being low.

"What is it? Rowan whispered.

Finn relaxed back into the seat. "It's nothing, don't worry," he said and kissed the top of her head. Eddie met his gaze in the mirror. Finn shook his head. It was acknowledged with a slight nod as his friend turned his attention back to the driver.

Rowan stumbled out of the car when it had finally come to a halt. "Sorry, half asleep," she murmured, as Finn moved quickly to her side. She stared at the detached sandstone building with its enormous windows. "You live here?"

"What were you expecting?" Eddie asked.

"I don't know, a terraced house, flat share, some sort of student digs?"

"None of the above. I am one of the lucky ones, two very affluent and generous parents. They bought me this house. I guess they wanted to ensure I was on the property ladder, even at my very respectable, though youthful age of twenty-two."

"I had pictured you as a student. So what do you do for a living, if you are not studying?" she asked.

"I'm what you would class as a computer boffin."

"You're an IT nerd," Rowan said, her mouth curved in a teasing smile.

"I prefer boffin to nerd," Eddie replied. He unlocked the front door and waved them inside.

"Not bad for a boffin," she said, as Finn removed her jacket and hung it on the coat hooks.

Indeed, the inside of Eddie's home was beautifully furnished in reds and creams. And surprisingly overflowing with flora, Finn thought.

"Ah, Lizzie wanted a few posies to brighten up the place," Eddie replied to Finn's silent question.

"She certainly has an eye for colour," Finn attempted without sarcasm.

"Too much?" Eddie asked.

"Yes!" Finn stated.

"No! The smell in here is divine," Rowan reassured.

"I'll get you both settled, and we can chat in the morning. The bathroom is upstairs and to the left. Your bedroom... I do take it you will be sharing with Finn, or is that too presumptuous of me?"

"We'll share," Finn responded before Rowan could.

"Okay, then. If you take the middle bedroom, the bed is more spacious, and comfortable for you both." Eddie winked.

"And here I thought we were going to have to sleep on that forsaken pull-out contraption that imitates a bed."

"If you miss it so much, you are quite welcome to take it."

"Not that much," Finn replied.

"Lizzie would have my nuts in a vice if she found out that I didn't offer my parents' room to you."

"Oh, please say we are not putting them out," Rowan said.

"No, they only visit twice a year but demand their home from home comforts."

"Would it be okay for Biscuit to join us?" she asked.

"Their precious poodle Sidney, aka Siddoms, is allowed to sleep in the room, so they can hardly complain about another mutt staying."

A deep growl reverberated around the entry hall.

"Apologies, Biscuit. I forget myself," Eddie replied.

"He's not a fan of pampered pooches," Finn explained to the grumbling bag. "Goodnight Eddie, and thank you."

Rowan reached for Finn's hand and together they climbed the spiral staircase, leaving their friend smiling impishly at the bottom.

Chapter Four
Kane

4 *Hours Later*
Bessantia's Cottage, Achavanich, Scottish Highlands

The creature moved to where the old woman had once stood and sniffed the air. Its cold amber eyes meeting Kane's glare with equal challenge, and mouth pulled back into a snarl that revealed large white fangs glinting in the moonlight.

"The power is gone. I cannot trace it, Commander."

Kane choked on his fury. "Tell me, Rivik," he demanded, "how is it even possible for her to escape?" Eyes burned with temper as Kane pointed an accusing finger. "Were you not watching her?"

Rivik scowled under the scrutiny of Kane's glare. "Closely," he snarled, "but she made no suggestion that she was casting, and you were—"

"Be careful," Kane warned, not caring for the creature to highlight his mistake or the distinct lack of judgement shown. The woman, after all, had borne the Master's mark.

The Fallen's claws raked the ground, but he was wise enough to make no further challenge. "What now, Commander?"

"Search the cottage. She may be hiding."

Rivik nodded and turned towards the building, tension rippling across his large hide. He sprinted away without a further word.

Alone, Kane stroked his chin and reflected on the night's events. Why has the Master made no mention of any mage existing in this world? A mage powerful enough to overpower my army and then miraculously disappear into the night? How could he not have known? Surely, the mark binds them?

Casting his mind back to his training, Kane frantically searched through his memories. As a child he had never believed such stories of the legendary Bessantia to be true, and he had sniggered at his fellow students for being so gullible. As far as Kane and his mother had been concerned, the old woman had been nothing but a myth, spun by the Fablekeepers to entertain on the anniversary of the Ancient Wars. The circumstances of Bessantia's death and sudden disappearance had been speculated on by so many, yet none, it would seem, could truly claim to know the truth. Tonight, the myth had indeed proved to be a reality.

An interesting turn of events...but who is she? What is she? What is the truth behind her source of power?

Kane's head ached as each question continued to tumble and spiral. How is it she still bears the Master's mark, and what is she doing here? Has she been here all this time?

His musings were disrupted by the sight of Rivik charging towards him. The creature's amber eyes glowed fiercely in the darkness. Kane sensed wild excitement and a hint of fear emanating from the Fallen. "Commander, you must come with me now."

His brow arched. "You've found the old woman?"

"No, something else. It is unlike anything I have sensed before."

Intrigued, Kane followed Rivik inside the cottage. The creature led him along a narrow corridor, passing through the kitchen destroyed by his earlier anger and to a door at the furthest end of the passageway. Kane's curiosity was piqued. A rune was carved into the wood, and although it was not one he had ever seen before, there was a strange familiarity to its marking.

"Can you sense it too, Commander?" Rivik asked.

Kane could indeed, and he licked his lips. His hand pressed against the wood, and a thrum of energy vibrated beneath his skin. Kane reached for the brass handle, but it would not yield. He scratched his chin and considered for a moment. Pulling a silver dagger free from his pocket, he carefully scratched a sigil over the top of the rune and waited to see if his suspicions would prove correct. Bright orange flames licked at the door and burned through the wood, scorching away the rune. When the last flame had extinguished itself, Kane reached for the handle once more. He held his breath, his hand trembling slightly as he opened the door to reveal...

... absolutely nothing.

It was quite the anti-climax as his eyes took in the sight of an empty room. Not one scrap of furniture was present. Nothing at all to account for the power that he had felt radiating beneath his skin just moments before. Kane entered, closely followed by a confused Rivik.

"I do not understand, Commander." The Fallen's footsteps echoed loudly as he padded the full circumference of the room. "There is something here, I can sense it. Yet..."

Kane crossed to the centre and cast his eyes down. "It's here," he growled as the thrumming resumed with an intense ferocity. It coursed through his body and fired every nerve. He inhaled sharply as a dark mist spiralled free from the floorboards and wrapped itself around his body, the warmth of its caress against Kane's skin welcoming him like a long-lost lover. It was a power unlike anything he had ever experienced before. Kane groaned involuntarily as he revelled in the feeling. His body palpitated with sheer desire and an unmistakeable need. Rivik shrank back against the wall and hissed a warning. The energy surrounding Kane continued to grow and consume. He released a purr of sheer gratification.

"Commander!" Rivik shouted.

Kane sensed his form had started to shift, felt the break of bones and his muscles quivering. The sensation was delicious.

"You leave me no choice," a distant voice warned.

From somewhere in the back of his subconscious mind Kane detected a faint movement and a sound of claws scraping into wood.

"Commander, step away," Rivik ordered.

"No, I want more," Kane argued in a voice that he barely recognised as his own.

A sudden high-pitched scream reverberated around the room. Was that me?

He collapsed to his knees, dragging the air into his lungs. The dark mist receded and relinquished its grip.

The Master's mark on his arm burned a fierce red. Tears cascaded down his cheeks as Kane lifted his gaze to meet Rivik's.

"You called him? Why?" he snarled.

Rivik's eyes were defiant. "You left me with no option. A second longer and it would have consumed you completely."

"I wanted it to," Kane spat out, glaring at the Fallen with sheer loathing. "The power was mine. I needed it. I..." He groaned in pain as the mark burned deeper into his skin.

The dark form of the Master manifested in front of them both. "Where is it?" he demanded.

"Where is what?" asked Kane innocently.

The Master instantly spun and threw Kane across the room. "Don't lie to me. I know you have tasted it."

Kane, winded by the blow, attempted to pull himself up. "I only felt it. I don't possess it," he managed between ragged breaths.

The Master turned towards Rivik. "Search the room. I know it's here."

"Forgive me for saying this, Master, but I do not think it is wise for me to..."

The Master's mouth twisted into a cruel sneer. "No need to fear. It will have little interest in the likes of you. Now, show me its location."

Rivik obeyed and moved tentatively to the centre. He sniffed the floorboards and shuddered. Taking a slight step back, he declared, "It lies beneath."

"Retrieve it and bring it to me," the Master snarled at Kane.

Kane reached to feel behind the back of his head. A sticky pool had formed. He rose with a grunt. "What if it happens again?"

"For your sake, ensure that it does not. It belongs to me, and if you try and use its power once more, I will feed you to the Weavers."

Kane lowered his gaze. He swallowed hard and pushed the swelling anger firmly below the surface.

The Master snarled, and a sudden gesture of hand had Kane's dagger slicing through his chest as it tore itself free from his pocket. The blade plunged itself into the wall furthest away from him and traced the motion of the Master's hand. A series of numbers were carved into the concrete.

"You will bring me what is mine to these coordinates," the Master instructed.

The dagger clattered to the floor once its work was finished. Kane moved quickly to retrieve it, and placed it back into his pocket before it gave the Master other ideas. "What about the Tracker and the girl?" he asked.

"You have found something much more valuable to me. Something that was stolen a long time ago. It is all that I need."

"But the prophecy?"

The Master's laughter sent a chill down Kane's spine. "There is nothing to fear now. The girl cannot compare to the power I shall hold."

"But, Mercadia has taken a number of risks sending the Tracker here. Why not possess them both, Master? Ensure that the Council of Elders are destroyed for good?"

The Master was silent for a moment. "You are right. I shall possess the girl and her power."

Kane turned to study the coordinates and etched them into his memory. "When will the portal open?"

"In two days. Take the Fallen and the girl and be at those coordinates. I will have an armed escort waiting for you."

"And the Tracker?"

"Kill him. I have no need of him now."

"At last," Kane said, releasing a deep breath as the burn from the mark subsided and the Master's form dissipated from the room.

"Commander?" Rivik asked, once they were alone.

Kane spun and glowered at the Fallen. "Betray me again and regardless of what you are, I will gouge your eyes out. Never forget who gave you the form and power," he snapped.

"I am sorry. However, my actions were justified."

We shall see, foolish creature. Despite what you are, you are of no match to me. Kane thrust his hand into the air and curled his fingers tightly in his palm.

Rivik howled as one by one, the bones in his leg splintered. Kane watched the Fallen's suffering with satisfaction. Only when he had achieved a small sense of retribution did he relinquish his grip.

Rivik panted on the floor, unable to shift his hideous bulk away from the perceived danger as Kane approached menacingly and reached for the dagger. He carved a healing sigil into the Fallen's thick hide.

"Let that be a lesson to you," he hissed.

Slowly, the bones cracked and fused together. Rivik writhed and hurled out curses in a foreign tongue.

Kane lost interest in the creature's suffering and turned his attention away. He moved cautiously to the centre of the room. Keeping his body firmly away from the main area and source of power, he plunged the sharp blade into the floor. The black mist swirled upwards and curled playfully around his fingers. Spellbound, Kane allowed it to intertwine, and felt that same ache of need and yearning in his gut as it caressed his skin. It enticed him to step forward and meld with it once more. The feeling was intoxicating, and he desperately wanted to feel such pleasure again. I must fight it for now, until I know...

Kane groaned his frustration and searched for the most painful of memories to combat the enchantment, the mist swirling evocatively around his hands with its promises of ecstasy.

He closed his eyes and hammered at the internal barriers he had erected in his mind to retrieve her memory, the most agonising one he possessed, recalling the scent of her perfumed skin and the softness of her rich lips as she'd turned to kiss him goodbye before thrusting the very same dagger deep into her chest. Her last words: "For you, my love."

A solitary tear escaped and slid silently down his cheek. Kane wiped it away before Rivik could see such weakness. The pain of losing the only woman he had ever loved was truly unbearable. His face hardened with hatred and his jaw clenched tightly as he pushed the memory behind the walls once more but held onto the emotions it stirred. His thoughts and heart were consumed with revenge. He would make them all pay.

The grief and anger were a sufficient distraction to give him the strength to reject the mist's alluring offer of an alliance. Kane levered the floorboards and threw them aside. Reaching down, he fumbled until his hand enclosed around a solid object. It felt smooth and cold. He retrieved it and placed it in front of him. It was a black obsidian crystal ball. The power continued to spill free and taunt him.

"Find me a bag," he ordered.

Rivik had only now been able to stand. "Yes, Commander."

The Fallen disappeared from the room and was back moments later carrying a thick heavy sack. He dropped it at Kane's feet and stepped away.

Kane scooped it up and opened it wide. It smelled of earth, and he screwed up his nose in disgust.

"It was all I could find."

Kane scowled and carefully lowered the cloth over the top of the obsidian crystal. He pulled the edges together and turned the sack slowly, forcing the obsidian to slide to the bottom.

"What now, Commander?" asked Rivik.

"Tear this hovel down."

Kane left the Fallen alone.

Outside, it was a clear night. He dropped to the ground and breathed the air in deeply. The wound on his head still smarted, and he sensed the bruises surfacing across his back. He had been right about the Master, and it would not be long before he carried through with his threat.

I must be ready, and strike before he strikes. Then I shall deal with her.

Kane felt his head and winced slightly at the dull throb. The blood still oozed in his hair. He braced himself and drew a healing sigil in the congealing pool, biting back the sharp sting as the wound knitted together.

The splintering sounds of wood and brick could be heard behind him as Rivik complied with his instructions.

Barrock suddenly appeared from the trees, closely followed by Gallo and two more of the Fallen. The largest of the two walked with a severe limp.

"Well?" Kane asked impatiently.

"Forgive us, Commander. They escaped behind some sort of force field," Gallo replied.

"We couldn't penetrate it," said another.

Kane appraised the one who had spoken with a scowl. "You are?"

"My name is Men-"

The creature exploded into several pieces before it could finish its name. Kane lowered his arm and turned to the one stood cowering against Gallo.

"And your name?"

"Please, I beg your forgiveness, Commander."

Kane paused as the Fallen bowed its head and lowered to the ground.

"My name is Grinn," the creature replied.

"I should kill you too," Kane snapped.

"We can ill afford to lose any more of our numbers, Commander," Barrock reminded him.

Grinn trembled as Kane considered whether he could even be bothered. Should I spare this miserable creature's life? They had indeed failed him.

He conceded that Barrock had raised a valid point, and he could not be sure how many of his army remained intact after the old woman's attack.

"We have been given new orders," he said and thrust the sack towards Barrock. "Take it."

"What is it?" Barrock scented the cloth. "It reeks of death."

"It belongs to the Master," Kane responded through gritted teeth.

Barrock nodded and reluctantly accepted as his Commander turned to address the others. "Make yourselves useful and assist Rivik. I want that hovel torn apart."

Grinn rose. He was careful to remain subservient.

Kane smirked.

"Yes, Commander, and thank you."

The two Fallen sprinted away to join Rivik. Barrock's amber eyes held an intense glow as he locked his gaze with Kane's.

"What next, Commander?" he managed through a mouthful of sack.

Kane glanced at the night sky. Dawn was swiftly approaching, and their time was running out. He considered the force field that the Tracker and girl had escaped behind and wondered. A portal, perhaps? It would explain why the Fallen could not travel through it. Only I grant them that power. I must be sure.

Withdrawing the spelled book from his pocket, he whispered an incantation. The pages turned back and forth by invisible hands, but refused to yield the Tracker's location. Kane snapped the cover closed and inhaled. After a count of three he released. With one hand placed on either side of the cover, he repeated the incantation with a little more fervour. Blood dripped freely from the book's spine and onto the ground. Kane's stomach tightened into a knot. The spell had been rejected. He ripped the book apart and threw the pieces onto the ground. How could this be? I do not understand.

Barrock inched slowly away from striking distance. "What is wrong, Commander?"

"Something has interfered with my magic. I cannot locate the Tracker."

"Perhaps the girl?"

Kane dismissed the possibility. How could this human be any match for my power?

"Gather what remains of your brethren and set up camp. I will be there shortly. Be sure to give Rivik the coordinates."

"Yes, I shall see to it at once. Er, Commander? My brethren need to begin their regeneration at once, their injurie..."

"They may retreat to their cocoons." Kane pointed to the sack that was gripped between the Fallen's teeth. "Leave that in my quarters."

"Very well, Commander."

Once alone, Kane closed his eyes and released his consciousness. It hurtled quickly through the void towards the Great Hall. The creature he had been attacked by drew close but did not harm him. "You are changing," it hissed.

"So I am told. What do you know of it?"

"More than you. Otherwise, you would not have returned."

It stopped following Kane, but he could still feel its presence as it watched from a distance. What is it waiting for?

An uneasy feeling travelled the length and breadth of his spine. This is no time for cowardice, Kane chided himself.

A momentary feeling of relief flooded his senses when he arrived in the Great Hall and landed in front of Morbae.

The Mistress's Guardian rose from the stone chair, his expression one of confusion. "Why have you come?"

"I need to speak with her. It's urgent."

Morbae studied him and then disappeared. The seconds passed and Kane tapped his foot. Finally, the chamber doors swung open, and Morbae waved him inside.

As he had seen her so many times before, she was stood in front of the fire, gazing into the flames. "What is so urgent?" she demanded.

"There has been a surprising turn of events, Mistress."

She glanced from the fire to meet his eyes. "Oh?"

"Bessantia," he replied, keenly observant to her reaction.

There was a sharp intake of breath. "What did you say?"

"Alive and well. She has been hiding amongst the humans all this time."

The Mistress clutched at her throat. "Does she possess it still?"

"It?" asked Kane.

"The Orb. Does she possess it?"

"No, I do. However, the Master interrupted me, and now he too knows of its existence. I have been ordered to return it to him."

Her scream reverberated around the room. She stormed towards him with a face full of fury. "It does not belong to the Master."

"He claims it was stolen from him."

"Then he lies," she spat out. "It was never his to possess."

"Be that as it may, I must obey him. You said this yourself. Otherwise, he will know the Lyboria bite failed."

"When?" she demanded.

"I have two days to return the girl and the orb to him."

The Mistress spun to Morbae with a questioning look. Kane watched on with interest as the guardian shook his head furiously. "The stars are not aligned; the risk is too great."

"Then I will strike a bargain with the Demon," she snapped.

Lines etched into Morbae's forehead. "The Demon is of an unknown origin. We cannot be sure it can be trusted."

"The Demon does not care for our world. It only seeks to claim the girl's."

"And what then, Mistress? It will have tasted a glimmer of your power. What if it should come for you, attempt to take your throne?" Morbae challenged.

"Then it would be a fool. Not only will I have the Orb, but a Nyrvallia standing by my side." Kane shivered involuntarily as she ran her fingers slowly and sensually down his arm. "Its darkness is no match," she purred.

He glared. "What do you mean? I have a right to know."

"In time," she replied and kissed his lips. "Can you feel it yet?" she teased.

He pulled his head back. "Feel what?"

"I can, and it will be soon."

"Mistress, precious time is wasted. We must prepare," Morbae advised.

She nodded. "I will be in contact with you before sunrise on the second day."

"The Tracker and the girl were aided by the Crone. I fear they have escaped through a portal. The blood can no longer locate them; something has interfered with the spell."

"Let me see," she demanded and wrapped her arms around his neck. Her tongue forced his lips apart as she plunged it into his mouth and explored. His groin stirred and he groaned with need. Blood roared in his ears as the kiss deepened. Kane's mind scrambled to lock down the memories from his past, secrets that he had no desire to divulge. Her breasts pressed against him. Her hands moved further down to the swell of his erection. Unsure where the strength came from, he caught hold of her and pushed backwards. She released a small gasp. Her eyes flashed fire.

"You go too far," Kane growled.

"You are still hiding things from me," she snapped.

"I hide nothing that is of interest to you."

"I doubt that. We will settle this matter soon. For now, I have seen all I need."

"And?"

"The Tracker and the girl were with Bessantia when you attacked. She will have been caught off-guard. Search the cottage; find something that belongs to the girl."

"Then what?" he asked.

"Then it is time to awaken one of the Nyrvallia's gifts."

"How?"

"Are you sure that is wise, Mistress?" Morbae interrupted. "Your blood did not take. You cannot be sure the Nyrvallia will serve you."

Kane caught the glint of a blade as she pulled it free from her robe. "Give me your right hand," she ordered.

He complied, and gave a slight wince as she sliced a deep cut across his palm. She repeated the same to her own hand and gave the dagger to Morbae. With her free hand she accepted the black cord that the guardian offered and then bound her hand to Kane's. He hissed as their palms connected. Morbae drew a symbol over their joined hands and muttered an enchantment. Perspiration beaded on Kane's forehead as the cut throbbed intensely against hers. Their blood mingled and dripped steadily from their locked palms.

"It is done," Morbae advised and untied the cord.

"Now we can begin. Fetch me the shard."

The guardian nodded and left. He was back in a moment, holding a small gleaming object in his hand.

She gestured to Kane. "He must be the one to do it."

Kane held out his hand to accept the object: a small piece of silver that appeared severed from a blade with a fine tip. "What is this?"

"All that remains of the previous Nyrvallia. It is a remnant of his power. It will awaken the gift that we seek."

"Which is?"

She laughed coyly and pointed to his third eye. "That you will discover yourself. But be sure when you sleep that you possess in your hand something that belonged to the girl."

"Why not the Tracker?"

"Bessantia will have prevented the gift from being used on the Tracker."

"How do you know this?"

"I know the power she possesses. If the Tracker has sought her aid, his mind will be protected."

"By the Shroud? I am trained to use it."

"My young apprentice, there is much about the Shroud you do not know. It selects one Master to wield it. He has been chosen already. The power does not lie with you."

"Are you saying the Tracker...?"

"No, its power was taken some time ago, by another who lives. Only he and he alone can wield the Shroud and take it from another. He has been to the place where none of us dare go."

"Do you know who he is?"

"I do not know his name. Only when free can I find him. He will join us."

"If he is pure of soul, he will not join us."

"He will have no choice. For I shall bear his child."

"I thought I was to rule by your side," Kane snarled.

She kissed him softly. "You shall rule, that is all you need to know."

He curbed his temper. "What am I to do with this?"

"Insert it into your third eye. Do it now."

The guardian smiled and licked his lips. "Be of no doubt that it will cause significant pain, but you will not die from it. You will become strong."

Kane prepared himself, determined not to feed the guardian's glee as he pushed the shard into his skin. A thousand drums boomed a painful welcome in his skull. Perspiration ran down his cheeks and he stumbled to the ground. His hands covered his ears to drown out the crashing and screaming. The Mistress peered down, her face drifting in and out of focus. He eventually lost consciousness.

It was only the sound of Rivik's persistent voice that woke him. "Commander? Commander?"

"What happened?" He rubbed the sharp stabbing pain at the centre of his forehead.

"We do not know," Grinn replied.

Kane moved to an upright position as Rivik met his gaze and eyed him suspiciously. He ignored the silent question and turned to Grinn. "I must find one of the girl's possessions."

Grinn's excitement was palpable. "I have found female garments discarded outside. The scent is strange. It does not belong to the old woman."

"Bring it to me and you will have earned my forgiveness."

The Fallen immediately bounded away, leaving Kane alone with Rivik.

"Why do you stare at me so?" he asked.

Rivik's mouth pulled back into a slight snarl. "I smell another's blood."

"What are you talking about?"

The creature within Rivik slithered to the surface. "I am no fool. Who is it that seeks to control your power?"

"What power do you speak of? What is it that you know?"

"I know what you are to become."

Kane glared with a sudden stirring of knowledge. "It was you. What did you do to me that day?"

"Your power is not to serve another. It does not belong to them."

"Then to who?" Kane growled. "You?"

Rivik's claws raked the earth. "That power is a gift bestowed by my ancestors. You are to align with me in accordance with our law."

"Your laws mean nothing to me. I align with no-one, do you hear me?" Kane shouted. His head ached and his blood boiled as the anger swarmed dangerously close to the surface.

"Be careful, Commander. Of this matter, you know extraordinarily little. If you are to survive the transition, you need me," Rivik bit back.

"I grow tired of the threats and innuendos. I am not anyone's pawn. I rule, I do not serve, and in time..." Kane realised he was ranting and bit down on his tongue before he exposed himself further. Instead he turned away, and yelled the last of his anger and frustration towards the night sky.

Grinn approached hesitantly with a bundle in his mouth. Only when the Commander appeared calm did he drop it at Kane's feet. It was a welcome distraction as Kane sifted through the clothing and lifted the strange-looking material to his nose. The scent of flowers filling his senses. He quickly discarded it.

"Bring them," he ordered Grinn.

The Fallen bowed his head and scooped the clothing from the ground.

Rivik made no further comment and lowered himself in invitation.

Taking the cue, Kane mounted the Fallen's back and hissed, "This is not over."

"Indeed," replied Rivik. Lifting his head to the night sky, the Fallen released a long howl.

Gallo sprung immediately from the rubble that lay behind them. "It is done, Commander. Barrock has sent word. The camp is ready, and my brethren are secured in their cocoons. We have their coordinates."

"Then lead the way, Gallo. Dawn is upon us, and there is much that I need to prepare."

"What of the girl and the Tracker?" asked Grinn.

"Do not concern yourself. I shall have their location by the time you awaken."

"Without the book?" asked Rivik.

Kane chose to ignore the sarcasm in the creature's tone. "I no longer need the book," he sneered, and kicked his heels sharply into the Fallen's hide. "Now go."

Rivik snarled in protest but made no other remark. The three broke into a run and headed towards the trees, Gallo leading the way.

Chapter Five
Rowan

esidence of Edward Throston, York, United Kingdom
R   Particles of dust blew into her face and hair as Rowan spun full circle, confused and suddenly alone, her dream all but a distant memory. She frantically rubbed the grit from her eyes and desperately fought to calm her emotions. The happiness she had experienced just a few moments earlier now sucked into the ether, leaving her trembling with the knowledge of what was to come.

The vision had jerked her with such a tremendous force, right out of the dreamscape. It should not have been possible. Yet, here she was, once again plunged into this strange and barren landscape. Her spirit guide, Charles, was unable to observe or hear her call for help.

The loud crack she had anticipated, and dreaded, echoed with the rupturing ground. It tore itself apart in front of her. As she stood on the precipice, she did not care to look down, already knowing what was there. The scent of death and decay hit her nostrils, and her stomach rolled in response. It was closely followed by the repeated screams of dozens of tortured souls. Her ears rang with their wails of agony as they called out and begged her for release.

Rowan fisted her hands at her sides and kept her gaze rigidly fixed ahead. She waited for it to come.

The voice that had previously warned her not to rescue them, however, remained silent.

"If I am not to help them, then why bring me back here?" she demanded.

No reply came.

"What do you want from me?" she shouted.

Still nothing.

Rowan's gaze flicked to the river of red below. It bubbled and hissed with each skeletal hand that rose and fell. She knelt on the ground, overcome with pain and despair.

"Beware, he comes," sang a ghostly voice—one she had not heard before.

The river of red stilled, and ice slithered down her spine. On the other side of the precipice stood a figure dressed in crimson velvet. Long silver hair streamed in a wind which claimed only him. His thin lips curved into a sneer as he studied her with eyes the colour of obsidian. She took in the rest of his appearance: distinct cheekbones, and a narrow protruding nose. His forehead was heavily lined with dark blue veins against sickly yellow skin. The pointed ears made him look almost feral, and when he widened his smile further, the flash of a white fang glinted.

"They belong to me," he laughed.

Rowan released a scream and bolted awake.

The bedside lamp bathed her in a soft light. Finn, his expression of fierce determination, had her held firmly in his grip, and he continued to shake her. With her teeth rattling in her skull, she fought to yank herself free from his hold.

"I'm awake," she yelled, with a jerk of her arm. "For heaven's sake, let me go."

He released a heavy breath. "Thank the saints," he said, and sank against the pillows.

She scowled at the rosy, pink marks on her skin. Just how long had he been trying to wake her?

"I thought..." his voice trailed away.

"You thought what?" she pressed.

"The Fallen. I thought they had taken you. Trapped you into an endless nightmare."

"Can they do that?"

"In their original form, they can invade and influence your dreams. Turn them into nightmares. Deprive you of sleep, drive you into madness."

She shivered. "I don't think it was the Fallen."

His brow furrowed. "But someone was there?"

Rowan nodded. "I had a vision the night before you came to me. And then tonight, the same vision, but different."

"Different how?"

"That's what I was going to ask," said a male voice.

Rowan shifted her gaze to the side of the bed, where Charles now stood.

"What are you looking at?" asked Finn.

"Charles. He wants the same answer."

"I don't blame him. Perhaps you can enlighten us both."

"Are you mad?" she asked.

"Not at you," he said. "I'm not sure who I am mad at."

"Would you be mad at me if I said all I wanted to do was go back to sleep?"

"Do you?"

"Yes."

Finn sighed and then kissed her softly. "Fine, then I guess we will both have to wait until morning. But if it happens again, I want an answer. Promise me?"

"I promise," she whispered.

Rowan spooned closer to him and silently communicated to Charles to be patient, her own eyes closing as she waited for Finn to drop asleep.

Charles's warmth roused her as she yawned and rubbed her eyes. She glanced blearily towards the alarm clock on the bedside unit. The illuminous numbers read two o'clock in the morning. Finn had rolled away and was snoring heavily into his pillow.

"What is it?" she whispered.

"We need to talk," Charles replied, his voice grim.

She slipped quietly out of bed and headed for the bathroom. The whirr of the extractor fan made her cringe as she bolted the door behind her and lowered the toilet seat to sit.

"You're worried," she said, attuning to his energy.

"I've spoken with the Lightkeepers, and they are concerned about the events tonight."

Rowan swallowed her irritation. "They're not the only ones," she muttered.

Charles heaved a sigh. "They, and I, need to understand what happened after you entered the Meridian."

Her stomach somersaulted. "Is something wrong?"

"The Lightkeepers are aware of an energy disturbance, a jolt in the space-time continuum."

"That must have been as we travelled through the portal. When we arrived here it was not as late as it should have been. The Meridian must have somehow adjusted the time to enable us to meet up with Eddie. Has it caused any damage?"

"A slight rip, but not significant. However, they have sent Alexander to repair it."

"Alexander?"

"He is a Sage like Eleanor, one of the oldest and most knowledgeable among them. Alexander is only ever enlisted in a time of great need."

"But you said it was only a slight rip?"

"So I am told. Yet the fact that Alexander has been sent to aid Tiberius suggests that there is more that the Lightkeepers are not telling me."

"Tiberius, if I remember correctly, is the Keeper of Time?"

"Yes. It is unusual for Tiberius to need aid," Charles said flatly.

Rowan sensed mistrust. "But why would the Lightkeepers withhold information from you? I just don't understand."

"I fear they believe I am too close to you."

"Which means, it is me that they doubt." The anger swirled like a hornet's nest provoked.

"The Meridian has changed you, given you powers that no human in this time should be able to possess. What you did this evening should not have been possible."

"I understand that they are concerned, and I can't deny that what I did tonight hasn't also frightened me, but I am still me. A human, not a demon."

"I know that, and the strength of your heart, the light that is inside you. But the Lightkeepers fear that in time this strange new power will consume you. If it does, Rowan, they will be forced into action and will not hesitate to banish you to the lower realms."

Rowan crossed her arms and huffed. "They'd have to kill me first," she snapped.

"If they believe you to have lost your soul, be assured that they will orchestrate the ending of your life."

"That is ridiculous. I would never..." her voice trailed off as she inwardly seethed. Should I tell him? Will that give the Lightkeepers more reason to believe I am losing my humanity?

Charles wrapped his arms around her. "I would never let them take you from me."

"I thought the Lightkeepers were the good guys?"

"They are, as far as this world is concerned, and the souls within it. However, they will take whatever steps are necessary to protect it. We must find a way for me to connect with you should you have need to go into the Meridian again. The only reassurance I had this evening was that those bombastic creatures could not enter either."

"Did you see what happened to the Fallen after we passed through the Meridian?"

"A barrier of light was raised the minute you entered. They were unsuccessful at penetrating it, as was I. Most frustrating, since I am a being of light."

Rowan drew back from his embrace. She bit down on her lip.

"What is it?"

"The moment we arrived in the Meridian, before Finn transformed back, it briefly connected its energy to me."

"Did you tell Finn?"

"No."

"Why not?"

"Because it showed me something and I felt I needed to talk to you first about it. Anyway, we were kind of occupied with the Fallen and then Enwen and—"

"Enwen?"

"A conversation for another time. The Meridian mentioned about the Guardian awakening, and said that this would be soon..."

"Go on," he encouraged.

"The voices I heard also mentioned a necessary transference of power to allow the chosen one to travel with me. It all happened so fast, and when it was over they showed me your face, only there was a strange marking on your forehead that I have never seen before."

"What mark?"

"I don't know. It looked to be some sort of hieroglyph."

"Can you picture it now, so I may see?"

Rowan nodded and closed her eyes. She visualised a black board and in her hand a piece of white chalk. Carefully, she drew the image she had seen.

"Do you recognise it?"

"It looks to be a Toki. It means courage and strength. Toki were worn by the Maori elders as a symbol of power, wisdom, and authority."

"Perhaps a previous incarnation?"

Charles was silent for a few moments. "If so, then it is odd I am unable to recall this."

"Nothing seems odd to me anymore. It did make me believe that when I enter the Meridian again, I should be able to connect with you."

"And when you leave with Finn?"

"I don't know," she replied, her voice barely a whisper.

Charles hugged her once more. "A conversation for another time. We don't seem to be doing well together or apart. I can't help but feel so far away from you. I guess I am not used to another man holding so much of your attention. It is a strange feeling."

"Strange it may seem to you, but not an uncommon one. I know we need to talk, Charles—truly talk—so both of us can make sense of everything that is happening to me, to us. I feel we are both holding important pieces of the puzzle. Somehow all of this connects. I just don't know how or what it means. You have to find out more from the Lightkeepers."

"I agree, and will do my best. I will be keeping a close eye on what is happening, as much as this new world of yours allows. At least I know I can trust him to take care of you. But I must go now. I've lingered too long, and Eleanor is summoning me. Finn is stirring too. I must ask before you leave as to whether you see the Toki now?"

She studied his face. There was no mark. "Perhaps it needs the Meridian to activate it?"

"Or you," Charles offered. "At least the Lightkeepers won't question me about it."

"I don't know how to activate a Toki."

He smiled. "I have a feeling the Guardian will know," he said and released his energy.

Rowan groaned loudly and laid her head against the cold tiling to soothe her battered thoughts. As if she did not have enough to worry about, now Charles's warning about the Lightkeepers had seriously unnerved her.

A gentle knock disturbed her thoughts.

"Rowan, are you okay?"

She rose and opened the door. Although it was too dark to see his face, she sensed his concern, and immediately flung herself into his arms.

"Hey, what's this all about?" he asked, hugging her tightly.

"Not here," she whispered.

She wrapped an arm around his neck as he lifted her into his arms and carried her back into the bedroom. Her head rested against her bare chest and her abdomen stirred with need, the strength of his body a welcome tonic. She gently caressed his skin with her hands as he placed her into bed and captured her gaze.

Finn blew out hard. "If you keep looking at me like that, we are both going to be in trouble."

"I'm sorry, I could not help myself. It is not often a semi-naked man sweeps me into his arms and carries me back to the bedroom. Besides, with the night I've had, I think I deserve a little pleasure," she teased.

His warm laughter soothed her nerves, and all she could think of was him. It was a far cry from those nights she had woken alone, grieving for the dream of one she believed she could never have.

Biscuit gave a soft growl as Finn's leg accidentally kicked him in his eagerness to press his body close to Rowan's, but the little dog was seemingly too tired to retaliate and fell back asleep swiftly.

Finn captured her mouth, and then withdrew, his lips seeking her neck to place soft kisses filled with the promise of the pleasure to come. She groaned as Finn's hand slowly travelled to the curve of her breast, his touch hesitant at first.

"I love you," he murmured against her skin. She reached for his hand to move it lower and let him explore the effect that his kisses had on her, but dropped it instantly when a soft click sounded and the room was suddenly cast into light.

Rowan's face instantly flushed at the realisation that she was semi clad, wearing only one of Eddie's shirts.

"Damn it Eddie, you have the worst possible timing!" Finn snapped.

Rowan pulled the duvet swiftly to cover herself and hide Finn's obvious erection.

"I'm sorry to be a buzzkill, but I need to talk to you. Something has got Lizzie really spooked. She sent me over here to check on you."

"Well, as you can see, we are fine. We would have been more than fine had you given us at least a couple of hours before intruding," Finn replied. He grinned at Rowan.

She rolled her eyes and then hit him over the head with a pillow. "I'll hold you to that."

Eddie shook his head. "Look, I was in the middle of some great pillow talk too, and then she sort of zoned out and came back into the moment screaming, and I hadn't even...well, you know."

"I can imagine how that would deflate a man's ego," Rowan grumbled.

"Seriously, it took me half an hour to calm her down. But she's got me spooked. I've never seen her like that before, and I felt something, and it weren't euphoria, believe me, mate." Eddie scratched his head. "Look, I feel really awkward. Is there any chance we can talk man to man, outside your love nest?"

"Sure," Finn said. "I'll see you downstairs in a couple of minutes."

"Thanks, and sorry again, Rowan. By the way, you really rock my t-shirt!"

Her laughter stopped when she caught sight of Finn's expression. "Surely not?"

"What? No. The jealousy thing? It's not that. I'm worried about Eddie. If he feels half of what I feel for you, something bad must have happened to have him leave Lizzie and come back here."

"Go talk to him. Maybe you can reassure him?"

"I don't suppose there's any chance in us picking back up where we left off, is there?"

"I think that ship has sailed, Tiger! But don't worry, I am on a two hours promise and I will hold you to that."

Finn kissed her hard and then left her alone.

Rowan sighed and laid her head back down. First Charles, and now Lizzie? What's going on? The time passed slowly, and her eyes grew heavier. Before Finn returned, she was sound asleep.

Chapter Six

Finn

R *esidence of Edward Throston, York, United Kingdom*
A gentle knock on the bedroom door disturbed his slumber. Groggily, Finn slipped out from beneath the covers and padded to the door. Eddie stood there holding two steaming cups. "A peace offering."

Finn grunted a thank you, and accepted the mugs. "Give us chance to drink these, and we'll be right down." He closed the door with his foot and moved to rest the mugs on the bedside unit.

Rowan stirred. "What's that?"

"Tea," Finn replied.

"Urgh, I prefer coffee first thing on a morning."

"I doubt you will find any of that hideous stuff here."

She flung the covers over her head and muttered something unintelligible.

"Eddie is downstairs waiting for us. We need to talk to you about last night."

Finn hoped this would spur her into action, although it was unlikely to put her in a better mood. He perched on the edge of the bed and patiently drank his tea.

Biscuit gave a yawn and stretched. He looked at Finn with hopeful eyes.

"I'm sure we can rustle up some breakfast."

The little dog barked an acknowledgement, and then proceeded to wash his ears. At the sound of the loud, squelching, licking noises, Rowan pulled her head free and propped herself up against the pillow. She muttered an expletive, her face drawn into a frown, before she reached for the cup and sipped slowly at the steaming liquid.

"I take it you are not much of a morning person?" Finn dared.

"Without a coffee, no!"

"So, do you want to talk about last night?" he asked.

"When you left the room with Eddie?"

"No, before that. When I found you in the bathroom, before we were so rudely interrupted."

"Not really," she replied grumpily.

"Were you upset about the attack, or has something else happened? Is it Charles?"

"Yes, Yes and No."

"Care to expand?" Finn persisted.

Rowan huffed and placed her mug down. "It seems that the Lightkeepers are getting twitchy about this strange new power I seem to possess."

"Who are the Lightkeepers?"

"I guess you could say they are like the Council of Elders in your world. They have expressed concerns to Charles."

"What sort of concerns? Have they threatened you?"

"No. As long as they know and can be reassured that I am still one of the good guys, I should be okay." She sighed.

"I'm sorry, this is all a bit much. I've suddenly gone from an ordinary, mundane life to an extraordinary, unimaginable one in a sheer matter of days. It's still hard to get my head around."

Finn placed down his empty cup and reached for her hand. "I can understand that, and for the record, I think you are doing amazing."

She gave him a weak smile. "I wish."

"How about a warm bath, and then some breakfast?" he offered.

Rowan's face softened. "That would be appreciated, thank you."

He risked a kiss on her cheek and left the bedroom.

Finn placed the soft piece of black plastic hanging from the chain into the plug hole and turned on the taps to let the water run. A few drops of the apple-scented liquid were deposited in the bath. Finn waited until the tub had filled and the top of the water was covered in soft rainbow bubbles. He checked the temperature was satisfactory, and then moved to scoop a delectable but still moody Rowan from the bedroom.

"When you're done, meet me downstairs," he said, then gestured to the little dog who had followed behind. "Come with me, Biscuit. Let's leave our lady to it."

Finn sprinted downstairs, Biscuit eagerly following him. Eddie and Lizzie were in the kitchen. Their conversation ceased as he entered. Eddie discreetly shook his head.

"Hey handsome, how are you doing?" Lizzie said. She managed a smile, but the strain on her face was evident.

Finn returned her smile. "Much better after a good night's kip. Rowan's just taking a bath; I hope that is okay. She'll be down shortly, and then I promise we'll leave."

Eddie nodded. "Not a problem, mate."

"Oh, that reminds me," Lizzie said, handing Finn a plastic bag. "Some clothes for Rowan. These should fit her nicely."

"And of course you can borrow some of my gear," Eddie said. "I noticed you didn't have any luggage with you when you both arrived."

Lizzie lowered to tousle Biscuit's fur. "We didn't leave you out either." She reached for two tin dishes on the counter and rested them on the floor. One was filled with water, the other with a strange-looking food. The little dog sniffed suspiciously at the biscuits and then quickly devoured them.

"Thank you, both of you. I'm sorry for the trouble we've caused." Finn said.

Lizzie sighed. "Well, it's not every day I can come to the rescue of an alien. I'm just sorry I freaked out last night. I can't explain my feelings to you. All I know is you have to go."

"I prefer Martian to alien," said Eddie, clearly attempting to lighten the mood.

"You know then, what I am?" Finn replied.

"It took Eddie some time to convince me that he was telling the truth, but yes, it all makes perfect sense now. Rowan, I understand, is human though?"

"A Teessider, not a Martian, she tells me," Eddie quipped.

Finn laughed. "Yes, she is the one I came in search of. I intend to take her back home with me."

Lizzie clasped her hands together. "Even knowing what you are, and Rowan being human, it doesn't change how I feel. I'm so sorry, Finn."

He shook his head, his voice solemn. "Rowan doesn't know anything yet. She was asleep when I came back up to bed, and wasn't in the greatest of moods when she woke."

"How much trouble do you think you are in?" asked Eddie with a frown.

"With Rowan?"

"No, I mean with you not being the only Martian who has landed," Eddie replied.

"There's more of you?" asked Lizzie.

"Not like me, and there's complications happening for Rowan too, but it's not my place to share, and to be honest, she doesn't even share it with me most of the time."

"Even more reason for you to go," Lizzie said.

Eddie turned to his girlfriend. "He's my friend, Lizzie. You've asked a lot from me and still cannot explain why."

"Don't you wish I could?" she snapped. "I like Finn and genuinely wanted to be friends with Rowan. This is hard for me, too."

Finn raised his hand before the pair descended into an argument. "Look, I appreciate you putting us up Eddie, but Lizzie is right, we cannot stay here. I don't want to bring any trouble to your door."

His friend nodded. "Is there anything more we can do to help?"

"You have done more than enough already. Rowan and I need to find something that belongs to her. I hope we can locate it today, and then we will be gone."

"I'm assuming it's best that I don't ask what?" said Eddie.

"The less you know, my dear friend, the better."

Rowan entered the kitchen. She was wearing a white robe, her hair wrapped tightly in a cloth. "I hope you don't mind, Eddie," she queried and gestured to the gown.

"Lizzie's brought you some clothes," Finn said, immediately handing over the carrier bag.

"There's a change of underwear for you too, and a toothbrush," Lizzie said.

Rowan peered inside, her cheeks flushed a warm pink. "Thanks. How did you know?"

"Eddie's explained who Finn is, and that you are not a Martian. I figured you would need fresh clothing, and Eddie never has any spare toiletries. I hope they fit okay. We look to be a comparable size."

"You're an angel," said Rowan. She turned to peck Finn on his cheek. "Thanks for the bath."

"Do you feel any better?" he asked.

"A little," she replied.

"How about some breakfast?" said Eddie.

"That would be great. If you'll excuse me, I'll get dressed first," said Rowan. She disappeared quickly from the room.

Lizzie turned a dial and clicked a button on the oven. A flame sparked into life. "You can sort the bacon, and I'll do the eggs," she said as she organised Eddie into action.

Finn dragged a chair out from beneath the pine table and sat. Biscuit curled up beside his leg, now contented with his full belly.

As he watched the interaction between Lizzie and Eddie, their clear display of affection, Finn could not help but yearn for the day when he and Rowan would share a home together and be at peace. The couple in front of him were well matched, and he was genuinely pleased for his friend that he had found someone that made him happy.

He suddenly flinched, his daydream disturbed by a deep gnawing ache at the centre of his guts, but it wasn't from the couple's banter. The hairs on the back of his arms rose to attention, and a faint breeze disturbed his hair. Finn automatically reached out with his senses and frantically searched the perimeter. His first thought was whether Kane had discovered their location already. Yet there was no sign of Kane nor his minions in the area—but something was most definitely wrong.

Sweat beaded Finn's brow and he shifted uncomfortably in the chair. His head throbbed as he waited for whatever it was to materialise. His eyesight shifted out of focus, allowing him to see a grey cloud of energy that loomed towards him. Without warning, he was dragged inside. Finn startled when a familiar pair of eyes stared back at him from the darkness.

"I see you, brother."

The voice was cold, and not at all how Finn remembered. He watched as Aaron raised his hand and wiped blood away from his cheek, his full features now coming into focus.

"What have you done?" Finn asked.

The hand paused in mid-air. His brother's eyes narrowed and gleamed in the gilt-framed mirror that had appeared, sending an icy chill down Finn's back.

"What I needed to," Aaron answered without emotion.

Fear gripped Finn's heart as he studied the reflection. "Need or wanted?"

"Does it matter?"

"Yes, it matters," Finn replied.

"Both."

Again, not a flicker of emotion from his brother.

"But why?" he pressed.

"Why not?" came the reply.

"Are you being forced to prove your loyalty?"

"No," said Aaron simply.

"Then I don't understand."

"Nor will you, brother."

Finn dragged his hands down his face. "You're making no sense."

"You shouldn't have come," his brother said firmly.

"But I wasn't the one who did the summoning," snapped Finn. "I don't even know how I've connected with you."

Aaron's face disappeared momentarily into the smoke that fanned around them. Finn waited as the minutes passed by in a deafening silence. Finally, he could bear it no longer. "There is a reason I am here, whatever instigated this meeting. Let me help you, Aaron."

"It's too late. This should not have occurred."

"But it did. It's never too late, brother. I can help you. Please believe me."

"You're a fool," Aaron said.

"Perhaps, but what does all this make you, brother?"

"Powerful."

"This isn't you. Talk to me. Where are you?"

"I have no time for this. Leave while you still can," his brother warned.

"And if I refuse?" Finn challenged.

"I am not alone. Break the connection before you are discovered. I cannot mask your presence in the Shroud, even if I wanted to."

"Something brought me here. We need to know what."

"You arrived at the moment my decision was made," Aaron said firmly.

"What decision? What are you talking about? I need to see you, Aaron. I must understand."

"You will see me soon enough. Our fates are sealed..."

"No, wait. What do you mean?"

Finn's words were met with silence.

"Aaron? Please answer me," he begged.

"Goodbye, brother."

"No, wait," Finn yelled. He jolted back to the bright, warm kitchen that smelt of bacon.

Eddie continued to wave his hand frantically in front of his friend's face. "Are you alright?"

Finn could not find the words to explain. He was so choked by emotion that all he could do was break down into tears. The pain of the reunion hammered deep into his soul, causing old wounds to resurface as he spun the conversation back and forth in his mind.

"Lizzie's gone to fetch Rowan. Hush, now," Eddie said, awkwardly patting Finn on his back. He was clearly at a loss as to what to do. No matter how hard Finn tried, he could not hush the sobs. Rowan rushed into the kitchen, Lizzie closely followed her. Her arms wrapped around him as he snuggled his face into her chest and continued to cry.

"What is it? What happened?" she asked.

"We don't know," said Lizzie.

"One minute he was okay, and the next this," said Eddie, with a shrug of his shoulders.

"Aaron." It was all that Finn could manage to say.

"Could you leave us?" asked Rowan.

"Sure, breakfast is done. We'll leave it here on the counter for when you are ready," said Lizzie, pulling at Eddie's arm. The two left the kitchen silently.

Rowan tipped Finn's head up and searched his face. He took a long steadying breath as she brushed his tears away with her sleeve.

"What happened?" she probed gently.

"My brother is in trouble."

"Did Mercadia tell you this?"

He shook his head. "Somehow I found myself in the Shroud. Aaron sort of told me himself."

Rowan pulled out a chair and sat beside him. "What can we do?"

"There is nothing we can do. I am not sure he can be saved."

"What about Mercadia? Could she not help?"

"It was the Council of Elders that sent him to the Master. I don't know if they would help him now, even if they did have the power to do so."

"But if they were the ones to have sent him to the Master, then surely they owe it to you to help," Rowan said angrily.

"He may be lost, even to them," Finn replied miserably.

"You have to try. What else have you got to lose?" she said firmly.

Finn heaved a sigh. "You're right. I owe it to him to at least try."

He wiped the last of his tears and straightened his back as he prepared to do battle. Rowan held his hand tightly as he felt for Mercadia's previous connection and forced it open.

"Are you okay?"

The Elder's words surprised him. "You know?"

"I sense your distress."

Mercadia was quiet for a few moments as she sifted through his mind. Finn did not have the energy to put up any resistance to the intrusion.

"I see," she said softly. "Bessie and I were afraid of the possibility of contact with Aaron, once you had commenced your training with her."

"So it was me who unwittingly instigated contact? Why did you not warn me, Mercadia? I could have been better prepared."

"We thought it best that you did not know. At least not until we could be sure that you even possessed the ability to tap into his connection with the Shroud."

"He's in trouble. You must help him," Finn insisted.

Mercadia sighed. "Your brother knew the risks when he agreed to the quest. It is too dangerous now for the Council to intervene. We are in a weakened state. If the Master even had a hint that your brother intended to betray him, he would kill him."

"But he's going to do something terrible. I can feel it."

"Your brother did what is necessary to keep up the charade. There were consequences to that. His life depends on us doing nothing at this moment in time."

"At what cost, though?" Finn argued.

"What is it you think he's going to do?"

"Aaron wouldn't say, but if he does go ahead with it, I fear I will lose him forever."

"Your feelings run deep with your brother. But even if you trust nothing else I tell you, you must trust me on this."

"I don't recognise him anymore," said Finn. "Something has to be done, before it's too late."

"I'm afraid that our hands, our fates, are bound. The Council cannot become involved; the consequences would be catastrophic."

Finn's temper unleashed and he hurled curses into the air. Mercadia released her connection and blocked him, only angering him further.

Rowan flinched as Finn slammed his fist into the table. "She won't help him."

"We'll find a way to save him," she assured.

"I fear there is no time," he said flatly.

"Then we must act now and save him ourselves," she replied.

"How can we? And what about your amulet? Kane and the Fallen?"

"Dammit, this is important to you. The amulet can wait one more day. We can get it tomorrow. Today, we must work together and find a way to save your brother. I don't know how yet, but we will. I promise you."

"You shouldn't make promises that you can't keep," Finn said. He registered the flicker of pain in her eyes and kissed her softly. "I'm sorry. Thank you; at least you are willing to try for him."

"Don't thank me yet," she said. "We've still to come up with a plan."

"You're prepared to try, and no matter how hopeless it seems, that is more than the Council would do."

"There's always hope, Finn. I firmly believe that," she said.

He nodded and managed a small smile.

Rowan stood and reached for the two plates on the counter. She passed one across to Finn. "Let's eat. I can't think on an empty stomach."

Chapter Seven

Rowan

Residence of Edward Throston, York, United Kingdom

Silence fell around them as Rowan and Finn ate the cooked breakfast that Lizzie and Eddie had prepared. Every so often, Finn's eyes would connect with hers, his sorrow and guilt evident. A part of Rowan felt incredibly guilty too, now that he was here, in her world. He had saved her from the creatures that stalked them, and continued to protect her, instead of immediately returning home to his loved ones, which she felt sure his instincts would demand from him.

Rowan could sense how conflicted Finn was, torn between adhering to the task that Bessie had insisted on and returning home to save his brother. If it had been the other way round, and Jake had been the one to be in danger, she would have been equally at a loss. How do you go about saving a man in another world?

Finn had not yet shared what had happened to his brother, or relayed the danger that he had sensed. Rowan continued to mull the conundrum over.

Is it possible that together, our combined gifts can protect him?

Finn really needed to open up to her, however painful. He had already told her that the Council of Elders had employed Aaron to spy on the Master. Surely, that would mean that they were obligated in some way to help?

She finished her sandwich and reached across to remove Finn's empty plate. He stared into space and failed to acknowledge her movement. With a deep sigh, she placed the dirty dishes into the dishwasher. The noise still had not broken his reverie. Rowan worried at her bottom lip and waited.

Finally, Finn whispered, "I feel so helpless."

She met his gaze, and offered her hands to drag him to his feet and into her warm embrace. Her voice filled with determination as she hugged him and told him firmly that, "We can do this, together."

Finn leaned into the strength she offered for a few seconds before he stepped away. His expression altered and a fire lit in his eyes.

"No, I can't fall apart now. I have to be strong, for you and Aaron," he said.

Rowan agreed as he led her by the hand and into the other room, where Eddie and Lizzie were waiting patiently.

"I've never seen you in such a state," Eddie said, his face full of concern. "Are you okay?"

Finn managed a small smile. "I will be, once I've managed to sort a few things out with Rowan."

"Do you two need more privacy?" queried Lizzie.

Rowan considered the young woman, who she now thought of as a friend. Lizzie was remarkably intuitive. But something about the interruption last night had set Rowan's nerves on edge. Lizzie's Spirit Guide was being decidedly guarded and refused to acknowledge her.

"If you do not mind, that would be great. Sorry, Eddie. We are completely taking over your house," she said apologetically.

"No problem. Lizzie and I will take Biscuit for a short walk."

Eddie gave Finn a manly hug and slapped him on his back whilst Lizzie went to retrieve their coats. She popped her head through the doorway. "I don't think Biscuit is for moving, so it'll just be Eddie and I."

"No problem. Thanks for offering," Rowan replied.

"See you later, mate," Eddie said.

The couple departed, leaving the two of them alone. Rowan lowered into the leather armchair and gestured for Finn to sit. She grimaced when he bounced down onto the springs of the settee.

What is it with men? Why can't they just sit like a normal person? Her brother was the same, throwing himself down dramatically as though his knees had suddenly ceased to work and gravity controlled him. She winced every time the furniture groaned its protest.

"What?" Finn asked innocently.

"Never mind. How about you tell me what happened to your brother?"

"Well, you already know that the Council of Elders asked my brother to infiltrate the Master's camp?"

"Yes," she prompted.

"It's just that the Master corrupts everything he touches, and everyone who has the misfortune to work for him. I fear that he has asked Aaron to do something terrible, something that will cause Aaron to be lost from me for good."

"You're worried that your brother will lose his soul if he does this?" Rowan said astutely.

Finn ran a hand through his hair. "Yes. I was pulled into the Shroud today. At least, I think it was the Shroud, or some version of it, although I did not enter it consciously, so I cannot be sure. I saw my brother in the reflection of a mirror. He told me I had arrived at the point he had made his decision."

"Did he say what that was?"

"No, but it was the way he looked at me. I have a bad feeling about it."

"Is there any chance you can go back into the Shroud? Find out what he is planning?"

"The fleeting time I had with Bessie to learn the Shroud was not enough. My brother has had years of training; there is no way I could access it undetected. He would block me from seeing the moment he sensed my presence there. Not to mention, he warned me that others were watching and he could not hide my presence."

Rowan leaned back into the cushions, her brow furrowed. She was determined to find a solution. If Finn can't enter the Shroud, would it be possible for someone else to? Someone Aaron could not sense?

"Do you know of anyone else who shares the same ability as your brother?"

Finn shook his head. "I don't..." he paused for a few moments. "But maybe the Council of Elders do."

"You've already said that Mercadia won't help," reminded Rowan.

"There is still Elios. He may be persuaded. It's worth a try."

"Have you contacted Elios before?"

"No. Mercadia is the only Elder known to be able to extend her power beyond the boundaries of our world. For me to reach Elios, it may take some time." He stood. "It is better that I attempt it alone. I'll use Eddie's room. I fear it may take too much energy."

"I can keep myself occupied. Lizzie and Eddie will be back soon."

Rowan eyed the collection of books on the bookcase, noting some of her favourite authors. Eddie had good taste in literature.

He gave her a chaste kiss. "Wish me luck."

"I have every faith in you, and if it doesn't work, we'll try to figure something else out."

Finn nodded and left her alone. Rowan moved across the room to browse the shelves. She selected a novel by Frances Hardinge and settled herself to read.

She'd only completed the first chapter in the book when a sudden pain split across her forehead and made her gasp. The book dropped to the floor as she staggered to her feet to call for Finn. Her vision blurred and the living room spun as she neared the door. She fell to her knees, groaning and holding her head. The slightest motion sent it clanging. Closing her eyes, Rowan willed the pain to subside.

An unfamiliar voice gave a deep throated laugh, and then said, "It worked."

The intrusion of her mind sent Rowan's heart racing and into a mini meltdown. She called out immediately for Charles.

"Open your eyes, girl," the male voice commanded.

Rowan refused to obey, and squeezed her lids tighter together. "Get out of my head," she ordered.

"But it is such a delight. I have been longing to meet you."

"Who are you?"

"Come now girl, surely you must know. Can you not feel my power?"

"Kane," she whispered. But how?

"Finally, we are introduced. I am looking forward to seeing you in the flesh."

"That's never going to happen."

"Oh, I beg to differ," he said.

"What do you want from me?" she whispered.

"Only for you to open your eyes. Let me see."

Rowan silently pleaded for Charles.

"Who is this man you call to? Another lover perhaps?" sneered the voice.

"None of your damn business," she snapped. Where is he? Charles? Charles?

"Such a temper. I shall have such fun with you."

Think Rowan, think. How the hell do I get this man out of my head? Her thoughts scrambled to her previous training. I have got to shut this connection down.

In the same way she rescued spirits, Rowan drew her awareness inwards and searched for the source of the invasion. She felt the measure of his energy, dark and orbicular, and the way it hovered threateningly around her third eye and waited for an opportune moment to burrow its way inside.

Rowan concentrated her power before the energy could grow. She cocooned it into a prism of light, and only when she was sure she had it sufficiently contained did she thrust the prism upwards. It went tumbling out through her crown chakra and was released into the ether. The voice cried out in anger with the final push of energy.

The pounding in her head instantly eased, and Rowan was relieved to sense there was nothing. Her thoughts were once again her own. She called out to Charles once more, relieved to note the connection of his energy to hers the moment the intruder was gone.

"What happened?" he asked.

"I was under what I can only describe as a psychic attack," she said wearily.

"But I sensed nothing," he exclaimed. "Are you sure?"

"It was the warlock, Kane. It would seem, like Finn, you cannot sense him either. He too is of another world."

"What did he want?" asked Charles.

"To flex his pecs," she answered, unable to keep the sarcasm from her tone. "He wanted me to open my eyes."

"It sounds as though he was trying to establish your location. How did you break free?"

Body trembling, Rowan dragged herself to her feet. She held onto the back of the settee for support. "In the only way I know how. Luckily, it was enough, but what if he should try this again? I'm not sure I'm strong enough to force him out a second time. Charles, he's got incredible energy. It's all-consuming."

Her guide was silent for a moment. "And in your sleep state, you will be even more vulnerable," he concluded. "We need to do a spell now. It will afford you some protection from him, and the lost ones. They too are growing more persistent. We are on the precipice of something, and I don't like it one bit!"

Rowan nodded. "I must speak to Finn. He's upstairs trying to contact one of the other Council Members. His brother is in danger of losing his soul, and he needs to find a way to help him."

"Then it would appear we need to act quickly. I will speak to Aliyah and ask her to prepare the spell. It must be done tonight." There was a gentle press of warmth on her forehead as he kissed her softly. "I'll be back soon."

With her legs steadier beneath her, she climbed the stairs. Finn was laid in Eddie's bedroom, his expression one of fierce determination. Rowan hesitated, not sure if she should interrupt his attempts. Yet the fact that Kane had been able to establish a psychic link terrified her. She sat on the edge of the bed and hoped he would sense her presence, his attention returned back to this world.

After ten minutes had passed with no acknowledgement, she gently nudged his leg. Finn's eyes sprang open. "Lost him again," he muttered.

"I'm sorry. I didn't want to interrupt you, but something's happened," Rowan explained.

Finn swung his legs to the side of the bed, manoeuvring to her side. "What is it?"

"I was attacked psychically, by Kane," she said.

Finn's eyes widened. "Say that again?" he asked, as though he had not heard her correctly the first time.

"Kane was inside my head," she repeated. "Charles couldn't sense him, and was somehow blocked from picking up my calls for help."

His jaw clenched, as he gripped her hand tightly. "Did he hurt you?"

Rowan shivered. "No, but he made threats. He said he was looking forward to meeting me in the flesh. Finn, I don't think he's far away. He was trying to get a precise point of our location by using my sight against me."

He rose and paced the floor, his hands gesticulating. "There is no way that bastard should possess this ability. It's a gift only given to a Mage Master, and then it must be with the Council's consent."

"I managed to force him out of my head, but it has left me weak. I don't have much energy," she continued.

"We need to leave here as soon as we can, and find your amulet."

"What about your brother? Did you have any luck with Elios?"

Finn heaved a heavy sigh. "I managed to establish a connection with him, but I have not been able to convince him to help. He advised the same as Mercadia."

She shook her head. "I really don't understand why the Council are withholding their support. Surely, even they must know that this will distract you from your mission."

"My what?"

Rowan frowned. "Your quest?" she offered.

"Ah, good point. I'm not giving up. I'll try to speak to Elios again, make him listen." He appraised her face. "You look tired. Why don't you rest?"

Her head shook emphatically. "Impossible. I can't take the risk of going to sleep and entering the dreamscape. I would be more open to another psychic attack. Charles is going to ready a spell to keep me safe. It will offer me some protection, but he cannot perform it until tonight." Rowan glanced towards the clock on the bedside. "Why don't you keep trying whilst I pack? Lizzie and Eddie will be back soon."

"Where's the fuzz ball?" asked Finn.

"Still snoozing under the kitchen table, I imagine." She moved to the landing and called out the little dog's name. There was no answering bark. Finn joined her and called out too, but he did not receive a response either. He walked down the stairs and poked his head around the kitchen door. "That's strange. He's not there."

Rowan investigated the rooms upstairs. "The bathroom window is open," she called out. "He wouldn't have gone out there, though. It's too high for him to reach, and it would be too big a drop for him to jump down. He's only got little legs."

"I wonder if he changed his mind about the walk?" Finn mused.

"But how would he even get out, or know where to go to catch them up?" Rowan moaned. "I'm an awful pet owner, not even thinking about his toileting needs. What if he has run off?"

"I very much doubt it," Finn said with confidence. "You go check out the front and I'll have a look out back. I promise you, he won't have gone far."

Rowan hurried down the stairs and in the direction of the front door. She lifted the latch and halted. As if on cue, there was a loud scratching on the wood. Biscuit sat on the front step, patiently waiting to come inside. He wagged his tail and trotted past her with a quick sniff of the air. How does he do that?

"It's alright, I've found him," she bellowed back to Finn. Following behind, she gently admonished the little dog, "Don't you do that again. You gave us quite a fright."

Finn studied Biscuit for a few moments. A knowing look seemed to be exchanged between the two males. Rowan was curious as to what it meant, but she did not comment. Biscuit, impervious to her appraisal, simply trotted off in the direction of the living room. Rowan shifted her attention back to Finn. "Try Elios again. Perhaps if he knew about Kane, he would realise we don't have the time to be distracted. It's not as if he can expect us to stand idly by and watch your brother lose his soul."

Finn agreed, and bounded up the stairs.

Rowan released a soft sigh and headed back to the living room. She was not surprised to see that Biscuit had curled into a ball on the sofa, ignoring her entry and making a point of going to sleep.

She tutted and flicked her gaze to the book that had been cast to the floor. Turning through the pages, she found where she had left off and let herself be absorbed once more into the story.

The time ticked away until at last Finn entered the room with a huge grin on his face.

"By your expression, can I assume that Elios is going to help?"

"Not exactly. He will not go up against Mercadia, and would not state his reasons. But, he advised me of another person that can help. One he once tutored in Astyllis. His power and knowledge of the Shroud would be able to challenge that of my brother."

"Who?" she asked.

Finn's smile broadened, now he was positively beaming. "Indigo," he said.

"Indigo?"

"My old friend, and so I know he will help us. I've just got to figure a way of reaching him. He and I were close at the Academy, and the connection is still there. It will give me something to work with."

"That's great news."

"Strangely, I've thought about him recently. I wasn't sure why, but now..."

She approached him and nudged his arm gently, breaking him free from his trance.

Finn continued, "I think I know the best way to reach him, but it will have to be tonight when he plays his pipes."

"Pipes?" she queried.

"Pan pipes. He's a musician, the finest in Valoria," he said proudly.

"Seems that we both have a lot to do this evening. We've not even considered the amulet yet."

Finn nodded and left the room momentarily. He returned with the rucksack and two jackets. "Eddie won't mind us borrowing these, and I've packed a change of clothing for us," he said.

"Speaking of which, don't you think they should be back by now?"

"Maybe they've gone back to Lizzie's," Finn suggested.

"I'll leave them a note. I saw a pad and pen on the bookcase." She paused, looking over at Biscuit, who was curled up on the settee, studying them. "Will we be okay to leave Biscuit here with Eddie and Lizzie? I know it's not ideal, but we don't have much choice. We can't bring him with us; it's too risky. This is going to be tricky enough without trying to keep him quiet and hidden too."

Finn sighed. "I suppose you're right. I'm sure they'll be fine. They seem to like him, and he's been on his best behaviour," Finn reassured her. He knelt beside the settee and ruffled Biscuit's fur, making eye contact with the little dog.

Whatever Finn had communicated telepathically, Biscuit seemed to understand, although he did not appear altogether happy as he let out a whine and lowered his head to his paws with a huff. Rowan gave him a reassuring scratch behind the ears.

"Good boy. We'll be back by lunchtime tomorrow; I promise. In the meantime, just be your usual charming self and try not to get into too much mischief, alright?"

Biscuit let out a soft woof of acknowledgment, nuzzling her hand.

"I'll write that note now for Eddie and Lizzie explaining the situation. Hopefully they won't mind the short notice," she said. Retrieving the pad and pen, she quickly scribbled a message, and then allowed Finn to help her slip on the blue denim he had brought for her. She rolled the sleeves up and then glanced back at her furry companion, biting down on her lip.

Finn already had his coat on and gave one last goodbye pat to the Scottie. "I'm sure it will be fine, stop worrying. We better get a move on; we've lost a good portion of the day," Finn said, shouldering the rucksack.

They left the house and headed back in the direction of the centre of the town, where Rowan hoped that along the way they would be fortunate enough to catch a taxi to the train station.

Chapter Eight

Kane

Somewhere Outside of Achavanich, Scottish Highlands

"How dare she?" Kane fumed, pacing back and forth in his tent and gesticulating wildly. The sheer audacity of this wretched woman. *Who is she to defy my power, and flick me away like a gnat? How was it even possible?*

From the moment they had connected, he had sensed no such ability from her, and there was nothing to suggest that she possessed any power to match his own at all. Time spent with these mortal women whilst waiting for darkness to fall had proved how little he had to fear from them. He was completely unimpressed with their simpering ways, and how they could be so easily manipulated with the flow of wine and a promise of a delicious meal.

Kane paused in his ranting to acknowledge that there had been one earth woman who had remotely impressed him: Nicki. He'd allowed her to live beyond her finite time with him. Possessed with such sexual prowess, unlike the wenches he had slept with back home, she had at least earned his leniency when the time had come to cut all ties.

Kane's thoughts momentarily drifted to the feel of that soft flesh beneath his, the rhythm of Nicki's body moulding to his own, and positions she'd informed him of that would have put a mysterious being called Kama Sutra to shame. A longing surged to have her there now, easing the heat of his anger. Instead, he was alone, in a remote location, with not so much as a local tavern or brothel house in walking distance—nothing to placate him as he waited for daylight to fade.

Kane pulled the opening of his tent apart, ignoring the slight tear as he roughly handled the material, and scanned the horizon to observe the position of the sun for what felt like the umpteenth time. The Fallen would soon be waking and awaiting their orders, yet, frustratingly, he still did not know the exact location of the Tracker. The only thing Kane could be certain of, when he had held the briefest connection to the girl's mind, was that they were no longer in the surrounding area. As incredible as it seemed, in the shortest of time, they had travelled a significant distance. The scent was far too faint for even the Fallen to trace.

Kane stormed to the oak table and manifested what remained of his wine store. A glass appeared, and he uncorked and poured. Swilling the honey-coloured liquid in his mouth, and then swallowing, he felt a sharp and fruited tang bit his taste buds and gave a slight shudder. It was not one of his finest, yet it would have to do. He continued to drink whilst considering the little information he had gleaned from the girl before she had so rudely sent him cascading into a strange oblivion of nothingness. She had been reading a moment before sensing his connection, and immediately shut off his vision. From what little he recalled of the words on the pages, the book was nothing but a fable, and gave no clue as to where the Tracker had taken her.

Kane frowned and rubbed his forehead where the shard had been inserted. The Mistress had said it would waken up an ability, and indeed it had. The contact directly to the girl's mind had been unexpected. But how to connect without her being aware of him?

Kane contemplated contacting his Mistress once again. Would she consider my constant interruptions a sign of weakness? She had given him the tool, although never fully expanded on the ability it would grant him. Would she be disappointed if I failed to learn how to use it? Kane had to be careful. Her time was nearing, and it would not be prudent for him to lose her faith in his abilities at this stage, and certainly not whilst he desired her mentorship. She would be the one to guide him through the change that he knew was inevitably coming. The Nyrvallia transformation, a curve ball which he had not foreseen. The thought of what additional power it would bring sent a sensuous thrill. Yet, there was still a slight thrum of fear, deep in his guts, as to what it would truly mean for him. Would I still be myself? Would it physically transform me, and into what? Kane did not care for his good looks to diminish or his sexual appeal to the females of his world to be destroyed. He still longed for an heir to continue his family line—once, of course, he had reasserted his family name and restored the power stolen from his mother.

He finished his drink and moved to lay once more on his bed, his hands seeking the soft material of the girl's clothing. There was still a faint scent of her perfume, delicate, and pleasing to his senses. She was a curiosity he fully intended to explore.

Closing his eyes, he felt for the shard inside him. The blade gleamed, and he caught a faint glimpse of his own reflection in the silver. His lips curved as a dark energy wrapped its arms around him and pulled into its embrace, sending him spiralling backwards. Kane fell through a deep chasm of blackness.

Finally, his feet landed on solid ground. The air stirred around him, and a thousand voices whispered in excitement.

A crone rose from her rocking chair and lifted her spectacles to peer closely at him. "Well, this is an unexpected surprise," she said.

"Where am I?" Kane asked.

She prodded him. "Don't you recognise your own kin?"

"Do not touch me." He glared a warning. "My mother was my only kin."

She cackled and pulled herself to her full height. For one so old, she was surprisingly tall. "Your mother was no match for me, and you, my boy, are no equal either. Your temper is wasted on me."

"Who are you?" he demanded.

"I am Ardella, Custodian of the Shroud. Eldest daughter of Rhydu."

Kane frowned. "My mother never mentioned she had a sibling."

Ardella snarled. "That sow always denied my relationship with our father. She could not stand the fact that my mother was born from a more powerful line. I bet

Kyranna whirled cartwheels the day I died. Little did she know."

Kane flinched at his mother's spoken name. "And how is it, Ardella, that you are Custodian of the Shroud? Its existence began well before your time. Even the historic scriptures are unable to confirm its true birth."

"My family have always been the Shroud's custodians. Even in death, we are called back to serve, and take over from the previous custodian. When my mother Ursula ascended, her time served in full, its call came to me, as it will to the next in line."

"Why am I here?" he snapped.

"The Eye granted that a descendant may call for my help, but I can only serve you this once. I sensed your need. Now, here you are. Be warned that you have only one favour to ask."

Excitement lit Kane's gaze and he laughed. "How interesting. Then I ask for you to make me a Master of the Shroud. I want all its secrets."

The crone shook her head. "That I cannot grant. The knowledge must be learned and time dedicated to the study of the Shroud. It must be honoured and respected. The Shroud will not accept anything less. Idleness will not serve as its Master."

Kane considered for a moment. "If it will not allow me full knowledge of its secrets, will it share one with me?"

Ardella cocked her head. "Perhaps. What is it that you seek, nephew?"

"I can enter another's mind, but not undetected. How do I use the Shroud to mask my presence from her?"

She smiled and crooked a finger. "Come closer, nephew."

Kane moved slowly towards her as she pulled a small pipe from her robes and lit it, taking a few puffs. The tobacco had a strange and sweet scent. When she was eye to eye level with him, she leaned forward and blew smoke in his face. Kane wafted a hand in front of himself as she murmured under her breath. The pipe suddenly extinguished. She tapped it against her side three times before placing it back within the thick material. Kane's eyes watered for a few seconds more. His throat felt tight, and he suddenly sneezed. The smoke filtered through his sinuses.

Ardella jabbed her spiny finger at the centre of his forehead. He cried out as the blade shattered into pieces. An incredible heat filled his head and perspiration flowed down his cheeks. The pieces melded together to form the tiny blade once more, the shard now burrowed deeper into his mind.

"The gift is given, nephew. You may ask no more of the Custodian."

Kane wiped his brow. "Will anyone be able to detect the power you have given me?"

"Only a Master of the Shroud can see it, and only two are known to have earned such titles. Unless you have a desire to declare it, the others that you fear will not discover it."

"I fear no-one."

"I see through your lie, nephew. For I, too, was a Master of the Shroud, and now, I am its Custodian. You cannot hide the truth from me."

Kane glared, "I do not intend to, crone."

She narrowed her gaze. "Before you leave, know that the gift you have been given will only serve you during darkness. It will remain dormant in the light of day."

His temper sparked. "How dare you trick me? I asked for the ability to be granted, and I expect its full power. You have no right to place a caveat as to when I may call upon it."

"The Shroud holds no fealty to the light or the dark. You are one with the darkness; therefore the ability granted will only serve you in darkness. Accept it, or I can remove it, and leave you with nothing," she snapped.

"I accept," he growled back, not caring for her tone.

Ardella's bony hands flung forward and pushed him away, causing him to stumble. Her sneer faded into the blackness as she bid him goodbye. Kane's gut wrenched as he soared higher through the chasm. A blast of light and he suddenly pitched forward off his bed and onto the canvas floor of his tent.

"Damn that crone," he muttered as he dusted himself off, and rose to his feet.

"What crone would that be?" asked Rivik, poking his head through a gap in the tent.

"None of your business," Kane barked, and signalled for the creature to enter.

Rivik sniffed the air. "What magic is this?"

"You ask too many questions, it would be wise to hold your tongue."

"Very well."

"Have the others risen?"

"Yes, although they hunger from the regeneration."

"And what about you?"

"My needs are no different."

"Look around you, Rivik. The source of flesh is somewhat limited here."

"Have you located the Tracker and the girl?"

"Not yet, but very soon."

"May I suggest we head south to the outlying villages? My brethren can feed whilst we await further orders."

"Very well, but we stay together, so you are prepared to move at my command."

"I thought you preferred not to watch us feed."

"No need to concern yourself. I shall be using my magic to locate the Tracker, and therefore preoccupied." Kane collected the soft material and turned to leave the tent. "Remind your Brethren to keep to the shadows when sourcing and consuming your food. Take only what is needed; this is not the time to be feasting."

"Yes, Commander."

Barrock's gaze met Kane's from across the campsite. He stalked forward, saliva dripping from his teeth.

"Pack up. We leave now."

"Where to, Commander?"

"South, to eat what you require in flesh and bone. You will follow Rivik's instructions. Do not speak to me or distract me."

Barrock nodded. "Symiar," he growled.

The largest of the Fallen approached and bowed its head. "Yes?"

"Dissemble it. We leave now."

Symiar, the Fallen's chosen one, turned and opened his mouth, blowing his foul breath onto the thick material as Barrock and Rivik walked away in silence.

Kane paused a few moments to watch the tent and all its belongings shrink in size, until it was small enough to consume and transport to the next destination. Kane still marvelled at his own ingenuity as Symiar lapped the miniature tent and swallowed it, the dry pouch held safely within the base of the creature's throat protecting it from choking. The Fallen bowed and waited for Kane's consent to leave. He nodded and gestured for Symiar to move.

All eyes followed the Commander as he strode forward to join the others. Symiar immediately took his position behind Barrock. Rivik lowered himself to the ground, allowing Kane to mount.

"The cocoons are dispersed. We are ready," Barrock announced.

Kane cast a gaze to the sky and smiled as the last ray of sun slipped beneath the horizon. The darkness embraced them.

"Proceed," he ordered.

Chapter Nine

Finn

York Train Station, United Kingdom
Finn appraised the train arriving on platform two. Although Rowan had tried to describe their mode of transport for today, nothing had really prepared him for seeing the real thing.

"You are a very trusting race," he muttered, eyeing the train sceptically.

The doors slid open and Rowan stepped onto the train. She turned when Finn didn't automatically follow, his legs refusing to cooperate and his feet firmly rooted to the spot.

"What's wrong?" she asked.

Finn stared at the open doorway with a frown. "Are you sure this is safe?"

Rowan pointed to a mother and two children embarking further down the train. The children laughed excitedly. "Look over there. Do they look scared?"

He glanced over and shook his head, his face hot and crimson. He cringed at how much of a coward he must look, his pride bruised as he noted the amusement in Rowan's eyes. Releasing a soft curse, he begrudgingly allowed her to pull him on board. A loud whistle sounded, and the doors closed behind them. It was too late to change his mind.

"Hurry," Rowan said, heading down the narrow aisle to find seats. Finn followed, his senses on high alert for any sign of danger.

As the train lurched to life, Finn noticed some seats facing the opposite direction. "Why do these chairs face the wrong way? Is this a trick? Are we being punished?" he asked.

Rowan laughed warmly. "It's not a punishment, I assure you. The train moves both ways, so they have seats pointing in both directions. Some people don't like travelling backwards."

Finn raised an eyebrow, unconvinced.

"Just relax, will you? You're going to make the other passengers nervous," Rowan scolded.

Glancing around, Finn observed their fellow travellers. An elderly man read a newspaper, a well-dressed woman gazed out the window wistfully, and the mother with her two arguing children sat nearby. The scene of the siblings bickering over candy felt familiar, making Finn yearn to reunite with his own family.

Interestingly, none of the passengers seemed perturbed about riding inside the metallic beast. I do need to relax, Finn conceded to himself, though he couldn't quite shake an uneasy feeling...

As their journey continued, the train wound its way through the lush English countryside. Rolling green hills dotted with farmhouses and pastures stretched out on either side. The gentle rocking motion began to lull Finn into a more relaxed state.

"It's quite beautiful, isn't it?" Rowan remarked softly, noticing Finn's gaze fixed on the passing scenery. "Different from your world, I imagine."

"Yes," Finn replied. "The colours in Valoria are more vibrant, the air fresher. But there's a serene beauty to this land, too." He described the dense forests and freely roaming animals back home, painting a vivid picture.

Rowan listened intently, transported by his words. As Finn spoke, some of the tension eased from his shoulders. Sharing memories of Valoria stirred a deep longing within him, but also reminded him of the vital purpose of his quest.

Hours passed as the train journeyed on. The food from the galley was disappointingly bland compared to Valorian cuisine or anything he had tasted in this world so far. Finn passed the time in conversation, finding comfort in Rowan's presence among the unfamiliar surroundings.

Finally, the conductor announced their approach to Cornwall. Finn gazed out the window as the train pulled into the station, a mixture of apprehension and determination settling over him. Though he had no idea what challenges awaited them, he knew one thing for certain: with Rowan by his side, he would face whatever lay ahead. Their bond had grown stronger with each trial they had endured.

As the train pulled into the station, Finn, and Rowan gathered their belongings and stepped out onto the platform. The sun had already begun to set, casting a warm golden glow over the bustling station.

Rowan frowned. "It's later than I thought," she said, turning to him. "The witchcraft museum will be closed by now. We'll have to wait until morning to go there."

"Are you sure the amulet is there?" he asked. It had been a long way to travel for a wild goose chase.

"Positive," she replied.

Finn nodded, suppressing a yawn. The journey had left him feeling drained, and the prospect of a comfortable bed was incredibly appealing. "We should find a place to stay for the night, then."

Rowan led the way out of the station and down a quaint cobblestone street lined with colourful shops and cafes. The salty sea air filled their lungs, and the distant cry of gulls could be heard over the chatter of passersby.

After a short walk, they came to a charming bed and breakfast with a blue door and flower boxes in the windows. Rowan queried availability and gave Finn a quick thumbs up. She checked them in, and then together they wearily climbed the narrow staircase to their room on the second floor. Before they had left York, Rowan had explained that she had written on the note to their friend Eddie that they would be back the following day to say goodbye and to thank him once again for his hospitality. Finn hoped that their absence would allow Lizzie to get over whatever it was that had got her so spooked as to insist upon them leaving.

As Finn entered the room, a sense of warmth and comfort enveloped him. The room was cosy, with soft, muted colours and simple, yet charming decor. A large window overlooked the quaint Cornish street below, allowing the last rays of the setting sun to filter through the lace curtains. Finn sat on the edge of the mattress, testing its firmness. "Well, it's not quite as soft as Eddie's," he remarked, bouncing slightly, "but it'll do for a night's rest."

Rowan joined him, running her hand over the slightly rough, handmade quilt that covered the bed. "It's perfect," she said, smiling. "It feels homey and comfortable; just what we need after such a long journey."

Finn leaned in to kiss her, but was interrupted by the low rumble of Rowan's stomach. She looked up, a slight blush colouring her cheeks. "I guess the train food wasn't quite as filling as I thought," she said with a laugh.

Finn rose and stretched his arms above his head. "Why don't we go out and find something to eat?"

Her eyes lit up at the suggestion. "That sounds lovely," she agreed, moving to the mirror to check on her appearance. "A quiet meal together, just the two of us, before we dive into the chaos of tomorrow," she said as she smoothed down her hair.

"You're perfect," Finn reassured her.

As they made their way downstairs, Rowan stopped by the front desk to ask for a recommendation. The owner, a kindly older woman with a warm smile, was more than happy to help.

"Oh, you must try the Oyster Sands!" she exclaimed, her eyes twinkling. "It's just down the street, right by the sea. They have the most marvellous seafood, and the atmosphere is just perfect for a romantic evening."

Finn thanked her, flushing slightly at the mention of romance. They set off hand-in-hand towards the restaurant. As they walked, they chatted quietly, their conversation a welcome distraction from the weight of their impending quest.

"I wonder what kind of seafood they have here," Finn mused, his eyes scanning the charming storefronts they passed. "In Valoria, we have these incredible iridescent fish that shimmer like rainbows in the sunlight."

"That sounds amazing," she said, leaning into Finn's side.

"I can't wait to try the seafood here and compare. Though, I doubt they'll have anything quite so magical."

As they approached the Oyster Sands Tavern, the sound of soft music and the tantalising aroma of fresh seafood greeted them. Finn led the way inside, more than ready to enjoy a moment of peace and Rowan's company before the challenges of the morrow.

The restaurant itself was charming, with soft lighting, nautical decor, and a warm, inviting atmosphere. A smiling hostess led them to a cosy table for two, a flickering candle casting a gentle glow over the crisp white tablecloth.

They settled into their seats, and a comfortable silence fell between them. The waiter arrived to take their order and returned again shortly with their drinks. Rowan took a sip of a rich, fruity liquid.

"This is delicious," she said, smiling at Finn. "Are you sure you don't want to try a sip?"

He chuckled, and shook his head. "Better not risk it."

Rowan nodded her understanding of his caution. "Fair enough. I guess we'll have to save the wine-tasting for when we're back in Valoria."

"I'd like that," he said, his eyes softening as he looked at her. "When this is all over, I want to show you everything my world has to offer."

"It sounds magical," Rowan said. "I can't wait to see it all with you."

Their conversation turned to the plans for the following day, and he sensed her mood become more sombre.

"Do you think the amulet will really unlock any power?" she asked, her brow furrowed with concern.

Finn sighed and toyed with his glass. "I hope so. Both Mercadia and Bessantia believe it will, and I suppose we must trust their guidance."

"Finn?"

"Yes?"

"Honestly, I'm a little scared. What if it's not real?"

"And what if it is?"

"But what if the Lightkeepers are right, and I can't control the power once it's unleashed?"

Finn reached across the table, taking her hand in his. "You're stronger than you give yourself credit for. I've seen the way you've handled everything that's been thrown at us so far. You have a good heart, and a strong will. That power is a part of you, and I believe you'll find a way to master it."

She squeezed his hand. "Thank you. I don't know what I'd do without you."

"You'll never have to find out," he promised, his eyes intense with emotion. "We're in this together, no matter what."

As their meals arrived, the conversation shifted to lighter topics. He asked her about her childhood, her favourite memories growing up, and the dreams she had for the future. She skipped over the pain of her father's death.

In turn, she listened as intently as he described his life in Valoria, the close-knit community he'd grown up in, and the mischief he'd got up to.

"I remember this one time," Finn said, chuckling at the memory, "I convinced Aaron that a squirrel had told me where to find a hidden treasure. He spent hours digging away in the forest, only to find an old, metal box."

Rowan laughed at the scene he described. "I bet he was furious."

"He was, at first," he admitted, smiling fondly. "But looking back, I wouldn't trade those memories for anything."

The mention of Aaron brought a sorrowful note back to the conversation, both acutely aware of his brother's predicament now.

"We'll save him," Rowan said softly, her eyes shining with determination. "I know we will."

He nodded, his jaw set with resolve. As they finished their meals, the conversation turned to their plans for the evening. Rowan settled the bill using a strange piece of plastic. Finn could not understand how it held such power, but the restaurant owner seemed satisfied, even suggesting they take a walk along a nearby hidden cove. As they made their way down to the secluded beach, the sound of the waves lapping against the shore soothed his nerves. It was a welcome sight to behold, and he could taste the tang of salt on the tip of his tongue.

Rowan sat beside him on the soft sand, the simple pleasure of enjoying each other's company without fear a rare opportunity Finn would forever cherish. For a moment, the worries of his quest faded away, and they were purely an ordinary couple, relishing the beauty of the world around them.

The night rapidly drew in colder, and the tide began to rise. It was with much reluctance that they made their way back to the bed and breakfast, lost in their own thoughts. Finn, ever the gentleman, gave Rowan the opportunity to bathe first. She showed him how to set the shower running before leaving him to undress. The warm water washed away some of the weariness.

Though his heart and body yearned for her, he knew that the time to consummate their relationship was not now. The events of the past few days weighed heavily on his mind, along with the concern of what tomorrow would bring.

Rowan took the bed, asking for him to give her some space whilst she sought contact with the mysterious Aliyah, an invisible witch who would help and protect her against Kane and his invasions into her mind. Finn agreed. It would give him the opportunity to contact Indigo, a conversation that he both looked forward to and dreaded at the same time.

He sat cross-legged on the soft carpeted floor of the dimly lit room. With his eyes closed, he concentrated on the memory of his friend and reached out with his mind, attempting to bridge the gap between worlds. The power and knowledge that the Meridian had bestowed upon him during the time they had spent with Bessie allowed him to focus his energy. The soothing melody of pan pipe music filled his mind as he made the connection, a reminder of the countless hours they had spent together in the forest.

"Indigo," Finn called out mentally, his voice echoing through the ethereal space between them. "I need your help."

Moments later, Indigo's presence materialised before him, his features coming into focus. The man's deep blue eyes held a mix of surprise and concern as he took in Finn's troubled expression.

"My friend," Indigo greeted, his voice warm, yet cautious. "It's been a long time. What troubles you?"

"It's my brother, Aaron. He's under the influence of the Master, and I fear he's going to do something terrible. I can't reach him through the Shroud. I can't follow him or watch him to know what he plans, or how I even go about stopping and saving him from the darkness. He knows I'm there, and he's told me others know I am there too."

"You were never one to be interested in the Shroud. Quite dismissive of its nonsensical hocus-pocus, if I recall correctly."

"I don't need to be reminded of my mistakes," Finn said grimly. "Aaron is a master of it now. I need to know what he's going to do. Can you help me?"

"Where was Aaron known to be last?"

"In the Master's faction."

Indigo stared at him. "Let me get this straight. You want me to use my knowledge of the Shroud and spy on Aaron right under the nose of the Master?"

"Yes, that pretty much sums it up," said Finn, his cheeks heating. "You're the only one besides Aaron who has studied the Shroud so closely. If anyone can help me and remain undetected, it's you. I wouldn't ask this of you if I wasn't desperate to save my brother."

Indigo fell silent, his gaze distant. The pan pipe music that constantly accompanied him grew softer, reflecting Finn's own inner turmoil and the gravity of the favour that he asked.

"What you want... it's dangerous. Going up against a Master of the Shroud, especially one as powerful as Aaron, is no small feat. But going up against the Master as well? It's pure insanity!"

His heart sank, but he understood his friend's reservations. "I know it's a lot to ask, but you're the only one I can turn to. My brother's life hangs in the balance, and I can't do this without you. I'd do it myself, but the Council have sent me on another quest. My balls are literally in a vice, old friend. Please help me."

Indigo met his gaze, the depth of their friendship reflected. The pan pipe music swelled, its melody determined and resolute. "Alright," he said at last, his voice steady. "I'll help you. But if I fail, you know Irina will come and hunt your sorry arse down. If I succeed, you owe me a Buckbear. She's been wanting one of those critters since my Grandmother passed away."

Relief and gratitude surged through Finn. "Thank you. And yes, when I return to Valoria I will track you a Buckbear down. I won't forget this, Indie. Good luck. Let me know as soon as you have any news."

Indigo smiled, the pan pipe music now a soothing backdrop to their conversation.

As the connection between them began to fade, the pan pipe music grew distant, but its comforting presence lingered on in Finn's mind. He joined Rowan in bed and scooted closer. In this quiet moment, they had each other. And for now, that would have to be enough.

Chapter Ten
Rowan

The Witchcraft Museum, Cornwall

"Are you sure we are in the right place?" Finn asked as they stood gazing at the entrance of the pretty whitewashed building.

Rowan rubbed absentmindedly at the crick in her neck, no doubt caused by the stress of going on her first shoplifting expedition. "I admit, it does seem smaller than I imagined, especially when it boasted to be the home of the largest witchcraft artefacts in the UK, but I do feel that we are in the right place," she replied.

"Need a hand with that?" Finn asked, producing a golden orb in the palm of his hand. He placed it on her neck and her eyes fluttered closed with the delicious warmth that spread out and eased the pain.

"Wonderful, I could have you do that all ..." She paused, suddenly conscious that they were in a public place. Across a small brook, an elderly couple were out walking their Jackapoo, who had been busy splashing in the water.

Rowan supressed a giggle when the older gentleman pulled off his spectacles and said loudly, "Vera, I think I need a new pair of glasses." He frantically rubbed a handkerchief over the lenses. "I could have sworn that fella over there, he erm.. he...well he..."

"For pity's sake, Duncan, spit it out."

"Well, he produced a magic ball of fire in his hand," Duncan continued, popping his glasses back onto his face.

There was no mistaking his wife's tut of exasperation, and she gave Rowan an apologetic smile. "Nonsense," she admonished.

"But..." he protested, scratching his chin.

"No buts. I think we'll get Doctor Herbert to review that medication, and perhaps your eyesight too." His wife pulled him away and across to the other side of the small bridge, the Jackapoo bounding after them.

Rowan was relieved to see them go. Thankfully, Finn's healing had not drawn attention from the other locals that had passed by.

He leaned in closer to inspect the noticeboard. "What's an entry fee?"

She turned her attention to the museum. "It means we have to pay to get in."

Finn's eyes widened and met her own. "You're joking, right?"

"No," she replied, then pushed the entrance door open.

She waved him inside, ignoring the look on his face. The assistant immediately stood and bid them a greeting. Rowan approached the desk, noting the name Jessica on the girl's ID badge.

"Welcome to the Museum of Witchcraft," Jessica said brightly.

A quick appraisal of the girl estimated her to be in her early twenties and attractive, with an enviable figure and manicured nails. Rowan inwardly sighed and glanced at her own hands, which were looking in desperate need of a manicure.

She felt an uncomfortable stirring in the pit of her stomach, and hoped Finn would not think her dull in comparison to the beauty in front of them. Conscious that she had yet to reply to the greeting, Rowan firmly placed the green-eyed monster that was threatening to emerge back in its box and beamed at the museum assistant. "Thank you, two adults please."

"That will be ten pounds."

Rowan fumbled in her pockets for the same card she had paid with the previous night, pleased that she had had the presence of mind to keep her purse in the rucksack before the Fallen had attacked. Intermittently, she flicked her gaze towards Jessica for any signs of potential flirting. She sighed in relief as the girl handed back the card from the merchant terminal. Rowan stuffed the receipt into her jacket pocket and turned back to Jessica to query the closing times. However, the girl had lost some of her earlier exuberance, and was looking quite uncomfortable. Inwardly groaning, she turned around to confirm the reason for the sudden change in her demeanour.

Well, she mused, she need not have worried whether Finn would find Jessica attractive. He was scowling at the pretty assistant as though she had just committed a highway robbery. Jessica coughed and cleared her throat nervously.

Rowan rolled her eyes to the ceiling and begged for strength as she counted to ten and pasted a smile on her face. She seized Finn's hand to distract him from his 'if looks could kill you would be six feet under' stare. Giving a quick peck on Finn's cheek, she crooned, "Now darling, I know you wanted to do archery today, but you did promise me."

Rowan turned back to Jessica with an exaggerated sigh. "I'm sorry. My husband is such a grump today."

The girl's posture relaxed. "I'll just get your tickets." The printer behind her whirred into life.

Finn's mouth immediately opened in protest. Rowan elbowed him in the ribs and silenced him before he could launch into the full tirade she had sensed was coming.

"That hurt," he hissed in her ear. She gave him an apologetic shrug.

"Here's your tickets and your information leaflet. If you follow the signs, they will direct you through the exhibits."

Rowan accepted the tickets. "Thank you. Come along dear, a promise is a promise."

"Enjoy the museum," Jessica called out cheerily as Rowan took Finn's arm and immediately steered him away from the desk.

She could hear the girl chuckling behind them as they followed the direction of the first sign indicating 'Exhibits this way'. Once they were out of sight of the front desk, Finn pulled his arm free from hers and strode purposefully in front. He disappeared into a room on the left-hand side of the corridor signposted 'Exhibit One'. She inwardly sighed and followed him inside.

Noting that there were other occupants in the exhibit room, she silently joined Finn, who feigned interest in one of the display cases. He made no acknowledgement of her arrival and kept his gaze fixed on the display in front of him. Tentatively, she slipped her hand into his. He was still angry, but he had not rejected her touch. The other occupants smiled politely and left the room.

Finn's voice broke the silence. "Why did you do that?"

"They would have been suspicious of us otherwise. You cannot just go around giving people evil looks because you happen to disagree with the way they do things."

"They have no right to charge. It's…what is that term that Eddie uses?…Oh, yes—daylight robbery."

"But the museum must make money to keep running. They have the building to maintain, wages to pay for," she explained gently.

"These are ancient artefacts that do not actually belong to them. They have no right to charge people to see them."

She rubbed her forehead. "I understand your feelings, I really do, but we honestly do not have the time to debate this now. Remember why we are here. We need to find my amulet, then figure out how we steal it from the museum without being caught," she whispered. Her stomach was in knots at the sheer thought of it.

Even in her wildest dreams she had never contemplated that she would fall into a life of crime, yet here she was, planning a museum heist.

Finn shoved his hands in his pocket and stubbornly kicked the floor like a petulant child. "It still isn't right," he growled.

"If you don't start acting normal and at least pretend to enjoy the museum you're going to make people suspicious," she hissed, "and we really don't need any attention being drawn to us right now."

"Fine," he grumbled.

Clearly it was not. "Well, could you tell your face that?" she said, noting that he still looked as though he were chewing a wasp.

"Tell my face what?" he asked, frowning at her.

"For goodness' sake," she said, pulling him towards her. She kissed him hard, extinguishing his anger. His mouth took control and the kiss deepened further, almost taking her breath away.

"Does that help?" she asked him breathlessly when they finally broke apart.

The corners of his mouth twitched and pulled upwards. "It's a start."

Rowan grinned. "Right. Let's find my amulet."

They moved through each of the exhibit rooms and searched the display cases. Rowan could not help but immerse herself in the history as she poured over the literature and pointed excitedly to some of the fascinating pieces that were on display.

"Look at this," she called out.

Despite his earlier protest, Finn's face showed a genuine interest.

"Better than archery, eh?" she said, giving him a playful nudge.

He winked back at her. "I'll let you have that one."

Rowan returned to the booklet she had been reading. "So much I never understood or fully appreciated before. What these poor women must have gone through. It's awful."

Finn nodded. "Another difference between your world and mine. We hold our mages in the highest esteem. They would never suffer the cruelty and torture that these people have been subjected to."

"I imagine had I been born in that time, my gift would have had me branded and hung or burned as a witch. It's a relief that times have changed, and my world is a little more tolerating to New Age practice and beliefs."

"A shame for these poor women, it didn't happen sooner."

They moved on to the next exhibit, falling into a thoughtful silence broken only by the sound of their footsteps as they ascended a set of winding stairs that led to a small room. Inside were mannequins wearing an assortment of brightly coloured robes and garments. There was a doorway at the back of the room signposted, 'Exit this way'. "Last room," Rowan noted with a heavy heart. Although she had thoroughly enjoyed the museum, she was disappointed to have not yet found the amulet.

Finn wandered over to a mannequin and touched the fabric of the gown. "Not unlike the robes worn in my world," he commented.

She smiled as he continued to examine the mannequins. Her eyes flicked to the last of the display cases in turn. She paused as something caught her attention on the far-right hand corner of the room. Almost tucked away and leaning against the back wall were three full length staves. Finn, absorbed in his appraisal, did not notice Rowan cross the room.

She examined each staff in turn. Her eyes fell on the last, which rested against the wall, and she was seized by an overwhelming urge to hold it. There were three bends in the crafting of the wood as she traced along with her finger and then peered closely at its tag. Is it too much of a coincidence that the wood was carved from a Rowan tree? Unable to resist its call, Rowan picked it up.

The wall of the museum completely crumbled away. Once again, she felt as though her body had been physically transported into the vision. This time she no longer stood in a world of desolation. Instead she was surrounded by lush green fields, and she was not alone.

A young boy scowled at her. "That doesn't belong to you."

Rowan gestured to the staff, still gripped in her hand. "You mean this? Whose is it?"

He spat on his hand and then rubbed the grime down the length of his beige linen trousers. "It's the Master's, and you know he will beat me if I do not return it. Now, give it back to me. You've had your fun."

"If this belongs to your Master, then how is it that it comes to be in my possession?" she challenged.

"Why, you stole it away from me," he said incredulously.

"How can I have stolen it? I've just arrived here."

The boy looked quizzical. "Has Freya given you one lump too many?"

"Freya?"

The boy stamped his foot. "Oh, it's not funny, Mordreya."

Rowan shook her head. "I'm not laughing, and my name is not Mordreya."

"Fiddle sticks it's not. Are you having one of your funny turns?" He eyed her suspiciously.

"What are you talking about? Do I look like your Mordreya?"

"Yes," he said.

Rowan huffed. "I don't know what this is, but I can assure you that I am not Mordreya."

"Fine, then you leave me no choice. Morvela can deal with you. He will not punish me half as much as what the Master will."

"Who?"

"Your brother," he shouted, his brow furrowed and hands resting firmly on his hips as he glared daggers at her.

Rowan could not stop herself. The hysterics suddenly broke free, which only infuriated the boy more.

"If you thought Freya was bad, wait until Morvela licks you good and proper with that cane of his. Then you will know what pain feels like."

"And why would my so-called brother lick me?" she asked.

"Because he hates you. Everyone hates you, including the Master."

"That's not a very nice thing to say," said Rowan.

"You're weak and stupid...you will never be one of them, never," screamed the boy. He turned and ran. "You'll see, you'll get what's coming to you," he called over his shoulder.

The vision ended with his last words.

Finn snapped his fingers in front of her face. "Did you hear what I said? I think I've found it."

"What?" Rowan asked shakily.

"Your amulet. Are you okay?"

"I...I..." she trailed off, not sure what to say to him.

Finn pointed towards a mannequin wearing a red velvet gown, a scarf printed with numerous Celtic symbols hung loosely around the neck to expose the emerald green pendant.

Rowan placed the staff she had been holding back against the wall and hurried toward it. "Why would this not be in a display case?" she whispered. Her fingers stroked the pendant and electricity sparked against her skin. She shuddered and withdrew her hand.

"Perhaps they didn't know it was there?" Finn said unconvincingly. He unclasped the pendant and placed it in her hand. "Put it on."

She searched the room, ensuring that they were still alone, and then lifted the necklace to her neck. Finn raised her hair gently whilst she fastened the clasp. Rowan slipped the pendant beneath her t-shirt so only the chain was partly exposed.

"Can you remember how the scarf was arranged?" she asked.

Finn nodded and tied the cloth tightly around the mannequin's neck.

"We need to get out of here," she said quietly, and with a final glance towards the row of staves, she headed towards the exit sign. Finn followed behind.

They climbed down a narrow staircase, pushed through another door, and were back in the reception of the Museum.

Jessica glanced up from her desk. "So, how was it?" she asked.

"Amazing, wasn't it, darling?" Rowan said, striding towards the desk. "Not that my husband wants to admit that it was a remarkably interesting and eye-opening experience. So sad what those women went through, the torture," she continued.

"Hard to believe that it all really happened," Jessica said.

"Well, thank you so much. I have really enjoyed it. We hope to visit again soon," Rowan said, laughing as Finn gripped her arm and led her towards the door. "Okay dear, archery next," she said with a smile and a wave back to Jessica.

"Was that necessary?" Finn hissed once they were outside.

"Quite," she replied, relieved that no security alarm had sounded.

He glanced around and nodded a greeting at a passing dog walker. "Over there." He gestured to a more secluded area, free from tourists.

With the amulet safely in her possession, Rowan followed Finn to stand beneath the sweeping branches of a nearby willow tree. The dappled sunlight filtered through the leaves, casting a soft, ethereal glow upon their faces.

Finn turned to Rowan, his eyes searching hers with a mixture of concern and curiosity. "Do you feel any different?" he asked, his voice low and gentle. "Now that you have the amulet, I mean."

She blinked, her mind still consumed by thoughts of the staff they had seen inside the museum. "No," she replied distractedly, her gaze unfocused. "I haven't really given it much thought, to be honest."

Finn frowned slightly, sensing her preoccupation. "What's on your mind? You seem distant."

She sighed, her fingers absently toyed with the amulet around her neck. "It's the staff, Finn. I can't shake the feeling that it's important, that we need to retrieve it as well."

His eyes widened, a flicker of apprehension crossing his features. "We can't just go back in there and take it. We've already got what we came for, and we need to get back to Eddie's."

Rowan shook her head, her expression determined. "I know it won't be easy, but I have to try. There's something about that staff. It's calling to me, like it's meant to be mine."

As he opened his mouth to protest, she vanished from sight, and in the blink of an eye, found herself standing before the staff inside the museum. Her heart pounded with a mixture of fear and exhilaration. Without any hesitation, she reached out and grasped the ancient wood, feeling a surge of energy course through her body.

Just as quickly as she had disappeared, she reappeared beneath the willow tree, the staff clutched tightly in her hands. Finn's mouth had not yet closed, his expression a mixture of relief and utter disbelief.

"How did you... What just... Rowan, what happened?" he stammered, his eyes darting from the staff to her face and back again.

She shook her head, equally stunned by her sudden teleportation. "I don't know," she admitted, her voice trembling slightly. "One moment I was here, and the next I was in front of the staff. It was like the amulet responded to my desire, and my need to retrieve it."

"This is... This is incredible! The power you possess, it's beyond anything I could have imagined."

She nodded, her grip tightening on the staff as a sense of purpose washed over her. "I know it's a lot to take in. But I feel like this is just the beginning, like the amulet and the staff are the keys to unlocking something greater. Something that will help us."

As they stood together beneath the willow tree, the amulet glowing softly against Rowan's chest, and the staff humming with ancient power in her hands, she knew that their journey had taken an unexpected turn. But as she held the staff, she couldn't help but wish it was less conspicuous. To her amazement, the staff began to shrink in her hand, diminishing in size until it was no larger than a pencil. With a grateful smile, she slipped the miniaturised staff into her pocket, marvelling at the amulet's ability to respond to her thoughts and desires.

Finn stepped closer, his hand coming to rest on her shoulder in a gesture of support and understanding. "I trust you, Rowan. If you believe this is what we need to do, then I'm with you, every step of the way."

With a shared look of determination, they set off towards the train station, ready to make their way back to Eddie's. The amulet glowed softly against her chest, a constant reminder of the power she now wielded, while the miniaturised staff rested securely in her pocket, a secret weapon waiting to be unleashed.

As they walked, Rowan couldn't help but feel a sense of anticipation mingled with apprehension. The journey ahead was sure to be fraught with challenges and dangers, but with Finn by her side and the growing strength of her abilities, she knew they were ready to face whatever lay in store.

As they approached the bustling train station, the amulet around Rowan's neck pulsed with a sudden warmth. She stumbled, her hand flying to her chest as a familiar, unwelcome presence pushed at the edges of her mind.

"What's wrong?" Finn asked, his hand on her elbow, steadying her.

"It's Kane," she gasped, squeezing her eyes shut. "He's trying to access my mind, to see through my eyes."

Finn's jaw clenched, his eyes scanning the crowded platform for any sign of danger. "Fight him. Use the spell, the amulet's power, whatever it takes. Just don't let him in."

Rowan focused on the energy emanating from the amulet, drawing strength from its ancient magic. She visualised a wall around her thoughts, a barrier that Kane could not penetrate. But even as she pushed back against his intrusion, she caught a fleeting glimpse of the train station through his eyes, a momentary slip that revealed their location.

With a final, determined effort, Rowan forced Kane's presence from her mind, the amulet flaring brightly as she severed the connection. She sagged against Finn, her breath coming in short, sharp gasps.

"It's too late, he knows where we are," she said, her voice trembling. "We don't have much time."

Chapter Eleven
Kane

Somewhere Outside of Achavanich, Scottish Highlands
S Kane paced restlessly, contemplating his next move. He had not meant to test the link again until nightfall, but his frustration had mounted with each passing moment until he no longer could help himself. The Tracker and the girl had eluded him for far too long, and his patience had worn thin.

Before his conscious mind seized back control, he had closed his eyes, focusing his dark power on the tenuous connection he had forged with the girl's mind. With a forceful push, he had broken through her defences, determined to uncover their location. Now what to do with the information?

A triumphant smile spread across Kane's face as he laid on his bed and closed his eyes. This time he had a different target in mind. Releasing his consciousness, he travelled through the vortex, paying no heed to the creature that continued to linger close by. The guardian, Morbae, sprung from his chair. "So soon, Warlock?"

"I know where they are," Kane declared. "We must act swiftly. I need you to seek the Mistress's aid in opening a small portal to their location. We cannot afford to lose them again."

"I shall petition the Mistress for her assistance," Morbae said. "Be careful, though. You push your luck in the help she is prepared to give."

Kane tapped his foot, the plan formulating in his mind, as he waited for Morbae to reappear. The time seemed to crawl as Kane waited, his anticipation building with each passing moment. Finally, Morbae returned, a large charcoal disc clasped in his stubby fingers. "One portal, one traveller. That is all you get. So, make it count."

Kane seized the disc and relinquished his consciousness, sending him hurtling back to the tent with such momentum that he bounced instantly onto his feet. He almost catapulted himself through the opening in the canvas.

"Rivik, now," he demanded, reaching his mind out to the Fallen. "Bring one of your brethren with you."

"Do you have a preference, Commander?" came the reply.

"As long as they are expendable, I don't care. Hurry, I have no time."

Rivik complied, nudging a reluctant Fallen towards Kane.

"His name is Mikoss."

"I'm not interested in his name," Kane spat and turned to the Fallen that studied him with suspicious eyes. He slung an item of clothing to the ground. "You will travel through this portal," he ordered and snapped the disc in two. "Find a suitable host, someone the Tracker and the girl will not suspect. Bite them, and give them this rag. I will control their actions from there. They will be my instrument in capturing the girl and killing the Tracker."

The Fallen hissed at the black cavernous mouth that had opened. It's amber eyes glinting with malice. "Yes, Commander," it rasped, its voice like the scraping of bone and stone. Lowering its head, it retrieved the cloth from the floor and stepped forward, its movements fluid and predatory. "Then, what?" it asked.

"Obey my next order. You will hear it no matter where you are," Kane said. "Now go."

Without hesitation, the chosen Fallen stepped through, vanishing into the swirling vortex. Kane closed his eyes, his consciousness following the creature as it emerged in a bustling train station. It moved swiftly, keeping to the shadows unseen by the humans milling about, until it spotted a young man smoking in a dark dank corner. The Fallen approached silently, its form nothing more than a shadow. It dropped the material it carried to the ground and, with a sudden lunge, sank its fangs into the youth's neck, injecting its dark essence into his veins. The young man stiffened, his eyes glazing over as the Fallen's consciousness merged with his own. Satisfied, the Fallen turned to leave and signalled for Kane's next order. It felt Kane's malevolence before its physical form crumbled into dust and was no more. The youth blinked, a slow smile spreading across his face as Kane's presence settled into his mind. He moved and retrieved the item of clothing from the floor and inhaled deep.

"Find them," Kane whispered, his voice echoing in the youth's thoughts. "The girl's scent will guide you. Do not fail me." The young man nodded and discarded the material into the nearest bin. His movements were jerky and unnatural as he made his way towards the train. Kane's essence thrummed through his veins, heightening his senses, filling him with an unnatural strength and speed.

As the train pulled away from the station, the youth stalked through the carriages, following the intoxicating scent of the girl. He could feel her presence, could sense the Tracker by her side. Anticipation coiled in his gut as he drew closer, his hand tightening around the handle of the knife concealed beneath his jacket.

Chapter Twelve
Finn

Train Station, Cornwall

Finn nodded grimly, his hand resting on the small of Rowan's back as he guided her towards the waiting train. "Then let's not waste any time. We need to get to Eddie's, collect Biscuit, and then be gone before Kane's minions catch up to us."

Boarding the train, Finn found himself moving with a newfound confidence, his previous apprehension about the strange mode of transportation all but forgotten in the face of the looming threat. They found their seats, Rowan's hand clasped tightly in his, the amulet's energy thrumming between them like a shared heartbeat.

As the train pulled away from the station, Rowan leaned into Finn, her head resting on his shoulder. "Do you think the amulet's power extends beyond just my teleportation?" she asked, her fingers tracing the intricate patterns etched into the metal.

Finn considered for a moment, his brow furrowed in thought. "It's possible. The artefacts of our world often hold multiple abilities, some of which are not immediately apparent. Why do you ask?"

Rowan bit her lip, a flicker of hope sparking in her eyes. "I was thinking... what if I could use the amulet to teleport both of us back to Eddie's house?"

Finn's eyes widened, the implications of her suggestion sinking in. "Teleporting yourself is one thing, but bringing someone else along... it could be dangerous. Let's not try that yet. Not until we know more and are sure."

Rowan twisted in her seat and peered at the other passengers. Her body was suddenly rigid and she whispered, "Something is wrong. Can you feel that?"

He turned his attention from one end of the carriage to the other. His hands balled into fists as he slowly stood. "Change seats," he ordered.

"Which way?" she asked.

"Left, and further back."

Rowan stood and casually moved several rows behind. Finn waited a few seconds before following her. He sat, his eyes fixed on the doors. "We need to get off this thing," he muttered.

"We can't while the train is moving."

A voice from behind startled them. "Tickets, please."

Rowan restrained Finn before he could leap out of the seat and swing his fist.

"He's not what we are sensing," she hissed, and quickly fumbled in her pockets.

Finn gritted his teeth together as they watched the mother of two small children hand something over. The man who had entered smiled and clipped the corner of three small cards with a silver instrument, he passed them back.

Finn studied every movement as the man approached an elderly couple. The husband continued to read the newspaper, leaving it to his wife to hand over the tickets.

"Keep it together, Finn," Rowan warned as they were approached next.

"Tickets?"

Her hands were slightly shaking as she passed them across. The man clipped the card and handed them back. "Are you alright, Miss?" he asked.

"Yes. We just skipped breakfast, that's all."

Finn's expression had not changed, and he felt a sudden nudge in the ribs. He immediately attempted to straighten his face, and forced a small smile.

"He's not had much sleep," Rowan explained.

The man chuckled and moved ahead, passing through the internal sliding doors.

Finn closed his eyes, reaching forward with his senses. The gnawing ache in his gut increased in intensity, his heart hammering inside his chest. It wasn't Kane or the Fallen, but something else was approaching.

His eyes sprung open, and he released Rowan's arm. "Call Charles. We need off this damned contraption now."

"He's already here, he senses it too. We must get these people into another carriage first," she said.

The train screeched to a sudden stop.

"I take it that's our cue," Finn said, rising.

"Charles and Aliyah have interfered with the train's operations, but they can't hold it for long."

Rowan stood. Her voice shook as she addressed the other passengers. "I'm so sorry, but we need everyone to clear this carriage."

The elderly man put down his paper. "Is this some sort of joke?"

"I am afraid not. Trust me, this carriage is not safe. That's why the train has stopped."

"Bollocks. I've been doing this journey for years," said the old man.

"Be that as it may, Sir, today you are required to change carriages, now," Rowan replied.

"And how do you know what this issue is?" asked his wife.

"I'm serious. Please do what I ask," pleaded Rowan.

"What are you? Some sort of psychic?" she laughed.

Finn was rapidly losing his temper, but stopped what he was about to say when Rowan raised her hand.

"Yes, I am. Please believe me, this carriage is not safe. You need to leave, now. Have you never watched that film? You know, the one where the boy has a premonition and gets off the plane?"

The mother of the two children studied Rowan. "You're serious, aren't you?"

Rowan's voice rang with desperation and fear. "Deadly. I'm not kidding, I assure you. Take the children and go into another carriage where it is safer."

"Mummy?" asked the little girl.

Finn stepped into the centre of the aisle, blocking the exit to the right. "Get out now, people," he insisted, "before someone gets hurt."

"I'm fetching the inspector," the elderly man said angrily. "You two are nuts." He collected his newspaper and stormed in the opposite direction.

His wife had stopped laughing. She followed him with a confused backward glance.

Rowan's eyes pleaded with the mother to listen. "Please, my partner is right. We don't mean to frighten you, but something is coming to hurt us, and we don't want you to get caught up in it."

"Listen to her," Finn said, his voice gentler.

"Mummy, I really think we need to do as the nice lady said," the little boy responded.

His mother collected her bag and reached out a trembling hand to both children. "I sincerely hope that whatever it is, you both will be okay." She turned abruptly and followed in the direction of the other passengers. The children did not utter another word.

Finn's relief quickly disappeared as he spun to the sound of doors sliding open from the entrance that he had been blocking. A youth in his early twenties with blond hair and a piercing in his nose stood in front of him, a knife gripped in his right hand.

Jet black coals locked with Finn's, and the youth released a slow and menacing snarl.

Finn completed a quick appraisal of the threat, taking in the youth's height, build and strength of body stance. Without removing his gaze from the intruder, he signalled for Rowan to move back. "This is Kane's handiwork," he confirmed.

"What are you going to do?" she whispered.

"Kill him," he replied.

"He's a human being! Can't you just knock him out or something?" she protested.

"Look at his neck," Finn said calmly. "He has an infected bite wound. It's too late; he's been bitten by the Fallen, his life force poisoned."

Finn took a step backward and prepared himself for the attack he knew was imminent.

The youth briefly flicked his attention to Rowan and licked his lips in a slow, languid movement. "The Master wants you really bad. I can see why," he hissed.

"Not a chance. If you back away now, I promise to kill you quickly," Finn said.

He sensed Rowan edging further away as he moved into a fighting stance.

"You're right, he has no soul." Her voice was small and quivered in fear.

The boy clasped his head and released an awful guttural sound.

"Kane's controlling him," Finn said, recognising the look in the youth's eyes.

Rowan screamed as a flash of silver suddenly struck out towards Finn. Anticipating the strike, he successfully dodged the blade and swung out both fists, landing punches to the face, then ducked away from the slash of silver metal. Seizing the boy by his centre, Finn drove the youth backwards and sent him crashing to the ground.

"Get Charles to open those doors," he shouted.

Kane's puppet recovered quickly, sprang to his feet, and charged again. Finn, this time, used the seats for leverage. He jumped and kicked out with his feet. Hitting the sternum hard, he sent the boy hurtling.

Spitting out a dark substance, the youth wiped his hand across his mouth and glared furiously. Finn motioned for him to try again. As he lunged a third time, Finn moved forward, and with a slight twist of his frame successfully caught his arm, and with a rotating sharp twist had gained control of the knife. The youth cried out as Finn forced his arm backward and spun him around. He threw him onto the nearest seat. His opponent landed with a loud grunt and was momentarily winded.

Finn paused as the boy stood and desperately dragged air into his lungs. A smile played across his lips as the youth realised that the knife was no longer in his possession. He screamed out in rage and dropped to the floor, frantically fumbling around the seats in a desperate search.

Finn spun his head briefly in Rowan's direction. "The door. Is it open?"

"Yes," she replied.

"Then get out," he told her.

"No," she stubbornly refused.

"I don't have time to argue about this, get out."

"Not without you," she insisted.

"Damn it, just do as you are told. I will follow, I promise."

Finn sensed her anger and fear, but there was no time at all to soothe her feelings. The youth becoming increasingly desperate, seizing clumps of his hair and wailing loudly.

Finn whistled. It was time to put him out of his misery. The boy looked up, his eyes filled with pure hatred, as Finn dangled the knife in front of him. He waited for him to scramble to his feet and lunge once more.

This time, Finn drove the knife deep into his abdomen and straddled him. He locked his hands tightly around the youth's throat, imagining it was Kane, and squeezed hard, watching the eyes bulge and arms flail as his feet kicked out.

Once he was sure that Rowan was nowhere in sight, Finn gave a violent twist to the head and snapped his neck. Rising slowly, he wrinkled his nose in disgust as a sticky black substance oozed slowly out of the boy's ears and nose.

Finn stared at the body for a few seconds. Another one to add to his not-so-finest hours. He darted down the aisle and jumped free from the train, sprinting to where Rowan was waiting. She trembled in his arms, tears streaming down her cheeks.

"I'm so sorry. I did not mean to get mad at you," he whispered.

"He tried to kill you," she said through gasping sobs.

"We need to move away from here. Kane will know his puppet is dead."

"What about the other passengers? They'll probably report us to the authorities," she said.

Finn cast a glance back towards the train that had begun to move. "The boy attacked us first. The danger came from him, not us. By the time they work it out, we will be long gone from here."

Taking her hand, he pulled Rowan forward and into a run.

They crashed their way through the wild growth of the field, Finn steering her in the direction of the forest that lay ahead. Neither stopped running until they had reached the perimeter.

"Are you okay?" he asked as she collapsed onto the grass. She nodded, unable to speak, as she fought to catch her breath. There were scratches on her arms where the wild plants had caught at her skin. He winced.

"Do we go in?" she asked.

Despite the stitch in his side, Finn moved to complete an examination of the trunks of the trees.

"What are you looking for?" Her eyes were filled with curiosity.

He laid on the ground, and pressed his ear to the earth.

They were in luck. Finn sensed the magical signature of a Fae clan. He rose and gestured to a gap in the trees. "Let's go."

"In there?" She looked unconvinced.

Although the sun had broken through the clouds, the forest was gloomy and cast dark shadows, as though in warning for intruders to beware.

"It's safe, I promise," Finn reassured.

"How can you be so sure?"

He took her hand and led her to one of the trees. "You see the ring of mushrooms around the trunk?"

"Toadstools," she corrected.

"Alright toadstools. Look closely to the right above them."

Rowan dipped onto her knees and peered at the tiny symbol etched into the wood. "What is that?"

"A sign that this forest is protected by the Fae," confirmed Finn. He moved through the gap and entered the forest. "Are you coming?" he called back.

Rowan hurried after him and linked her arm through his. "What are we going to do now?"

"Seek help from the Fae, of course. We need to get back to Eddie's before dusk. I'm worried about him and Lizzie."

"Can't you...you know..."

"Even with four legs, I couldn't get us there fast enough." Finn judged by the level of light breaking through the branches of the trees, and the increasing temperature of the forest, that they were approaching noon.

"Are you sure they will help us?" Rowan asked.

She froze at a sudden snap of twigs ahead of them and to their left. Finn held a finger to his lips and focussed his senses in the direction of the sound. He reached his sight forward, through the bushes, and sensed the doe. Magical energy surrounded her. The deer studied him for a few moments, attuned to his energy. He did not doubt that the Fae were using the doe to check on the intruders and advise as to whether they posed a threat to the sanctity of the forest.

Finn opened a connection, his spirit binding to the earth. The trees bowed and rustled their leaves in greeting. The doe lowered her head; she had acknowledged his request. The Fae would receive his message of greeting, and a request for their help. Finn retrieved the citrine crystal that had been gifted from Mercadia when he had first arrived and placed it on the ground in front of him. He held his breath and hoped that the offering would be accepted. A whoop of joy disturbed the birds in the forest, as the earth shivered and the stone slipped beneath its surface. The hand of friendship had been accepted, and an alliance confirmed. The trees rustled loudly, applauding the union.

"The Fae have accepted our offering, and agreed to help," Finn beamed.

A sudden breeze gathered, and stirred the air around them. With its arrival, a gift was dropped at his feet. Finn picked up the acorn and turned it over in his hand, noting the tiny symbol etched in its skin and the rune beneath it.

"Would you look at that?" he murmured, passing the acorn to Rowan.

"You know what it is?" she asked.

"This emblem here," he said, pointing, "is a family crest of the Fae, but I never would have believed they had kin in this world. The rune here, this grants the bearer the ability to use the acorn as a portal. It's more than I could have hoped for."

Rowan's mouth dropped open. "But that's amazing, and all this given to us in exchange for a small rock?" she asked.

"Not just any rock," Finn replied. "The citrine crystal is imbued with the power of abundance. I am quite sure the Fae will be overjoyed to receive such a gift."

Rowan cleared her throat. "They're not likely to use it, to do something..." Her voice trailed away, her face flushed with embarrassment.

He grinned, "Do not worry. They are not evil, and they have no interest in the humans of this world. But they will protect their home and forest if threatened."

"I understand that," she replied, and lowered to the ground. Her fingers stroked the spot where the crystal had sunk beneath, and she whispered a thank you.

Chapter Thirteen
Kane

Somewhere Outside of Achavanich, Scottish Highlands

Kane slammed his fist on the table, his anger boiling over like a volcano ready to erupt. The glass of wine he had prepared for his moment of triumph teetered precariously before smashing to the floor, the vibrant red liquid spilling across the now dirty and worn canvas. He eyed the stain with disgust, his lip curling as he pushed his chair back with a violent scrape.

"How is it that one so pitiful continues to defy me and my army at every turn?" he demanded, his voice a low, menacing growl. In a fit of rage, he kicked the wooden frame of his chair, watching with a small measure of satisfaction as it shattered, splinters flying in every direction.

"Look at us," Kane raged on, his eyes blazing with barely-contained fury. "Stuck in this hovel like common rats. It is beneath me, beneath my station!"

Rivik's amber eyes appraised the scene of destruction. With an air of exasperation he tried to reason with the warlock. "A temporary necessity until nightfall, Commander," he said, his voice low and even. "What do you value more? Your comfort, or your life?"

Kane spun on his heel, his face contorted with rage. "You dare to threaten me?" he snarled, his hand twitched to cast.

Rivik bristled. "It is not I who threatens you, Commander," he snapped, his words sharp and biting. "The Master loses patience with our failures, with your failures. Do not forget where the true power lies."

"I am perfectly aware of our position," Kane interrupted, his hand curling into a fist so tight that his nails drew blood from his palm. "Do not presume to lecture me, Rivik. I am still your superior. Your Commander."

The Fallen licked his lips, a gesture that was both unsettling and calculating. "Then forgive me, Commander, but what do you propose to do next? Nothing you've tried has worked so far. And the Master expects us to be at his coordinates tonight."

Kane jerked his fist into the air, his anger palpable. "Remember your place, fiend!"

Rivik stalked closer, his movement predatory. "Be careful, Commander," he warned, his voice barely above a whisper. "You forget exactly what I am, the power that I wield. I am not like the others, the lesser Fallen. The darkness inside me, it grants me abilities beyond your comprehension."

Kane's eyes narrowed, his posture stiffening. "And what abilities might those be? What secrets have you kept from your Commander, your Master?"

A slow, cruel smile spread across Rivik's face. "I can teleport. Move through space in the blink of an eye. It is a gift granted to me by the darkness that courses through my veins."

Kane's anger flared, white-hot and all-consuming. "And you didn't think to mention this before?" he roared, his voice echoing off the walls. "I could have had them by now, the Tracker and the girl. Your secrecy has cost us dearly."

The Fallen's own anger rose to match Kane's. His eyes burned with an unholy light. "You never asked, Commander. Never informed me of your plan. Had I known, I would have executed the original plan without fail, without the need for such wasteful sacrifices."

For a moment, the two stared each other down, the tension between them thick enough to slice with a knife. Kane's hand twitched once more, but he hesitated, the gears in his mind turning.

"Very well," he said at last, his voice low and dangerous. "Then let us not waste any more time. When night falls and I have ascertained the girl and tracker's location, you will teleport to them. Keep them prisoner, and send word to your brethren. They will bring me to you, and together, we will finally have our victory."

Rivik nodded. His eyes glinted with a dark satisfaction. "As you order it, Commander. They will not escape us this time."

Kane stepped closer, his face inches from Rivik's. "See that they don't. For if you fail me again, the consequences will be severe. For you and for your precious brethren. Do I make myself clear?"

The Fallen bowed his head, but there was no submission in the gesture. "Crystal, Commander. The Tracker and the girl's fate is sealed. Their suffering will be legendary."

As the two prepared for the coming confrontation, the air in the tent seemed to grow colder, the shadows deeper.

Kane poured a fresh glass of wine. He had come too far, sacrificed too much, to let his prey slip through their fingers once more. This time, he would emerge victorious, no matter the cost. And woe betide anyone who stood in their way.

There was no doubt in his mind he would be the one left standing, his enemies broken and defeated at his feet. His Master and Mistress no more. It was only a matter of time. The darkness within him relished the thought of the suffering to come.

Chapter Fourteen
Rowan

Residence of Edward Throston, York, United Kingdom

R   The world seemed to twist and bend around Finn and Rowan as they stepped through the shimmering portal, the acorn clutched tightly in Rowan's hand. The sensation was unlike anything she had ever experienced, a kaleidoscope of colours and sensations that left her breathless and disoriented. But as quickly as it had begun, the journey ended, and they found themselves standing in the middle of Eddie's living room, the familiar surroundings a welcome sight after the chaos of the day.

Eddie and his girlfriend Lizzie were seated on the couch, their eyes wide with shock and disbelief as Finn and Rowan materialised before them. For a moment, no-one spoke, the silence broken only by the ticking of the clock on the mantelpiece.

"Finn? Rowan?" Eddie finally managed, his voice hoarse with surprise. "How did you... where did you come from?"

Finn stepped forward, his hand momentarily resting on Eddie's shoulder as his friend rose to greet him. "Best you don't know, friend."

Lizzie's face paled, her hands trembling as she gripped Eddie's arm. "What's going on, Eddie? What have you got us into?"

Eddie shook his head, his expression a mix of confusion and concern. "I don't know, Lizzie. Finn and Rowan needed a place to stay, and of course, I offered to help. I had no idea... I mean, I knew they were different, but this..."

Rowan swayed on her feet, exhaustion washing over her like a tidal wave. Finn caught her, his arms wrapping around her waist to steady her. "I'm sorry," she whispered, her voice barely audible. "I'm just so tired, and after what happened in Cornwall..."

Finn's face darkened, his jaw clenched with barely-contained anger. "We were attacked," he said, his words clipped and precise. "A youth tried to kill us, and kidnap Rowan. We don't know who he was—"

"And we've spent a long time being interviewed by the police," Rowan interrupted.

Lizzie's hand flew to her mouth, her eyes wide with horror. "Oh my God, that's awful. Do you think the police will catch him?"

"Honestly? I don't know. They have his description."

Eddie stood, his hands held out in a placating gesture. "Lizzie, we can't turn them away, not now. Look at the state of her. She's drip white."

Rowan stepped forward, her eyes pleading. "Please, I know this all seems strange, and I wish I could give you more of an explanation, but I can't."

"Just one more night, and then we'll be gone. I promise," said Finn.

Lizzie hesitated, her gaze shifted between Eddie and Rowan. "I don't know," she said, her voice trembling. "I had a bad feeling last night, a sense that something terrible was going to happen. And now, with you two here, and all this talk of attacks... I'm scared."

Eddie wrapped his arms around Lizzie and pulled her close. "I know, love. But we can't let fear rule us. Finn and Rowan are our friends, and they need us. One more night, that's all they're asking."

Lizzie sighed, her shoulders slumped in defeat. "Alright," she said, her voice barely above a whisper. "One more night. But after that, they have to go. I can't... I won't risk our safety, Eddie. Not even for friendship."

Rowan nodded. Tears welled in her eyes. "Thank you. I know this isn't easy, and I appreciate your kindness, more than you can know."

Despite the compromise, the atmosphere in the room was still tense, the weight of the day's events hanging heavy in the air. Eddie cleared his throat. His eyes darted between the two couples. "Why don't we go out for tea?" he suggested, his voice falsely bright. "A double date, just like normal couples do. It might help take our minds off things, at least for a little while."

Lizzie nodded. A small smile tugged at the corners of her mouth. "That's a lovely idea. We can go to that little Italian place down the road."

Finn glanced at Rowan, a silent question in his eyes. She nodded, the prospect of a few hours of normalcy too tempting to resist. "We'd love to," she said, her voice stronger than she felt. "Thank you, both of you."

The exhaustion etched on her face was evident to all. "Hey, why don't you go grab an hour or two of sleep first?" Finn suggested gently, placing a hand on her shoulder. "I know you're beat. I'm going to go check on Biscuit and smooth things over after we left him behind yesterday. Eddie and Lizzie will keep me company."

Rowan rubbed her bleary eyes. "Wake me up when it's time to get ready?"

"Will do," Finn promised. "Now go get some shuteye."

As the night drew in, the four friends prepared to leave. Lizzie glanced at the steak she had set out to defrost on the kitchen counter earlier, now ready to be cooked for her and Eddie's dinner. With a sigh, she picked it up and carried it over to Biscuit's bowl, dropping it in with a soft plop. "Enjoy, little one," she said, scratching the Scottie dog behind the ears. "At least you'll have a good meal tonight."

Biscuit wagged his tail, his eyes bright with anticipation as he dove into the unexpected feast. Rowan, now rested, smiled at the sight, a moment of pure, uncomplicated joy amidst the chaos of their lives. She was relieved that Biscuit had accepted their apology and seemed happy to be left alone again, at least for a few hours, whilst the couples enjoyed a meal out together.

The Italian restaurant was everything Lizzie had promised, with fairy lights twinkling in the garden like captured stars. Finn sat close to her, his hand intertwined with hers beneath the table as she sipped her wine and spoke about her family and her close relationship with her brother, Jake. For a few precious hours, they were just a normal couple, enjoying a romantic evening with friends.

But as the night wore on, the exhaustion began to take its toll once more. Rowan's eyelids grew heavy, her head nodding forward as she fought to stay awake. Eddie signalled for the cheque, and although she had enjoyed the evening, she was relieved when the four of them agreed to make their way back to Eddie's house.

As they prepared for bed, she marvelled at the amulet that hung around her neck. "What do you think it can do?" she asked Finn.

He shook his head, his expression serious. "I don't know. But I don't want you to try anything else until you've had a chance to speak with Bessie. You need some guidance and mentoring on how to use it. The amulet is powerful, and we can't risk unleashing something we don't understand."

"You're right," she said and yawned. "I'll wait until we can talk to Bessie. She'll know what to do."

They climbed into bed. His warm body fit securely to hers, like two pieces of a puzzle. Finn pulled her close. His lips brushed against her forehead in a tender kiss.

As if reading her thoughts, he chuckled softly, his breath warm against her skin. "I want our first time to be special, and without an audience." He glanced down at Biscuit, who had curled up at the foot of the bed, his eyes already drooping with sleep. "And that includes our furry little friend here."

"You're right," she said, snuggling closer into his embrace. "When we're alone and safe, we'll make it a night to remember."

They drifted off to sleep, lulled by the sound of each other's heartbeats and the soft snores of the Scottie dog at their feet.

In her dreams, Rowan found herself in a beautiful country cottage, the sun streaming through the windows and the scent of freshly baked bread wafting from the kitchen. Finn was there, his arms around her waist as they watched their two children, a boy, and a girl, playing in the garden.

It was a vision of the future, a glimpse of the life they could have together when all of this was over. But even in the depths of her dreams, Rowan couldn't shake the feeling that something was amiss, a sense of unease that prickled at the back of her neck.

She woke with a start, her heart racing in her chest. The room was dark and still, the only sound the gentle breathing of Finn and Biscuit. But something had woken her, a presence that tugged at the edges of her consciousness.

Quietly, so as not to disturb the others, Rowan slipped out of bed and padded downstairs, her bare feet silent on the carpeted steps. She opened the front door, stepping out onto the pavement, the chill night air raising goosebumps on her skin.

The street was empty, the houses dark and silent. But she still felt that someone, or something, was watching her. She rubbed her arms, the thin fabric of Lizzie's nightgown doing little to ward off the cold.

Her gaze drifted to the street sign on the corner, the letters illuminated by the pale glow of the streetlights. London Road, Y056 7ZZ. The name meant nothing to her, but she found herself committing it to memory, as if it held greater significance.

Across the street, a row of flowerbeds bloomed in the darkness, the heady scent of night-scented stock drifting on the breeze. Rowan breathed deeply, the fragrance calming her racing heart. She chastised herself for being silly, for letting her imagination run wild in the depths of the night.

With a final glance at the quiet street, Rowan turned to go back inside, her hand resting on the brass number seventy two that adorned Eddie's door. For a few seconds, the number seemed important, but the thought slipped away as quickly as it had come, lost in the haze of exhaustion and lingering dreams.

As she climbed the stairs, Rowan heard a soft rustling from the bedroom, the sound of Finn stirring in his sleep. She quickened her pace, not wanting to worry him with her midnight wanderings.

But as she slipped back into the room, Finn was already sitting up, his hand reaching for the t-shirt he had discarded on the floor. "Rowan?" he whispered, his voice rough with sleep. "Is everything alright?"

Rowan nodded, climbing back into bed and nestling into Finn's arms. "Everything's fine," she reassured him, her voice soft and soothing. "I was just still a bit spooked from today, that's all. I needed some air."

Finn held her close, his chin resting on the top of her head. "I understand," he murmured, his fingers tracing gentle circles on her back. "But we should probably leave in the morning, just to be safe. We don't want to put Eddie and Lizzie in any more danger than we already have."

Rowan nodded, her eyelids already growing heavy once more. "You're right," she said, her words slurring with exhaustion. "We'll leave first thing, find somewhere safe to regroup and plan our next move."

As she drifted back to sleep, Rowan's dreams returned, the vision of the country cottage and the laughing children filling her mind once more. In Finn's arms, the worries of the day seemed to melt away, replaced by a sense of peace and belonging that she had never known before.

They would face the challenges ahead together, hand-in-hand and heart-to-heart. And when all of this was over, when the darkness had been vanquished and the world set right once more, they would build a life together, a future filled with love and laughter and the promise of forever.

For now, in the stillness of the night, in the warmth of each other's embrace, they could rest, their dreams a sanctuary from the storms that raged beyond the walls of Eddie's house. Tomorrow would bring new trials, new dangers, but tonight, they had each other, and that was enough.

Chapter Fifteen

Kane

Somewhere Outside of Achavanich, Scottish Highlands

In his tented domain, Kane sat in silent contemplation, his eyes closed and his breathing slow and measured. The room around him was dark, the only light emanating from a single candle that flickered on the table before him. The shadows seemed to dance and writhe in the corners, as if alive with a malevolent energy that mirrored the darkness within Kane's own soul.

For hours, he had been probing Rowan's mind, seeking a way to manipulate her thoughts and actions without her knowledge. The Nyrvallia's gifts, bestowed upon him, had granted him new powers, abilities that even he had not fully comprehended. But with each passing day, each whispered incantation and blood-soaked ritual, he could feel his strength growing, his connection to the darkness deepening.

And now, as he sat in the stillness of his chamber, Kane reached out with his mind, gently nudging Rowan's subconscious, planting the seed of an idea, a compulsion that she would not be able to resist. He could feel her stirring, the unease that had haunted her dreams slowly drawing her from the warmth of her bed and the safety of the Tracker's arms.

Kane smiled, a cruel twist of his lips that held no warmth or joy. He watched through Rowan's eyes as she padded down the stairs, her bare feet silent on the carpeted steps. He felt the chill of the night air as she stepped outside, the goosebumps that rose on her skin as she rubbed her arms for warmth.

Through Rowan's gaze, Kane drank in the details of the street, the houses that lined the road, the gardens that bloomed in the darkness. He saw the street sign, the letters illuminated by the pale glow of the streetlights – London Road, Y056 7ZZ. And there, on the door of the house where Rowan had emerged, the brass number seventy two.

Kane's smile widened, a triumphant gleam in his eyes. He had them now, the girl and the Tracker, and there would be no escape. With a final, lingering caress of Rowan's mind, he withdrew, his consciousness snapping back into his own body like a rubber band.

The candle on the table guttered and died, plunging the room into darkness. But Kane hardly noticed, his thoughts consumed by the knowledge he had gained and the plan that was already forming in his mind.

He rose from his chair, his movements fluid and graceful despite the long hours of meditation. With a snap of his fingers, the canvas parted, revealing the hulking form of Rivik waiting beyond.

"You have news, Commander?" the Fallen asked, his voice low and rough like the grinding of gravel.

Kane nodded. His eyes glinted with a feverish light. "I have the location of the girl and the Tracker. They are hiding in a house on a London Road, protected by the Tracker's friends."

Rivik's lips curled into a sneer, his disdain for the humans who would dare to stand against them evident in every line of his face. "Then let us go and retrieve them, Commander. The Fallen grow restless, eager for the taste of blood and the thrill of the hunt."

But Kane held up a hand, his expression calculating. "No, Rivik. We must be smart about this. The girl and the Tracker are not to be underestimated, and we cannot risk them slipping through our grasp once more."

Rivik's brow furrowed, confusion and frustration warring in his eyes. "Then what do you propose, Commander? We have the location, we have the power. Why delay the inevitable?"

Kane smiled, a cold, cruel thing Rivik admired. "Because we have an advantage that the girl and the Tracker do not. We have you."

Rivik stood tall, his eyes gleaming with a fierce, unholy light. "You want me to go alone, Commander?"

Kane nodded, his gaze unwavering. "You have the power to open portals, Rivik. To travel instantly from one place to another. Use that power now. Go to the house where they are hiding. Kill anyone who would stand in your way, anyone who would dare to protect them."

Rivik's nails dug into the canvas. "And the Tracker, Commander? What of him?"

Kane's smile widened, a predatory gleam in his eyes. "Kill him. Make him suffer for the trouble he has caused us, for the humiliation he has brought upon your kind. Break him, body and soul."

Rivik nodded. "And the girl, Commander? What would you have me do with her?"

His expression hardened, his voice as cold as the grave. "Take her alive. Bind her, gag her, do whatever you must to keep her subdued. But do not harm her, not yet. She is mine to break, mine to punish for her insolence and her defiance."

Rivik bowed his head, his voice thick with anticipation. "As you command. I will not fail you."

Kane placed a hand on Rivik's shoulder, his grip tight enough to bruise. "See that you don't. For if you do, the consequences will be beyond your darkest nightmares."

With a final, crushing squeeze, he released his hold on the Fallen, his eyes boring into the creature's soulless pit. "Go now."

With a final, feral grin, Rivik's form vanished into the darkness. Kane watched him go, his heart pounding with a fierce, savage joy. Soon, very soon, the girl and the Tracker would be his.

Kane turned back to the table, his hand hovering over the candle that had long since gone out. The candle flickered and danced into life, the only witness to the madness that consumed the warlock's mind. And in the depths of the night, the Fallen hunted.

Chapter Sixteen
Rowan

Residence of Edward Throston, York, United Kingdom

R The night was cold and still, the houses on the quiet road sleeping under the watchful eye of the moon. In the bedroom of number seventy two, Rowan and Finn lay wrapped in each other's arms, their dreams filled with the promise of a future together, free from the darkness that haunted their steps.

Downstairs, Lizzie moved quietly through the house, her mind restless and her heart heavy with the weight of the secrets she now carried. As she entered the kitchen, her thoughts turned to the strange and wonderful couple sleeping upstairs, and the incredible journey that had brought them into her life.

But as she reached for the kettle, a sound from the hallway made her freeze, her hand clamping over her mouth to stifle the scream that threatened to escape. There, in the shadows, a figure moved with a predatory grace, its form twisted and grotesque in the dim light.

Lizzie's heart raced, her mind reeling with the realisation of what she was seeing. Without a second thought, she fled, her feet carrying her out of the house and into the night, her silent scream of terror left behind.

Upstairs, Rowan woke with a start. Beside her, Finn stirred, his eyes blinking open in the darkness.

"What is it?" he asked, his voice rough with sleep.

But before she could answer, a crash from along the hallway made them both bolt upright, their hearts in their throats. Rowan leaped from the bed, her feet carrying her to the door and down the hall towards the source of the disturbance.

There, in the shadows, she saw him. Eddie, his body broken and lifeless, the lamp table beside him shattered on the floor. And standing over him, a figure of pure nightmare, its eyes gleaming with a malevolent hunger.

Rowan's scream shattered the silence as it stared at her from the shadows. The lifeless body of Eddie lay contorted at its feet. Locating her within seconds, her spirit guide Charles shouted her name repeatedly, trying desperately to tear her free from the fear that shackled her. Her eyes were wide and had locked onto the creature in front of her. It surveyed her from the shadows. Drops of blood fell to the floor as the creature pulled back its lips and bared its teeth. Rowan could feel its lust, and her stomach lurched in response. An unseen force slammed into her, causing her momentarily to lose her balance, and she crashed into Finn, who had entered the room behind her.

Charles's voice finally broke through and snapped her to attention. "Rowan, get out now," he yelled. The creature snarled and sprang towards her. Charles intervened and focussed his energy, forging a barrier of light between the creature and his ward. It howled as the light made contact and hurled it with considerable force back into the shadows of the deathly scented room. A welt appeared against its skin and the creature's eyes watered with tears of rage and pain. Rowan turned her back on the Fallen and used all her strength to push Finn outside into the hallway. He cried out in dismay as he struggled to move past her and save his friend. He was clearly angry and scared, shouting curses for her to listen.

"It's too late," she repeated and gripped his arm tightly, dragging him to the stairs.

"What about Eddie and Lizzie?" he yelled, attempting to twist himself free.

"He's dead and we will be too if we don't get out of here." Her eyes pleaded with him. "I don't know how long Charles can hold it off."

"But I might be able to heal him." Finn's voice broke.

"No, you can't. His soul is gone."

Another crash sounded from the room. The roar of the creature snapped Finn back into reality.

The couple raced down the stairs, their hearts pounding in their chests, the sound of their own blood rushing in their ears. Out into the night they fled, the cool air shocking against their skin.

"Watch out," shouted Rowan as she pushed Finn out of the way. Shards of glass rained down from the window above them. The creature's scream made her blood run cold as she looked up to the window. She prayed that Charles was okay.

Finn grabbed her hand and they ran, her bare feet painfully slapping the pavement. As they reached the end of the street, Rowan skidded to a halt, her eyes wide with horror. "Biscuit," she gasped, her hand flying to her mouth. "We forgot Biscuit."

Her heart clenched, her mind raced with the thought of their companion, trapped inside. But even as she turned back, a familiar bark made her cry out in relief.

There, bounding towards them through the shadows, was Biscuit, his fur gleaming in the moonlight, his eyes bright with a fierce, protective love.

"Biscuit!" Rowan cried, dropping to her knees and gathering the little dog into her arms. "Oh, thank God, you're alright."

The roar of fury from the Fallen ricocheted down the street. They had little time left to escape to safety.

"This way," Finn said, his voice low and urgent. "We need to find somewhere to hide. Somewhere to disguise our scent."

The three companions raced through the streets, moving through the twisting alleys and narrow passages. Rowan gritted her teeth against the sting of the numerous cuts that were carved into the soles of her feet. And then, just when it seemed she could take no more, Finn found it: a small, hidden alleyway, its entrance concealed by a pile of rubbish and discarded boxes. The stench had her stomach heaving.

Finn dove inside, dragging Rowan behind him. Their bodies pressed against the cold, damp walls, their breaths coming in ragged gasps. Rowan shivered, her thin nightgown clearly doing little to ward off the chill of the night air. Finn, clad only in the t-shirt and boxer shorts

Eddie had lent him, fared no better. He wrapped his arms around her, his body heat seeping into her skin.

For a long moment, they simply held each other, their minds reeling with the horror of what they had just witnessed. The grief and guilt of Eddie's death weighed heavy on Rowan's heart.

"What do we do now?" she whispered, her voice small and lost in the darkness. "Where do we go?"

Finn's mind raced with the possibilities. "I don't know," he admitted, his voice heavy. "But we can't stay here. They'll find us, sooner or later."

Rowan's hand drifted to the amulet that hung around her neck, the metal warm against her skin. "I could use this," she said, her voice trembling with a mix of fear and hope. "I could try to teleport us somewhere safe, somewhere far away from here."

But Finn shook his head, his eyes filled with a deep, abiding concern. "No. It's too risky. You've never used magic before, not like this. We don't know what the consequences could be."

Before Rowan could argue, a sound from the mouth of the alley made them both freeze. A figure loomed in the darkness, its form hunched and shadowed in the dim light.

Finn pushed Rowan behind him once again, his body tense and ready for a fight. But as the figure drew closer, they saw that it was not one of the Fallen, but an old homeless man, his face weathered and lined with age.

"You two alright?" the man asked, his voice gruff but kind. "Heard a commotion out on the street, thought I'd better check."

Rowan stepped forward, her eyes wide and grateful. "We're alright," she said, her voice shaking slightly.

The old man nodded, his eyes taking in their absence of suitable clothing and bare feet. Without a word, he shrugged off his own tattered coat, draping it around Rowan's shoulders. "Here," he said, his voice gentle. "You look like you could use this more than me."

Rowan's eyes filled with tears. She swallowed a lump of gratitude for this small act of kindness, especially in the midst of such darkness.

"Thank you," she whispered, her voice thick with emotion.

The old man simply nodded, his eyes drifting to the pile of cardboard boxes stacked against the wall. "You two can rest here for a bit," he said. "Ain't much, but it's out of the wind, at least."

Finn and Rowan exchanged a glance, but in the end, exhaustion, and desperation won out, and they sank down onto the boxes, their bodies huddled close together for warmth.

The old man watched them for a moment, his eyes filled with a deep, unfathomable sadness. And then, with a sigh, he gathered up his few meagre belongings, stuffing them into a battered shopping trolley.

"Best be moving on," he said, his voice low and weary. "You two take care now, you hear? When you can, I suggest you both get to the nearest walk-in centre. Those cuts on your feet look pretty bad."

And with that, he was gone, his form swallowed up by the shadows of the night. Finn and Rowan sat in silence for a long time, their minds reeling with shock. Neither acknowledged the old man's last words. Beside them, Biscuit curled up on the ground, his warm body pressed against their legs, a small comfort.

"Cuts?" Finn finally said. He glanced at his own feet and then looked towards Rowan's. "Oh no...I didn't think...the blood..."

"What's wrong? Are we in trouble?"

"Yes," Finn hissed, then pulled her to her feet.

Footsteps approached, and then, from the shadows at the mouth of the alley, a figure emerged, tall and lean and radiating a malevolent power.

Behind him, the Fallen gathered, their nightmarish forms filling the alley, their amber eyes gleaming with hunger.

The trio were trapped, with nowhere left to run.

Biscuit barked furiously.

"Who is that?" Rowan asked, although deep down she knew the answer.

"Kane."

The warlock stepped forward, his eyes fixed on Rowan, his lips curled into a sneer. "Well, well, well," he said, his voice dripping with a mocking condescension. "Look what we have here. The famous Tracker and his wench, caught like rats in a trap."

"If you have any ideas, Rowan, I am open to suggestions," Finn whispered.

She called for her guide, but he did not arrive. "I can't make contact with Charles."

"Try one of the others," he suggested.

Rowan's voice trembled. "No-one can hear me."

Under the moonlight, Kane inspected his fingernails and then looked towards them. Smiling in satisfaction, he waved. It was like a red rag to a bull for Finn, and his temper ignited. Rowan's hand slipped into his and pulled him back from the brink of stupidity.

"Don't," she hissed, sensing his anger.

Biscuit barked for attention.

"What is it?" Finn asked. The bark changed in tone and became more aggressive.

"What's Biscuit saying?"

"Prepare."

She knew that dogs had a protective instinct in them, and would defend their owners no matter what the cost. "No, Finn. If he tries to attack Kane, or the Fallen, he wouldn't survive."

He grabbed her and began moving them both slowly backwards. She resisted. "No, wait! What are you doing?" Her panic rose further and she attempted to break free from his grip.

Finn only tightened his hold. "Trust me," he said.

Kane looked on in amusement. "Am I supposed to fear this rat?"

Finn did not respond.

Biscuit's bark grew louder and deeper until it was replaced by a sound that made Rowan shudder. She felt the hairs raise on the back of her neck.

"Biscuit?" she ventured.

Biscuit's small body began to convulse, and trembled with a power that seemed to radiate from every inch of his being. He shook from side to side, his tail, once short and stubby, now extended behind him, long and muscular and adorned with a series of wicked-looking spikes. His once small and round head was now angular and fierce, with two great horns curving back from his brow, and eyes of the most piercing emerald green. His body grew, stretching and expanding until he towered over them all.

Rowan's hand flew to her mouth, her eyes wide. She almost stumbled and narrowly avoided the sweep of his tail as she clung onto Finn.

A cracking reverberated loudly through the alleyway, and Rowan instinctively shielded herself as two giant wings broke free from Biscuit's back. They punched two holes in the alley wall, sending bricks clattering to the ground.

Biscuit stretched his wings upwards and moved them slowly up and down. As the air stirred around them, Rowan and Finn coughed from the dust inhaled.

She glanced at Kane, who was no longer lingering at the entrance of the alleyway. The warlock simply stood there, mouth agape.

Biscuit turned his attention to his friends. Rowan let out a squeal as her eyes were captured by giant green jewels. Fearing that her legs would buckle beneath her, she gripped Finn's arm as the dragon appraised her.

"It's okay," Finn reassured her.

Her breathing was coming out in short, sharp gasps.

"Look at me, Rowan." He turned her around to face him.

Her eyes were wild, her brow covered with a clammy sweat that also trickled down her spine.

"His name is Roark, but he's still Biscuit...in heart and nature."

It took her a few moments to formulate words. "He's a bloody dragon, Finn!"

It was all that she could manage as her head tried to process what her eyes were seeing.

"I know, it's amazing. He's magnificent, huh?"

She scowled at his attempt to lighten her fear.

"Impossible," Kane snarled. "The Braeden are extinct, wiped out centuries ago."

Rowan continued to stare. Her mind reeled from the revelation. "Dragons don't exist in this world."

Roark attempted to smile, but it only made her pale at the sight of the huge fangs that gleamed at her.

"Maybe attempt that again at another time," Finn advised.

Sudden movement from the shadows reminded them that they were not alone. The Fallen had recovered from their own shock and had slowly started to advance. Their eyes radiated a hunger and a malevolence that made the very air suffocating. Each pair of amber eyes bored into her from the darkness, their blood lust driving them into a frenzy as thick saliva glooped from their teeth.

Roark turned his attention to Kane, who held up his hand. The Fallen froze and waited impatiently. Their claws scraped against the concrete cobbles, clearly eager to launch their attack.

"Foolish boy to bring a dragon here, and one of the Braeden too. I shall certainly be well-rewarded tonight."

"Don't be so sure of yourself, Kane," Finn called out, ignoring Rowan's protests as he lifted her onto the dragon's back.

"On the contrary, it is you who have underestimated me. I mean to have your girl and the dragon. The Master will have your head on a platter whilst the Fallen enjoy the feast of your remains," Kane snarled.

Finn scrambled onto Roark's back, sitting in front of Rowan. His hands gripped scales as Rowan wrapped her arms around his waist.

She closed her eyes and pressed her face against Finn's back.

Kane issued a command. Three of the Fallen broke away from the pack, and sprinted towards them, their intention to kill.

Roark reared up and breathed a flame of fire. The Fallen stopped in their tracks as they faced a wall of smoke and heat. They screamed in outrage as their putrid skin singed.

"Now, Rivik," Kane ordered. The large Fallen disappeared, and then reappeared in front of the flames. It sprang, it's mouth wide with savage fangs, ready to pierce bone and flesh. At exactly the same time, Roark spun and lashed out with his tail, sending Rivik through the flames and smashing into the others. Rowan screamed with the force of the movement and clung on for dear life.

With a great beat of his wings, the dragon launched himself into the air before the creatures could recover.

The wind whipped at Rowan's face, the ground falling away beneath them.

From below, Kane's shouts of rage echoed through the night, a promise of retribution.

Rowan tightened her hold around Finn's waist as they soared through the sky, the city sprawling out beneath them like a glittering jewel.

Chapter Seventeen

Finn

Northeast Region of England

They had been flying for what felt like hours, the city lights fading into the distance, replaced by the inky blackness of the countryside below.

Grief and anger warred within Finn, the events of the night replaying in his mind. Rowan witnessing Eddie's lifeless body, the Fallen's nightmare forms, Kane's cruel sneer—it all swirled together in a dizzying kaleidoscope of the horror she had never known existed, and he had brought it all to her door.

And then there was Biscuit, the loyal canine companion, who had transformed into a creature of legend before his very eyes. It was too much to process, too much to comprehend for Rowan. For him, there had been a feeling that Biscuit was much more than he let on, but could he have guessed that Biscuit was Roark, a mighty Braeden dragon?

"Finn," Rowan called over the rushing wind, her voice hoarse and strained. "We need to land. I can't... I need to rest, to think. My mind feels like it's spinning out of control."

Finn nodded his understanding. "I know, love. It's been a hell of a night. Roark, can you find somewhere to set down? Rowan needs a break, and honestly, so do I."

The dragon rumbled his assent, his wings angling downward as he scanned the ground below. After a few moments, he began to descend, his body cutting through the air with a grace that belied his size.

They landed in a small clearing, the grass soft and cool beneath their feet. Rowan slid from Roark's back. She sank to the ground and rested her head in her hands.

Finn watched her with concern, his heart aching for the pain and confusion he saw in her eyes. He longed to take her in his arms, to hold her close and promise her that everything would be alright. But he knew she needed time to process, to come to terms with all that had happened. And so, he set about making a fire, gathering wood from the surrounding trees and arranging it in a neat pile.

Roark settled himself nearby and watched Finn work with an amused expression. Surely the dragon wasn't expecting him to waste the rest of the night rubbing sticks together.

"Could you?" Finn wasn't sure why he had to ask.

Roark leaned forward, a small flame sparking from his nostrils and igniting the kindling.

Finn settled himself beside Rowan, wrapped an arm around her shoulders, and pulled her close. She leaned into him, drawing from the comfort he offered.

"I'm here," he murmured, his lips brushing against her hair. "I know it's a lot to take in."

"I just... I can't believe Eddie's gone. And Lizzie... do you think she's...?"

Finn sighed, the ball of emotion difficult to swallow. "I don't know. I hope she at least got away, that she's safe somewhere."

For a long while, they sat in silence, the crackling of the fire and the soft rustling of the trees the only sounds in the still night air. Rowan kept glancing towards Roark. It was almost as though her mind was still struggling to reconcile the mighty dragon with the little dog she had known and loved.

Finn squeezed her shoulder, a silent reassurance that he was there.

When it appeared Rowan would not talk further, Finn took the opportunity to seek the connection he shared with Mercadia. He felt her presence and began to relay all that had transpired.

Mercadia interrupted when he told her of the strange staff that Rowan had found in the museum. The one she believed to be important, though neither of them knew why. Her response was sharp and anxious, her concern palpable, even across the vast distance that separated them. "The staff has revealed itself?" she asked.

"I said, '**a** staff,' not '**the** staff.' What is '**the** staff'? What aren't you telling me?"

"Nothing," she snapped. "You are to guard it with your life. In the wrong hands, it could bring untold destruction upon both our worlds. That's all you need to know."

Finn frowned, his curiosity piqued. "Don't you think I have enough to deal with? What's so special about it?"

The Elder remained silent for a long moment, and he sensed her hesitation, her reluctance to reveal the secrets she held close. "There are some things that are better left unsaid. Some knowledge is too dangerous, too powerful, to be shared lightly, and especially with you!"

His frustration flared hot and bright in his chest. "We're risking our lives, dammit. We deserve to know more."

But the Elder was immovable, her will as unyielding as stone. "I've guided the fate of our world for longer than you can imagine. I know what is best, and what must be done."

Finn bit back a sharp retort, knowing that arguing would get him nowhere. Instead, he changed tack, his voice softening with a note of pleading. "Well, can you at least open a portal and bring us home? I've done what you asked, found what we came for."

The response was immediate and fierce. "No. You cannot leave without Bessantia. You must find her and bring her back with you. Only then can your task be considered complete."

"So she's still alive?"

"Sort of."

"What is that supposed to mean?"

"Find that out for yourself."

Anger warred within him. "Why don't you bring her back? I need to go return. I haven't heard from Indigo about Aaron. I'm worried about them both."

The Elder's fury was a palpable thing, cold and sharp as a blade. "What have you done?" she demanded, her voice trembling with rage. She ransacked his mind, seeking the answer. "You sent someone to infiltrate the Master's ranks without my knowledge, my consent? How could you be so foolish, so reckless?"

Finn set his jaw, refusing to be cowed by her anger. "I did what I had to do. Elios knew, and he even suggested it after you refused to help me. We needed information to know what we were up against."

Mercadia was silent for a long moment, and Finn could feel the weight of her disappointment, her disapproval, pressing down on him.

"You must contact Indigo immediately," she said at last, her voice tight and controlled. "Tell him to abort his quest, to get out of there as soon as possible. If the Master discovers ..." she trailed off, unable or unwilling to finish the thought.

Finn could sense the fear that lay beneath her words, the unspoken dread.

"I will," he promised.

The Elder's presence began to fade, her mind withdrawing from his. He opened his eyes, his heart heavy with the enormity of the task before him. Rowan reached to take his hand, her fingers intertwining with his.

"What is it?" she asked softly. Her eyes searched his face. "I assume it was Mercadia? What did she say?"

Finn sighed. His shoulders slumped. "She won't bring us back without Bessantia. We must find her. And Indigo... I must warn him, get him out of there before it's too late. I told her of the staff too, and she says we must guard it with our lives!"

"Oh, God! Finn, it's back at Eddie's, with our clothes!"

"Then we will have to go back for it before we find Bessantia. A piece of cake, really, when you consider we've got a dragon... a freaking awesome dragon!"

Roark gave a deep cough.

Finn rose and moved to the fire. He threw another stick into the flames, watching as the sparks danced and swirled in the night air. "We'll have to go in the morning when it's safe."

"No. If it is as important as Mercadia says, we go back for it now."

"Are you crazy? Kane could go back there. And then there's Eddie..." his voice cracked.

"I'm wearing the Amulet. I can do the same as I did back at the witchcraft museum. Teleport in and out. It gives me a chance to grab the rucksack and our clothing. We can't float around half naked all night."

"But I can't go with you!"

"I'm not arguing about this, Finn."

He yelled out as she disappeared in front of him. "Dammit, woman," he cursed at the air.

As the minutes passed by, he paced back and forth.

Roark connected his mind to Finn's. "She's stronger than you give her credit for."

"She's impulsive and reckless," Finn snapped.

"The amulet she wears. It will keep her safe."

"And how do you know that?"

"I just do," Roark replied simply.

Finn released a deep breath when Rowan reappeared unscathed. She was now dressed in a pair of jeans and a hooded top. She dropped the rucksack and two jackets onto the ground. "I've got it. There was no sign of them. Charles was with me. He's okay. Anyway, I pinched some more of Eddie's clothing, and what Lizzie had left behind. Thankfully, her trainers fit me. There's a pair of Eddie's boots in the bag for you, too." She sighed. "Don't look at me like that. I feel awful about Eddie and Lizzie, but it's not like either of them is going to need them. We need to survive."

Finn grabbed her and kissed her hard. "Don't you ever do that to me again," he said, when he came back up for air.

Rowan dismissed his words with a wave of her hand. She ignored his glare and sat down on the grass to watch him dress. Finn muttered under his breath. He could see the hint of her smile from the corner of his eye.

"You know, you are quite attractive when you get all huffy," she said.

"Funny," he replied, and sat beside her. "I need a distraction." He gestured towards the dragon. "Roark, can you tell me more about how you came to be in this world? Why you were hiding as Biscuit all this time?"

Roark replied telepathically. "She cannot hear my story, though?"

"I'll relay it, as you tell it," Finn confirmed out loud.

"Very well," the dragon sighed. "It is a long and complicated story," he said, his voice a low rumble in Finn's mind. "One that begins many centuries ago, in the time of the Ancient War of the Fathers."

Finn leaned forward, his eyes fixed on Roark's face, his interest piqued. When the dragon started to talk, he began to recount his tale to Rowan.

"My rider was a young mage named Bessantia," Roark began. "She was brave and beautiful, with a heart as fierce as any dragon's. But she was also proud, and prone to the same weaknesses that plague all mortal creatures."

He paused, his eyes distant, as if seeing into the depths of the past. "Bessantia was in love with a man named Morvela, a powerful mage with a talent for dark magic. Their love was passionate, all-consuming, the kind of love that burns hot and bright, but often it ends in tragedy."

Finn felt a deep sorrow welling in his chest. He could sense the pain in Roark's voice, the weight of the memories he carried.

"Morvela had a twin sister, Mordreya," the dragon continued, his voice growing darker, more sombre.

Rowan gasped, but would say no more. She indicated for Roark and Finn to continue.

"She was as powerful as her brother, and her heart was pure, untainted by the lust for power that consumed him. The two were close, as only twins can be, but as they grew older, they began to drift apart, each drawn to different paths."

"I've heard the names mentioned once when I was a child. What happened to them, Roark? How did their story end?"

The dragon twitched his tail restlessly in the grass. "Morvela and Mordreya were each given a powerful artefact by one of the Ancient Fathers. Mordreya received a staff imbued with the ability to control the minds of others, to bend them to her will. Morvela was gifted an orb, one that could see into the hearts of men, reveal their deepest desires and darkest secrets."

Finn's eyes widened. "The staff from the museum... it was Morvela's, wasn't it?"

Roark nodded. "Yes. And the orb... it was hidden away by Bessantia when she realised the extent of Morvela's madness, the depths of his depravity."

Finn's mind raced. "What did Morvela do? What could have been so terrible that Bessantia would turn against the man she loved?"

The dragon closed his eyes, pain etched into every line of his face. "Morvela killed his sister Mordreya, and then used the staff and the orb together to enslave the minds of thousands, to build an army of mindless thralls who would obey his every command. He became drunk with power, consumed by his own ego, his own twisted desires."

"And Bessantia... she didn't try to stop him? To reason with him?"

Roark shook his head. "Bessantia was blinded by her love for Morvela. She believed that she could change him, that her love could redeem him. But in the end, she realised the truth—that Morvela was beyond saving. That he had become a monster in mage form."

Finn's eyes narrowed. A sudden thought occurred to him. "The Braeden dragons... your kind. Which side did they fight for in the war?"

Roark met his gaze, his eyes unfathomable, ancient. "The Braeden were neither good nor evil," he said, his voice a low rumble in the stillness. "We simply obeyed the commands of our riders, the ones to whom we were bonded. Some fought for the Ancient Fathers, some for Morvela and his army. In the end, it mattered little. The war decimated our numbers, left us broken, a scattered remnant of what we once were."

Rowan rose and moved closer to Roark. She rested her hand on his chest as Finn completed the story.

"I'm so sorry," she whispered. "I can't imagine the pain you must have felt, the sacrifices you made."

The dragon leaned into her touch. A deep, rumbling purr vibrated through his chest. "Tell her it was a long time ago. The wounds have healed, though the scars remain. But I have found a new purpose, a new hope."

"Thank you, Roark," he said, joining Rowan at the dragon's side. "For everything you've done, for everything you are. We couldn't do this without you."

Roark bowed his head, a gesture of respect and affection. "It is my honour, Finn." He turned his head towards Rowan as she called out his name.

"Just for tonight, would you return to Biscuit please?"

The dragon nodded his acquiescence, and with a shudder transformed in front of them. The little Scottie dog that they knew and loved stood before them. Rowan stroked his fur as Biscuit nuzzled close. A silence fell around them, disturbed only by the occasional hoot of an owl. Her eyes drifted close.

Finn, too tired to contemplate what the morning would bring, soon joined her. Before the fire had burned low and the stars began to fade in the sky, he had fallen asleep with Rowan nestled in his arms and Biscuit laid with his head in her lap.

Chapter Eighteen
Kane

York, England

Kane paced the length of the narrow alleyway, his fury rising with every agitated step. Rage blazed in his eyes with a madness bordering on the edge of reason. The girl and the Tracker had slipped through his grasp like wisps of smoke carried away on the wind, and with them, the legendary Braeden dragon.

"Impossible," Kane snarled, his voice a guttural growl reverberating off the close walls. "How could they have concealed such a powerful creature right beneath our very noses?"

Rivik observed the fuming warlock warily, sensing the barely-contained danger simmering just below the surface. "Commander," he said in a low, soothing tone, attempting to balm Kane's frayed nerves, "I understand your anger and frustration. But we mustn't allow this setback to cloud our judgement or blind us to the opportunities now revealed."

Whirling on him, Kane spat venomously, "Opportunities? What opportunities, Rivik? They possess a Braeden, a being of immense ancient magic. How can we possibly stand against such might?"

Rivik's expression remained a mask of calm reassurance. "I have knowledge that will make this discovery more bearable, perhaps even grant us an advantage over our foes."

Interest flickered in Kane's eyes, momentarily piercing his blinding rage. "What knowledge? Speak plainly, and do not test my patience."

Bowing his head in deference, Rivik replied, "Of course. But we should discuss this somewhere more private, away from prying eyes and listening ears."

Kane hesitated, his paranoid gaze darting to the Fallen lurking in the shadows, their eyes glinting. Though he knew they were bound to him by the dark magic flowing through their veins, he was still reluctant to fully disclose his plans, to unveil his closely guarded secrets.

"Very well," he acquiesced tersely. "We ride to the city outskirts where we may speak freely without interruption."

A small, knowing smile played at the corners of Rivik's lips. "As you wish."

The Fallen lowered himself for Kane to mount. Melting into the shadows alongside his brethren, they blended seamlessly into the enveloping darkness. An uneasy flicker of doubt pricked at Kane's mind, a sense that Rivik held even more secrets that he had yet to uncover, despite all his power and cunning. Brushing the thought aside, he focused instead on the tantalising possibilities ahead. Could Rivik's knowledge truly grant him an advantage? They were due to rendezvous at the Master's coordinates imminently, and Kane knew tardiness would not be tolerated. But surely news of the Braeden dragon would justify a delay—and provide an opportunity to redeem himself in the Master's eyes.

Turning to the remaining Fallen, Kane commanded in a low growl, "Hunt, feed, grow strong. We will have need of your strength and savagery in the coming days. Join us when you've had your fill."

Heads bowed in obedience, the Fallen dissipated like wraiths, melting into the night until they were lost from sight. Kane's heart pounded with fierce, savage joy as Rivik carried him in the opposite direction. The night air whipped cool and crisp against his face as they left the twinkling city lights behind, venturing into the wild, untamed countryside illuminated solely by the moon and stars.

As Rivik's paws pounded against the hard-packed earth, Kane placed his fingers on the Master's mark and closed his eyes, reaching out with his mind. The connection was faint, but he sensed the pulsing thread of energy binding them.

"Explain," the Master demanded.

"I have located the tracker and the girl. They are in my grasp, but I need one more day to bring them to you. I promise you, victory will soon be ours. You will have the girl and the Orb." Kane paused with bated breath, wondering if it would be torture or death for his delay. He could only hope that the additional find of the Orb would make the Master more amenable to his request.

"You have one more day," the Master declared before severing the connection. Kane had felt the tiniest ripple of approval, a warmth suffusing his being with unshakable strength and conviction that his gamble had paid off. The Orb was clearly of great importance, and the Master needed Kane alive to bring it to him.

At last they reached a dense, secluded forest pulsing with ancient, primal energy. Rivik scanned the still shadows for any hint of danger before nodding his affirmation to Kane. Dismounting, the warlock settled himself on the ground, his expression one of anticipation and impatience.

"We are alone. Now, speak. Tell me this secret that will grant us an advantage over the girl and tracker."

"Commander," Rivik began, his voice trembling with the gravity of his revelation, "what I am about to divulge will shake the very foundations of your understanding. But I expect you to trust in the truth of my words."

Suspicious, yet intrigued, Kane nodded for him to continue.

Taking a deep breath, Rivik explained, "I was once known by another name, forgotten by all but a few. I was Morvela's dragon, his bonded companion and most loyal servant."

Shock registered in Kane's widening eyes. "Morvela? The dark mage who sought to enslave the world centuries ago? Impossible... his dragon perished alongside him. The histories are clear."

"The histories are incomplete," Rivik countered. "When Morvela fell in battle, his body destroyed and essence scattered, I thought I too would die, as is a bonded dragon's fate. But with one last act of defiance against the natural laws of magic, he ensured our survival."

Leaning forward intently, Kane asked, "How? What spell could defy death itself?"

"An ancient incantation that merged his essence with mine, binding his soul to me in a way transcending life and death. We became a single entity, never to be truly parted."

"You mean... you are Morvela? You possess his memories, knowledge, power?" Kane asked in disbelief.

Rivik chuckled ruefully. "Not quite. I am the being born from that merging. I hold some of his memories and knowledge, but I am not truly him. I am something different, straddling the line between dragon and mage, life, and death. For centuries I've wandered, moving from host to host."

Realisation dawned on Kane. "Which is how you found a Margorian Shade and absorbed its power, then moved on to the Fallen when I gave them form."

Rivik nodded. "I used the same incantation that bound me to Morvela to merge my essence with theirs. I sensed the power flowing through your veins, the dormant potential within you, and now the potential of Nyrvallia's power."

"Tell me more of this power," Kane pressed.

"Soon," Rivik promised. "But the Orb's temptation nearly destroyed you. Without Morvela's full knowledge to wield it, you would have been reduced to a husk, consumed by its power if I had not stopped the bonding ritual."

"The Orb could have destroyed me," Kane repeated grimly. "But how do I claim its power if neither you nor I fully comprehend it?"

"There is one who knows, who holds the key to unlocking your potential," Rivik revealed. "One who already keeps you close, guiding your destiny since your mother's death. The Mistress, Morvela's twin sister Mordreya."

Shock and fury warred within Kane. "Mordreya is dead, slain by her own brother's hand! How could she manipulate me from beyond the grave?"

"Death is but an obstacle to one as cunning and powerful as she," Rivik explained. "Mordreya found her own path to immortality, subtle and insidious. She is a master of manipulation, driven to claim the power she believes is rightfully hers. But she is the only one who can guide you to your destiny."

"And what do you seek for yourself in all this?" Kane demanded suspiciously.

A sly smile curved Rivik's lips. "I seek to capture Roark, the last Braeden dragon... and my brother. By consuming his essence, I shall reclaim my true draconic form and might. And with you as my rider, my equal, we shall be unstoppable."

Kane's eyes gleamed with dark interest. "How do you propose we capture a dragon?"

"With the Eye of Malachite," Rivik revealed. "An ancient stone imbued with the power to prevent dragons from shifting forms. Even the mightiest dragon would risk all to possess it. I believe your Master holds this treasure. Convince him to relinquish it and I shall lure Roark into our trap."

Kane's face split into a vicious grin as Rivik outlined the details of his plan. When the Fallen returned, he dismissed them to feed and rejuvenate, summoning only Symiar to prepare his lavish tent. Reclining on furs with a goblet of rich wine, Kane gestured for Rivik to continue.

"I am connected to Roark still," Rivik explained. "When opportunity arises, I shall teleport to him, tricking him into his weaker form to be ensnared. This will surely bait the girl and Tracker as well. But first, I need you to provide the incantation to craft the necessary illusion."

"Well then," Kane purred, "let us proceed. With a dragon in our grasp, even the Master will bow to our might."

Rising to his feet, Kane strode from the tent, Rivik prowling at his heels. With a snap of his fingers, Kane conjured a roaring campfire. Raising his arms, he drew a rune symbol above the flames that leaped and danced, morphing into a swirling vortex.

From the churning flames, a shadowed figure began to take shape. The Master himself. "Why have you summoned me?" he demanded.

"Master," Kane began, bowing deeply, "I come bearing news of a great opportunity. The chance to capture a Braeden dragon."

The Master's eyes narrowed. "A bold claim, given none live. And how do you propose to accomplish this miraculous feat?"

"One has survived, hidden all this time under the protection of Bessantia. I have a plan to capture him in his alternate form and bring him to you, as my sign of my devotion and in recompense for my failings. But I need the Eye of Malachite to capture him."

The Master was silent for a long, considering moment. "You have failed me before, Kane. Why should I trust you with not just one, but two powerful artefacts?"

Kane met his gaze unflinchingly. "Because with a dragon under our command, we shall be unstoppable. The girl and the tracker will be helpless against us. And the Eye will ensure the Braeden cannot escape our grasp. I have already learned my lesson regarding the Orb. You are its rightful Master."

"Hmmm. And if you fail?" the Master pressed. "If the dragon slips through your fingers and the Eye is lost?"

Kane's jaw clenched. "Then I shall accept what punishment you deliver."

The Master studied him intently, seeming to weigh Kane's resolve.

Kane held his ground, refusing to waver beneath that penetrating stare.

"Very well," the Master said at last. "I will grant you the Eye. But know this, Kane: if you fail me again, death will be a mercy compared to what awaits you."

He waved a hand, and the flames flared brilliantly. From their depths, a green stone with black striations appeared, eerily glowing with eldritch light. Kane reached out to take it, but the Master held it back.

"Understand the gravity of what I am entrusting to you," he warned.

"I understand," Kane assured him solemnly. "I will wield it only as you command."

Seemingly satisfied, the Master relinquished the stone. Kane closed his fist around it, feeling the thrum of ancient magic against his palm.

"I will not tolerate further failure," the Master intoned ominously before his image dissipated like smoke. The flames died down.

Kane held aloft his prize.

Rivik smiled. "Perfect timing. I've located my brother."

Kane handed the stone over. "I take it that this will not harm you?"

"I am not fully Braeden. It will only bind me in my current form when the incantation is uttered."

"Then wake Barrock and give him the coordinates before you go, and remember what is at stake. I shall meet you there."

"Yes, Commander."

Chapter Nineteen
Roark

Northeast Region of England

The night was dark and still, the only sound the gentle rustling of leaves in the breeze and the soft, even breathing of Rowan, Finn, and Biscuit as they lay curled together beneath the shelter of the trees. Exhausted from the day's events, the trio had drifted off into a deep, peaceful slumber, their bodies, and minds surrendering to the warm embrace of sleep.

But as the night progressed, Biscuit began to stir, a gnawing sensation in his belly rousing him from his slumber. He lifted his head, blinking owlishly in the dim light, his mind still foggy with the last vestiges of sleep. The hunger in his stomach grew more insistent, and he knew that he would not be able to ignore it for much longer.

With a soft, huffing sigh, Biscuit rose carefully to his feet, mindful not to disturb his sleeping companions. They needed their rest, and he would not be the one to steal these precious moments of peace from them. Quietly, he padded away from the campsite and into the surrounding woods, his nose twitching as he scented the air for any hint of prey.

Once he deemed himself far enough away, Biscuit reached deep within himself, tapping into the ancient primal magic that was his birthright. Power surged through him, and he felt his body begin to change, to shift. Soft fur melted away, replaced by gleaming scales of deepest black. Horns emerged, curving wickedly against the night sky. Wings unfurled, catching the starlight. With a powerful downbeat, Roark launched himself skyward, his emerald eyes gleaming with pleasure.

He kept his flight path close, not wanting to stray too far from Rowan and Finn. His keen draconic senses quickly picked up the scent of cattle in a nearby pasture. Roark dove, descending upon an unsuspecting cow with swift, deadly precision. Razor-sharp claws and fangs made quick work of his prey.

As he began to eat, the rich, coppery taste of blood filling his mouth, a sudden sound made Roark freeze, instantly alert. Heavy, purposeful footfalls crunched through the underbrush with a strange bouncing light. He tensed, powerful haunches coiling, ready to spring skyward and vanish into the night.

But then, a strange sensation engulfed him. An insistent tugging in his mind, urging him to shift back into his canine form. Perplexed and unsettled, but compelled by the unfamiliar magic, Roark allowed the transformation to overtake him once more. His body condensed, wings furling, scales absorbing back into skin and fur, until Biscuit stood in the dragon's place.

No sooner had he completed the change than a glimmer of light caught his eye. A crystal, suspended from a low-hanging branch, pulsing with an eerie green radiance. An inexorable pull drew Biscuit forward, an invisible force he could not resist. Warily, he crept closer, seeking shelter beneath the boughs.

The instant he reached the crystal, a blinding flare erupted and gleaming silver bars shot up from the earth, forming a cage around him. Biscuit yelped in shock, flinging himself against the unyielding metal, but to no avail. Panic rising like bile in his throat, he reached for his magic, desperate to shift back, but the ability had been severed, cut off by the same strange power that held him captive.

"Well, well, well," a familiar voice purred in his mind, rich with cruel amusement. *Losiah? But how is that possible?*

"How the mighty have fallen. The last of the great Braeden, brought low, nothing more than a helpless pup in a cage. How fitting."

Biscuit snarled, lunging at the bars. "Release me!" he projected fiercely. "Face me as I am, you coward!"

Mocking laughter filled his thoughts, cold and cutting. "So proud. So arrogant, even now. Struggle all you like, little brother. That cage is wrought with dark magic, the same that keeps you bound in this pitiful form. You are powerless. And soon, you will be delivered to the warlock."

Icy dread pooled in Biscuit's gut at the mention of Kane. He knew the warlock sought Rowan, hunted her relentlessly, and now he was just as sure that he would use Biscuit as bait, a tool to lure her into his clutches, before handing her over to the Master.

"I'm going to savour breaking you," Losiah hissed, malicious anticipation dripping from every word. "By the end, you'll be nothing but a whimpering, shattered husk, pleading for the release of death."

The cage jolted, rising slightly into the air as Losiah held it gripped in his powerful jaws. Biscuit crouched low, trembling with mingled terror and rage as his prison swayed and spun. Losiah carried him off into the night.

Time lost meaning, the land below blurring into a dark, featureless mass. With every passing moment, Biscuit felt the yawning chasm of distance stretching between himself and his companions, an aching void where the comforting warmth of their presence should have been. He cast his thoughts out desperately, straining to reach Finn, to send him a warning. But the magic that bound him strangled the connection, muted it to a maddening, unreachable whisper.

An eternity seemed to crawl by before he felt the cage drop to the ground in the first wan light of dawn. It settled with a harsh clang in a bleak area, the sound of water running close.

"We wait here," Losiah's mental voice informed him, almost offhand in its nonchalance. "The Commander will arrive soon. And then, dear brother... then your torment truly begins."

Biscuit squared his small shoulders. "Do your worst," he spat across their bond, defiance, and despair warring within him. "I don't care what you inflict upon me."

But his captor's presence only receded with a last contemptuous chuckle, abandoning Biscuit to his isolation, with nothing but the cruel bite of fear and the drumbeat of his own galloping heart for company.

Rowan began to stir from slumber and reached instinctively for Biscuit, seeking the comforting warmth of his small body curled between them. But her questing fingers met only cool, empty earth.

She bolted upright with a gasp, sudden dread seizing her heart.

"Biscuit? Roark?" She whipped her head around, voice shrill with budding panic. "Where are you?"

Silence. Only the sound of the wind through branches and the growing, ghastly certainty that something was profoundly, terribly amiss.

Finn gained his feet, an expression of grim resolve settling over his features like a mask. "I can't sense him."

"Kane's got him, I am sure of it. There is no other explanation. He would have answered by now." She closed her eyes and muttered, "Two can play at his game."

"What the hell are you doing?" Finn shouted.

She opened her eyes. "He's got him alright, trapped in a cage."

Finn blew out a breath. "Do you have any idea what you've done, contacting him voluntarily? He can see exactly where we are."

"What does it matter now? He has Biscuit, and he knows we will come for him."

Finn went silent.

"We are going for him, aren't we? Surely you don't expect me to leave him behind?"

"Biscuit—Roark—can take care of himself."

"I have to go to him." The words spilled from Rowan's numb lips as she spun to face Finn, already gathering herself as she reached for her amulet. "Just as I know you will have to come for me."

Before Finn could do more than open his mouth in protest, Rowan closed her eyes and fixed her mind on Biscuit and her desire to be with him.

Light exploded behind her lids, searing, blinding. A sickening wrenching sensation, a plummeting fall and Rowan slammed back into solidity. She did not register the danger until it was far, far too late.

Chapter Twenty

Biscuit

Outskirts of York, England

O   Just as he was sinking into a grey fog of helplessness, a sudden flurry of activity intruded on the edges of his awareness. Biscuit raised his head wearily, peering out through the bars of his cage, and growled at the sight that greeted him.

Fallen—a dozen or more—milled about in a loose half-circle, a parody of an honour guard, claws flexing, teeth bared in eager rictuses. Anticipation poured off them in a noxious wave, palpable even to Biscuit's numbed senses.

And there, striding through their midst like a conquering king, was Kane.

The warlock's lips curved in a smile of malicious satisfaction as his gaze lighted on Biscuit's prison, pale eyes glinting with a vicious, feral hunger, barely restrained.

"Well done, Rivik," he purred, the unfamiliar name settling coldly in the pit of Biscuit's stomach. *Losiah? Rivik? How many faces does my brother wear? How deep does his treachery run?*

Kane crossed to the cage and crouched down, bringing himself eye to eye with Biscuit. The dog glared back defiantly, even in the face of the mage's overwhelming dark power.

"Such spirit," Kane mused, almost fondly. "Such fire. I can see why you want him so much, Rivik." He straightened, turning to cast his gaze over the assembled Fallen. "The Master will reward us richly for this prize. Rivik, you have exceeded all—"

The words died on his tongue, his eyes going abruptly distant. For a moment he stood, head cocked, as if listening to some unheard voice. Then a slow, awful smile unfurled across his face like a blood-drenched banner.

"It seems," he said softly, "that we have a rare opportunity before us. The girl deigns to reach out to me. She demands to know if I have had a hand in the disappearance of her beloved pet."

"No!" The thought ripped from Biscuit in a ragged projection of pure, white-hot denial. He flung himself against the bars, snarling and snapping. "You leave her be, you sadistic bastard!"

Kane laughed, a sound like ripping silk. "Peace, little beast," he crooned. "I do you a kindness reuniting you with your mistress. Shouldn't you be grateful?"

Ignoring Biscuit's continued stream of projected invective, the warlock closed his eyes, brow furrowed in concentration.

"Rowan..." Kane's tones were a mockery of warmth, of care, oozing false concern. "Come swiftly, before he suffers further."

He showed her an image of Biscuit's familiar small form, huddled and shaking within a cruel cage. Terror and pain emanated from the vision in choking waves, underpinned by a piercing, desperate plea for her to help.

R owan wrenched her head up, her gaze clashing with piercing eyes, alight with cruel triumph.

"Rowan." Her name on the warlock's tongue was an obscenity, a mockery. He smiled, baring teeth. "So good of you to join us."

The Fallen closed in around her with taunting snarls.

Rowan screamed, and in the cage beside her, Biscuit howled.

Chapter Twenty-One
Finn

Northeast Region of England

N A ragged cry tore from Finn's throat as Rowan vanished in a blaze of blinding light, her final, anguished apology still echoing in his ears. For a moment he stood frozen, staring at the empty space where she had been just a heartbeat before, his mind reeling, refusing to comprehend the horror of what had just happened.

Then, with a choked gasp, Finn's legs gave out, and he crumpled to his knees in the loamy earth, fists clenching in the detritus of leaves and twigs. Despair crashed over him in a suffocating wave, driving the air from his lungs, crushing his ribs like a vice. They were gone. Both Rowan and Biscuit, the two souls in all the world he cherished most. Stolen from him in an instant, spirited away to face unimaginable torment at the hands of their greatest enemy.

And he had been powerless to stop it.

Finn squeezed his eyes shut against the hot sting of tears, a low, keening moan building in his throat. He had failed them. Failed to keep them safe, to protect them as he had sworn, as he had promised. Some Tracker he was. Some friend.

But even as hopelessness threatened to engulf him, to drag him down into the yawning abyss of grief and self-recrimination, a small, stubborn spark kindled to life in Finn's chest. A glimmer of determination, of sheer, mulish refusal to surrender. No. This could not be how it ended. He would not let it be.

Slowly, almost painfully, Finn raised his head, fixing reddened, resolute eyes on the verdant canopy overhead. He drew in a deep, shuddering breath and released it in a rush.

"I call upon the Fae," he said, surprised at the steadiness of his own voice. "I beg of you to aid me. Help me reach my friends before it's too late."

For a long, stretching moment, there was no response. Only the faint wind through leaves, the distant twitter of birdsong. Finn swallowed past the hard lump of trepidation in his throat and pressed on.

"I will owe you a boon, bound by oath. Any favour within my power to grant, in exchange for the means to open a way to Rowan and Biscuit. I swear it, by the earth and sky, by all I hold dear. Please." His voice broke on the final word, exhaustion, and desperation cracking the facade of composure.

He nearly wept when, between one blink and the next, an acorn appeared nestled in a tuft of moss near his knee. A relieved half-sob escaped him as he reached out to cradle the precious seed in his trembling palm, marvelling at the opalescent shimmer of its surface. The Fae had heard. They had answered.

Finn clutched the acorn to his chest like a talisman, feeling a wild, reckless hope surge through him, chasing back the shadows of dread and despair. He had a chance now, a glimmer of possibility. He would not waste it.

Securing the rucksack across his back, he closed his eyes and turned his focus inward to the well of power that pulsed beneath his breastbone in time with the steady thrum of his heart. He cast his mind to the endless hours spent under Bessantia's tutelage, to the exercises and meditations she had guided him through with infinite patience.

Carefully, methodically, he began to weave the ribbons of his telepathic bond with Rowan and Biscuit into the shimmering fabric of the Shroud, pouring every ounce of will and intent into the working, willing the ancient magic to knit them together, to forge a path to his lost companions.

He knew it was a desperate gamble. Accessing the Shroud in full wakefulness was an incredibly difficult feat to achieve, and though Finn was many things—a tracker, a shapeshifter, a being with an innate connection to the beasts and wilds—he had only ever walked that liminal realm, as most did, through the doorway of sleep and dreaming.

But this was no time for doubt or hesitation. Rowan needed him, and Finn would run any risk, dare any feat, to reach her before Kane and his foul minions could harm them further.

Slowly, gradually, an image began to take shape behind Finn's closed lids. Indistinct at first, hazy like a scene viewed through thick fog, but with each passing second it sharpened, growing clearer, more defined.

A dense forest, ancient and sprawling. Towering evergreens and gnarled oaks, their branches twining together overhead to form a dense canopy. Through the centre of the wood ran a wide, swift-flowing river, spanned by a massive bridge of weathered sandstone.

And there, in a small, barren clearing on the near bank, a sight that made Finn's heart lurch painfully in his chest was Rowan, crumpled and surrounded by a ring of Fallen. The creatures circled her with macabre glee, their cruel laughter, and malicious chatter assaulting Finn's ears even through the Shroud-borne vision.

Beside them, imprisoned in a cage of glowing silver bars, Biscuit flung himself against his prison again and again, heedless of the wounds he inflicted upon himself. His frantic, animal howls of rage and distress knifed through Finn like shards of jagged ice.

With a gasp and a shudder, Finn wrenched himself free of the Shroud's grip, his heart pounding like a war drum against his ribs. He held the memory of that place tightly in his mind. And now that he had seen the horrific tableau awaiting him there, he wasted not a single second more.

Clutching the acorn tight in one white-knuckled fist, Finn surged to his feet, his jaw set with grim determination. He reached for his power once more, but this time there was no subtlety or finesse to the working, only raw, desperate need, a fierce, all-consuming imperative to be with Rowan and Biscuit, to save them from the hell they endured.

The world wrenched sideways, reality folding in on itself like a collapsing telescope, and then...

Finn stumbled as his boots slammed into earth and leaf litter on the far side of the stone bridge. For a moment he reeled, disoriented, stomach churning with the aftereffects of the translocation. But he mastered himself quickly, pushing back the nausea and vertigo to focus on the scene before him.

Kane now clutched Rowan in his arms, the Fallen still taunting and tormenting her with sadistic delight. Biscuit slumped in his cage, sides heaving with exhaustion and pain.

"Good of you to join us, Finn," Kane drawled.

"Didn't want to miss the party," he replied, not giving Kane the satisfaction as his eyes completed a quick surveillance.

"And quite the party I have put on for you," Kane said. "My guests have been so looking forward to getting acquainted with you."

"That's nice," Finn said. He reached out with his senses to get a closer visual of the cage.

Biscuit's mind connected to him. "It's the crystal suppressing my ability to transform."

Think, Finn. He pulled back and opened his eyes. Kane was studying him closely. "Where did you get the crystal from? I didn't think a man such as yourself would be interested in such knickknacks."

Finn hoped that Rowan would understand the meaning behind his question.

"Oh, you would be amazed what I can procure. I mean, I do have your girl after all. I shall enjoy all that her flesh has to offer."

Finn fought back the desire to sprint across the bridge and pummel the warlock's face as Kane spun Rowan to face him and forced his lips on hers. Rowan instantly pulled back, her face one of revulsion, and she slapped the warlock across the face.

"Don't," Biscuit's voice warned him. "He's baiting you."

"She's got such spunk," Kane said, rubbing his jaw. "I shall look forward to breaking her in. Especially as my friends cannot scent you on her. You are a fool not to have claimed her when you had the chance, to feel her delectable body beneath you. When you die, Finn, be sure that it will be with the thought of me and her together. It will be my name she screams in ecstasy. Only I can satisfy such passion in such a spirited filly."

Rowan spat in Kane's face. "I'm no bloody horse, and you're disgusting. I'd rather die than have you inside of me."

Finn's self-control was teetering on the edge.

"You're about as attractive as that crystal there. The only man who ever comes close to taking my place is Charles," he called out pointedly.

Rowan turned in his direction and met Finn's gaze. He nodded his encouragement.

"Yes, I heard her call out his name before. What a disappointing prospect you offer her, if she thinks of another man whilst in your arms."

"And can you give me what I need?" Rowan asked. "Make me forget?"

"Try me! I am a far better lover then the offerings you've had before you."

She turned away from Kane, as if to give his words further consideration.

"Forgive me," she mouthed towards Finn.

Now what is she planning? No! No way, I think I'm going to hurl!

Rowan spun and clasped Kane's head in her hands, dragging him forward to her mouth. She kissed the warlock with fervour. Kane moaned, his hand sliding and groping at her body.

Finn watched, appalled as the warlock gyrated and rubbed an obvious erection against her, enjoying the misery he knew it would be causing Finn.

Kane was too distracted to note the subtle movement as the cord of the crystal was slowly unknotting and loosening from Biscuit's cage.

A faint clang as the crystal hit the metal bars had the couple pull apart.

"What was that?" Kane snarled.

Rowan seized his hand and thrust it to her breast, "I don't know. Perhaps your guest doesn't like to watch," she suggested.

Kane smirked.

Finn's fists clenched and unclenched by his side. *You better hurry your arse up, Charles, before I go over there and kill him!*

Rowan ignored Finn's murderous gaze and pulled Kane's head lower to her chest as her hand frantically gestured behind her back. She moaned loudly and crooned Kane's name. It was enough to mask the slight creak of a cage door opening.

Finn himself had almost missed the sound as he clamped down on his desire to storm across the bridge and seize Rowan from his nemesis's grip. The warlock was getting far too handy for Finn's liking.

"Well, it looks like the party is over," Kane said when they finally broke apart. "Rowan and I will be moving on to have our own private party. "

Finn stole a glance in the direction of the cage, and was relieved to note it was empty. "Are you sure? It seems my party is about to get started."

Kane turned in the direction of the cage. "You fools," he bellowed, and threw Rowan to the ground. She didn't hesitate for a second, and scrambled onto her feet, running towards Finn with a fierce determination. The Fallen were too distracted gawping at the now empty cage.

Finn pulled her into a hug and then pushed her behind him. She peered her head around his shoulder. "And just for the record, Kane, you're a lousy kisser."

The warlock's face turned the colour of a beetroot and he waved his hand, sending one Fallen hurtling into the air and crashing to the ground.

"Didn't your mother teach you how to be a hospitable host?" Rowan goaded.

Finn didn't know whether to gag her or applaud her. He had never seen Kane so furious.

"I could crush you both," he spat out.

"Except you won't, because the Master wants us, or at least her, alive." Finn said.

Kane stalked towards them. Finn and Rowan backed up slowly.

Where the hell was Roark?

"The Master will forgive me for losing the whore, and technically it won't be me or my army that sends you to your grave. For such insolence, I have something better."

Finn noted that the rest of the Fallen looked extremely nervous, and they too retreated. Kane drew out his dagger and sliced his palm. The blood pooled to the ground as the warlock whispered an incantation.

"Another Nyrvallia gift, you have awakened."

"Nyrvallia?" Finn whispered.

"What's wrong?" Rowan nudged him. "What's a Nyrvallia?"

"If what he says is true, we are in trouble. Big trouble."

Kane laughed hysterically.

Finn stared in horror as the dark substance oozed and bubbled in front of him. It began to pulsate. He could see something forming in its centre which was rapidly growing.

Finn looked up at Kane as realisation dawned. "It can't be," he said, his face unable to mask the horror of what Kane had done.

"This will be the last time that you underestimate me." Kane smiled.

"You are crazy, bringing that thing here. There is no conceivable way you can control it."

A grotesque transmutation took place. It screeched and writhed as three exo-skeletal limbs protruded from its mass.

"What the hell is that thing?" Rowan shouted.

Finn knew he should be putting some distance in between them and it, but he could not force his feet to move. "An Abaddon," he responded.

It wailed as three more appendages burst free.

Kane's face was pure delight.

Rowan covered her ears.

The Fallen pawed nervously at the ground.

"It's mine to control," Kane said.

"You're deluded. There is a reason the Master banished those things," Finn told him.

"Am I? We shall see. Well, you won't, as you will be dead in a few minutes."

"Wrong again," Finn shouted. "Only an idiot would summon an Abaddon on his side of the bridge."

Kane spun as two of the Fallen were tossed aside. Black tar oozed from wounds to their abdomens. "Kill them," he demanded, and pointed in Finn's direction.

Roark landed in front of them with a thunderous crash as the Abaddon turned, its limbs chittering and skittering sickeningly as it moved towards them. The dragon reared back and breathed out a scorching wall of fire, cutting the creature off. The flames illuminated its grotesque form, a writhing mass of spindly limbs, pulsating flesh, and glinting obsidian eyes that gleamed with malevolent hunger.

"What kept you?" Finn yelled telepathically, his heart pounding.

"Why are you both still standing here?" Roark challenged back, his deep voice reverberating through Finn's mind.

A putrid, sulphurous smell filled the air, making Finn's nose wrinkle in revulsion as the Abaddon spewed forth a sickly yellow substance from its gaping maw. The viscous liquid sizzled as it hit the flames, subduing them and allowing the nightmare to cross through.

Finn grabbed Rowan roughly and practically threw her onto the dragon's back. But as he went to leap on behind her, one of the Abaddon's jagged limbs whipped out and wrapped around his ankle in a vice-like grip, yanking him away. Rowan screamed in horror as the creature began dragging Finn towards its eagerly-clacking mandibles.

"Get her to safety, now!" Finn shouted. The dragon hesitated for a split-second, but self-preservation won out and Roark spread his great wings, preparing to take flight.

However, Rowan was having none of it. With a string of colourful obscenities, the small woman hurled herself off the dragon's back. Roark barely managed to catch her flailing form in his front claws as he took to the air, Rowan punching and kicking as she tried to wriggle free, desperate to get to Finn.

The Abaddon paused in its attack, distracted as it observed the fiery scene unfolding in the sky above with its multiple glittering eyes. Finn seized his chance. Coiling his free leg up to his chest, he smashed his boot into the joint of the limb holding him with all his strength. The creature let out an ear-splitting shriek, and its grip loosened just enough for Finn to yank himself free.

Scrambling to his feet, Finn took off into the forest at a dead sprint. His heart jackhammered against his ribs and his breath came in ragged gasps. Behind him, trees groaned and snapped as the enraged Abaddon gave chase, its bulk crashing through the underbrush.

"There's something you should know—" Roark's voice invaded his panicked thoughts.

"If it's the fact that she's the Guardian and your Rider, I already figured that out," Finn shot back between panting breaths as he wove between the trees, trying to evade the creature hunting him.

"Then you know I'm coming for you," Roark said, his tone dark.

"No!" Finn barked. "Invoke the Oath of Dragoria. Release yourself from her foolishness!"

Roark hesitated, conflicted. "She won't be happy about this, Finn."

"Something we'll both have to live with," Finn gritted out. "But right now I need her somewhere safe!"

He felt a pang of guilt even as the words left his mouth, knowing the betrayal Rowan would feel. But he pushed it aside. Keeping her out of the Abaddon's reach was the only thing that mattered now.

To Finn's immense relief, he sensed Roark stop circling and finally wing his way east, away from the bridge and the nightmare that pursued them. Rowan's furious shouts faded away.

The Abaddon let out a high-pitched wail that made Finn's skull vibrate. He risked a glance over his shoulder and immediately wished he hadn't. A seventh limb had punched out of the creature's back - a long, flexible appendage tipped with a wickedly spiked and blackened barb dripping with viscous fluid. It lashed back and forth, leaving sizzling holes in the earth where the poison struck.

"Time to get the hell out of here," Finn muttered. He pushed himself harder, lungs and legs burning, ducking under branches and hurtling over fallen logs in his path.

Desperation rising, he reached out with his mind, casting his thoughts out into the ether. "I owe you another boon if you can get me out of here," he called to the Fae, his inner voice ragged. "I can't fulfil my first oath if I'm dead!"

Just ahead, a round portal shimmered to life, its iridescent surface undulating and beckoning him forward. Finn arrowed towards it, the stench of the Abaddon thick in his nostrils as it narrowed the gap between them. He heard the sharp whistle of its tail slicing the air and instinctively dropped into a roll. The tip missed him by a hair's breadth, crashing into a tree trunk and sending a spray of splinters flying.

Finn threw himself back to his feet and sprinted the last few strides, hurling himself headlong at the portal. White light enveloped him as he fell into the shimmering gateway. For a moment he was weightless, suspended between worlds.

Then the ground rose up to meet him and he landed hard on the other side, the impact driving the air from his lungs. Gasping, Finn dragged himself up onto his elbows, glancing around wildly. He'd emerged in a dense patch of forest, the trees packed tightly together. Of the Abaddon, there was no sign.

Heart still racing, he pushed himself to his feet. He needed to find the others and regroup. As he took a step forward, a wave of dizziness crashed over him and he stumbled, barely catching himself against a tree trunk.

Breathing hard, Finn squeezed his eyes shut and tried to collect himself. His whole body ached and his head was pounding, but he couldn't afford to rest. Not with that thing on the loose. Gritting his teeth, he pushed off from the tree and staggered onwards, determined to find a way to stop the creature before it was too late.

Around him, the forest had fallen eerily silent, as if it too sensed the malevolent presence that had been unleashed.

Finn shuddered, remembering the Fallen's terrified faces as they scattered into the trees. Even Rivik had looked shaken.

Finn picked up his pace, ignoring his body's protests. He let out a yell when he collided into a soft and hairy figure. Chocolate brown eyes peered over him. There was something familiar about its appearance. The small creature sniffed at him before enthusiastically thumping the ground with its hind leg.

"Mortimus?" Finn ventured.

"Oh, thank the heavens, Master Finn. I have found you at last," the hare replied.

Finn rose and rubbed his back. Every muscle and ligament screamed out in pain.

"Are you injured?" Mortimus asked.

"Not from the Abaddon, at least," Finn sighed and then slumped against a tree. He dragged his hands down his face.

"Did you say an Abaddon?"

"Yes, Kane decided this world didn't have enough to put up with with his stinking presence and summoned one up for the shits and giggles."

Mortimus blinked at him. "I don't see how—"

"Never mind," Finn cut in. "Where are we?"

"Not far from Mistress Bessantia's cottage, or at least what is left of it."

"Perfect, an Abaddon-free zone. Shame that the love of my life happens to be on the other side of that portal and somewhere that thing can still get to her." Finn groaned. "How the hell do I find her now?"

The hare seemed to consider for a few moments before it spoke again. "Let me ask you this, Master Finn. How did you find her the first time?"

"Mortimus, you're a genius."

"Not quite, but one day I hope to return to Valoria and finish my Mage training."

"I take it this isn't your true form."

"Good grief no, although I am not as young as I once was."

"Can you change at will?"

"I'm afraid not. I can only return to my human form at night when the spell was first cast and then from dawn, I am back to this."

"Didn't I also see you as a statue on Bessie's porch?"

"Yes, you did. Bessie and I were experimenting with the spell to see if I could maintain my human form for longer periods of time. Sadly, the magic is not the same here as it is in our world. It did come in quite handy whenever she had visitors. Amazing what things I overheard, especially from Old Lady McGinty. What an oddball she was. Still, her flapjack was quite palatable."

"Old Lady McGinty?"

"Mistress Bessie's bingo partner. Totally bonkers, that one. Knew everything that happened in that village. Her nose was in everyone's business. Tongue as sharp as knife if you crossed her. She had a soft spot for Mistress Bessantia, although that could have been the effect of the sugar cube that we spelled and dropped in her tea," he mused.

"What happened to Bessie that night?" Finn asked.

Mortimus sighed deeply and allowed a solitary tear to escape. "I do not know. She sent me and Albion away before the warlock arrived. We were told to come and find you both in two days."

"Where is Albion?" Finn asked.

"Trapped on the other side of that portal."

"So it was you who had opened the portal, not the Fae?"

"I doubt there would be any Fae in that forest if the Abaddon was allowed to enter it."

"They may not have had a choice."

"Don't be too sure."

Finn sighed. "Is Albion like you?"

"Not exactly. By day he takes his true form, and then by night that of a dragonfly. He was born in the Crystal Caverns of Elyssia and—"

"You've got to be kidding me... a dwarf?"

Mortimus peered closely at Finn. "And what, pray tell, is wrong with a dwarf?"

"Apart from the fact that they are bad-tempered and selfish?" Finn countered.

"Yes, well, Albion is not your average dwarf. His mother was a dwarf, his father was Fae."

Finn's jaw dropped. "You seriously expect me to believe that?"

"Have you ever seen a dwarf with wings?" asked Mortimus.

"No," replied Finn.

"There you are. Why do you think Albion's form is that of a dragonfly?"

"Mortimus, I haven't seen an actual dragonfly, and neither have I seen a dwarf with or without wings."

"Until today, I bet you had not seen an Abaddon either. Just because you have not seen something with your own eyes does not mean it does not exist. Your foul-smelling friend back there is proof of that."

Finn nodded. "I take your point."

Mortimus glanced upwards at the sky. "How about some breakfast?"

"Is rabbit is out of the question?"

Mortimus folded his paws across his chest.

"Just kidding," Finn said.

He tracked his way through the forest, Mortimus following behind, until they had reached a small stream. Taking his boots and socks off, Finn rolled his trouser leg up and stepped into the chilly water and waited. He closed his eyes and reached out with his senses. Instinctively he plunged his hands into the water and, cupping the fish, threw it onto the bank. He continued until he had caught enough to feed them both.

Stepping back onto the bank, he heaved a sigh of relief as the warmth of his footwear eased some of the icy chill from the water.

Mortimus had obviously been busy gathering firewood.

"You haven't lit this?" Finn queried.

"Forgive me, Master Finn, but it is a skill I have never learnt. Not much call for it as a hare."

Finn chuckled. "I guess not. Here, let me show you." Finn took the branches and arranged the campfire, setting a ring of stones from the stream's bank around it. He then raised a hand above and drew the elemental sigil of fire. It dissipated over the wood and set it alight.

"I have never seen an elemental sigil used in this way," Mortimus said.

"It does take practice."

Mortimus tapped his paw against his chin. "You're really not what I thought you would be."

Finn smiled. "In a good way, I hope."

"Oh, yes. Why don't you rest now, whilst I prepare the fish? That, I can at least do."

Chapter Twenty-Two
Rowan

North Yorkshire Coastline of England

Refusing to let him offer any assistance, Rowan stubbornly thrust herself from the dragon's back. It was a decision she instantly regretted as she slid to an undignified heap on the ground. Ignoring his amused look, she cursed under her breath at her own foolishness as she pulled herself to her feet and swiftly brushed the dirt off her jeans.

Roark arched a brow and glowered at her in response, his large green eyes piercing her own as he let out a small growl of warning. She did not falter as she placed her hands on her hips for good measure and matched his expression with equal ferocity. Admittedly, she had not yet mastered the art of telepathy; however, she was damn sure that Roark was under no illusion now as to how pissed-off she was feeling. He had blatantly ignored her pleas and left Finn stranded with that hideous creature. She inwardly seethed when he rolled his eyes upwards and snorted in annoyance before turning and almost tripping her with his tail. He settled himself on the earth and closed his eyes.

Her hands flew into the air as she let out a scream of frustration and marched towards the cliff edge. The sea was a sharp contrast to her own emotions as the waves broke gently against the rocks below. *How dare he,* she thought. *Finn at this very moment could be lying there injured—or worse, dead—and the bloody dragon is taking a nap!* Closing her eyes, she focussed on her breathing, attempting to quell the turmoil of emotions swirling in her abdomen. Both anger and fear waged a war inside.

Yes, she was grateful that Roark had saved her, but what was the point if he left Finn there alone to face that thing? She needed Finn alive. *Bessie needs Finn alive. How could he?* she raged. She glanced back and scowled at Roark. He opened one eye and looked at her briefly before closing it again. She sank to the ground, almost wanting to stamp her feet in sheer temper and frustration. Instead, she called out to Charles.

"What is it?" he asked, immediately responding to her call.

"I need to be able to communicate with him."

"Who? Finn or the Dragon... where is Finn?" he asked.

Rowan's voice caught, and she swallowed the lump in her throat. "Roark refused to turn around and go back for him. He left him alone with that thing."

"I don't understand," he said.

"Neither do I. That's why I need to communicate with Roark now. He needs to go back for Finn. Can you help?"

"The Lightkeepers have called an emergency meeting following its entry into our world. They allowed me to leave when I heard your call. Let me go back and speak to them. For what you are asking me to do, I will need their consent and their help."

She nodded. "Quickly, Charles."

Pulling her knees up to her chest, she searched her own feelings. *Surely if Finn were dead, I would know?* Something inside her gave her a little hope.

Charles, as she knew he would, returned minutes later, although she was a little taken aback when he was not alone. She allowed the spirit energy to connect with hers and received a vision of an older lady with long ebony hair wearing a deep burgundy velour gown.

She spoke with an accent that Rowan could not place. "My name is Eleanor."

"Eleanor is one of the Sages," Charles explained.

Rowan smiled. "Thank you so much Eleanor, for agreeing to help me."

"It has been a long time since I have seen a dragon in this world," Eleanor replied.

Rowan turned to look at Roark. "I don't know how to communicate with it."

"I can help with that, but Rowan, you must understand that once done this cannot be undone," Eleanor replied.

Charles placed a hand on Rowan's shoulder. "The Lightkeepers have agreed to enhance your telepathic communication. With this gift comes a great deal of responsibility, and you are going to have to learn how to control it, as we cannot take this back. As the dragon is not of this world, Eleanor has agreed to work with Roark to enhance his telepathic connection to your own."

"I accept the responsibility, and I understand what you are saying about Roark. Please hurry."

"I must have consent from the dragon first, Rowan," Eleanor responded. "Wait, Charles," she instructed him.

Rowan turned to watch Roark as she felt Eleanor's energy pull away from her. She was grateful that Charles remained close, continuing to rest his hand reassuringly on her shoulder. Her stomach somersaulted as Roark suddenly rose and met her gaze.

"It's okay, Roark," she said, giving him a small smile. Her heart thumped wildly in her chest as she waited for his response. A strange silence fell around them both. Roark eventually nodded and closed his eyes.

"Now, Charles," Eleanor called out.

Rowan's entire being pulsed with an electrical charge as Charles instantaneously combined his energy with her own, sending strong and powerful currents surging along pathways and lighting her from within. Her eyes glazed over and her vision distorted, the existing landscape gradually disappearing in a blur and plunging her momentarily into darkness, before a brilliant white light burst through and enveloped her.

She desperately wanted to rub her forehead to soothe the centre, which throbbed and tingled as her third eye continued to vibrate and open wide, but her arms stubbornly refused to move. An upwards tug from her crown had her gasping as she levitated onto the tips of her toes. She was suspended there for a few moments before being gently released. As the last of the electrical currents dispelled from her fingers and feet, she wept with joy.

"Are you okay, Rowan?" Charles asked, concerned.

Her voice shook as she replied, "I'm fine. I just need to catch my breath." She slid to the ground and rubbed her temples in a slow circular motion, easing the pressure and hoping it would deter the headache that was threatening. She felt him draw close and place his hand on her shoulder.

"Are you okay?" she asked in return.

She could hear the weariness in his voice as he replied, "I'm afraid it has spent a lot of my energy."

Rowan winced and reached her own hand upwards to join with his. "I'm so sorry. I know it was a lot to ask of you."

"Yet we both know this to be necessary," he reassured her. "You must prepare yourself for what is to come. This gift is one that takes time to master."

Silence fell between them as Rowan contemplated his words. Her life had already been altered beyond all recognition following the arrival of Finn. Would this new gift change her completely, too?

A female voice snapped her to attention. "It is done."

Rowan instantly turned in the direction of Roark, who was laid on the ground, eyes closed and breathing heavily.

"Is he okay, Eleanor?" She noted Roark's eyes flicker at the sound of her voice but remain firmly shut.

"Indeed he is, although he must sleep now whilst his body adapts to the changes we have made."

There was something in Eleanor's tone that had alarm bells ringing. "What changes?"

"I must take Charles back to the Sages for healing. Your dragon will wake in a couple of hours."

Eleanor had deliberately evaded the question. It was on the tip of her tongue to push for a response when she felt his hand restrain her. Rowan bit back her question.

"Come now, Charles," Eleanor insisted.

"But she will be alone."

"She will not be alone, another companion draws close. I have given him a helping hand," Eleanor stated.

Rowan turned nervously to look around them. Except for Roark sleeping, they were alone.

"Who?" she asked.

"We must go," Eleanor insisted.

Rowan's temper bubbled below the surface. Whilst she had the greatest of respect for the Sage, she was less than impressed with being ignored for a second time.

"I promise you I will be back soon," Charles reassured her.

Before she had the chance to protest, they were both gone.

Rowan let out a cry of frustration and stamped her feet on the ground. Roark, she noted begrudgingly continued sleeping, oblivious to her outburst.

Just great, she thought angrily. *Finn is either dead or injured, Roark is sleeping, and I am stuck here on the top of a cliff alone waiting for who or what to arrive to keep me company. But hey, don't sweat it Rowan. You're completely safe. Yeah, right.*

Rowan flinched as something flew into her line of vision. She glanced down as it landed softly on her knee and stilled its wings.

A dragonfly!

She watched with fascination, having never seen one this close before. It really was quite stunning, she considered, although a little odd for it to behave in this way. Still, its arrival did give her a welcome distraction from her inner turmoil, so she did not dwell on its behaviour too much. The dragonfly had a surprisingly calming effect on her mood and she noted her earlier temper and frustration beginning to ebb away.

Without meaning to, she slipped into a dreamless sleep.

It was almost dusk when Roark eventually stirred and stretched. Opening his eyes, he turned and growled as he rose to his feet. The dragonfly immediately took flight.

"Really, Roark, did you have to do that? You have frightened it away," Rowan scolded as she rubbed the sleep from her eyes.

The dragon stared and eyed her carefully in the dim light. Her mouth fell open when his connection to her mind proved successful. "I hope for that witch's sake you can hear me."

Rowan resisted her automatic instinct to respond verbally and instead pushed her thoughts towards Roark. "Yes, but can you hear me?"

"I can," he responded. "What is it I am supposed to have frightened away?"

Rowan stood and let out a whoop of joy. She danced around in a circle and wiggled her hips.

Roark eyed her sceptically. "You're behaving very strangely," he told her.

"I can't believe it's worked," she exclaimed. "Oh, and it was a dragonfly you scared away."

"A dragonfly, you say?"

"Yes, it kept me company whilst you were napping."

Roark let out another growl. "I was not napping. It was that witch, and you can hardly talk, since you were snoring like a hunting horn."

"I was not," she protested.

Roark grinned at her.

"Of course you weren't napping, you were just resting your eyes, and Eleanor isn't a witch, she's a Sage."

Roark rolled his eyes and let out a sigh. "Whatever she is, she made my head hurt."

"That bloody dragon better behave itself," a voice called out. Roark spun quickly, swinging his tail out towards the small figure approaching them.

Rowan watched warily as the figure automatically jumped out of the way and stood with small hands on hips. "For pity's sake, Roark, this really does grow tiresome."

Roark let out a roar of laughter. "Well, Albion, you are still alive, I see."

"Bessie's Albion?" Rowan asked.

"The very same," Albion responded, continuing towards them.

Roark pulled back his lips, exposing his huge teeth. Rowan could not make her mind up whether he was deliberately trying to scare Albion, or attempting a sneer. Albion, however, clearly was not fazed by this and scowled as he passed. "I preferred you when you were a mutt," he said.

"And I prefer it when you're hanging from a window," Roark retorted.

It did not take a genius to figure out that the pair of them clearly did not get on.

"What are you doing here, Albion?" she asked.

"Bessie sent myself and Mortimus to join you the night before the warlock attacked. She told us both to come to these coordinates in two days. Slightly a few hours underestimated, but still, here I am, and here you are."

"Where is Mortimus?" Roark asked. "I don't see him with you."

"Typical. You still favour the bloody rabbit," Albion snapped.

Rowan intervened before Roark could respond. "Where is Mortimus?" she repeated.

Albion sighed deeply. "With Master Finn, I imagine. They both went through the portal before that abomination could catch him."

Rowan almost sobbed in relief. "Finn's alive? He escaped?"

"Yes, a truly amazing accomplishment. Not many men have ever escaped from an Abaddon," Albion replied.

A huge weight fell away from her shoulders.

"You need to take us to him. Now, please."

"I am not getting on the back of that bloody dragon," Albion snapped.

"Fine, then you can stay here," Rowan said simply.

She glanced across at Roark and did not miss the glint in his eyes as he stared at the dwarf.

"See? He's doing it already."

"Doing what?"

"Looking at me like a prized rump steak."

"I'm sure he doesn't want to eat you."

Rowan bit back a smile as Roark teasingly licked his lips. Albion turned with his hands on his hips and his eyebrows quirked.

"Rowan, wait."

Stifling her laughter, she signalled for them both to be quiet as his energy connected. "What is it, Charles?"

"It's the Abaddon, we cannot leave that thing there. It is has taken a life and is destroying the forest. How soon will it be before it finds the city? The Lightkeepers want it destroyed."

His words had an instant sobering effect. "What can I do, Charles? This is beyond anything I have ever seen before."

"Not you, Rowan, the dragon."

"Roark?"

At the mention of his name he turned, connecting his thoughts to hers. "What is it?"

"The Lightkeepers want you to destroy the Abaddon."

"I see," he replied.

She rubbed her temples slowly, a familiar sickly feeling clamouring in the pit of her stomach. "Cannot the Lightkeepers do anything? You can't expect me to risk Roark's life like this."

"You underestimate the power of your dragon."

"You've seen the Abaddon, felt its energy, the darkness it holds within. I cannot ask Roark to do this."

"Eleanor would not request this lightly. Neither would I, knowing how much he means to you," he replied softly.

Tears threatened. "Eleanor has no right to ask this, and neither do you."

Drawing closer his energy enveloped hers as he attempted to offer some measure of comfort. "You must believe me. We will not allow any harm to come to your dragon."

For the first time, she rejected him, finding no solace in his words. "What if it is you who underestimates the power of the Abaddon? You know nothing of its world. How can you guarantee he will be safe?"

No answer. She deliberately kicked out at a pebble, watching it skip across the ground.

Still no answer. Sinking to the ground, she ground her teeth and inwardly seethed.

Albion sat beside her and placed a hand on her shoulder. "What is it?"

She shook her head, unable to formulate the words. Her eyes lifted and caught Roark's gaze. Sensing her need, he moved in response, wrapping himself gently around her. She pressed herself against him, grateful for his closeness. Neither of them spoke. Time passed; how much, she was not sure. Her thoughts and emotions were a jumble.

"Rowan?"

He was back, but this time she sensed he was not alone.

"I hear you, Charles, and I know you're there too, Eleanor."

"Charles has explained your concerns, Rowan," she replied.

Rowan could not help herself. "What you ask is unfair."

"It was also unfair to bring this into our world and risk the lives of so many innocent souls. Yet, this is the position that we find ourselves in."

"It's not like I deliberately asked for any of this, Eleanor."

This time she accepted him as his energy connected with hers. "Rowan, please. You need to hear this."

She heaved a sigh. "I'm sorry. But surely you can understand why I am not happy about this. Roark's life is of value too."

He acknowledged her apology with an embrace, the warmth of his love and concern soothing the guilt of her earlier rejection.

"Listen to her," he whispered, pulling his energy back. She sensed a shift and Eleanor's authority step forward.

"You forget that I have connected with Roark's energy. I am aware of his value and I do not request this lightly. What you do not realise yet, as you are clouded by your emotions, is the sheer depth of his strength and power. It is not to be underestimated. Neither, Rowan, is yours. The impossible has been made possible. A dragon has returned to our world, and with it, the rising of a dragon guardian. You shall therefore go with Roark and destroy the creature."

Rowan sensed his shock. "Absolutely not, Eleanor. That is not what we discussed."

"Charles!" Eleanor warned him.

She ignored the unspoken exchange between them both as Eleanor's last words echoed in her ears. "Wait, rewind. You want me to go with Roark?"

"Yes," Eleanor replied.

Charles remained quiet as she quickly stood to her feet. Ignoring Albion's confused expression, she flicked her gaze across to Roark.

"What have they said?" Roark asked.

"They? You sensed her?"

"I felt the witch return, yes."

"Just give me a minute, Roark. I need to find out more, but the main headline is they want me to go with you."

She watched Albion flinch as Roark let out a growl. "The witch is deranged. Finn would be furious if I agreed to that."

"Well Finn isn't here, and it's my decision."

"What in the blazes is going on with you two?" Albion demanded, jumping up and down.

She felt a pang of guilt as she deliberately ignored him, directing her attention back to Eleanor. "What is it you expect me to do, Eleanor?"

"Believe, Rowan, is all I need you to do. You are the Guardian, a dragon rider. You must believe in the strength of your bond, its light. When the time comes, you will know what to do."

"What is that supposed to mean?"

No response.

"Eleanor? Charles?"

No response.

Throwing her arms in the air, she stalked to the edge of the cliff and released a steady stream of expletives.

"Feel better?" Roark asked when she had finally run out of steam.

"Will someone please tell me what is going on," Albion shouted, stomping his feet.

Roark rolled his eyes. "It would seem that Rowan and I are to fight the Abaddon."

Albion's face turned a deeper shade of red. "Are you crazy? Miss Rowan, you cannot. Master Finn would be furious!"

"Master Finn isn't here," she snapped, instantly regretting her words as Albion stared at the ground, his shoulders hunched. Guilt knocked the last of the wind out of her sails, leaving her exhausted. "I'm sorry, Albion, but this is something that Roark and I have to do."

As she flicked her gaze across to Roark, his expression told her all that she needed to know. She smiled.

"It's madness."

"That may be, Albion, but the decision has been made."

"Then I shall come with you, too."

"No, Albion, I need you to stay here. If this does not end well and we do not return, I need you to find Finn for me. Tell him that I love him and that he must promise to take care of my mum and Jake."

Albion's voice broke. "Please don't let it come to that."

She dabbed at her eyes with her sleeve. "I'll try."

He sniffed. "I'll find some firewood, have a camp ready for when you return."

He did not wait for a response.

"Who knew dwarfs were so sensitive?" Roark commented once they were alone. "Are you ready?"

Taking a deep breath, she nodded.

Rising to his feet, he gently cupped her in his claws and placed her onto his back. She laid her head against his glistening scales.

"Let's do this." she whispered.

"Together," he replied, unfolding his wings and raising them into the sky.

Chapter Twenty-Three

Rowan

Outskirts of York, England
O   The unearthly howls and shrieks of the Abaddon echoing through the forest turned Rowan's blood to ice. Trees snapped like matchsticks under the abomination's relentless rampage, their trunks toppling with groans of splintering wood. The very earth seemed to shudder in revulsion at the creature's presence. All around, the denizens of the forest scattered in absolute terror, their frantic rustling and skittering adding to the cacophony.

A putrid stench wafted up to where Rowan clung to Roark's back, so foul it seared her throat and made her gag. She swallowed hard against the rising gorge. "I'd forgotten how bad that thing smelled."

"Be grateful you only have tiny nostrils," Roark growled as he climbed higher, wings beating powerfully. The rancid odour slowly dissipated as they gained altitude.

Banking into a hover, the dragon craned his neck to look back at her, pale eyes glinting in the afternoon sun. "Do you have a plan?"

Rowan was silent for a long moment, her mind racing as she listened to the cacophony of horror echoing from the shadowed forest canopy far below. The snap and crash of the Abaddon's brutal passage, the discordant symphony of destruction. Finally, she spoke, her words grim. "I do, but you're not going to like it much."

"I do not like any of this much," Roark rumbled, "but the Lightkeepers have tasked us with stopping this abomination before it can slaughter more innocents. What did you have in mind?"

"We need to bait the Abaddon. Draw it out of the forest and onto the bridge."

"Then what?"

She blew out a shaky breath. "That's as far as I got. We'll have to make the rest up as we go along. But I'm figuring dragon fire would be a start."

Roark snorted, a puff of smoke jetting from his nostrils. "You're right, I do not like it. But seeing as we have little choice, I will go along with it." He shifted restlessly beneath her, muscles coiling like steel springs. "Are you ready?"

Rowan squeezed her eyes shut, heart pounding a desperate tattoo against her ribs. Unbidden, thoughts of the innocent life the Abaddon had already claimed flashed through her mind. Of the devastation it would wreak if it reached the city. Anger and determination crystalized the fear in her gut to diamond hardness.

"As I'll ever be," she said, voice hard as flint. Her hair whipped about her face in the wind of their passage, having long since torn free of its confines.

"Then hang on!" Roark roared.

The bottom dropped out of Rowan's stomach as the dragon folded his wings and plummeted into a precipitous dive. Icy wind tore at her hair and clothes, stinging her face and stealing her breath as they hurtled downwards. The treetops rushed up to meet them in a dizzying swirl of green and brown. At the last possible second, Roark snapped his wings out, catching the air and levelling their flight.

The thick, foetid stench of the Abaddon clogged Rowan's nostrils, leaving an oily coating on her tongue. They skimmed just above the forest canopy, so close she could feel the lash of leaves against her legs. Roark's spiked tail sliced through the upper branches like a scythe, leaving a trail of shattered limbs in their wake.

An eerie quiet descended over the forest below, the sudden absence of crashing and shrieking more unnerving than the cacophony that had preceded it. Neither Rowan nor Roark were fooled by the seeming tranquillity. Lips peeling back from dagger-like teeth, the dragon summoned a challenging bellow from the depths of his massive chest. The roar shook the air like thunder as he angled their flight towards the stone bridge spanning the gorge ahead.

The Abaddon's answer came swiftly: a piercing, ululating wail that scraped like nails down the spine and set the primal lizard-brain gibbering in horror.

A splintering crash from directly behind made Rowan whip her head around, heart leaping into her throat. The sound was terrifyingly close, the shockwave of the impact palpable. She stared in mute dismay as another massive tree toppled, reduced to kindling by the creature's passage. It was gaining on them far faster than she'd anticipated.

"I'm not sure this was such a good idea," she yelled over the rushing wind.

"Too late now," Roark snarled, pumping his wings harder. The strain showed in the quivering of his flight muscles and the laboured rasp of his breathing.

Rowan cast another desperate glance over her shoulder at the trail of destruction cutting through the forest behind them like a festering wound. "Can't you fly any faster?"

"I'm a dragon, not a jet engine," Roark snapped, voice tight with effort and annoyance.

"Roark, if you don't shift that scaly arse of yours, we're both going to be Abaddon kibble!"

"Kibble?" he growled, the single word dripping with draconic indignation. But he redoubled his efforts, the rhythmic clap of his wings pummelling the air.

Despite the deadly gravity of their situation, a slightly hysterical giggle burst from Rowan's lips. "Well, at least you're moving quicker now."

"Perhaps you'd like to jump off," Roark shot back acidly. "Then I'll move a lot faster."

A blood-curdling screech from below was their only warning. Rowan screamed, fingers scrabbling frantically for purchase on Roark's scales as he wrenched them into a desperate corkscrew roll. A cruelly barbed limb punched through the canopy where they'd been a mere heartbeat before, sending an explosion of splintered wood raining down.

"It's directly below us!" Rowan cried, her eyes huge with terror. She cringed back against Roark's neck as another nightmarish appendage struck out at them like a spear, the wind of its passage ruffling her hair.

"Will you be quiet and let me think?!" Roark roared. He grunted in pain as the tip of the Abaddon's flailing limb caught him along his flank, leaving a weeping gash in the iridescent scales.

Roark surged higher with a laboured beat of his wings, fighting to put distance between them and the horror crashing along below. "It grazed my hide," he panted, "but otherwise I'm alright."

Rowan bit her lip hard, tasting copper as she stared down into the violently churning sea of leaves. The Abaddon seemed to boil up from the depths of the forest itself, a seething mass of limbs and teeth and insatiable hunger. It thrust multiple appendages up through the canopy, groping and stabbing blindly as it searched for its prey.

"How many bloody legs does that thing have?" Rowan breathed, nausea rising in her gorge.

"Enough to ensure we do not outrun it," Roark said grimly. A shudder rippled down his sinuous length from snout to tail-tip. "We need to rethink this, Rowan."

She swallowed hard, trying to push down her fear. The bridge was tantalisingly close now, the weathered stone just visible through the thinning tree line ahead. "It's not much farther," she said, injecting more confidence into her voice than she felt. "We're almost there."

"We need to slow it down," Roark growled.

"How? You can't use your fire, the whole blasted forest will go up in flames!"

"I have a plan," the dragon rumbled, "but you're not going to like it."

Despite herself, Rowan barked a harsh laugh devoid of humour. "Now who's being funny?"

"I apologise," Roark said, suddenly contrite. He took a deep, shuddering breath, the exhalation gusting hot over Rowan's face and stirring her hair. "This is what I propose: I will engage the creature on the ground and remove some of its limbs. You must take that opportunity to fly to the bridge. I will follow, and the Abaddon will follow me."

Rowan's stomach turned to lead, horror rising in a strangling tide. "You want to FIGHT that thing? Are you insane?"

"Have you a better idea?" Roark demanded.

She opened her mouth. Closed it again. Glared at the back of his horned head in furious, terrified silence.

"I thought not," he said flatly.

Rowan shook her head hard, sending her hair flying. Rage bubbled up to mingle with the fear, burning through her veins like acid. "And what if that thing injures you? Or worse, kills you? What then, you overgrown lizard?"

"Then you will do what must be done," Roark said simply. An awful finality undergirded his words, immovable as the bones of the earth. "You must prepare yourself, Rowan. It's happening now."

And with those words, the dragon folded his wings and dove, angling his flight in a precipitous embankment. Rowan's shrieks of protest were lost to the rushing wind as they hurtled downwards, the forest canopy rising to meet them with horrifying speed. At the last possible second, Roark flung his wings out, catching the air and levelling their descent.

They struck the ground with a bone-jarring impact, Roark's talons gouging deep furrows in the earth as he skidded to a halt amidst a storm of torn leaves and broken branches. The dragon hunched low to allow Rowan to slide from his back. She stumbled away on watery legs, breath coming harsh and fast.

"Run," Roark snarled, the basso rumble of his voice making her very bones quake. His eyes blazed like molten gold, pupils slitted to razored black lines. Rowan stared at him for a long, awful moment, heart cracking behind her ribs. Then she turned and fled into the waiting trees, Roark's parting roar chasing her heels.

Thorny undergrowth snatched at her legs as she crashed through the forest, heedless of direction save for the imperative to move, to put distance between herself and the sounds of rending scale and shrieking monster at her back. Fear turned the world syrupy slow and preternaturally sharp, every gasping breath, and rabbit-thump of her pulse magnified.

Distantly, through the haze of exhausted terror, Rowan felt for her connection to the dragon. Perhaps she could use his sight to navigate the gloom, see what he saw. Desperately, she tried to cast her mind out as she ran, to form the connection required. But there was only the ragged tatter of her own thoughts skittering uselessly in her skull.

"Roark, can you hear me?" she screamed into the void, into the horrible empty spaces between the trees and inside her own head where his presence should be.

And then, like a key turning in a lock, like a circuit completing, something snapped into place. Her dragon. His voice, resonant and achingly familiar, filled her mind: "I am with you, Rowan. I am always with you."

The trees fell away, and suddenly she stood in a clearing dappled with fading daylight. At its centre, the Abaddon reared up in all its putrid, skittering horror, a mass of limbs and teeth and insatiable hunger. And before it, wings mantled and jaws gaping in challenge, stood Roark.

The dragon seemed to glow from within, his scales limned in shimmering opalescence. As Rowan watched in breathless awe, he lunged forward, faster than anything that large had a right to move. Talons flashed, and a gout of foul ichor sprayed the air as Roark ripped one of the Abaddon's limbs away in a shriek of sundered chitin.

The creature screamed, the sound like shattered glass dragged over exposed nerves. It skittered backwards on its remaining legs, its movements jerky and uncoordinated. Roark pressed his advantage, lashing out with teeth and claws in a whirlwind of iridescent scales and fury.

But the Abaddon was far from defeated. With blurring speed, it struck like a snake, its barbed tail whipping around to catch Roark across his bleeding flank. The dragon roared in pain, the sound like rending metal, as poison sizzled and smoked against his hide.

"Feel me with you," Rowan whispered desperately, clenching hands into fists. "Feel my strength."

And somehow, impossibly, he did. Roark surged to his feet with a Herculean effort, his movements steadying. Slit-pupil eyes met Rowan's across the ravaged clearing, and in that moment, they were one mind, one heart, one soul.

Dragon and Rider, bound by something far deeper than mere flesh and bone.

Together, they turned to face the horror that crouched before them, its remaining legs scrabbling at the earth and its tail lashing the air. Roark reared back, chest swelling with impossible breath. And when he roared, when he unleashed the maelstrom within, the Abaddon burned.

Later, Rowan would remember only fragments - the flash of dragon fire painting the afternoon crimson and gold, the stench of charred chitin and roasted meat, the Abaddon's final, agonised wail spiralling into the uncaring sky.

But in that moment, as the flames died, and the echoes faded and the creature that had haunted them lay smoking and still, none of it mattered. Because Roark was limping towards her, broken and bloodied but alive, gloriously alive, and nothing else existed save the space between them.

Exhaustion and relief and a soul-deep weariness turned Rowan's legs to water. She sank to her knees in the churned earth, heedless of the blood and muck, and buried her face in the warm, solid scales of her dragon's neck. The tears came then, hot and cleansing, and she let them fall unhindered as great, shuddering sobs wracked her narrow frame.

"It's over," Roark rumbled, his voice a soothing bass thrum that she felt in her bones. "We did it, Rowan. We won."

She managed a watery laugh, lifting her head to meet his luminous gaze. Dried blood crusted her temple and ran into her eyebrow, pulling the skin tight. "I think I'm going to be sick," she said, only half-joking. "That thing smelled even worse cooked."

Roark huffed a laugh, a puff of smoke curling from his nostrils. "Be grateful your nose is so small, then." He cast a critical eye over her, taking in the rips in her clothes, the scratches marring her skin. "You're hurt."

Rowan reached up to touch the wound on her brow, wincing as her fingers came away sticky with half-dried blood. "It's just a scratch. I'll live." She eyed the gash in his side, still weeping sluggish rivulets of crimson. "You, on the other hand... We need to get you someplace safe, get that looked at."

"It will heal," Roark said dismissively. He shifted his weight gingerly, favouring his injured leg. "I've endured worse."

"Not on my watch, you stubborn beast," Rowan said, hauling herself to her feet. The world swayed alarmingly, and she swallowed hard against a surge of nausea. "Come on. Let's get out of here before something else decides we look like a tasty snack."

"You have a plan, I assume?" Roark asked, a hint of weary amusement in his voice.

Rowan managed a smile, swiping at her filthy, tear-streaked face with an equally filthy hand. "I do, as a matter of fact." She took a shaky breath, steeling herself. "We return and tell the Lightkeepers the deed is done, and the Abaddon will terrorise the innocent no more."

Roark inclined his great head, eyes gleaming with fierce approval. "I am with you," he said simply. An oath, a vow, a promise. "Always."

As the sun dipped towards the horizon, painting the sky in a riot of orange and pink, Rowan, and Roark winged their way back to the clifftop where they'd left Albion. The cool evening air felt blessedly soothing against Rowan's skin after the foetid heat of the Abaddon's pursuit, and she closed her eyes for a moment, savouring the sensation.

Roark landed with a soft thump on the rocky outcropping, folding his wings neatly along his sides. Albion was waiting for them, a small fire crackling merrily at his feet. The tantalising aroma of roasting meat made Rowan's stomach rumble, reminding her sharply of how long it had been since she'd last eaten.

"I thought you might be hungry," Albion said by way of greeting, his weathered face creasing into a smile beneath his bushy beard. He gestured to a makeshift spit over the flames, where several skewers of meat sizzled and popped. "It's not much, but it should take the edge off."

Rowan slid down from Roark's back, her legs wobbling slightly as they took her weight. "Albion, you're a saint," she said fervently, moving to warm her hands over the fire.

The dwarf chuckled, passing her a skewer. "Hardly that, my dear. Just practical." His keen eyes raked over her, taking in the rips in her clothing, the dried blood matting her hair. "You look like you've been through the wars."

Rowan huffed a laugh, tearing into the meat with gusto. "You could say that," she mumbled around a mouthful. She swallowed, then sobered. "The Abaddon is dead. It won't be threatening any more innocents."

Albion let out a low whistle. "That's no mean feat," he said, respect and a hint of awe colouring his tone. "Well done, the both of you."

Roark rumbled deep in his chest, a sound of weary satisfaction. "It was a near thing," he said, settling himself near the fire. "The beast was... formidable."

"But you were better," Rowan said firmly, reaching out to lay a hand on the dragon's flank. Roark leaned into the touch, a silent acknowledgement of the bond they shared.

For a few minutes, there was no sound save the crackle of the flames and the distant calls of night birds as Rowan devoured the contents of several skewers. But as the last light faded from the sky and the stars began to wink into existence overhead, a new urgency thrummed through her veins.

"We need to get back to Finn," she said abruptly, tossing the stripped skewer into the fire. "He'll be worried sick."

Roark raised his head, pale eyes glinting in the firelight. "You need rest, Rowan," he rumbled, a note of warning in his voice. "You're exhausted, and those wounds need tending."

She shook her head stubbornly, rising to her feet. "I'll rest later. Right now, I need to see Finn. I need to know he's alright.

The dragon heaved a sigh, smoke curling from his nostrils. "Very well. But don't say I didn't warn you."

Rowan turned to Albion, apology in her eyes. "I'm sorry to eat and run," she began, but the dwarf waved her off.

"Nonsense," he said briskly. "You've done a great thing today. Let's go find your young man."

"You'll ride on the dragon?"

"Yes; for you, I will." Albion replied.

Rowan managed a smile, reaching out to clasp Albion's rough hand in her own. "Thank you," she said simply.

Albion harrumphed, but there was a telltale glimmer in his eye. "You behave yourself, now," he warned.

Roark snorted, lowering his head to allow Rowan and Albion to clamber onto his back. "You should be honoured, dwarf," he said, a thread of amusement running through his voice. "It's not every day a Rumpelstiltskin such as yourself gets to ride a dragon."

Albion humphed, settling himself behind Rowan. "Just keep the fancy aerial acrobatics to a minimum, eh? Some of us aren't built for loop-the-loops."

Roark's rumbling laughter shook them as he spread his wings and leapt skyward, powerful strokes carrying them rapidly away from the cliff and out over the forest.

The flight back to Finn passed in a blur for Rowan, her mind consumed with a whirlwind of emotions. Relief that the Abaddon was dead warred with anxiety over Finn's welfare. Anticipation at seeing him again mingled with a sudden, shyness. Would he be angry that she'd risked herself so recklessly? Would things be different between them, after everything that had happened?

All too soon, and yet not quickly enough, Roark was spiralling down towards a small clearing nestled amongst the trees. As the dragon back winged to a landing, stirring up a cloud of leaves, Rowan could make out a small campfire burning, two figures silhouetted against the flickering light.

Her heart leapt into her throat as one of the shadows detached itself and came running towards them, a painfully familiar voice calling her name.

"Rowan!"

She was off Roark's back and running before the dragon had even fully touched down, exhaustion forgotten in the overwhelming need to close the distance between herself and Finn. They crashed together in a tangle of limbs, Finn's arms coming around her like bands of iron as he crushed her to his chest.

For a long moment, they simply clung to each other, Rowan's face buried in the crook of Finn's neck as she breathed him in. He smelled of wood smoke and sweat and something uniquely him, a scent that meant safety and home.

Finally, Finn pulled back just far enough to cup her face in his hands, his eyes raking over her features as if he could hardly believe she was real. "Are you alright?" he asked urgently, thumbs stroking over her cheekbones.

Rowan managed a watery smile, her hands fisting in the fabric of his shirt. "I'm fine," she assured him, leaning into his touch.

Finn's gaze hardened, a muscle ticking in his jaw. "You went after it, didn't you? The Abaddon. You and Roark."

Rowan looked at Roark. "Snitch," she hissed. Finn stood with his hands on his hips, his face awash with fury and concern. She bit her lip, in the face of his intensity. "We did," she said. "But we didn't have a choice, Finn. It had already killed, and if we hadn't stopped it..."

"You could have died!" Finn burst out, his hands tightening on her shoulders. "Rowan, when I think of what could have happened, I..." He broke off, throat working as he visibly struggled for control.

"But I didn't," Rowan said firmly, reaching up to cradle his face in her palms. "I'm here, Finn. I'm right here, and I'm not going anywhere."

They were interrupted by a pointed clearing of a throat. Mortimus stood nearby, a knowing look on his weathered face. "Much as I hate to intrude," the old man said, eyes twinkling, "perhaps Master Finn could heal our dragon? He looks fit to drop, and I don't particularly relish the thought of spending the night under a giant lizard."

Rowan felt her cheeks heat. "Of course," she said.

Roark released a long sigh as the healing orb set to work. Once he was settled, Finn steered Rowan towards the campfire.

As they settled themselves close to the crackling flames, he drew her hand into his lap, examining the myriad cuts and scrapes that marred her skin with a critical eye. "Let me," he murmured, holding his other hand palm up. Another glowing sphere appeared and coalesced just above his skin, pulsing gently.

Rowan watched, fascinated, as Finn passed the orb over her injuries, the energy sinking into her flesh with a pleasant, tingling warmth. Everywhere it touched, her hurts faded, leaving unblemished skin in its wake.

"That's amazing," she breathed, flexing her newly healed fingers. "Thank you."

Finn smiled, the glow of the orb casting his features into sharp relief. "I couldn't do anything about the Abaddon," he said softly, "but I can do this, at least."

Across the fire, Mortimus harrumphed. "I'd say you two have done quite enough for one day," he said, but there was no censure in his voice, only a gruff sort of pride.

Rowan glanced over at the old man, taking in the deep lines graven into his face, the wild thatch of white hair, the keen intelligence sparking in his rheumy eyes. In that short time, Mortimus, as too Albion, held a special place in her heart. Mortimus, a grandfatherly figure full of wisdom and dry wit, a steadfast ally in their quest to save Bessie.

"I don't know what we would have done without you, both," she said impulsively. "Truly. Thank you, for everything."

Roark rolled his eyes as Albion blushed with pride.

Mortimus smiled. "Ah, you'd have managed," he said with a wink. "You two are made of sterner stuff than most. Though I dare say our timely advice and dashing good looks didn't hurt matters, eh?"

Finn barked a laugh. "And your modesty, old man, don't forget that."

Rowan shook her head, a bemused smile tugged at her lips. So much had changed in such a short span of time: the world, her understanding of it, and her place within it. But there were constants, too, she was coming to realise. The steady presence of her companions, the strength of the bonds they'd forged. The power of love, in all its myriad forms.

Finn's arm slipped around her shoulders, drawing her close against the solid warmth of his side. "We should try to get some sleep," he murmured, lips brushing her temple.

"Dawn will be here before we know it, and we still have to find Bessie."

Chapter Twenty-Four

Kane

Outskirts of York, England

O Kane's eyes blazed with barely-contained fury as he watched the Abaddon lumber after Finn into the dense forest, branches snapping under its immense weight. The sound echoed through the trees, a cacophony of destruction that sent birds scattering from their perches in a flurry of wings and panicked cries.

His jaw clenched, and a muscle twitched in his cheek, as the bitter realisation sank in. The girl called Rowan and the dragon had slipped through his grasp. The knowledge sat like a lead weight in his gut, a failure he could barely stomach.

The loss of two of his Fallen to the creature had only added insult to injury, a stinging reminder of his own hubris. He had paid the price.

But even as the anger coursed through his veins, Kane forced himself to focus, and to push aside the rage. He needed to think clearly, and could not afford to let his emotions cloud his judgement; not now, not when so much hung in the balance.

Reaching out with his mind, Kane attempted to connect with the Abaddon and determine if it had successfully tracked and eliminated the tracker, Finn. But there was only a void, a deafening silence where the creature's presence should be. Kane's eyes widened momentarily, a flicker of uncertainty passing over his features as the truth sank in. He truly had no control over the monstrosity he had summoned. A low, guttural growl escaped his throat, a rage that simmered just beneath the surface.

But dwelling on this miscalculation was a luxury he could not afford. The human world, with all its trivial concerns and fragile inhabitants, meant nothing to him. It was only the promise of delivering the girl and the dragon to the Master upon their return through the portal that consumed his thoughts. The weight of his failure bore down on his shoulders like a suffocating burden.

Kane turned to Barrock, his voice low and commanding, his tone leaving no room for argument. "Finn's fate is of no consequence. But the girl and the dragon must be retrieved at all costs. Failure is not an option. We have until sunset tomorrow to bring them to heel. Regroup to the forest; have Symiar prepare my quarters."

The urgency in his voice was a tangible force that hung heavy in the air. Barrock nodded in grim understanding, his expression hardened with renewed determination.

As they melted into the shadowy depths of the forest, Symiar began erecting the tented quarters and all its luxurious furnishings with his usual practised efficiency.

Inside the tent, Kane sat at the table, his fingers steepled before him, his mind churning with dark thoughts and sinister machinations. Rivik entered, his head bowed in deference, a tension crackling between them. Kane's piercing gaze met Rivik's, a silent challenge hanging in the air. "We cannot return empty-handed," Kane said, his voice a low, menacing whisper. "We need to change our approach."

Kane commanded Hymorious' table to manifest an item of the girl's clothing that Mendip had previously brought to him. He closed his eyes, delving deep into his Nyrvallia gifts. The ancient power coursed through his veins. Reaching out, tendrils of his consciousness snaked through the ether, seeking Rowan's mind. Images flooded his thoughts. Memories of Rowan and her brother Jake, their laughter echoing through his skull; moments shared with her best friend Jennifer. The warmth of their bond seared his very soul. And the three of them together, their camaraderie sickening to his palate.

A low, malevolent smile spread across Kane's face as an idea took root. A twisted plan blossomed in the darkest recess of his mind. His eyes snapped open, locking onto Rivik's with a frightening intensity. "We return to where we first entered this world. We will capture her friend and brother, use them as leverage to lure the girl to us," he declared, his voice dripped with sadistic anticipation.

Rivik's eyes glinted with understanding. A cruel smile tugged at the corners of his lips. "The Fallen have rested, Commander. The afternoon grows darker, the sun hidden behind overcast skies. We should act swiftly," he urged, a hunger for violence simmering just beneath the surface.

Kane rose from his seat, his movements fluid and purposeful, a coiled serpent ready to strike. "Agreed," he declared. "Break camp and gather the others. We move out at once."

Mounting Rivik's back, Kane led the Fallen through the shadows, his mind consumed by the sinister plan unfolding before him. They emerged at the new coordinates as the sun began its descent, painting the sky in hues of blood red and ominous orange.

From their concealed vantage point, Kane watched as the one he knew to be Jennifer and a strange man exited her home, making their way towards the local tavern. His lips curved into a predatory smile. A twisted sense of anticipation thrummed through his veins, his dark heart pounded with excitement. Even at a distance, Jennifer moved with an eye-catching grace, her long hair tumbling down her back in glossy waves. Kane could sense the vibrant energy radiating from her, a tantalising draw he could not resist.

As the couple disappeared into the tavern, Kane turned to his companions, his eyes gleaming with excitement and a steely resolve. "The game begins now," he said, his voice a low, conspiratorial murmur. "Remember, tread carefully. Trust and loyalty are earned through cunning and persuasion, not brute force. Rivik, you will accompany me inside, but remain in the shadows. The others will remain hidden, outside, and be ready to strike at a moment's notice," he instructed, his voice a low, menacing whisper.

Rivik nodded, a cruel smile played on his lips. "As you command, Commander," he replied, a perverse sense of eagerness evident in his tone.

Kane entered the tavern, and was immediately assaulted by the clamour of voices, and the thick scent of ale and sweat mingling. His eyes scanned the room, searching for his quarry. And then he saw her, illuminated by candlelight in the far corner: a vision of loveliness that shockingly stole his breath.

Up close, Jennifer was even more stunning, her delicate features and sparkling eyes an alluring siren song. Kane watched, transfixed, as she laughed at something her companion said, her melodic voice rising above the tavern's din like a bell.

As if feeling the weight of his gaze, Jennifer glanced up. Her eyes locked with Kane's across the crowded room. In that moment, the air seemed to crackle with an inexplicable energy, a magnetic pull he could feel in his bones.

Kane made his way to the couple's table. A charming smile played about his lips. He moved with a feline grace that drew every female eye, his presence commanding attention even as he tried to blend in. Rivik had already evaporated into the shadows, unseen to anyone other than Kane.

"Pardon the intrusion," he said smoothly, his voice a rich, velvety purr. "I couldn't help but notice you from across the room. I'm Kane."

A becoming blush stained Jennifer's cheeks as she took him in. He sensed her pulse fluttering wildly in her throat. Everything about him clearly thrilled and unnerved her. His chiselled good looks and the dangerous air that clung to him like a second skin, he knew no woman could resist.

"Jennifer, although my friends call me Jen," she replied softly. "And this is Simon."

Rivik watched intently, a glimmer of amusement danced in his eyes, as Kane slipped into the booth beside the girl. In one swift motion, he pulled her into his arms. His mouth claimed hers in a hungry, possessive kiss before she could utter a word of protest. The anger emanating from her lover only spurned Kane on, a twisted sense of satisfaction coursing through his veins.

As Kane pulled away, he flashed a slow, lascivious smile at the girl, revelling in her wide-eyed shock and the way she turned to her lover, shaking her head in a futile attempt to defuse the situation. But it was too late, as the fuse has been lit, and the explosion was imminent.

Simon leapt to his feet, murder blazing in his eyes as he grabbed Kane by the collar, his face contorted with rage. Temper slithered in the pit of Kane's stomach, a venomous serpent ready to strike at the sheer audacity of this pitiful creature who dared to challenge his superiority.

Rivik tensed, his muscles coiled and ready to spring into action at a moment's notice. Kane, however, remained calm, a cruel smile on his lips as he met Simon's furious gaze with a chilling intensity.

"Simon, no," Jen warned as he pulled back his fist, ready to deliver a blow. Kane felt a rush of adrenaline surging through his veins, a twisted sense of anticipation that built in his chest. But the strike never came. Instead, a pair of large hands grabbed Simon from behind, dragging him away from the table.

"Not in here, you don't. Get out now. You too, arsehole," a gruff voice commanded, the authority in his tone unmistakable.

Kane's eyes flicked to the newcomer, a large, heavyset man with a shaved head and a broken front tooth. He had Simon by the scruff of his neck, holding him in a vice-like grip. Kane decided to let the insult slide, too amused by Simon's pathetic struggles to break free.

Turning his attention back to the girl, Kane fixed her with a commanding gaze. "Come with me now," he ordered, his voice low and imperious.

Jen stood. She grabbed her coat and bag, helpless to resist the power of Kane's will. A smile tugged at the corners of his lips as he revelled in her subservience. The intoxicating rush of control flooded his senses.

The heavyset man escorted them outside, his eyes narrowed as he assessed the situation. "Are you okay, Jen?" he asked, the concern evident in his gruff tone.

Kane's eyes bored into Jen's, holding her captive within his penetrating gaze. She was powerless to break free. Her voice trembled as she stammered, "I'm fine, Stan."

Stan's gaze shifted between the three of them, suspicion and unease etched into the lines of his face. "You start anything out here, and the police will bang the lot of you up. Gav's already called them," he warned, his voice low and menacing. Turning to Jen, his expression softened slightly. "If you have any sense, you'll ditch both these losers and go home. If you come back in, Jen, I'll get you a taxi."

But Jen was lost, trapped within the web of Kane's influence. "It's fine, Stan. I have a ride home sorted," she assured him, her words sounding hollow.

Pleased by her response, Kane reached out and pulled Jen to him, a possessive gesture. She let out a small gasp as he ran his tongue along the sensitive skin of her neck, a twisted promise of the dark delights that awaited her.

Stan shook his head, disappointment, and resignation etched into his features. With a shrug of his shoulders, he admitted defeat. "If you're sure, Jen," he muttered, casting one last wary glance at the two men before retreating into the pub.

As soon as they were alone, Simon whirled around, anger and disbelief burned in his eyes. "So, you're going to go with him? A man you barely know?" he demanded, his voice dripping with contempt.

Kane felt Jen waver beside him, her resolve faltering under the weight of Simon's accusations. He dug his fingers into her side, a sharp, warning pressure that snapped her back to attention. Before she could pull away, his hand travelled to the swell of her breast, his fingers moving in a slow, circular motion that sent bolts of pleasure and pain coursing through her body. She inhaled sharply, her face flushed with a mixture of desire and shame. "Yes," she whispered.

Simon's face contorted with rage and disgust and he launched himself at Jen. Kane moved quickly to seize his hands and twisted him around and away before they could connect with Jen's neck. He sent her stumbling backwards in the process as Simon yelled for release. "I don't like my women spoiled," Kane snarled, his voice low and dangerous.

Jen watched in horror at the agony on her boyfriend's face. A scream tore from his throat.

"Simon!" she gasped, her eyes wide with shock and disbelief.

Simon's legs buckled beneath him, and he sank to the ground, his body wracked with pain. Kane leaned in close, a cruel chuckle escaping his lips as he tightened his grip. The satisfying snap of bones echoed in the night air.

"Simon," he repeated, his voice dripping with mockery. "You're no match for me."

Jen turned to Kane, desperation etched into her features. "Let him go. He's worthless. You know it's you I desire," she pleaded, her voice trembling.

Kane considered her words. His grip never wavered, even as Simon's sobs filled the air. Jen leaned in closer, her lips brushing against Kane's ear as she whispered, "Let him go for me, please. Look at him. He's not worth your time or energy. Save it for me, for us."

For a moment, Kane was caught off-guard. A flicker of confusion passed over his features as a familiar feeling stirred within him. Against his better judgement, he released his grip on Simon, watching as the man crumpled to the ground, cradling his broken hand.

Simon looked up at Kane. Hatred and fear burned in his eyes. "You're a total nutter," he spat, his voice laced with pain and anger.

Kane's gaze narrowed, a dangerous glint in his eyes. "You have no idea what I am," he warned, his voice low and menacing, a promise of untold horrors lurking just beneath the surface.

Stumbling to his feet, Simon turned to Jen. "You really want to bed this creep?" he asked, his voice dripped with contempt.

"Or stay with a spineless insect like you?" Kane retorted. "I can satisfy her in ways you could never imagine."

Simon's eyes flashed with a mixture of fear, anger, and revulsion. "Slag," he spat, the word dripping with venom.

Kane's jaw clenched, as he fought to control his temper in front of the girl. "I suggest you leave now, before I break your other hand or, worse, your neck," he warned.

Simon met his gaze. A flicker of understanding passed between them. With a final, contemptuous glance at Jen, he turned and walked away, his shoulders hunched in defeat.

Un-noticed, Kane locked eyes with the sinister figures lurking in the shadows. He passed a silent command to Barrock who detached from his brethren, with a wicked gleam in his eye. "Deal with him," Kane ordered coldly. "Make sure you leave no trace."

"Of that, you can be sure, Commander," Barrock replied. Flashing his master a savage grin, the Fallen stalked off in pursuit of his prey, a wolfish hunger in his every move. Jen shuddered at the full import of Kane's words, but he drew her close once more, his lips brushing her temple as he whispered soothing words of comfort and reassurance.

"Don't be afraid, my sweet," he crooned, "I would never let any harm befall you."

His body purred in satisfaction as he sensed all her misgivings fade, swept away by the force of his power. As they lost themselves in each other, Rivik materialised from the gloom.

Jen tensed, her fear spiking through her at the sight of this creature not of her world. Kane adjusted his hold, radiating a calming anchor.

"Hush now," he breathed against her hair. "My army means you no harm. He is my most loyal guardian."

Rivik bowed as Kane gently steered her hand to place upon his hideous head. "Do not fear him. He serves me, and his brethren will serve you. Gallo, step forth."

The Fallen obeyed, and lowered itself in front of the human girl.

"Your sworn protector as well."

"But why? I don't understand..."

Kane smiled, a soft, knowing expression. "You are precious to me, Jen, more precious than you know. And there are forces in this world, in the worlds beyond, that would seek to use you against me."

Gathering her hands in his, he held her gaze. The intensity of it made her shiver. "Gallo is here to make certain that no-one, and nothing, can ever come between us. He will be your constant shadow, watchful, vigilant, and utterly dedicated to your safety."

Slowly, hesitantly, Jen nodded. "I trust you," she murmured, reaching for his hand, and squeezing his fingers. "If you say Gallo is my guardian, then I will accept him as such."

At this pronouncement, Gallo inclined his head, a gesture of deference and allegiance. For a long moment, the quiet reigned, heavy with unspoken things.

Finally, Kane stirred, drawing Jen close once more. "The hour grows late," he mused, "and there is much yet to be done. You must return home and make your preparations. Say your goodbyes. We have but a scant few hours before we must be away."

"Away?" she echoed, a thread of anxiety evident in her voice. "Away where?"

A secretive smile tugged at the corner of Kane's mouth. "To your destiny," he said simply. "And mine."

Looking up at him, her eyes shone with a desperate longing. "Why me?" she whispered and wound her arms around his neck, her lips parting, granting him access to the sweet depths of her mouth. As the kiss deepened, something shifted between them. A dark hunger awakened. She responded with a fervour that matched Kane's own, a depravity that sent shockwaves of desire coursing through his body.

Kane broke away, momentarily caught off-guard by the intensity of his own feelings. A fire scorched the pit of his stomach. It was a need he had not felt in longer than he cared to remember, not since the death of...

Jen growled in frustration as he broke away, the realisation dawning.

Her eyes were dark and wild with hunger. "Who are you?" she panted.

Kane screamed in triumph. "Alyssa."

"I... Alyssa...no, Jennifer..." she frowned. "But you're mine...my Kane... you have always been mine...no, wait.... Oh God, what am I saying? I don't understand. What is happening to me?"

Kane took her mouth and silenced her questions. When they finally broke apart, he whispered, "You're awakening. Soon, my love, all will be as it once was."

He snapped his fingers, summoning Gallo to his side. "Escort Jen home. Keep watch over her. See that no trouble befalls her."

Gallo grunted his assent, moving to take up a protective position at Jen's side, though keeping to the shadows.

"A few hours," Kane reminded her gently, tucking an errant strand of hair behind her ear with a ghost of a caress. "That's all the time we can spare. Best use it wisely, my love."

Swallowing hard, Jen nodded. Before she could overthink it or second guess the mad impulse, he brushed a fleeting kiss across her lips, a hint of the passion to come.

She hurried off into the night, Gallo a looming shadow at her heel.

Kane watched until she was swallowed by the darkness. He could still taste her sweetness and feel the warmth of her soft skin. It called to him, and he ached to answer. But not yet. There was strategising to be done.

"Rivik?"

"The girl was to be our bait," the Fallen started. "But now..."

"Now she is mine," Kane finished smoothly. "Jen belongs to me, body and soul. She will be coming with us, a new and valuable addition to our cause."

"But what of our plan?" Rivik pressed, the frustration simmering beneath his implacable exterior.

A wicked gleam sparked in Kane's eye. "Ah, but she is only one piece on the board. Her connection to the girl's brother is still a pressure point we can exploit. One way or another."

Chapter Twenty-Five

Finn

P itlochry, Scotland

Finn jolted awake, heart pounding as sheer panic slammed into his mind.

"Finn! Wake up, right now!" Indigo's voice screamed with frantic urgency.

Rowan stirred sleepily in Finn's arms as he concentrated, opening their telepathic link. Nearby, Mortimus sat up with a startled grunt, his rheumy eyes wide and confused. Albion zipped agitatedly around the old man's head.

"Indigo? What the hell is going on?" Dread prickled over Finn's skin as he braced for the flood of Indigo's memories.

"I... I found Aaron." Indigo's mental voice shook with barely restrained horror. "But what I saw...it's just...I don't think I can find the words... You were right... All hope is gone... He's lost to us."

The vision unfolded like a deranged nightmare tapestry. Aaron's ghostly form shimmered among the twisted trees, weaving strands of inky black magic.

"Mother," the illusion crooned in a sickening mimicry of Aaron's voice. "I need your help. Finn is in trouble. We need you. Please come alone. If the Council of Elders found out that I'd abandoned my quest to help Finn, they would punish us both... please... he's... he's hurt."

Inside the castle walls, Myrialle froze at the sound of his voice through the Shroud, her hazel eyes wide with alarm. She didn't question the strange pull in her gut as she wasted no time in responding to his pleas. With silent practice, she stole past the sentry guards on duty and slipped out of the castle towards the forest.

"Aaron, where are you?" she called out, frantically searching for the son who had left her many seasons ago. "What happened to—"

Her words died as Aaron stepped from the trees, his face twisted in a cruel sneer of revulsion.

"Hello again, mother." He barked a harsh laugh as inky tendrils lashed around Myrialle's slender frame. "Did you miss me?"

Denial and sickening realisation battled across Myrialle's face as she took in the malicious stranger wearing her son's skin. Her eyes blazed with hurt and disbelief before hardening like steel.

"My son ..." Agony laced her voice as she swept her arm out, a wicked sword appearing in a blaze of light. Its blade shimmered with ethereal power. "What darkness has consumed your soul?"

Aaron laughed and produced his own sword, pulling it from thin air as though it had always been there, waiting for the battle to begin.

Myrialle released a heavy sigh and moved into a fighting stance. "If you have truly given yourself to darkness, then you leave me no choice. I will not let you threaten those I love!"

All hell broke loose. Through Indigo's eyes, Finn watched in awe and growing dread as Myrialle flew at Aaron, her sword flashing in a whirling dervish of deadly light. She moved like quicksilver, her feet blurring into afterimages as she spun and leapt, parried, and slashed with inhuman speed and grace.

She fights like a freaking Fae warrior! Finn marvelled through the disbelieving dread. *Where'd she learn killer moves like that?*

The sound of Aaron's teeth drawing back in a feral snarl distracted his musings. He looked on in horror as a sickly blue flame erupted from his brother's free hand in a blinding inferno, lashing towards Myrialle.

Her radiant blade arced through the fire, dispersing the firestorm in a prismatic shower of sparks. But the split-second distraction had cost her.

Aaron flew at Myrialle in a cyclone of slashes and stabs, the wicked blade humming a dissonant note as it sheared the air and bit deep into Myrialle's sword arm. She screamed as the obscene metal seared her flesh, the coppery tang of blood filling the air as smoke rose from the wound.

"I will rip the Shroud's power from you," Aaron vowed, face contorted into a twisted mask of dark bliss and rage. "And then nothing will stand in our way!"

"Aaron, please!" Myrialle gasped out, staggering back as her guard began to crumble beneath the relentless onslaught. "Don't do this!"

But her words fell on deaf ears. With a vicious snarl, Aaron hammered at her defence, bludgeoning through her weakened parries until her sword was finally torn from her grasp.

It clattered among the dead leaves as Myrialle dropped to her knees with a choked cry, clutching at her ravaged arm. Aaron loomed over her, his hand glistening with her blood as he flexed his fingers.

"Enough!" he roared. "Your meddling ends now."

With a violent slashing motion, night-black tendrils burst from the earth, lashing around Myrialle's limbs and torso to wrench her into the air. A strangled scream ripped from her throat as Aaron's free hand curled into a claw, light pulsing between his fingers.

Indigo's view pitched and yawed queasily as the very fabric of reality seemed to shudder. Profane runes blazed to life in the air, hovering and rotating in sinister spirals as they syphoned off Myrialle's life essence in scorching ribbons of shimmering rose-gold. "He's... draining her magic," Indigo rasped, revolted to his core. "Absorbing her power!"

Myrialle's agonised wails crescendoed into a throat-shredding shriek before tapering into weak, rattling gasps, her struggles growing feeble as more and more of her life force was ripped away.

With a final, brutal wrench, the last mote was torn free to vanish down Aaron's gullet. He shuddered as it suffused him, a look of obscene ecstasy contorting his features. As Finn watched in blank, numbed horror, the hideous wounds scoring Aaron's face and arms knit closed, healing completely in a matter of moments.

His expression going cold and pitiless, Aaron flicked his fingers. The shadow bonds released their hold and Myrialle dropped to the blood-soaked earth like a discarded puppet, crumpling into a pathetic heap.

Aaron stooped to snatch up her fallen sword, testing its weight and balance before levelling the razor-sharp tip at her exposed throat with a sneer of dark triumph.

"The seeds you've sown," he intoned with grim finality, "now bear their bitter fruit."

"NO!" Finn's psychic scream choked in his mind as the blade seemed to draw back in slow motion.

Indigo's presence wrenched violently away a split-second before the sword scythed down in a grotesquely efficient blur of silver. The truncated gurgle and the meaty thud that followed painted a vivid enough picture to rend his heart in two.

The vision released him and Finn surfaced with a ragged, anguished sob, instinctively curling himself around Rowan's sleeping form as if to shield her from the horror. Bile seared his throat, and he swallowed convulsively, fighting down the urge to vomit.

"By the saints..." Mortimus breathed, his weathered face ashen. Albion's agitated buzzing took on a sickly, keening note.

"It can't be real!" Finn raged at Indigo, desperate for any thread of doubt to cling to. "Tell me that wasn't real! My mother can't be dead!"

"I'm so sorry, Finn." Indigo's mental voice was leaden with sorrow and regret. "I swear on all that's sacred, every second of that horror show was real. Myrialle fought with the heart and fury of an army, but Aaron's power, that THING possessing him... It was just too much. He bled her dry."

Finn released a low, wounded noise, dull disbelief warring with a sickening, inescapable reality. "The magic," he forced out around the lump of icy dread lodged in his throat. "Tell me it's not true. Tell me that's still—"

"Gone," Indigo cut him off, his voice a lifeless rasp. "The instant Aaron drained Myrialle's essence, I felt the Shroud... SNAP. Like a branch stressed beyond its limits. It's not just weakened, Finn. It's fractured. I can't feel the flow anymore, I can't touch the power. This contact has cost me more than you know." Indigo's mental presence flickered, as if fighting to maintain their link. "The magic that's sustained our realms, the energy that fuels all our gifts... it's been completely severed."

Albion's frantic loops tightened, the dragonfly nearly crashing into the old man's head.

A yawning chasm of despair and panic opened in Finn's chest. "Then it's all real," he whispered, the words leaden on his tongue. "The prophecies of doom, the warnings of the Elders... A world-ending storm is coming. And my own brother, is he its true harbinger?"

"There's no limit to the destruction he and the Master can unleash." Indigo sounded hollow, scraped raw. "Finn, maybe it's best you stay where you are. There is nothing to come back to. Return and you will die, like the rest of us will soon."

The connection abruptly winked out.

Finn jack-knifed upright, yanked back to the cold, horrific reality. His breath expelled in shallow, uneven gasps as he fought to master the wailing tempest of grief and horror shredding his insides. On pure panicked instinct, he reached out with his mind, groping for her familiar presence, only to find a yawning, empty void where Mercadia's essence should be.

He tried again, cursing, and pushing harder, searching for even the barest flicker of her. Nothing. Just a terrible, echoing absence that drove the breath from his lungs and the strength from his limbs.

"No, no, no; this can't be happening," Finn moaned, clutching at his head. But the truth was a noose, tightening around his heart with every passing second.

Heedless of the hour, he shifted his focus and called out again, desperately seeking the ancient, steadying resonance of Elios' psychic signature. But again, there was only crushing, damning silence. The tether was gone.

"Finn, what's happened?" Mortimus asked urgently, reaching out to grasp the younger man's shoulder. Albion settled on Finn's knee, his wings finally stilling.

When Finn brought his attention back to the harsh reality, his eyes opened to reveal Rowan holding his face in her hands, Mortimus, and Albion hovering anxiously at his side.

"What's going on?" Rowan asked, her voice tight with fear.

Roark was watching him closely, and when his mind connected with Finn's, the dragon released a heavy sigh. "I see," was all he could say.

Finn reached for Rowan's hands and lowered them from his face. He turned to include Mortimus and Albion in his haunted gaze.

"Valoria has fallen, my mother is dead, and we need to find Bessantia, now!"

Chapter Twenty-Six
Mercadia

King Gregor's Castle, Elyssia, Universe of Morvantia
In the heart of King Gregor's castle, an emergency council convened in the war room. Elios stood before the King and Mercadia, his weathered face set in lines of grim determination.

"Your Highness," he began, his deep voice resonating through the chamber, "I come bearing news of the utmost importance." He reached into his robes, withdrawing a tattered parchment. "After months of searching, I believe I have at last discovered the location of the Margorian Compass."

King Gregor leant forward in his seat, his eyes widening. "The compass? But I thought all were lost centuries ago, during the Ancient Wars."

Elios nodded and unfurled the parchment to reveal a complex map, riddled with arcane symbols. "Indeed, it was believed that all five compasses were destroyed. But it seems one was stolen away and hidden until the day when its power might be needed again."

He pulled out a small, stained scrap of parchment from his pocket and pointed to a small, intricate symbol in the corner of the map. "And this, this is the key. The sigil that marks the entrance to the catacombs where the compass lies."

Mercadia rose and moved to study the map. She raised an eyebrow at Elios, a question in her eyes. He looked away, a scowl passing over his face. "Don't ask," he muttered. "You don't want to know how far I had to go to to retrieve that bit of parchment from that wretched mouse."

Her lips twitched, but she did not press the issue. Instead, she traced a finger over the twisted lines of the map. "These catacombs... they run beneath the castle itself. But I've never seen any entrance..."

"The door is hidden, concealed by magic." Elios tapped the strange sigil. "Only this symbol, when pressed, will open the way to the tunnels that lead to the compass's resting place."

"Just as well it does not require magic to open it, since..." She could not bring herself to speak the words out loud. The discovery of Myrialle missing and the loss of the connection with the Shroud had been a devastating blow. She did not know how it had happened, but she knew by the empty and sickening ache in her heart that Aaron had followed through on the Master's order and ended his mother's life right under their very noses. If Kyle had been alive, he would have struck her down for all the pain and suffering they had unwittingly brought to his family.

King Gregor stroked his beard, his expression thoughtful. "And with this compass in our possession..."

"We could turn the tide of this war, undo some wrongs," Elios finished grimly. "The Margorian Compasses were crafted to allow their bearers to navigate the currents of time itself. With one in our hands, we could—"

The rest of his words were lost as a deep, bone-shaking BOOM echoed across the castle grounds. The three froze in a split-second of pure, shocked silence that reigned supreme before chaos.

"The Astylliss Cannon!" Mercadia gasped, her face drained of colour. "But that would mean—"

"The Gydgen are on their way." King Gregor surged to his feet, his expression hardening.

As if to punctuate his words, the chamber doors burst open and two soldiers stumbled through, their faces pale and streaked with sweat beneath their helms.

"Your Highness!" the first man gasped, dropping to one knee. "The outer defences have fallen!"

"The Gydgen?"

"No, your Highness, it is the Master's Assassins who have breached the castle walls!"

"Drey Balor leads them," the second soldier added, his voice shaking. "They... they'll be upon us at any moment!"

Mercadia released a moan at the mention of her former love. Her hand flew to her throat. Elios gripped her shoulder. "There's no time," he said urgently. "We must reach the compass before Drey and his forces overrun us completely." He turned to King Gregor, his ancient eyes ablaze. "Your Highness, you must come with us. The compass is our only hope now."

The King hesitated for only a heartbeat before nodding, his jaw set with resolve. "The castle is lost. We must salvage what we can." He strode to the far wall and wrenched aside a tapestry to reveal a hidden panel. "This passage will take us to the lower levels, and the entrance to the catacombs."

Elios had already moved to follow him. "Then let us pray we can reach it before—"

A second, even louder explosion rocked the chamber, showering them with dust and debris. Screams and the clash of steel echoed from beyond the doors, growing louder with each passing second.

"Go, now!" King Gregor barked, shoving Mercadia and Elios through the secret door. To the soldiers, he snapped, "Hold them off for as long as you can. Buy us the time we need."

The men bowed, drawing their swords with shaking hands. "To the last breath, sire."

Mercadia choked back a sob as Elios dragged her through the hidden portal. King Gregor was on their heels. The panel slid shut behind them, plunging them into musty darkness. They moved as quickly as the darkness would allow along the passageway, Elios leading the way. "Quickly," he urged, his voice muffled in the close confines of the passage. Mercadia did her utmost to navigate through the murky and dank blackness as she tried to ignore the ring of steel in the distance. And then from beyond the walls, there came a sound to chill her blood and a sharp, echoing of boots on stone. Drey's call was underscored by the mocking laughter of his fellow Assassins now in pursuit. Mercadia shuddered, bile rising in her throat.

They descended in a tense silence broken only by their heaving breaths and the scuff of their feet on ancient stone. The air grew colder and damper the deeper they delved until their breath misted and their fingers grew numb with the chill.

After what felt like an eternity, the passage bottomed out into a long, low-ceilinged corridor. The walls were slick with moisture and crawling with pale, twisted roots that seemed to writhe in a guttering witch light that had appeared.

"Keep going; they are not far behind," King Gregor whispered. Mercadia now had to slither on her belly, swiping cobwebbed threads from her face and ignoring the sickening squelch under her gown. The twists and turns continued, and she almost released a cry of joy when the ceiling rose, allowing them to pull themselves to their feet. The light was now sufficient to quicken their pace. The Assassins had not given up on their pursuit.

"The entrance should be here," Elios said. He came to a halt before a smooth expanse of wall, indistinguishable from any other save for a small, half-eroded sigil etched at chest height.

Mercadia reached out with trembling fingers to trace its curves, frowning when nothing happened. "How do we open it?"

"Like this." Elios laid his palm flat against the symbol. He took a deep breath, then pressed with all his strength. For a moment nothing happened, and then, with a grinding rumble of shifting stone, the wall pivoted inward to reveal a low, dark aperture.

A gust of stale, tomb-like air washed over them, heavy with the scent of dust and ancient magic. Mercadia gagged and covered her mouth and nose with her sleeve.

Elios peered into the exposed tunnel with a grim frown. "The catacombs. Hurry, we've not a moment to lose."

But before they could take more than a step, a voice rang out behind them. A voice at once familiar and utterly, terribly changed.

"Ah, there you are, my faithless love."

Mercadia's body snapped rigid, her face drained of colour. Slowly, she turned to face... "Drey," she whispered, her voice breaking. His face, once so beloved, was a bone-white mask above the midnight black of his leathers. His eyes blazed with a fervour that bordered on madness.

King Gregor snarled, drawing his own sword, and placing himself between the Assassins and his companions. "You will not harm her, traitor! Not while I still draw breath!

Drey's eyes flicked to the monarch and his lips curled in a sneer. "Bold words, old man. You'll choke on them."

He flicked his wrists and twin daggers appeared in his hands, their edges glinting with a sickly sheen that promised a slow, wasting death to any they cut. "But first, I think we'll have a little sport."

With a hissing cry, the three deadly warriors surged forward, a tide of flashing steel and billowing shadow. At the same moment, Elios seized Mercadia around the waist and hurled her and the map through the open catacomb entrance.

"GO!" he roared. "Find the compass. We cannot let the King fight alone!" He slammed the hidden door shut behind her, sealing himself and King Gregor in the passage.

"NO!" she screamed, scrabbling at the seamless stone, her nails breaking against the unyielding surface. "Elios! Gregor! Please, please, don't..."

From beyond the wall came clashes of steel on steel, the meaty thud of a blade sinking into flesh, and a gurgling cry abruptly cut short. Mercadia sagged against the door, a wordless sob tearing from her throat.

"The compass..." Elios's voice was a thready rasp, muffled and fading. "Mercadia, you must... find the..."

A wet, tearing sound. A scream of pure agony. The sickening crunch of bone.

Then Drey's mocking laughter, awful and triumphant. "Foolish old men. As if you ever had a chance of stopping me." A beat of terrible silence, then, crooning, "Don't weep, my love. You'll join them soon enough."

Mercadia bit down on her fist, fighting back the wail building in her chest. Tears streamed down her face as she forced herself to turn away from the door, from the horror she knew was playing out beyond.

The compass. I must find the compass. I'm the only one left, the only one who can stop this nightmare. I must keep going. I must be strong.

It hurt like nothing she'd ever known, a tearing grief, with the crushing sense of failure. Her love turned to a monster, her dearest friend, and liege butchered before her very eyes... *No!*

She shook her head and viciously, dashed the tears from her eyes. *No, I will not break. Not now. Not when they sacrificed everything to give me this chance.*

Drawing a shuddering breath, Mercadia squared her shoulders and retrieved the map from where it had landed. She memorised the route, every twist, and turn imprinted to her memory, before pocketing it into her tattered robes. With her face set in determination, she strode forward into the waiting dark of the catacombs.

The tunnels seemed to go on forever, a winding labyrinth of narrow passages and crumbling stone. The air was thick and heavy, rancid with the stench of decay and the skitter of unseen vermin in the shadows. More than once, Mercadia had to drop once more to her belly and crawl, the ceiling so low it scraped her back, tearing her robes further and showering her with grave dirt—the pulverised bones of long-dead things.

But she did not stop. She could not stop, not with Drey and his killers so close behind. She could hear them in the distance. Their footsteps and snatches of cold, cruel laughter echoed through the tunnels. It was only a matter of time before they caught her.

Just as she was beginning to despair with the conviction that she'd lost and failed and was now doomed to share Elios's fate, she stumbled into a brightly lit chamber that made her breath catch in her throat.

It was a perfect circle of smooth, bare stone, its walls curving up and in to form a dome high overhead. In the centre of the floor was a shallow depression filled with what looked like quicksilver, its surface as still and unbroken as a mirror.

And there, resting on a plinth of the purest obsidian that rose from the pool... was the compass.

Mercadia's legs nearly gave out at the sight of it. A hysterical little laugh bubbled up in her throat as she stumbled forward, barely daring to believe her eyes.

I found it. I actually found it! Oh Elios, if you could only see...

The thought of her Elder brother sobered her instantly, the grief and urgency crashing back in. Shaking herself, Mercadia stepped to the edge of the pool, squinting against the compass's otherworldly glow.

It looked exactly as described: a disc of some strange, blue-black metal, veined with threads of glimmering silver. Arcane symbols chased around its circumference, pulsing in time to the shimmering light that swirled in its depths like captured starlight.

Mercadia reached for it with trembling fingers... then hesitated, a sudden, dreadful thought striking her. Elios didn't mention guardians. But an artefact this powerful, surely it wouldn't be left unprotected...?

As if in answer to her unspoken question, the surface of the pool exploded upwards in a geyser of freezing, stinging liquid. Mercadia yelped, leaping back as a nightmarish shape burst from the churning quicksilver.

It was massive and easily twice her height, a writhing, serpentine horror of oily black scales and razored fins that glinted like metal in the light. Lamprey jaws gaped in a face that was neither fish nor eel but some awful amalgamation of the two. Milky eyes rolled and teeth gnashed as it lunged for her with terrifying speed.

Mercadia shrieked, throwing herself aside in a desperate bid to evade the nightmare's strike. She felt the wind of its passage, the foetid gust of its breath as its jaws snapped shut a hair's breadth from her face.

"Oh, by the saints," she gasped, scrabbling backwards on hands and knees as the creature reared up above her. Its bulk filled the chamber and blotted out the light. "Elios, you old fool, you might have warned me!"

But Elios was beyond hearing, beyond all aid or comfort. Mercadia was alone, the last of the Elders, facing a horror that was dredged up from the primordial dark. She had no weapon save herself, no allies save desperation, and time—well, time was swiftly bleeding away.

She could hear them drawing ever nearer. The tramp of booted feet, the ring of drawn steel... and beneath it all, Drey's laughter, growing louder, harsher, closer with every hammering beat of her heart.

He's coming. They're coming, these wolves of shadow and spite and twisted ambition, slavering for my blood. And the compass her only hope. If she failed, there would be no-one left to stand against the tide of annihilation except Finn and a girl from another world. And there would be no-one left to mend the unravelling weave of time, no magic that survived, unless Bessantia was still alive and could be returned to their world.

I cannot fail, I cannot, I must not, I—

The monster lunged again. Its jaws seized her arm, and needle teeth crunched through cloth and flesh and into bone. Her mind dripped white with a blinding, shrieking agony. Her feet left the floor as it wrenched her off the ground, shaking her like a rag doll even as her screams ripped the air.

In that moment, as the pain crested, and the world greyed out at the edges of her vision, a strange, crystalline clarity descended. Time seemed to slow, to fracture, the monster's movements turning sluggish and disjointed as Mercadia looked up... and locked eyes with the compass.

It whispered to her, its light pulsing and swelling, tugging at her mind, the remnants of the magic she had previously possessed, the secret core of power that had been gifted to her bloodline by the great ones of before.

With the strength of that whisper filling her, Mercadia no longer felt the teeth in her arm, the venom burning in her veins. She felt only the compass's call, only the sure and certain knowledge of what she must do.

Gritting her teeth against the agony, she fixed her gaze on the artefact and thrust out her free hand, pouring every shred of her will, her desperation, into a single, world-shaking command.

"COME TO ME!"

The words ripped from her throat in a scream that seemed to shatter the very air. For an instant, the universe held its breath...

And the compass leaped from its plinth in a blaze of searing silver light, and smack into Mercadia's palm with bruising force.

At the same instant, an unholy shriek split the air as the monster convulsed, Mercadia's arm still clamped in its jaws. Its coils hammered the floor, the walls, cracking stone and sending geysers of stinging quicksilver spraying in all directions.

Mercadia screamed again as the bones of her arm snapped under the force of the thing's thrashing. But she did not let go of the compass, not even when a particularly violent spasm finally tore her free of the nightmare's jaws and sent her flying across the room to smash into the far wall with bone-breaking force.

She crumpled to the floor in a broken heap, her ravaged arm twisted at a sickening angle, blood sheeting down her side. But the compass was hers, throbbing in her grip like a second heart, and with it clasped tight to her chest, the pain receded to a distant roar.

Slowly, agonisingly, she pushed herself upright, swaying on her knees as she stared down the length of the chamber at her seething, shrieking nemesis.

The monster writhed in the ruins of its pool, ichor geysering from the ruin of its face where the compass's light had seared it to the bone. It seemed diminished somehow, its substance waning as the artefact's power ascended.

But she could spare no thought for the guardian, not now. For beyond the chamber door, drawing ever nearer, she heard the one sound in all the world that could slice through the pain, through the numb haze of her fading strength: Drey's laughter, cruel and exultant.

Even as despair yawned like a bottomless chasm beneath her feet, the compass flared in her hand. Its light washed over her, through her, burning away the cobwebs of confusion and the deadening shroud of defeat.

"No," whispered a voice at the back of her mind, ancient and knowing. "No, child, you are not alone. Never alone, so long as you hold me close."

Fresh strength poured into Mercadia's limbs, chasing away the last of the venom's numbness. With a grunt of effort, she staggered to her feet, cradling her mutilated arm against her chest as her gaze found the door and the inky shadows boiled on its other side. Drawing a deep, shuddering breath, Mercadia closed her eyes and steadied herself. Then, with all the strength and surety of her lineage, of her love and her rage and her adamantine refusal to bend, she slammed her will into the compass and screamed her demand to Morvantia.

"TAKE ME FROM THIS PLACE!"

Power exploded through her like a supernova, whiting out thought. For an instant, she was everywhere and nowhere, then, and now, and everywhere in between. The currents of time lashed around her, tides of might and memory that buffeted her incorporeal form like a leaf in a hurricane. And then she was gone, vanished into the liminal spaces of the universe as if she had never been. In her wake, the chamber lay empty, its guardian dissolving back into the quicksilver depths with a final, rattling hiss.

Seconds later, the door blasted inward in a hail of shattered stone, and Drey stalked through the settling dust, his Assassins fanning out behind him. His eyes raked the room, lingering on the bloodstains marring the floor, the walls, the quicksilver pool... but of Mercadia, of his love and his betrayer, there was no sign.

"Where is she?" he snarled, rounding on the other men with a vicious slash of his hand. "Find her, find her! She can't have gone—"

His gaze fell on the empty plinth where the compass had once rested, and his words died in his throat. For a long, terrible moment he simply stared, realisation and the purest, blackest fury warring across his features.

Then, slowly, awfully, he laughed, a jagged, rending sound like the death of hope itself.

"Oh, my love," he whispered, shaking his head as a smile of utmost cruelty twisted his mouth. "You poor, deluded thing. You think you've won, don't you? You think you've beaten me."

He turned to his accomplices. The shadows writhing at his feet danced to the tune of his rising madness. "But I promise you this, Mercadia: there is nowhere in this world or any other that you can hide from me. Nowhere where my Master's reach does not extend."

His eyes blazed like hellfire as he raised his fist. "I will find you, my faithless love. Find you and break you." He started to laugh again, the sound building and building until it filled the chamber and drowned out all other noise, all other thought.

And in the depthless reaches of time, hurtling through the spaces between heartbeats... Mercadia screamed.

Chapter Twenty-Seven
Kane

Outskirts of Guisborough, England

Kane watched as the Master's form retreated into the flames, his final orders still ringing in his ears. It was time to return home, and whilst Kane was pleased to return and had seemingly been forgiven of his most recent failings, Kane was still beyond frustrated that the Master would not divulge what had turned their hand, resulting in the downfall of the Council of Elders. His time away from the Moren clearly had impeded his own progression and status with the Master. He could only take a small measure of comfort in the knowledge that Rivik had given him, and the advantage this would give in the battle for supremacy.

Kane turned his attention to the Fallen. Their eyes gleamed with a mix of anticipation and unease. Barrock, he noted, gazed at Rivik with a contained aggression as he stood by his side.

Kane smiled to himself as, one by one, the Fallen lowered their heads in deference. All except Barrock, who bared his blood-stained teeth in a snarl as Rivik deliberately did not bow and instead shifted closer to Kane, reinforcing his position as first-in-command.

The tension crackled between the two Fallen, the air growing thick with the intoxicating energy of their rivalry. Kane breathed it in, letting it seep into his pores, savouring the delicious flavour of impending violence.

"Yield," Rivik growled, his skin rippling with the barest hint of the darkness lurking beneath.

Barrock sneered, contempt etched into every line of his cruel face. "You forget your place, mongrel. When we return to our world, I will remind you of it, painfully."

Rivik's eyes flashed, his voice dropping to a lethal purr. "Yield, or I will end you here and now."

"You had your chance at the Gantalei and failed," Barrock spat. "You may have stolen leadership for now, but you will never be one of us."

Rivik's lips curled in a coldly amused smile. "On that, we agree. I will never be Talei. I am something far more to be feared." He cocked his head, a predator scenting blood. "This is your last warning, Barrock. Yield."

Barrock dragged his tongue across his jagged teeth, his eyes fever-bright. "I still remember the taste of your blood, whelp. Surrender, or I will drink you dry."

Rivik turned to Kane, a question in his gaze. Kane nodded approval, his curiosity piqued by the history between the two creatures.

Rivik's skin split with a thunderous crack, the darkness billowed forth like smoke to hover above his discarded flesh. Barrock's eyes bulged, disbelief and dawning horror writ large across his face.

"A Margorian Shade. Impossible!" he whispered. His words were lost in a howl of agony as the writhing mass of shadow engulfed him and devoured him whole.

The rest of the Fallen threw back their heads and a rising cacophony of terror and confusion screeched through the air. Symiar was the first to break, falling to his knees in supplication.

"Spare us!" he begged, the others were quick to follow suit. "Please, spare us!"

"Join with me," the darkness hissed, its voice a thousand screaming souls. "Embrace the glory of the Hive."

They surrendered without hesitation, prostrating themselves before the nightmare that was once Rivik. Kane looked on in avid fascination as shards of living shadow splintered away, burrowing beneath the skin of each grovelling Fallen.

Their bodies convulsed, eyes rolled back in their heads as a viscous, oily substance bubbled up from their gaping mouths. Symiar, the first to recover, staggered to his feet and hacked up great gouts of the foul ooze. The last globule splattered to the ground... and slowly, horribly, began to move and slither back towards him.

It hovered before his face for a long, taut moment... then forced itself up his nostrils, disappearing. Symiar shuddered, his eyes fluttering closed... and when they opened again, they blazed with an unholy light.

One by one, the rest of the Fallen rose, reborn and remade in the image of their new master. The darkness seeped back into Rivik's reformed flesh, the transformation complete.

"My children," he crooned. "My Fallen, bound to me now, and forevermore."

Kane clapped slowly, a frisson of unease beneath his outward nonchalance. "Quite the show. And now you have your army."

"Just so," Rivik agreed, turning to face him. In the gloom, his eyes glittered like chips of bloody ice. "You have not forgotten the plan?"

Kane smiled thinly. "Certainly not. But these new developments warrant clarification. Your children, they are independent of the greater Hive? Autonomy must be preserved."

"They are an extension of my will," Rivik said. "They know what I know, want what I want."

Kane nodded, unease growing. "And the Master? They understand discretion is paramount?"

Rivik's head cocked, a bird of prey sighting a trembling rabbit. "They will play their parts, as shall I. The Master will suspect nothing... until it is far, far too late."

He gestured languidly to Symiar and breathed a substance directly into his nostrils. "For Gallo."

Symiar lowered and allowed Kane to mount. Once he was astride, the Fallen took off at lightning speed.

Rivik ran at Kane's side as Symiar surged onwards, the landscape blurring past. There was no need for words; they both knew their destination.

Jen. My love, my curse, my obsession. Kane's blood sang with a fever-bright need, an addiction that went beyond the physical, beyond reason or mercy. He would have her, all of her, no matter the cost.

They reached the outskirts of the village in a matter of moments, the shadows seeming to congeal around them. To Kane's surprise, they passed unchallenged, as if shielded by an unseen hand.

He filed the oddity away as they came to a stop before a nondescript house, indistinguishable from its neighbours save for the silhouette framed in the upstairs window.

"She is not alone," Rivik murmured, disquiet threading his tone. "I will await you here. Symiar will deal with Gallo and bring him forth. Be swift in your business, as we have tarried in this realm too long."

Kane moved toward the front door, drawn like iron to a lodestone. But before he could raise his fist to knock, she pulled him away and pushed him down onto the lawn. She pressed her hand against his mouth and shook her head, warning him to be silent. He arched a brow, and she moaned against him before crushing her mouth to his. It was a kiss that both claimed and surrendered. He met her with a matched hunger and desperation, her fingers winding in his hair. Her nails dragging deliciously against his scalp sent his pulse charging.

When they finally broke apart, she whispered, "My father locked me in. I had to sneak out."

"I will kill him," Kane snarled.

"No, just take me away from here."

Kane rose and lifted her to her feet. Symiar moved past him and nodded his affirmation to the silent question asked. Gallo followed on and slipped into the shadows to join his brethren. Jen reached for Kane's hand and pulled him away from the house. They walked for a short time, the Fallen following in the darkness. When Jen seemed satisfied with the distance, she spun and kissed Kane again, scraping her teeth against his lobes as she whispered her desires.

"I have something for you," he said softly, reaching to unclasp a necklace from around his neck and dropping it into her outstretched hand. It was a finely wrought silver chain with a pendant teardrop of polished obsidian.

Jen stilled, her breath leaving her in a sharp, sibilant rush. "I... I know this." She held the pendant up with a trembling hand. Wonder and disbelief warred across her face. "How do I know this?

"It belonged to the only woman I've ever loved," Kane said simply, taking the necklace from her slack fingers. "Look again, Jen. Remember."

He fastened the chain around her neck with a curiously familiar gesture, the pendant nestled in the hollow of her throat like it was made to rest there.

Jen shuddered. A low, wrenching moan tore from her lips. Her eyes, fluttered open but were no longer a warm, inviting brown.

Instead, a depthless black stared back at him, fathomless and echoing with lifetimes Kane had only ever dreamed of, before turning to a brilliant violet hue.

"My Amore," she breathed, wonder and recognition suffusing every syllable. "Oh, my love...my heart...how I have missed you."

"Alyssa," Kane whispered, a prayer and a promise. "My anima, my soul. You've come back to me."

She smiled, radiant and terrible, and in that moment, he knew her, beyond the veil of this single mortal life. The taste of her tears, the heat of her fury, the wrenching ecstasy of losing himself in her, over and over, through centuries and worlds and the wheeling dance of stars.

"I did not anticipate you to return to me so completely. How?" he asked, already guessing the answer, seeing the threads of fate that bound them, one to the other, tighter than blood, than death, than reason.

"I made a promise," she replied, her eyes luminous and brimming with shadows. "Not even oblivion could keep me from you. Not forever."

She leaned into him, fitting against his side like she was made to rest there. Kane's groin ached with a need that he could have taken her there and then. He was desperate to re-consummate their love, the vicious and intoxicating passion as their bodies joined and soared to hideous heights of pleasure. He could teach her more of such pleasures, the manipulations of ecstasy that he had mastered following his time spent with the delectable Nicki and her Kama Sutra tutelage.

"My Master," Kane said as he regretfully turned his thoughts away from his bed. "He's waiting for us. We cannot delay. But there is something I need you to do for me first. Jake. I need you to lure him to us."

Alyssa sighed, resignation and calculation passing across her face. "Must we? He has been... a friend, in this life."

"All the more reason to tie off that particular thread," Kane said gently, implacably. "He is part of your past, my heart. We must look to our future, and all that it demands of us. Plus, I have a score to settle—one which will bring what the Master desires."

For a long, taut moment, she was silent, her gaze distant and shuttered. Then, slowly, she nodded. "You're right," she murmured. "What must be done... must be done. For us, and all that we are destined to become." She turned to him, holding out a hand, her smile a thing of knives and broken promises. "Shall we, my Amore?"

Kane intertwined his fingers with hers. The buzz and hum of barely leashed power thrummed beneath his skin as he thought of the road that lay ahead, the worlds that would shatter and burn in the wake of his glorious ascension...

... and he smiled, wide and bright and hungry.

"Oh my love... let's."

Alyssa gestured for Gallo to approach. His expression betrayed no surprise at her changed countenance. Instead, he merely raised an imperious brow as she mounted his broad back.

"You've changed," she mused, running a considering hand along his flank. "There is a... difference in your resonance. A new frequency to your power."

Gallo inclined his head, a movement somehow both respectful and mocking. "As have you, Mistress. Your soul sings with the chorus of ages."

Alyssa smiled, sharp and bright as a new-forged blade. "Just so. Shall we attend to our unfinished business, then?"

"How will you do this?" Kane queried.

Alyssa pulled a small device from her pocket and tapped out a sequence. She placed it to her ear. "Jake, I need you. Please come..."

Kane watched in admiration as the lies tripped easily from her tongue. She gave a location and then returned the device to her pocket.

"We are a few minutes away from where you will meet him. It is secluded; no-one ever visits there at this hour."

"My love, you please me," Kane said as he mounted Rivik.

"My Amore," she purred, her eyes dancing. "Don't I always?"

They set off at a ground-eating lope, the night folding around them like a lover's embrace. In a matter of moments, they'd reached their destination, an enclosed land of greenery she had called a park.

Alyssa dismounted. There was a strange expression flitting across her face as she stared up at the rustic facade. If Kane didn't know better... he'd almost have called it a pang of regret.

She shook it off quickly and straightened her spine as she marched to a wooden seat. Kane and the Fallen faded into the deeper shadows of the treeline, watching, and waiting.

Jake sprinted towards her, the concern etched into the strong lines of his face. "Jen? What's wrong, why are you—"

He stopped as she pulled the device out of her pocket once more and tapped out another sequence.

"I'm sorry," she whispered. Even from his place in the shadows, Kane could hear the threads of real sorrow in her voice. "I'm so sorry, Jake... Yes, ambulance, please," she said clearly. "There's been an accident."

Jake stilled, confusion and dawning terror washing across his face in sickening waves. "I don't understand," he said slowly, taking a step back. "Jen, what the hell is going on?"

A twig snapped in the underbrush, and Jake whirled, searching for the source. But it was already too late.

Rivik and Gallo exploded from the treeline, all glistening teeth and razor-tipped claws. Jake screamed as Rivik barrelled into him, bearing him to the ground in a tangle of flailing limbs.

Kane stepped out of the shadows, drinking in Jake's terror, the delicious stench of his desperation. Rivik crouched over Jake's thrashing form, teeth bared in a macabre grin as he forced the boy's head back, exposing the vulnerable line of his throat.

"Do pass on my regards to your sister," he taunted, relishing the whimper that escaped Jake's bloodless lips.

Rivik bit down, but before he could tear out Jake's throat, a sudden, bone-deep chill pervaded the clearing. Kane staggered, his breath pluming in the frigid air as an unseen force slammed into him, driving him to his knees.

Rivik and Gallo fared no better, their triumphant snarls turned to yelps of pain as they were hurled away from Jake's prone form by an invisible hand. They landed in a tangle of limbs, struggling to rise against the crushing weight of the strange power bearing down on them.

"What is this?" Alyssa hissed, staggering to Kane's side. Her eyes were wide, darting around, seeking the source of the attack. But there was nothing to see, only the emptiness of the clearing and the steadily gathering cold.

"You will pay for this, Warlock." The voice came from everywhere and nowhere, a sibilant whisper that crawled down Kane's spine like a living thing. "Abandon this fool's errand, or face the consequences of your hubris."

Kane snarled, forcing himself to his feet through sheer will. "Show yourself, coward!" he roared, power sparking at his fingertips. But the voice only laughed, a sound like cracking ice and shattering bone.

"We will have our reckoning. But not this night." The unseen speaker seemed to smile, a sensation like a blade's caress across the back of Kane's neck. "Pray you do not cross our path again."

And then, as suddenly as it had begun, the presence was gone. The oppressive cold lifted, and the force pinning Kane in place released. Rivik and Gallo climbed warily to their feet, their eyes wide as they scanned the treeline for any sign of their attacker.

But the woods were silent, still. Even the night birds had fallen quiet, as if cowed by the power that had so recently held sway here.

Kane growled, flexing his hands as he struggled to master his fury, his unease. "We need to leave, now," he bit out, already striding towards Rivik and Gallo. "The damage has already been done by the Lyboria bite. I have had my revenge."

Alyssa lingered a moment longer, staring at Jake's limp form. Then, with a shake of her head, she rose and joined Kane, her legs shuddering under the effects of the unseen force. Kane boosted her onto Gallo's broad back, the Fallen having only managed to gain their feet.

The couple rode in silence as night approached dawn, Kane's mind whirling with questions, a sick certainty that they had stumbled into a game whose rules they could not yet fathom.

But there would be time enough to worry about that later. For now, they had more pressing concerns.

They reached the portal at the coordinates delivered by the Master, its swirling surface painting the clearing in eldritch hues of purple and blues. Kane and Alyssa dismounted, the Fallen flanking them as they approached the shimmering vortex.

"Are you ready, my love?" Kane asked softly, taking her hand.

She met his gaze, shadows, and stars whirling in the depths of her eyes. "For this?" She smiled, sharp and fierce. "I was born ready."

As one, they stepped into the portal, the world falling away in a dizzying kaleidoscope of light and colour. Kane felt the familiar tug of translocation, the gut-wrenching sensation of being unmade and remade in the space between heartbeats...

... and then they were through, stumbling out and into the Citadel's courtyard.

He dismounted. "Welcome home, my love," Kane murmured, steadying Alyssa as he helped her down.

But before she could respond, before she could do more than flash him a quicksilver grin... Kane doubled over with a scream. Agony lanced through him like a thousand burning blades.

He could only dimly hear her shout his name, or feel her hands on him as he crumpled to the unnaturally warm earth. The Master appeared, but his entire presence, his words, were drowned out by the roaring in Kane's ears and a sickening crack and pop of bones shifting and reshaping themselves beneath his skin.

He convulsed, back arching as a fresh wave of pain crashed over him, his spine lengthening, his vertebrae expanding and multiplying as his shoulders broadened, his limbs stretching grotesquely. Maroon-coloured scales erupted along his arms, his legs, his back, as wicked talons burst from his fingertips in a spray of blood.

Wings unfurled from his shoulders with a snap of leather and a reek of brimstone, their span blotting out the sullen sky. He threw his head back, a roar tearing from his throat as fangs crowded his jaw, pushing past his lips in a twisted parody of a smile.

And through it all, woven into every searing second of his metamorphosis... memories flickered past his mind's eye. Memories of blood and battle and aching hunger. Memories of who—of what—he truly was. The truth of him, seared into the fabric of his being like a brand.

"I am Nyrvallia. I was Laybardi, and now I am Kane."

With a final, shuddering crack, the transformation completed. Kane rose slowly to his feet, the power thrumming through him in an ecstatic rush.

He turned to Alyssa, drinking in her awestruck expression, the trembling wonder in her eyes as she beheld his true form at last.

"Magnificent," she breathed, reaching up to trace the razor edges of his jawline, heedless of the way his scales sliced her fingertips to ribbons. "Oh, my Amore... my dark prince."

Kane smiled, a slow, savage grin that bared his fangs. "No more waiting," he rumbled, his voice a grating, sibilant rasp. "No more hiding. The time has come to claim our birthright."

The Master laughed. "You serve me, Nyrvallia."

"I serve no-one," Kane rasped.

He gathered Alyssa into his arms and lifted her into the air, soaring above the Citadel. The Master's roar of rage died in the wind.

"Together, we will shake the stars from the heavens. We will carve our names into the wailing throats of worlds."

Alyssa shivered against him, a fierce, feral light kindling in her eyes. "Let them burn," she hissed, molten hunger in every syllable. "Let them all burn, and rise anew in our image."

The Master turned his gaze to where the Fallen had stood, but they had disappeared into the dark, leaving him alone to consider his next move.

Chapter Twenty-Eight
Charles

The Ascended Spirit Realms

T he Ascended Spirit Realms
In the shimmering, ethereal halls of the spirit realm, Charles floated, his form a shifting kaleidoscope of light and memory. Around him, the towering shelves of the Akashic Records stretch into infinity, each scroll a glowing testament to the lives and fates of every soul to walk the mortal plane.

But today, the normally serene hush of the Hall was shattered by a rising tide of discord and unease. Scrolls flitted back and forth, rearranging themselves in increasingly agitated patterns, their radiance flickering like candle flames caught in a rising wind.

Charles frowned, a ripple of disquiet passing through his luminous form. In all his aeons, he has never seen them so disturbed, so... unbalanced. Something was wrong, a fundamental shift in the delicate weave of destiny itself.

But what could possibly...

Before he could complete the thought, a chiming summons echoed through the Hall, a clarion call that resonated in the core of his being: Nicolai, calling him to council.

With a last, troubled look at the swarming scrolls, Charles gathered himself and streaked upward, a comet trail of silver light in his wake. In a matter of moments, he materialised in the Chamber of Illumination, the sacred heart of the spirit realm.

The Lightkeepers were already assembled, their forms towering and radiant, suffused with the pure, unfettered glory of the Divine. They were the archangels of mortal legend, the shepherds of the spirit guides, charged with maintaining the balance between the realms of flesh and faith.

But now, as Charles took his place among the lesser lights of his fellow guides, he could sense the tension humming through the assembled host, the grim anticipation crackling like lightning in the sacred ether.

"Charles." The voice of the first Lightkeeper, Nicolai, rolled through the chamber, a tsunami of sound and psychic pressure. "You know why we have called you here."

It was not a question, and Charles bowed his head in deference, fighting down the flare of trepidation in his core.

"I have sensed it," he murmured, his voice a thin thread of silver in the encompassing radiance of the Chamber. "The Records... they are in turmoil. Something has altered the weft of fate, sent ripples through the skein of causality."

"More than ripples," Raphael intoned. "What has been set in motion threatens the very foundations of the Great Design."

A murmur passed through the assembled spirits, a frisson of fear and awe that set the ether thrumming like a plucked harp string. Charles's essence trembled in response.

Dread, and a strange, burgeoning sense of destiny, warred within him.

Nicolai raised a hand, and the murmuring ceased instantly. "The Orders of Being have been breached," he said, each word a tolling bell of dire portent. "The Lost Ones have found a way through, and even now, they sow the seeds of ruin in the mortal realm."

Images flashed through the collective consciousness of the Chamber: writhing shades of anguish and malice, the twisted remnants of human souls forever barred from the light. Charles shuddered as their essence washed over him, a foetid tide of jealousy, rage, and despair.

"Possessions," another Lightkeeper murmured, their voice a crack of solar thunder. "Demonic incursions into the bodies and minds of the innocent. We have seen them in our scrying of the mortal plane. Men and women and children subsumed, hollowed out and filled with the howling madness of the Lost."

Charles felt a wrench to his core, a sickening lurch of horror and sorrow. He saw them now in the cascading visions shared by the Lightkeepers. Families huddled in terror as their loved ones thrashed and screamed, eyes black as pitch, voices grating with the discordance of the Abyss.

Priests, haggard and ashen, fighting a losing battle against the tide of darkness, their prayers, and rituals flickering like guttering candles against the rising leviathan of shadow.

"But how?" Charles burst out, unable to contain the question burning at the heart of him. "How could this happen? The Orders have held since time immemorial, the boundaries between realms inviolate. What could have possibly..."

"The strangers from the world of Valoria." The statement fell like a stone into the roiling sea of horror and confusion, and Charles felt the truth of it settle into his essence like lead. "It is their incursion into our world that has led to this. The summoning of that bombastic creature! Its death has heralded the rise of hell on Earth."

"And now the way lies open," Nicolai said grimly, "for the Warlock's legions to break upon the shores of the mortal realm, borne on the dark edict of his so-called Master."

"My ward." Charles straightened, a sudden urgency blazed through him. "Rowan. She is the key, the fulcrum upon which all our hopes must turn." He met the ineffable regard of Nicolai. His essence flared with the force of his conviction. "We must keep her safe, guide her on this path. With her gifts, her strength, she may be the only chance we have of driving the Lost Ones back, of sealing the breach before it is too late. And of saving another world in the process."

"And what of her brother?" another Lightkeeper asked, their form shimmering with troubled hues of azure and gold. "The attack he has suffered, the darkness that even now rends at his spirit..."

"Jake." Grief lanced through Charles, sharp and bright. He saw the boy in his mind's eye, struggling against the oily coils of some unspeakable sentience, screaming as it twisted its way into the secret chambers of his heart. "That...thing, inside him...it is not of the Lost Ones. It is something else, something... other."

"All the more reason to bring the girl into play," Nicolai declared, his voice a clarion call to arms. "She must be made ready, her path illuminated. The fate of worlds rests upon the strength of her soul, the light she carries within."

Charles nodded, resolve crystallising within him like a diamond. "I will go to her," he said, a quiet conviction ringing in every word. "I will guide her home, shepherd her to the thinning places where the veil runs weak. There, she can begin her work: the exorcising of the Lost Ones, freeing the taken vessels, forging alliances with other lights in the darkness."

A ripple of assent passed through the assembled spirits, a silent vow of aid and succour. They would not let Rowan walk alone; every guide, every shining soul would lend their strength to her cause, to the desperate battle against the rising tide of shadow.

"Go then, with our blessing," the Lightkeepers intoned as one, their voices a symphony of thunder and starlight. "Find the girl, and set her upon the path. The hopes of worlds go with you, Charles... may your light never waver, nor your purpose falter."

Charles bowed his head, a solemn oath kindling in the core of his being. He would not fail, could not fail. Too much depended on the choices to come and on the courage of one mortal girl, and those who would follow her into the hungry dark.

But as he raised his head, ready to descend once more to the mortal plane... a gasp ran through the Chamber, a ripple of shock and awe that set the very ether trembling.

"Look!" A Lightkeeper cried, their form flashing with incandescent brilliance. "Upon Charles's brow... a sign, a portent!"

A sudden warmth suffused him, a glow of power and purpose that seemed to emanate from the very centre of his essence. Slowly, hardly daring to believe, he raised a hand to his forehead...

... and felt the thrumming, pulsing heat of a rune etched in living light upon his spectral skin. A Toki, the glyph of guardianship, of destiny, shimmering like a captured star above his widening eyes.

"The Toki," the Lightkeepers whispered, their voices reverent, exultant. As one, they bowed before Charles, their radiance dimming in deference to the Toki's glory. "Charles, beloved of the light...you have been Chosen. Anointed by the Purpose that moves us all."

Charles could only stare in mute wonder. A burgeoning awe crashed through him like a tsunami. The Toki, the mark of the Guardian... blazing upon him like a beacon, a promise of trials and triumphs to come.

He thought of Rowan then, his brilliant, beautiful ward. The girl who carried the fate of the worlds on her slender shoulders. And he knew, with a certainty that sang in his very soul, that their paths were now inextricably intertwined, their destinies woven together by the glorious, inexorable tapestry of the Toki's design. Wherever she went, he would be able to go.

"Guardian of Light," the Lightkeepers murmured, their essences bending and swaying like candle flames caught in a sacred wind. "Go forth, Charles. Go forth... and let the radiance of your purpose light the way for us all."

Charles closed his eyes, feeling the Toki's power thrumming through him, suffusing every particle of his being with unshakable resolve.

When he opened them again, it was to the shimmering expanse of the mortal realm spread out beneath him, a patchwork quilt of shadow and luminance, despair, and yearning.

And there, a glimmering beacon amidst the darkness... Rowan. His ward, his charge. The lynchpin upon which the fate of realms now turned.

"I'm coming," Charles whispered, the Toki burning like a second sun upon his brow. "Hold fast... for the light is on its way."

Chapter Twenty-Nine
Finn

Pitlochry, Scotland

Finn stared at the ruins of Bessie's cottage, the anger continuing to fire in the pit of his stomach as he took in the full wake of the destruction. Bessie's home, once so warm and welcoming, now stood in ruins. He could sense Rowan's pain and sorrow as she approached, the shock clearly etched on her face as she stumbled aimlessly across the rubble towards him. He moved quickly, seizing her arm as her foot caught in debris, breaking her fall.

Freeing herself, she lifted her gaze and gave him a weak smile. He searched her face and noted how close the tears were to falling.

"I'm okay," she mumbled, turning away from him.

Sensing her need to take a few moments, he released his grip. Her breath hitched as she fought to regain composure.

"They've destroyed it all," Roark said, breaking the silence.

Eyes hard as steel met Finn's own, the sentiment of the dragon clearly conveyed.

"No doubt, the gardens too," Rowan whispered, her tone laden with sorrow. But as they approached the once-lush and vibrant patch of earth, a gasp escaped her lips. "Finn, look! The gardens... they're untouched!"

Finn blinked, hardly daring to believe his eyes. But there it was, a verdant oasis amidst the ruin, the flowers, and herbs swaying gently in a breeze he couldn't feel. A soft, pulsing glow emanated from the very soil, a shimmer of power that made his skin prickle.

"The Meridian," Roark rumbled, awe and disbelief colouring his tone. "Its energy... it must have protected this place. Redirected itself to shield Bessantia's sanctuary."

Mortimus joined them. "Remarkable," he murmured. "Bessantia's power endures, even in her absence."

A dragonfly zipped past Finn's nose, its iridescent wings catching in the moonlight. It hovered for a moment before Rowan, then darted into the garden.

"Albion seems drawn to it as well," Finn observed.

Rowan stepped forward as if in a trance, her hand outstretched. The moment her fingers brushed the edge of the garden, the glow intensified, tendrils of light curling around her like living things.

Finn started forward, a cry of warning on his lips, but Rowan shook her head. "It's alright," she murmured, her voice distant, dreamlike. "It's... speaking to me. Calling me."

She moved deeper into the garden, the light enveloping her, welcoming her. Her four companions could only watch, transfixed, as she reached the centre and knelt, pressing her palms flat against the earth.

For a moment, nothing happened. Then, with a suddenness that stole the breath from Finn's lungs, Rowan threw her head back, a cry tearing from her throat. Light exploded outward from her hands, from her eyes, her mouth, a supernova of power that made Finn shield his face and Roark rear back with a roar.

When the light faded and Finn could see again, Rowan was on her feet, her eyes blazing with an inner fire. She turned to him, and the smile on her face was a thing of pure, incandescent joy.

"Bessie," she said, her voice ringing with certainty. "She's in the Nether plane. And I... I know how to find her."

Finn gaped, hardly daring to hope. "How? What did the Meridian tell you?"

She shook her head, wonder, and determination warring in her gaze. "No time to explain. I must go, now."

Finn squared his shoulders, pushing down the myriad of questions bubbling up in his throat. Rowan needed him, needed his strength and his faith. Everything else could wait. "I'm coming with you," he said firmly, stepping forward.

But Rowan held up a hand, stopping him in his tracks. "No, Finn. I must do this alone."

Finn opened his mouth to argue, to insist, but the look in her eyes made the words die in his throat. There was a certainty there, an unshakable resolve that he knew he could not sway.

Mortimus placed his hand on Finn's arm. "She'll be alright, lad," he said gently. "Have faith."

So instead, Finn simply nodded, pulling Rowan into a fierce, desperate embrace. "Come back to me," he whispered into her hair.

She pulled back, cupping his face in her hands. "I will always come back to you."

And with that, she turned and stepped into the heart of the garden. Finn watched her disappear, his heart in his throat, his hand clenched white-knuckled by his side.

Time lost all meaning as he paced the perimeter of the garden, his nerves strung wire-tight. Mortimus kept vigil with him, his presence a steadying anchor despite the dragonfly zipping to and fro in agitation.

Roark kept watch as well, a silent, stalwart presence, his eyes fixed unwaveringly on the spot where Rowan had vanished. He could sense the tension building with every minute that passed, his tail repeatedly lifting and then falling to the earth with a soft thud.

"Could you cut that out?" Finn hissed, finally standing still.

"If you stop grinding your teeth and wearing a hole into the earth," the dragon bit back.

"Peace, both of you," Mortimus chided. Albion flittered persistently in agreement.

Arms folded, Finn cast a glare towards the dragon. Roark ignored him but did cease flicking his tail.

It could have been minutes, but it felt like hours or days for Finn, when a light shimmered and warped, disgorging two figures onto the lush grass. His heart leapt into his throat as he recognised Rowan, her arm wrapped tight around a second, frailer form.

Bessie. Alive. Whole.

He was running before he'd made the conscious decision to move, Roark, Mortimus, and Albion hot on his heels. They reached the women just as Rowan sank to her knees, exhaustion, and relief robbing her legs of strength.

"Well, that was close," said Bessie.

"Rowan!" Finn skidded to a halt beside her, dropping down and pulling her into his arms.

"Patience, Finn. Let her catch her breath," Bessie ordered. Mortimus nodded in agreement, while Albion circled them in concern.

Rowan sagged against him, her head falling onto his shoulder as she let out a shuddering breath.

"I found her," she mumbled, her words slurring with fatigue. "I found her, Finn."

"You did," he agreed, wonder and awe thick in his voice. "You brilliant, impossible, miraculous girl. You did it."

Bessie, looking wan but smiling, reached out to lay a hand on Rowan's arm. "She saved me," the old mage said softly, her eyes bright with unshed tears. "Fought through horrors I can scarcely imagine, horrors no living soul was meant to face. And she did it for me."

"I don't ever want to see that thing again," Rowan said.

"I knew I should have gone with you," Finn said with a bite to his tone.

Bessie placed a restraining hand on his shoulder. "Rowan's life was never in danger, and she wasn't alone."

"The lass had help from beyond," Mortimus added sagely. Albion bobbed in the air, as if nodding.

Rowan lifted her head. "She's right, I wasn't alone."

"Would someone care to explain?" Finn demanded.

Bessie ignored him. "Are you alright, dear?"

"Does it look like it?" Finn snapped, losing his patience.

"Would you like me to teach you some manners?" Roark snarled and lifted his tail into the air.

"Settle down my old friend," Bessie said, and then to Rowan, "Perhaps you are now ready to tell Finn what happened dear?"

Releasing her from his hold, Finn gently cupped her chin, their eyes locking. "Tell me?"

She nodded, "I'm okay, Bessie was right I was not in danger myself. Although I cannot deny that what I witnessed did not terrify me,"

"Go on," he managed, his jaw clenched tightly.

"I crossed a bridge into the Nether and the first of seven planes of existence. I could sense Bessie calling my name, but I just couldn't make my feet to move. It was so dark and barren, I simply froze, I don't know how long for. Then I felt a hand against my back. At first, I thought it might be Charles, but it wasn't. I have no idea who he was, but he had the most amazing eyes, full of such warmth and kindness. I could hear his voice in my head as he reached for my hand. He told me to wait for the others who were coming. Suddenly I was surrounded, so many voices in my head urging me to step forward, reassuring me that I was safe."

"Who were they?" Finn asked, turning to Bessie.

"The Ancestors of Old, first of Earth's Mages," Mortimus answered, his voice hushed with reverence.

"They guided me to Bessie, through the void and onto the next plane. Each plane did seem slightly better than before, brighter, warmer and a little less frightening. I found Bessie on the fifth. On the way back down, after we crossed into the second plane, I thought I had felt something watching us. By the time we reached the first Nether plane, I knew it had followed. The Ancestors told us to run, not to stop, not to look back. I could see you and Roark ahead through the light, and I am sure it could see you both too. At the point we reached the bridge, I couldn't help it; I had to see what it was, how close it was. The Ancestors pushed us over the bridge the moment I turned my head. They blocked my view, but I had already seen its eyes, hideous yellow pools of hatred and rage. It wanted you dead."

"Me?" Finn asked.

Her eyes shifted. "No, Roark."

Finn shook his head. "And you still expect me to believe that neither one of you were in danger?"

Bessie sighed. "The only danger was that thing latching on to one of us and bringing it back into this world. It would not have attacked us. We were under the protection of the Ancestors and safe. Rowan, I imagine, more so, given her connection to Roark."

Albion buzzed agitatedly, as if echoing Bessie's words.

Finn let it go, although his stomach still churned at the prospect of what could have been.

Rowan gave him a quick kiss. "It's okay," she whispered before turning to Bessie.

Roark connected to Finn's thoughts. "I understand your fear, but she is stronger than she looks. They both are."

Finn glanced at the two women as they hugged and he blew out a breath. "You're right, I'm sorry for my rudeness earlier."

"Forgotten," Mortimus said kindly. "Whatever IT was that tried to follow them through, the fact it wanted Roark dead suggests that it did have something to fear. Take comfort from that."

"Right, now it's time we go home," Bessie said.

The group watched as she walked the perimeter of the Meridian and then lifted her hand to draw a rune in the air. A ray of golden light burst free, and sparks of gold and purple light danced from her fingers. She closed her eyes, her feet automatically guiding her along with not so much as a stumble. When she had completed a full circuit of the Meridian and lit it with a gold and purple hue, she returned to its centre and murmured an incantation. Then, finally, she gestured for them to join her.

Roark, Finn, Mortimus, and Albion moved forward automatically, but when Rowan did not, Finn turned to appraise her. What he read in her face made his heart clench. Her eyes looked to the left of her, as she nodding slowly. The colour had fully drained from her face, her forehead beaded with sweat and, she was rubbing her hands anxiously at her sides.

"What is it?" Finn asked in concern.

"My brother, Jake... he's..."

Finn pulled her into his arms, holding her close and stroking her hair.

"Breathe," he instructed.

Roark roared and lurched back towards them, Mortimus and Albion following. "Who's done this?" the dragon demanded.

"I swear I am going to kill him," Finn muttered darkly.

"What's that damn Warlock done now?" Roark's gaze locked onto a trembling Rowan.

"Save your anger, both of you. It's your strength she needs right now," Bessie scolded, moving quickly to join them, Mortimus at her heels and Albion hovering beside her. "Tell me," the old mage ordered gently.

"The Fallen have attacked my brother. I need to see him. Charles said he's currently in a coma. He's not yet like the boy on the train, but something has happened to him. His guide is keeping him in a coma in case he wakes and attacks my mother, or anyone else for that matter."

Mortimus made a distressed sound while Albion's wings fluttered agitatedly.

"Then of course you must go, both of you," Bessie said firmly. "I can use the portal and get you there faster. Do you know where he is, dear?"

Rowan turned to face her. "He's at the General Hospital in my hometown of Middlesbrough."

"Come with me."

They followed Bessie to the centre of the Meridian, Rowan gripping tightly to Finn's hand, Roark, Mortimus, and Albion close behind. The old mage spoke another incantation and a portal opened. Retrieving a small crystal from her pocket, she whispered to the stone and then threw it into the swirling vortex.

"What was that?" Finn asked.

"Quartz," Bessie replied, turning to Rowan. "Roark, Mortimus, and Albion will remain here with me. The portal will send you straight to the hospital, although I imagine at this time of night they will not let you in, dear. I have taken the liberty of adjusting the portal by eight hours ahead. It will be morning when you arrive."

"How is that possible? Will there not be any consequences?" Rowan asked, worry creasing her brow.

"Neither of you will have any memories of the last eight hours, although you will still have aged. You may also have a slight headache, but no other major catastrophe that I can foresee. I will send a portal for your return as soon as time has caught up. I am afraid I cannot delay our departure beyond that, and so I can only give you a few hours."

Rowan nodded, determination settling over her features. "Any time that you can give me is appreciated, Bessie. I need to be there, protect my mum, find a way to save him somehow."

Finn ran a hand through his hair. "Is there nothing that will cure him?"

"Not in this world," Bessie replied grimly.

Wait, Finn thought, latching onto her words. "No cure in this world, but what about ours? Is there a cure in our world?"

"There may be a way, but the poison will have consumed him, and if he should wake before we can even hope to return with a cure—"

"Charles?" Rowan interrupted, a small smile touching her lips as her gaze returned to Bessie.

"What is it, dear?" the old mage asked.

"Charles wants to know if a cure does exist for my brother in your world. He thinks he may know of a way to keep Jake in a coma until our return."

Bessie nodded slowly. "If there is any way your guardian can give us more time, then yes, we can source a cure for him."

"That won't be easy," Roark growled.

"No," Mortimus agreed. "But for the lass, we'll move mountains if we must."

Albion zipped around them in a dizzying pattern, his agreement clear.

"The Council Elders will owe Rowan a debt of gratitude," Bessie said. "Therefore, easy or not, it is the least that can be done for her."

Rowan's eyes shone with unshed tears. "Thank you," she whispered.

Finn squeezed her hand. "Are you ready?"

She took a deep breath and nodded. "Yes. How long do we have, Bessie?"

"I can give you a couple of hours from when you arrive through the portal. You will need to go through one at a time."

Finn stepped forward, resolution etched into every line of his body. "I'll go first. See you soon."

Epilogue
Rowan

M *iddlesbrough, England*
"You'll get the hang of this." He laughed as the portal closed behind them. She scowled and brushed the dirt away from her knees. It was a feeble attempt she considered to improve her dishevelled appearance. She doubted her mum would be convinced of such a pitiful excuse as the car breaking down en route from London to explain the dirt and grime. She glanced around the hospital car park and was relieved to note that no-one had witnessed the humiliation of her falling flat on her face. "How do I look?"

"Beautiful... apart from the smudge of dirt on your forehead."

"Seriously, could you be any more helpful?"

Before she could stop him, his finger was wetted and enthusiastically rubbing the dirt from her face. She batted his hand away. "For pity's sake, I'm not a two-year-old."

"Thanks for your help, Finn," he muttered.

She sighed. "Is it gone, then?"

"What?"

"Are you seriously out to wind me up today? The dirt?"

"Yes, I just managed to clean your face before you unjustly whacked my hand." He grinned.

Damn him, she thought, trying to smother her laughter. He always managed to find a way to prevent her from being mad with him.

"I'm sorry."

The humour fell from his face. "Look I understand you're scared for Jake and worried about your mum. I don't want you to feel my pain..."

"Yes, but I shouldn't take it out on you. You've done so incredible coping with your mother's death and Aaron..." her voice trailed away.

She allowed herself to be pulled into his arms, her face nestled against his chest as she selfishly enjoyed the few precious moments, knowing the horror that was to come. In tune with her needs, he allowed her to take what comfort she needed from him, despite his own pain carried.

"Are you ready?" he asked.

She swallowed hard and then turned in the direction of the hospital building. Finn held her hand as they walked into the white, clinical building. His expression was one of disbelief as they passed the wards and headed along the corridors. "I don't think I will ever understand your world."

"I guess, not what you are used to seeing?"

"Why are there so many here? Do they not have mages in your world?"

"Some are visitors, not necessarily patients who have come for treatment. Our mages are called doctors and nurses, they are specially trained in medicine. Sadly, they do not possess any magical powers and so it takes longer for people to heal. In some cases, people cannot heal at all, and will either die or live their lives as best they can with supported care until it is time for them to cross over."

They reached the lifts, and she pulled him inside. "Not a word," she hissed in his ear.

He shifted uncomfortably as the lift began its ascent. A ping and a voice announced the second floor. Finn almost fell through the doorway at speed. "Why would anyone choose an iron box to travel inside?" he muttered.

"It's called a lift, and is perfectly safe."

He did not look convinced.

With her heart thumping in her chest she pressed the button on the ward door. A nurse answered, "Can I help you?"

"I've been told that my brother Jake Thomson has been admitted here."

"And you are?"

"His sister Rowan, this is my fiancé Finn. Sorry for our unannounced arrival. We received news he had been hurt and have travelled back from London."

The nurse allowed them entry to the unit. "If you could just wait here for a few moments."

Finn's eyes widened as he took in the sight.

Moments later, the nurse returned with Rowan's mum. "Oh thank god you're here. Where have you been? I've had no contact from you for days, then Jake... and I still couldn't reach you...I..." Her mother broke down and sobbed on Rowan's shoulder.

"You can talk in the relatives' lounge, there is no-one in there. I will be along shortly," the nurse told them.

Finn followed behind as she led her mother into the small room on the right. They sat down uncomfortably on the sofa. Finn kept his distance and rested back against the wall.

Her mother smiled through her tears. "I guess the business trip is going well? Although—"

"Don't ask, mum. It's been a difficult journey and neither of us wanted to wash and change before we came here. I just wanted to see you both."

"I'm pleased, I've missed you so much."

"Me too. I'm sorry I haven't called. I—"

"It doesn't matter; you are here now. Perhaps you can fill me in later. So, how did you know about Jake?"

"From Jen." It was the safest choice given how close their parents were.

Her mother's face changed, her tone one full of contempt. "That girl!"

"I don't understand. What happened, Mum? Why are you angry with Jen?"

"Jake was over at Sandra's house. He rang to say he would be late back as he had to rescue Jen from her new boyfriend. Derek couldn't go, as Jake feared he was too angry and would end up doing the lad damage. Shortly after, I get a call from the hospital to say Jake has been found injured and admitted to Critical Care. And where the hell is Jen? Nowhere to be seen. Sandra assumed she'd changed her mind and disappeared with this mysterious boyfriend!"

"Wait, what new boyfriend? I thought she was with Simon."

"That is what Sandra thought initially. Jen went out with Simon to the pub and then returned without him, claiming she'd split up with Simon and was in love with another man. She claimed it was love at first sight and they were moving in together. Derek hit the roof and locked the doors. She snuck out of the window, apparently, and then later phoned your brother saying she'd made a terrible mistake. Jake had just calmed Sandra and Derek down and was due to come home when the call came from Jen.

"But it doesn't make sense, mum. Does Sandra know who he is?"

"Only that his name is Kane, but they'd never heard of him until last night."

The colour drained from Rowan's cheeks and she cast her gaze to Finn. The anger was evident in his face. She shook her head, urging him not to let his feelings escape.

"It seems to me too much of a coincidence that he goes off to help her and then ends up in hospital less than an hour later. If she has rung you, I can only assume she was the one who phoned for an ambulance. The caller did not identify the name to the emergency services, and when they found Jake, he was alone."

Her mind raced, trying to piece it all together. Jen and Kane?

"How is Jake?"

"They've managed to stabilise him for now, although they tell me he is still critical. He's lost a lot of blood and is in a coma."

A soft knock at the door, interrupted them. The nurse entered and took a seat opposite them. "Have you brought Rowan up to date on Jake's condition?"

"We were just getting to that, Emma," her mum answered.

"Okay. So, we have managed to stabilise Jake, but he is still very poorly. The wound is infected, and he is showing symptoms of an allergic. We have started him on intravenous antibiotics and we're keeping him in a coma to aid his recovery."

"Can I see him?"

"Yes, but not for long."

They followed her in silence, Finn, she noted, keeping a slight distance behind, allowing mother and daughter their space, but still close enough for her to seek support should she need to. Her mother waved her inside the side room.

"You go on in. I just need a quick word with Emma."

"I also have some consent forms I need you to complete. The doctors would like to run some further tests."

"That's fine. Go on, Rowan, it will make a difference to him knowing you are there."

She nodded and automatically reached behind her. Finn's hand immediately found hers. "Come on, you can do this," he whispered in her ear. Taking a deep breath, she pushed open the door and entered the room.

Her brother looked so small against the pillows, his hair slicked with sweat, his skin grey in colour. There was a large bandage across his shoulder and chest. Taking a seat beside the bed, she reached her hand forward and gently placed it on his arm.

"Be careful, Rowan," Finn warned.

A voice spoke to the side of her. "I'm keeping him in a coma, Rowan."

"Harry?"

"Yes."

"Is he suffering?"

"His soul is in torment. We released him to give him respite and when he flatlined, an entity tried to take possession, so we had no choice but to return him. We've had our best healers trying to protect his light from the infection in his physical body, but it is too strong, and it's a magic we've never come across before."

"You know what he will become?"

"Charles told me about the attack on the train."

"How would an entity move that quickly to possess his body?"

"Since the night of the storm...it's triggered..."

"Harry!" Charles warned. He turned to Rowan. "His physical body is compromised. We summoned the Sages the moment it happened to stop the spread of infection through the energy centres, but they failed. Our only option is to keep him in a coma."

"Is it true? Did Jen have something to do with this?"

"She was with the Warlock when the creatures attacked. She did nothing. She left with the Warlock voluntarily. The cord to her guide Daniel was severed; we do not know how. Daniel had to be taken to Eleanor for healing. It has never happened before to a guide."

Finn gently touched her shoulder. "What is it?"

Her mother entered the room, preventing her from answering him.

"Are you okay, Rowan?"

"It's just tough seeing him like this, Mum."

Her mother leaned over to kiss Jake's cheek. "The doctors want to run more tests on him."

Her brother's eyes suddenly snapped open. His hand seized her mother by the throat. A guttural sound escaped his lips. It all happened so quickly. Rowan watched in horror as her mother struggled to free herself from Jake's grip, her face turning a deeper shade of red and tears streaming down it. Charles shouted for Harry to fetch Eleanor whilst he tried his best to restrain Jake with his light. But then Finn was by her mum's side and attempting to prise Jake's fingers away from her throat. When all attempts failed, he pulled his fist back and punched Jake hard in the face. Jake's grip released, and he slumped into the pillows. Coughing, her mother stumbled backwards, her face filled with pain and horror. "His eyes, Rowan," she exclaimed.

Her gaze met Finn's.

"I'm so sorry, I had no choice," he told her.

"That wasn't my son," her mother murmured as she accepted the cup of water her daughter offered.

"Sip it slowly." Rowan glanced across at her brother, his face already showing signs of bruising. "Can you heal that before the hospital starts asking questions?"

"I'll give it a go. I don't want the healing to wake him back up."

Eleanor's voice replied. "We have eight sages here restraining him. He will not waken."

"I'm assured he won't wake if you heal it. Go ahead, Finn."

He released the healing orb. It entered Jake's skin momentarily then extinguished. Finn shook his head sadly as the bruising faded. "It's healed the damage, but not cured his affliction."

"Did you expect that it would?" Rowan asked.

"No, but a part of me had somehow hoped it would. I feel responsible for this," Finn said miserably.

"It's not your fault, Finn."

Placing her cup down her mother turned her eyes to Finn. "Who are you? What did you do to Jake?"

"I punched him?"

"I'm no fool, Finn. You and I know that was not what I asked. I could see the light leaving your hands. You are dating my daughter, therefore, I have a right to know."

"I'm sorry, Christine. I didn't mean to take you for a fool." His eyes pleaded for Rowan to intervene. She sighed, knowing they could no longer evade the truth.

"Mum, there is a lot I need to explain. But right now I need you to trust me. I need to concentrate, find out what is happening."

"Charles?" Finn asked.

"Your imaginary friend?"

"You know about him?"

"I thought you had grown out of it. Rowan, this is all really confusing."

"Please Mum, could you give me a couple of minutes?"

Her mother fell into silence, staring at Finn, who shifted uncomfortably.

Charles hugged Rowan. "Are you okay?"

"Yes, I think. Where's Harry?"

"He is in complete shock. He lost his connection to Jake when he attacked your mother. Eleanor told him to keep away for the moment. She and the others are still working on your brother."

"Is the bond severed for good, like Jen's?"

"No, only temporarily disconnected."

"Is there anything more they can do? Will he waken again?"

"This magic is stronger than human medicine. We've done all we can and interfered as much as we can. Eleanor and the others can keep him restrained, but only for a few hours. They will have to leave to restore the energy they are losing to keep him under. I'm afraid death will be his only release. I'm so sorry we could not give you the time I had optimistically hoped."

Rowan slumped to the cold, tiled floor, the tears sliding down her face. "He's going to die. They can't keep him in the coma," she told Finn. He was beside her, holding her close and whispering soothing words.

"He's not going to die," said a female voice.

Finn jerked and released Rowan from his embrace. He dragged her to her feet and spun in the direction of the one who had spoken.

"Who are you?" demanded her mother.

"Mercadia," Finn replied.

"Will someone tell me what the hell is going on?" her mother shrieked.

"Mum, quiet!" shouted Rowan.

"I do not have time to explain. Give this book to Bessantia. And here, this is for your brother." She dropped the vial into Rowan's hands after she had passed the book to Finn.

"What is that?" he asked.

"Blood from the Red Scorpion. It will keep her brother in a permanent state of sleep until you find the cure. But he will not be as he once was. That is all I can give you. I cannot linger in this time or world. There is a note that explains everything in the Journal, for Bessantia's eyes only."

Rowan flipped the lid of the vial, pulled Jake's mouth open and emptied the contents in. She wiped his lip clean with her sleeve so there was no trace of the liquid he had consumed.

"Will it work straight away?" she asked.

There was no reply. Mercadia had gone, her mother had fainted and Finn was on the floor fanning her face.

Rowan filled a cup from the jug on the bedside table and then chucked the contents over her mother's face. Finn grimaced as some of the water splashed onto him. Her mother sprang up, spluttering.

A nurse walked into the room.

"She fainted," Rowan explained. "Perhaps we all need a break. Can we use the relative's room again?"

"Sure," said the nurse. She checked the monitors before leading them away.

Once alone, Rowan turned to her mother. "Do you promise to keep an open mind?"

"I will do my best, that is all that I can promise."

"Just know that I am not crazy, Mum."

"You're scaring me now."

Rowan took a deep breath... *Here goes*.

She watched and waited. Her mother masked her emotions well. Rowan could not tell whether she believed her or not. The minutes passed, Finn shifted uncomfortably beside her.

"Is there a cure for Jake?"

"There is, but we need to go back to Finn's world and retrieve it."

"I see."

Finally, her mother turned to face her daughter and recited what Rowan initially thought to be a strange, yet familiar poem. But she couldn't fathom out why. Until Finn spoke up, the surprise evident in his voice.

"You know of the Prophecy?"

"Mum?"

"Since the night you left, Rowan's father has visited me in my dreams and read to me those words. I didn't understand why until now. I believe you."

"Dad?" she managed as she swallowed the lump in her throat.

"Yes," her mother laughed and dabbed at her eyes with her sleeve. She turned her attention to Finn. "Do you love my daughter?"

"Yes, I came across time and space to be with her. When all this over, and with your blessing, I intend to marry and make a life with her."

"And where will you make your home?"

"My world has more to offer."

"Your world is at war. If you love my daughter as you say you do, why knowingly take her into danger?"

"Both our fates are tied to the prophecy, and neither of us can escape from that, no matter how much we want to. I could be selfish and remain here with Rowan, try and build a life, but my world would be destroyed. I could not live in this world knowing I let my own world die."

"Mum, the people in Finn's world can save Jake. We need their help just as much as they need ours."

"I guess none of us have a choice. I thank you for your honesty, Finn, and I believe you when you say you love my daughter."

Rowan hugged her mother tightly. "Thank you. We need to go. Jake will remain in the coma, so you have nothing to fear. I'll come back soon with the cure and save him. I promise. I love you, mum."

Her mother nodded sadly. "I love you, too. Keep her safe, Finn."

"I will," he said.

Navigating back through the hospital, Rowan's only focus was the main exit. Her feet broke into a run as soon as she cleared the building. She ignored Finn's calls to slow down. She could not stop. She could not think. The tears flowed freely as she swerved to avoid crashing into an elderly couple.

"Are you alright, pet?" the woman called after her, but she did not answer. Her brain somewhere registered Finn calling her name repeatedly. She sensed he was still behind her, and yet she continued running. When he finally caught hold of her, he spun her straight into his embrace. She shattered against him.

Time passed as they stood holding on to each other tightly. Finally, she could cry no more. Her eyes were sore, and her throat dry from the effort. Finn's shirt, she noted with a grimace, was soaked in her grief.

He lifted her chin, forcing her to look at him. "I'm sorry, Rowan."

"It's my fault. Kane must have found about them through me. I just don't know how he convinced Jen to help him."

"He can be very manipulative, you know that."

"Is she still with him? I don't understand. I've known her all my life. She's been like a sister to Jake. How could she do it?"

"He's clearly forced her."

"No, Finn, there's something else. She severed her connection to her guide. That just is not possible. She herself somehow must have played a conscious part in that happening."

"I guess the only way for you to know for sure is to ask her."

"Oh, believe me, I will, and if I find out that this was deliberate, I will kill that bitch."

"What do you want to do now?"

"Aside from beating my best friend senseless? Bessie will re-open the portal in a few minutes. I guess we wait here. There's nothing more I can do for Jake and I need to keep my promise to my mother."

There was a sudden thrum and a whisp of silver light.

"You ready?" Finn asked.

"Yes," she replied, and followed him without hesitation to the other side.

Bessie reached out a warm hand and gave a gentle squeeze. "I know, dear."

Mortimus moved forward, concern etched into the weathered lines of his face. Albion hovered nearby, his wings a blur of iridescent motion.

"How?" Rowan asked.

Roark approached. "I felt your pain. The Warlock has much to answer for."

"Not just the Warlock. It seems my best friend has betrayed me, too."

Mortimus shook his head. "Betrayal cuts deep, lass. But you've got friends here, and a purpose. Hold tight to that."

Albion bobbed in the air, as if in agreement.

"We will end him, Rowan," Finn told her.

"I'm ready."

"Roark and I have prepared the portal for our return. Whilst you are a dragon guardian, Rowan, you are still new to our world. Therefore, I must ask that you ride with Roark through the portal. Finn, you will be with me. I will need your immediate assistance," Bessie said.

Mortimus's eyes narrowed. "Trouble on the other side, I take it?"

"A welcoming party?" Finn asked.

"Did you expect anything less?" Bessie replied with a wry smile and signalled to Roark.

Rowan could see something glinting in the dragon's claw as he offered the object to Finn.

Finn held the blade out in front of him. "Nice. Where did you get it?"

"Stolen many moons by a young beau of mine. Its previous owner was none too pleased. The sword has been anointed, and now will serve only you," Bessie explained.

Mortimus whistled low. "That's quite the gift, lad. Wield it well."

Rowan watched as Finn swung the sword confidently around his torso, lunging and slicing through the air, changing direction and hands with each swing of the blade. She had to admit, he looked hot!

Bessie winked at her. "Not bad, eh?"

She blushed. "Whilst he does look all He-Man like, I am not sure I like the thought of you both on the ground and us in the sky out of harm's way. Can't we just burn them?"

"Absolutely not," Bessie exclaimed. "The Fae would be furious if their forest was destroyed."

Albion's wingbeats took on an agitated tempo at the mention of the Fae.

"Well, why would the Fae even let whatever it is into their forest?" Rowan countered.

"The Fae do not involve themselves in our war unless their own clan are threatened," Finn explained. "We go burning down their home, it will force them to take action and choose sides."

Mortimus nodded sagely. "Aye, and you don't want the Fair Folk as your enemies. Capricious bunch, they are."

"But you said before, they wouldn't allow those creatures into their forests?" Rowan pressed.

"Those creatures are born from dark magic, something different altogether."

"So, what then?"

Finn turned to Bessie for the answer.

"No creatures, dear, Finn and I are safe on that score. However, let's say my juju informs me of a scout team close by; our arrival won't go un-noticed."

"Then you should ride Roark too," Rowan insisted.

Smiling, Bessie rolled up her sleeves and cracked her fingers together. "I am hardly what you would call a defenceless old woman."

Mortimus barked a laugh. "That you are not, Bessantia dear. That you are not."

Admitting defeat, Rowan gestured to Roark. He softened his spikes and slipped his tail gently around her waist to lift her high on his back. Reluctantly, she settled against him. As though sensing her unhappiness, he connected his thoughts to hers. "Don't worry. I shall be keeping a very close eye on them both from above, regardless of those winged fleas," he reassured.

"Can they hear us?" she asked, surprised when no retort came from below.

"No. Our connection cannot be heard by others, as dragon and rider."

She peered down at Finn, his sword firmly in his hand and extended out in front of him. "That's good to know."

Finn met her gaze and mouthed the words, "I love you."

She blew him a kiss.

Mortimus cleared his throat pointedly. "If you two lovebirds are quite finished..."

Albion zipped around them in dizzying loops, his excitement palpable.

"Ready?" asked Bessie.

"As we'll ever be," Rowan shouted and clung on tighter to Roark.

Bessie drew symbols into the air and delivered an incantation. A strange silence fell. Roark shifted beneath her. "Here it comes," he warned.

There was a thundering crack. The Meridian tore away and plunged her into nothingness. She focused on her connection with Roark and sought access to his sight once more. Her eyes adapted to the gloom that surrounded them. She was reassured to see Finn still standing below with one hand entwined with Bessie's and the other gripped tightly to the sword. Mortimus stood beside them, his own magic primed while Albion hovered overhead.

A sound shattered the silence. The hum, a continuous melody that soothed and yet excited at the same time. She memorised the song, wondering why it resonated so deeply. A spark of a memory long-forgotten, held in the deepest chasm of her soul. It teased and tormented, refusing her demands to be shared. There was an explosion of white light.

"Quickly Roark, there's not much time," Bessie's voice shouted.

The dragon beat his magnificent wings and lifted her into the air. They followed their companions into the darkness of Valoria, Mortimus's determined figure and Albion's shimmering form soon swallowed by the portal's swirling mists.

To Be Continued...

Releasing July 2024

Gentle Ben
By
Kirsty F. McKay

In the heartwarming and bittersweet tale of "Gentle Ben," follow the extraordinary journey of Ben, a Labrador dog who found his forever home after a troubled past. Rescued at the age of three, Ben quickly formed an unbreakable bond with Binx, a clever and lovable cat. Together, they brought immeasurable joy and laughter to their family's lives, showcasing the incredible benefits of having dogs as companions.

Ben's presence brought comfort, happiness, and unconditional love to his family. His playful nature and unwavering loyalty provided endless moments of joy, while his protective instincts made him a cherished member of the household. Through heartwarming anecdotes, witness the transformative power of a dog's love and the profound impact they can have on our lives.

However, the story of "Gentle Ben" also explores the pain of loss when Ben crossed over the rainbow bridge. As the family navigates the heartache of saying goodbye to their beloved furry friend, they learn to cherish the precious memories they shared and find solace in the enduring bond they continue to feel.

"Gentle Ben" is a touching tribute to the incredible joy and benefits dogs bring into our lives, as well as the profound grief experienced when we have to bid them farewell. It is a testament to the enduring power of love, friendship, and the everlasting impact our furry companions leave on our hearts.

Releasing July 2025

The Gift That Keeps On Giving
By
Kirsty F. McKay

In a world where understanding is scarce, Olivia's journey unfolds as a testament to resilience and unwavering spirit. "The Gift That Keeps on Giving" is a captivating tale based on true experiences, where the fictional character shares her raw and heartfelt account of living with Fibromyalgia and battling through the challenges of peri menopause.

Step into Olivia's shoes as she unveils the complexities of her life with a disability, shedding light on the hardships and misconceptions that surround her. With courage as her guide, she bravely reveals the invisible struggles and the profound impact they have on her daily existence.

Through her narrative, Olivia becomes an inspiration, forging a path of strength and determination that defies the odds. This remarkable story not only sheds light on the realities of living with chronic illness but also serves as a powerful reminder of the resilience of the human spirit.

"The Gift That Keeps on Giving" is an unflinching exploration of the power of empathy and the transformative nature of storytelling. It is a heartfelt invitation to embrace understanding, compassion, and the beauty that lies within the struggle. Prepare to be moved and enlightened by this captivating journey of self-discovery and the unbreakable spirit that resides within us all.

Don't miss out!

Visit the website below and you can sign up to receive emails whenever Kirsty F. McKay publishes a new book. There's no charge and no obligation.

https://books2read.com/r/B-A-IWAZ-FIFBD

BOOKS 2 READ

Connecting independent readers to independent writers.

About the Author

Kirsty McKay, born in Middlesbrough in 1976, is an author driven by a lifelong passion for writing. From a young age, she immersed herself in the world of books, frequenting the library every week and devouring stories from various genres. While she appreciates all types of literature, Kirsty's heart lies in the realms of fantasy and the paranormal, where her imagination soars.

With a loving marriage spanning twenty seven years, Kirsty is the proud parent of three children and dotes on her four grandchildren.

Kirsty's writing journey took flight when she joined a writing development group, igniting her creative spark. After the publication of her first book, The Veils Of Valoria, The Chronicles of Morvantia Series, she founded The Book Dragon, a platform dedicated to self-published and independently published authors. Fuelled by her frustration of the lack of support for self-published and indie authors,

Kirsty is passionate about nurturing fellow writers and helping them achieve their dreams, while keeping hope aflame. Since its inception on 4 July 2022, The Book Dragon has grown into an award-winning business, fostering a supportive community, and providing abundant opportunities.

Despite managing Fibromyalgia and Osteoarthritis, Kirsty seamlessly weaves her disability into her work, thanks to the unwavering support of her family.

Kirsty is a Reiki Practitioner and a Crystal therapist. Grounded in her Pagan philosophy, Kirsty embraces values and practices that resonate with her core beliefs, drawing upon her clairvoyant abilities in her healing work.

In her spiritual journey, Kirsty finds guidance from her Spirit Guide, Charles, who she lovingly describes as a young Mel Gibson lookalike, and who was an American Quaker in the 1600's that she was married to in a previous life. She also connect with Jack, a loveable scoundrel, and a renowned Galleon Sea Captain in his time, who playfully teases Kirsty about her distinct lack of sea legs.

Kirsty's life is a tapestry woven with creativity, compassion, and unwavering dedication to empowering others through her words and actions.

About the Publisher

Welcome to The Book Dragon Ltd, a publishing company committed to championing the voices of self-published and indie authors. We understand the unique challenges faced by these talented individuals and are dedicated to providing a platform for their work to shine. With our passion for storytelling and unwavering support for independent voices, we strive to foster a community that celebrates creativity and empowers authors to share their stories with the world. Join us on this exciting journey as we bring exceptional literary works from self-published and indie authors to readers worldwide.

Address: Book Dragon Ltd, 6 West Row, Stockton on Tees, TS18 1BT, United Kingdom

Facebook: www.facebook.com/thebookdragonteam

Open to Submissions – Fiction All Genres, Adults & Children's Books, Non -Fiction & Poetry

Supporting Self Published and Independently Published Authors

Editor in Chief: Tim Marshall

Email: tim@thebookdragon.co.uk

Business Executive & Founder: Kirsty F. McKay

Email: kirsty@thebookdragon.co.uk

Testimonials:

The Book Dragon's commitment to supporting Indie and Self-published authors is unmatched, and their selection of books is sure to have something for everyone. I highly recommend this bookstore to anyone looking for their next great read or to any author looking for business support. **Author Eleanor Dixon**

I really appreciate The Book Dragon's support of indie authors and all the creative ways they employ to drive that support. **Author Wayne Kramer**

The Book Dragon is an amazing partner and I am so grateful to be working with such a dedicated and passionate team, devoted to self-published and indie authors. Thank you for everything you do and keep up the good work. **Author Fiona Lowry**

Read more at https://www.thebookdragon.co.uk/.

Milton Keynes UK
Ingram Content Group UK Ltd.
UKHW022003310524
443378UK00014B/604